PIRATE

Also by Duncan Falconer

The Hostage
The Hijack
The Operative
The Protector
Undersea Prison
Mercenary
Traitor

Non-fiction
First Into Action

DUNCAN FALCONER

PIRATE

sphere

SPHERE

First published in Great Britain in 2011 by Sphere
Reprinted in 2011

A CIP catalogue record for this book
is available from the British Library.

ISBN HB 978-1-84744-411-0
ISBN CF 978-1-84744-412-7

Typeset in Bembo by Palimpsest Book Production Limited,
Falkirk, Stirlingshire
Printed and bound in Great Britain by Clays Ltd, St Ives plc

Sphere
An imprint of
Little, Brown Book Group
100 Victoria Embankment
London EC4Y 0DY

An Hachette UK Company
www.hachette.co.uk

www.littlebrown.co.uk

To Jamie Seward: a rich pirate to be sure but one of the good guys!

Prologue

Dinaal Yusef had lived in Bogota for five years before he learned why he had been ordered to begin a completely new life there. He first arrived in the Colombian capital on vacation: or at least that was the way his leaders wanted it to look. In reality he was there to carry out a preliminary assessment of the city. And to ascertain what he needed to do to be able to apply for a resident's visa. Yusef was a tall, handsome and athletic man in his late twenties, and he was well educated, having attended university in Barcelona, where he had lived for fifteen years. He'd been born and grown up in a small town on the Kashmir border in Pakistan. But a wealthy uncle living in Spain had adopted Dinaal and brought the boy to live with him after his mother and father, a policeman, had been killed in a dawn raid by the Indian army.

In the second week of Dinaal's month-long visit to Bogota he met a young local girl. He frequented the street café where she waited on tables. After just a few days he'd charmed her, completely turned her head. It had been easy enough for a man of his looks and intelligence to convince the girl, who had left her village only a few months before to find work in the city. It was almost as easy convincing her parents. After a brief but passionate affair, he flew back to Spain promising to return to marry her. Three months later he was as good as his word.

It was a union of love for the Colombian only. For Dinaal, it was one of convenience. It meant he acquired his permanent resident visa. And completed the first stage of his assignment. Dinaal had been sent to Colombia to set up an undercover operations cell. So he needed to be married. It was a necessary tool. It allowed him to stay in the country for as long as he wanted and to travel abroad at will and return at will. Without having to deal with the usual visitor's visa complications.

He waited a year before he travelled out of Colombia. Dinaal went back to Pakistan for the first time since his youth. On arrival he took the first of many trips into Afghanistan to meet his bosses. These visits, mostly into Kandahar, never showed on the pages of his passport. Because he was always guided in and out through the mountainous, arid borders by people who knew how to avoid Pakistani troop patrols and Western Coalition forces.

It took close to three years to get the Bogota active unit numbers up to operational strength. The secret cell was made up of six other men, all of whom had been recruited from madrassas in various parts of the world that taught an extreme form of Islamic jihad. The seven men had subsequently attended jihadist training camps once a year for weeks at a time, and on one occasion for two hard months straight. They'd learned the art of terrorism. They'd taken weapons and explosives training and been drilled relentlessly on how to conduct themselves undercover. Only one of the men was a native Colombian. The others were from Pakistan, Indonesia and Saudi Arabia. In the final weeks of training they'd focused on the skills required to conduct independent and unsupported attacks in foreign countries. By now they had solid small arms skills. They could handle pistols and assault rifles. At this point they learned how to construct simple but lethal explosive devices using locally purchased materials.

When Dinaal was sent to Colombia to set up the active service unit, the leaders didn't tell him why. He would have to wait another two years before learning of its purpose. But he had been able to wait because he was a patient man.

In truth, the men who had recruited and sent Dinaal to Bogota didn't know what the task would be either. They were following a directive that came down from on high. They had been ordered to set up as many active service cells as possible in just about every significant country in the world. The cells were to remain asleep until given orders to become operational.

It was during one of Dinaal's visits to Islamabad, while receiving training in the use of wire-guided missiles and anti-vehicle mines, that he got called to attend a meeting. The gathering, which included other cell commanders, was held on a country estate a few miles inside Afghanistan on the Kandahar road beyond the Spin Boldak border checkpoint. Much to his surprise, Dinaal's bosses were men he had never seen before. It was like there had been a complete changing of the command guard. Many of the new leaders were younger than their predecessors and were far more politically savvy. They were also ruthless and ambitious.

The meeting lasted a whole day. One by one the cell commanders were called to give account of their units. When it came to Dinaal's turn, he described his men, their enthusiasm and their eagerness to do anything they were asked in the name of Islam. He also emphasised they were all willing to die for the cause. At the end of it, Dinaal was given what seemed a strange sequence of instructions. But he was not permitted to question them nor to divulge them to any living person outside the members of his cell.

On his return to Bogota, Dinaal assembled his team at the first opportunity and relayed the instructions. His men were equally bemused. He assured them that ultimately it would lead to a significant task: all he could say was that they were taking part in a truly global operation, one that would have a greater impact than the Twin Towers assault on 11 September 2001. Dinaal also warned the six men not to ask questions about the task nor to discuss any aspect of it beyond the walls of the secret cell headquarters. He didn't lie to them: if they disobeyed the order they would be killed.

The Colombian, the Indonesian, the two Pakistanis and the two Saudis assumed Dinaal knew the real purpose behind the weird task. He did not let them think otherwise. He was well aware that information was power and that if you didn't have any, it was always best to let others think that you did.

He spent a week carrying out day and night reconnaissance of the target area on his own. He looked at it from every position until he was satisfied. When he had decided on the location and timing, he took his two best men out on the ground to explain the plan in detail. He showed them where it would take place and precisely how they would carry it out.

He had one relatively minor obstacle in the preliminary plan: the procurement of a rifle. Dinaal wasn't worried about ammunition being a major issue since he required only one bullet. And getting hold of a rifle was easy enough in Colombia. But it had been impressed upon him that the acquisition of the firearm had to be as clinical as every other part of the operation. It had to be a clean weapon, untraceable back to them. No member of the cell could be associated with a firearm in any way, shape or form. This was vital to the future of the cell. Dinaal knew he had to take it extremely seriously.

It was the Colombian who managed to achieve this level of secret acquisition, quite by chance. He stole the weapon from the military without them knowing who had done it. He was driving towards a country road checkpoint late one night, common enough just about anywhere around the Colombian capital, and the barrier was up. He was waved through by a single soldier and noticed a dozen or so others asleep, weapons out of hands. Instantly inspired, he drove for about another hundred metres, around a couple of bends and pulled the car off the road. He crept back through the bush on foot. He took not only a rifle but a pouch full of magazines.

After detailed questioning of the Colombian, Dinaal was satisfied that security had been maintained and that it would remain so as long as the weapon was never found in their possession and they kept it hidden until they needed it.

Finally the night of the task arrived. The seven men climbed into a van and they drove into the city. The van belonged to Dinaal, a second-hand Transit with windows at the front and in the back doors only. It was rusty in places and looked well worn but Dinaal ensured the engine was always in good condition. The Colombian was at the wheel. They kept to the highways and after a while they hit Calle 17 and headed into the much less populated agricultural area to the north-west. The traffic had been heavy in the city but as soon as they turned on to the farm road it disappeared. The surface of the road was hard-packed crushed stone that wound through small, cultivated fields. A handful of farm houses were dotted about. The land was as flat as a billiard table in every direction.

Less than a kilometre along the lane, the vehicle turned into an even narrower track and came to a stop under some trees, which provided complete cover from the moonlight. The Colombian turned off the lights and the engine.

The two Pakistani men climbed out of the back of the van and skipped into the bushes. They looked at the few houses in sight, their lights on inside. Otherwise they couldn't see any sign of life.

Dinaal hardly took his eyes off his watch. The others waited quietly and patiently. 'Let's go,' he said finally.

The double doors at the back opened and the men climbed out. Two of them were carrying a long wooden box. Dinaal and the Colombian driver joined them.

'You have three minutes to set up,' Dinaal said.

One of the Saudis and the Indonesian climbed over a low, wooden fence and took the box that was handed to them. Then they all hurried along the edge of a ploughed field. The ground began to slope away a little as they reached the end of the field, where they stopped. Beyond them they could see a wide trough of marshy water that reflected the moonlight.

'One minute,' said Dinaal.

They placed the box on the ground and opened it. Inside was the rifle, a standard 5.56mm ball Galil IMI. The Saudi who had been elected weapon preparer lifted the weapon out of the box. He was handed a magazine and he pushed it into its housing, cocked the breach that loaded the chamber and handed the weapon to the Indonesian, who was standing ready and waiting to receive it. He was short and stocky, low centre of gravity. He took it, placed the stock into his shoulder and looked directly at Dinaal.

'That way,' Yusef said, holding his arm out. The Indonesian adjusted his position so that he was aiming the rifle into the sky in the direction indicated.

'Hold him,' Dinaal hissed at the Saudi.

The man took a tight hold around the Indonesian's waist.

'Safety catch,' Dinaal said.

The Indonesian removed the safety catch.

Dinaal searched the skies behind them, in the opposite direction to the aim of the rifleman.

After about fifteen seconds they could all hear the distant sound of an approaching aircraft.

The rifle pair didn't move, they just remained focused skywards, their backs to the oncoming aircraft, while Dinaal and the others stared into the black star-covered sky.

'There,' said the Colombian, finding a couple of tiny, piercing lights moving together through the thousands of stars. A large, commercial passenger plane soon took shape, increasing in size as it descended directly towards them, its landing lights searching ahead.

Dinaal glanced at his gun team, who remained in position. 'Get ready,' he said.

The Indonesian regripped the weapon that he held tightly into his shoulder. His number two squeezed him slightly harder, arms clamped around the man.

The scream of the jet engines grew rapidly louder as the craft began to fill the sky. Dinaal could see the cockpit windows now. He felt a fleeting satisfaction with his timing and positioning perfectly beneath the large craft's flight path. As it roared overhead the Indonesian aimed at its underbelly, which was not difficult – it practically filled his vision.

'Now!' cried Dinaal above the deafening shriek of the turbines.

The Indonesian fired a single shot. The report, like Dinaal's shouted command, was consumed by the intense high-pitched whine of the big bird's huge engines.

The Indonesian lowered the barrel but his partner still held him and they all stared at the tail of the thundering airliner as it continued to descend towards the bright parallel lines of airfield approach lights in the field before the runway.

'Quickly!' Dinaal shouted.

The Indonesian shoved his partner away and placed the gun back inside the wooden box. They picked it up and hurried along the field to the fence, which they scurried over. The two lookouts held the doors of the van open for them. The team stepped up and inside and pulled the doors closed. Dinaal joined the driver in the front and the engine burst to life. The Colombian reversed the vehicle out of the narrow track on to the stone lane, turned on the lights and drove them back the way they had come.

A line of suitcases of various shapes and colours oozed from beneath a curtain of twisted black rubber strips. They lay on a well-worn conveyor track that looped through the drab and humid baggage hall of Bogota International Airport. A porter plucked one of them from the line, placed it on a rickety trolley and followed a tall, casually dressed man to the customs desk. The man showed the official his diplomatic passport and was promptly ushered through to the arrivals hall.

On the street outside, the Englishman was led to a smart bulletproof limousine. He climbed inside, his suitcase was placed in the trunk and the vehicle drove off.

Forty-five minutes later it arrived at the entrance to the British Embassy, where it passed through several layers of robust security to gain entry. A few minutes after that the man wheeled his suitcase into a large second-floor office in the three-thousand-square-metre building. The room was well appointed, had everything such an office should have, including a big ornate lump of a desk. An older man in a dark suit sat behind it.

'Ah. He has arrived,' the man behind the desk said, grinning and getting to his feet. 'Good flight?'

'Bearable,' the Englishman said, letting go of his suitcase and placing a laptop bag on a chair. 'You've caught a bit of sun since I left.'

'A round of golf with the American Ambassador.'

'Did you win?'

'Tried hard not to but his putting was frightful. Whisky?'

'Yes, but this one's on me. And I have a treat for you.'

The tall Englishman placed his suitcase on a chair and opened it. He took out a couple of shirts and looked at them. They were wet in his hands. He put them down and picked up the wooden box nested in the centre of the case. The contents of the box tinkled, made the sound of broken glass. The man turned it in his hands and an amber-coloured liquid dribbled from a hole in the side of the box.

'Oh dear,' the old embassy man said as he approached. 'What a waste.'

With his index finger, the Englishman probed the two neat holes on either side of the wooden box. It led him to investigate the lid of the suitcase. It had a neat hole in the centre. He lifted the case to discover a corresponding hole the other side. 'It's a bloody bullet hole,' he muttered.

'So it is,' the other man said, looking quizzically at his colleague.

1

Stratton sat in complete darkness on a grey rocky slope in a treeless, moonscape wilderness. He was wearing an insulated jacket and hard-wearing trousers, heavy boots and a thick goat-hair scarf wrapped around his neck to keep out the chilly night air. He looked like he had been camping in the outback for days without a clean-up.

He was in a comfortable position, his back against a rock, knees bent up in front of him, elbows resting on them, supporting a thermal imager in his hands. He was looking through the electronic optical device at a house half a mile away. It was one dwelling among a cramped collection of them, practically every one small, single-storey and built of mud bricks or concrete blocks. He slowly scanned the village, pausing each time the imager picked up a human form.

A mile beyond the village the land abruptly ended in a dead-straight horizontal line across his entire panorama, beyond it a vast black ocean and a lighter cloudy sky.

Stratton lowered the optic, letting it hang from a strap around his neck. He picked up a large pair of binoculars and took another view of the area. There was enough light coming from some of the houses for the glasses to be effective. Headlights suddenly appeared beyond the village, coming from the direction of the highway that followed the coastline. He shifted the binoculars on to them.

'Vehicles approaching from the south-east,' a voice said over Stratton's earpiece. 'Looks like two Suburbans.' The communications were encrypted and scrambled should anyone else try to listen in.

'Roger,' Stratton said as he watched the two pairs of headlights bump along a gravel road. The vehicles drove into the village, lights occasionally flashing skywards as they bumped over the heavily rutted ground. They came to a halt outside the house Stratton had been watching.

He switched back to the thermal imager and focused on the lead vehicle. He could see the bright white of the car's brake discs and exhausts. He watched as the Suburban's rear doors opened. A couple of men climbed out. The thermal imagers graded them down the scale from the superheated components of the car. The bodies were lighter than the buildings behind them and the ground under their feet. Stratton could see the men's hands and their heads, brighter than their clothing. Both men were carrying rifles, the cool metal almost black in their white hands, but just as visible because of the contrast.

One of the men went to the front door of the house. As he approached, it opened and two men came outside. There appeared to be an exchange of words. One of the men from the house walked to the Suburban and looked to have a conversation with someone in the back.

'Do you have eyes on?' the voice asked over Stratton's earpiece.

'Yes, though I can't identify anyone. But it's the right time, the right place and they look pretty cautious,' Stratton replied. 'I'd say it's safe to assume our man's there.'

'Enough to do the snatch?'

'Why not? It's like fishing. If we don't like what we catch, we can always throw it back.'

'Is that what you normally do?'

'If there was a normal way of doing things like this, everyone would be doing it.'

Stratton picked up a large reflector drum lens on a tripod with a device attached to the optic and looked through it. Because the image was highly magnified, it took him a few seconds to find the vehicles. He saw a man climb out of the back of the lead Suburban and talk with the one from the house. Stratton pushed a button on the device, which took several still recordings of the man. They were all of his head but more of the back than the front or sides.

The man walked towards the house. Just before going in he turned to the vehicles as if someone had called to him. Stratton quickly recorded several images of the man before he turned and entered the house.

Stratton viewed the images he'd taken and selected several of the man's face. He downloaded the images on to the satellite phone attached to the lens. He scrolled through the address book, selected a number and hit send. A few seconds later a window confirmed that the file had been sent.

He took up the thermal imager again, carried on scanning the house and the two vehicles. The two armed men stood off a couple of metres from the SUVs. The engines of the Suburbans were still running, their exhausts bright white on the imager.

'If it makes you feel any better,' Stratton said, 'I just sent London some images of a possible. They should be able to confirm.'

Less than a minute later the satphone gave off a chirp and he looked at the screen message: *Image 3. Target confirmed.*

Stratton disconnected the drum lens and put it in a backpack. 'Hopper?'

'Send,' said the voice.

'London has replied. If we catch this fish, we can keep it. I'll see you at the RV in two.'

'Roger that,' Hopper replied.

Stratton got to his feet, tied up the pack and pulled it on to his strong shoulders. He checked the ground around him, pocketed the wrapper from an energy bar he had eaten and searched for anything else. He made a three-hundred-and-sixty-degree scan of his surroundings using the imager. It picked up nothing save a few goats a couple of kilometres away. He wondered what the bloody things ate. It didn't seem possible that anything could grow in this barren land.

He headed down the gravelly incline into a gully that took him out of sight of the village. Stratton dug a cellphone from his pocket and hit a memory dial.

'Prabhu? Stratton. We're in business. We're towards you now, OK?'

Then he pocketed the phone and clambered on down a steep channel to a stony track barely visible in the low light. He paused to look around and listen. The sound of stones shingling downhill came from the slope opposite him. He continued walking and watched the shadowy outline of a man grow clearer as it made its way down the rise towards him.

The man joined him on the track and they walked alongside each other. The man was a similar age and build to Stratton, his lighter hair cut short. 'That was a pleasant few hours,' Hopper said. 'I would like to have seen the sunset though. Could you see it from where you were?'

'Not quite.'

'If the demand for gravel ever equals oil, Yemen will make a bloody fortune,' said Hopper. 'Never seen a country with so much dry rubble. The entire place looks like it's been bulldozed. A few trees would help. I don't know how the bloody goats manage. You could scratch around here all day and not find anything to eat. And water? The riverbeds must have water in them no more than a couple of days a year.'

Stratton listened to his partner talk. Hopper was a passionate man at heart to be sure. He felt sympathetic to people whose lifestyle he judged to be of a lower quality than his own. And he assumed that if they could, they would like to live the way he did. It made Stratton feel cold and unconcerned by comparison and Stratton didn't regard himself as particularly cold. He didn't resent Hopper for it though. Nor did he think the man was soft. But the way Hopper talked, with his emphasis on human kindness, it was a tad over the top, as well as being a potential weakness in their business. Yet that was Hopper. Stratton had known him on and off for ten years or so. He had worked with him hardly at all and knew him more socially than anything else back in Poole.

'You happy with this next phase?' Stratton asked.

'Yep. No probs. You talked to Prabhu?'

'He's on his way to the RV. Have you done a snatch like this before?'

'A few. One in Iraq. A handful in Afghanistan.'

'This should be easier. I don't expect the target to be as twitchy here. This is generally a quiet neighbourhood.'

'You operated in Yemen before?'

'Did a small task in Aden a couple years ago,' said Stratton. 'I've never been here before.'

Hopper checked his watch. 'Helen'll be putting the boys to bed about now,' he said. 'We usually let 'em have a late night Saturdays.'

Stratton had met Hopper's wife a few times. At the occasional family functions the service ran. She was nowhere near as chatty as her husband, certainly not with Stratton at least. But that stand-off attitude was not unusual. He had a good idea what most of the wives thought about him. He was single for one. And he never brought a girl to the camp gigs, which suggested he did not have a steady girlfriend. There was ample evidence to prove that he had normal tastes when it came to females. It was just that nobody he hooked up with appeared to last very long. Add that to his reputation as a specialised operative, exaggerated or otherwise, and most of the wives, other than those of his closest friends, put up a barrier when he was around.

But Stratton never felt completely comfortable operating alongside men like Hopper because they brought their families with them. Hopper was always thinking about them or talking about them in conversation. He seemed unable to disconnect while away on ops. Hopper never saw it as a disadvantage being a family man as well as an SBS operative. He regarded himself as pure special forces. He only talked to civilians beyond casual exchanges if he had to. He viewed them as potential security leaks. All of his friends were serving or former military personnel.

All of which meant several things to Stratton. Hopper would be fine and he would do the job well enough. But he would have preferred it if Hopper had not been chosen for this operation. He was better suited to large-scale ops. But at the end of the day Hopper had a reputation for being reliable, for being steady, and Stratton had no doubt he would do well.

'We weren't talking the day I left for here,' Hopper went on. 'Had a bit of a row. Not the best thing when you're off on an op. By the time I get home it will all have blown over. Helen doesn't hold on to things like that for long. You've met Helen before, haven't you?'

'Yes.'

'Course you have. That last service family barbeque. I never associate you with those kinds of bashes.'

'I think I got back from somewhere that day and just happened to be there.'

'That would explain it.'

'We're getting close to the RV,' Stratton said. He wasn't concerned about being overheard. They were still a long way from the village. But the family chat was getting him out of the right frame of mind. It didn't feel right to be talking about Hopper's family life. It was precisely the reason why he didn't like working with married fads.

They came to a broader track that connected the coastal highway with the village. A short distance further along they hit a track junction, the other route leading way up into the hills.

A narrow wadi ran alongside the track and through the junction at that point. Stratton stepped down into it. Hopper joined him.

'This is ideal,' Hopper said. 'Far enough away from the village and the highway.'

The air was still. Both men heard the quiet sound of boots on loose stones and they looked along the track that led up into the hills to see a figure approaching along it. The man was short and solid-looking and carrying a small backpack. He stopped on the edge of the wadi and squatted on his haunches with an economy of energy.

'Ram ram, Prabhu,' Stratton said, by way of greeting.

'Hajur, sab,' Prabhu replied.

'Sabai tic cha?' Stratton asked. It was more of a formality

than anything else because Prabhu would have warned him as soon as something was not OK.

'Tic cha,' Prabhu replied in his calm, easy manner, a hint of a smile on his lips. He had a flat, ageless face, short dark hair. He was a former British Gurkha officer and had completed twenty-four years in the battalion, rising through the ranks to major, one of the few who did. 'Ramlal is waiting in the vehicle around the other side of the hill,' he said.

'Good man. Take this pack back with you. We'll do the snatch here as planned. Soon as it goes off, you drive down and pick us up.'

'No problem, saheb,' Prabhu said, exchanging packs with Stratton.

'Don't forget your gas masks,' Stratton said with a smile. He had a soft spot for the Gurkha soldier but especially for Prabhu who he had worked with before in Afghanistan and Iraq.

'Don't worry. We won't forget.'

The ex-major set off back the way he had come and Stratton pulled a gas mask from the pack and handed it to Hopper, who stuffed it into one of the large pockets in his coat. Stratton took another mask for himself, which he pocketed. Then he took a large, heavy, jagged metal coil from the pack. He carried it along the wadi for a few metres and stopped to inspect the track.

'This'll do,' he decided.

Hopper climbed out of the wadi and Stratton handed him the coil. Hopper crossed the track, placed it on the ground, removed two metal pins from the brutal-looking device and pushed them into holes in its sides. He removed his scarf, bundled it on to one of the pins and gently hammered the pin home with a rock. He repeated the process with the other pin until the device was held securely, and wrapped the scarf back around his neck. As he walked back across the track to rejoin Stratton in the wadi, he unwound a coil of steel wire, the final part of the installation.

Hopper pulled the wire just enough to make it taut, then he put a rock on it to keep it in position on the edge of the wadi.

'We're good to go,' Stratton said and they both walked back to the track junction.

Stratton took a final item from the pack – a cardboard box – and opened it to expose half a dozen canisters, ring-pulls attached. They looked like smoke grenades but smaller. He handed three to Hopper. 'The lead car will open their doors as soon as they stop,' he said. 'That's the best time to pop them in.'

'We found that smashing the windows and dropping them inside the vehicle was quicker,' Hopper said.

'What if the glass is armoured? They'll lock the doors and you won't get in.'

'Unlikely, but I get your point.'

'You take the rear vehicle and I'll take the lead.'

'Roger that. Good luck,' Hopper said and he made his way back along the wadi to the cable, where he sat down and made himself comfortable.

Stratton sat back so that he could see the village, and stretched out his legs. He felt tired. The past few days had been long ones.

The operation had started in Washington DC three days earlier. He had flown in to attend a meeting of British and US special operations. Discussions about strategic alignments for Afghanistan and North Africa. It had finished with a global assessment of the Islamic offensive to date. Not surprisingly to Stratton, the Americans pegged Somalia, Djibouti and Eritrea as focal points for future operations. Somalia had become a mess on just about every level and was threatening to get worse. The world's centre for piracy and large-scale kidnappings was fast becoming a conduit for hard drugs and arms smuggling. And the ops guys talked about another, possibly greater concern: Somalia had begun to emerge as an operational front for international Islamic terrorism.

It wasn't Stratton's kind of meeting. All too hypothetical for him. But he hadn't been able to avoid it. With his level of experience he was expected to contribute to alliance planning strategies that included British special forces. His fears of one day getting permanently dragged into the office, desk, operations administration system had gone up a notch. But luckily for him, on this occasion someone in London thought they needed him more than the Washington think-tank did.

As the second day of meetings came to an end, Stratton received a high-priority message to make his way to the

British Embassy. Just him, no one else. Not the two SBS officers and the sergeant major from C Squadron he had arrived with. The message couldn't have been clearer. The faint odour of an operation wafted through his nostrils. He couldn't get out of the US Navy Intelligence offices quickly enough and grabbed a taxi to the other side of town.

On arrival at the embassy he was met by an aide. After brief formalities and security clearances, the aide walked Stratton up to the third floor, along cream-coloured corridors, and invited him to attend a private briefing inside the bubble chamber – the electronically sealed room designed to prevent eavesdropping. Stratton had been expecting several people to attend the brief. But he was mistaken. It was just him and the aide. The younger man, clearly from MI6, started talking. He was erudite, polished and intelligent.

Without the use of visual aids, he described how a month previously a British Airways flight arriving at Bogota International Airport from London Heathrow had been shot at from the ground. There was no doubt that the attack had happened while the aircraft was on its final approach to the Colombian capital. It could never have happened while taking off from Heathrow. And certainly not during its flight across the Atlantic and the eastern edge of the South American continent. There wasn't a rifle made that could fire a bullet vertically for seven miles. And it had been a single bullet fired into the underbelly of the aircraft. The bullet had been recovered – a 5.56mm which was common enough and suggested a military issue rifle. As to the make, that was impossible to determine. The incident had initially been labelled as nothing more than vandalism. People loosed off shots at commercial aircraft all the time, particularly in poorer, more unstable parts of the world. But when the same thing happened a week later to a French commercial airliner on its final approach to Nairobi, ears pricked within the Western intelligence community.

Yet it wasn't until several fine threads of intelligence were weaved together from various sources that the two attacks began to take on the form of something more significant.

Stratton sat quietly absorbing every detail. The MI6 man spoke methodically without pausing to take questions. Stratton would observe the usual protocol, which was that all queries be left until the briefer had completed his task.

The MI6 man kept talking. They had seen a spike over the previous twelve months in the interest among certain known terrorist arms providers in ground-to-air missiles. This interest had gradually become refined to the hand-held, man-portable variety of the weapon. That was always enough to set alarms ringing. But it was nothing new. The threat had been there ever since the Americans handed the Afghans large numbers of Stinger missiles during the USSR's invasion of their country. The mujahideen had used them against Soviet aircraft with great success.

A subsequent sting operation conducted by the CIA netted a handful of potential buyers of ground-to-air missiles but the trail to the ultimate end-users was never uncovered to any satisfaction.

A few months ago the interest in the deadly weapons

seemed to dry up, said the MI6 man. This was significant and had happened for three possible reasons. One, the end-users had failed to acquire the weapons and given up the effort, perhaps redirected their energies into a different scheme. Or two, they had just changed their minds about whatever they were planning to use the weapons for and no longer needed them. Or three, they had managed to find a reliable source for the deadly weapons.

The intelligence community had been speculating that the third option might be the case and that Islamic terrorists had managed to acquire portable ground-to-air missiles. Whereas it was always wise to prepare for the worst, it was also dangerous to assume anything. What they needed was some 'A1' category evidence – A1 being hard evidence witnessed by an intelligence organisation's own personnel. The source of the weapons couldn't be identified but there was still talk of them going round. For a time the rumour was thought to be the result of a collating phenomenon. Like Chinese whispers. One intelligence organisation asks another if they know anything about a given topic, such as the purchase of man-portable ground-to-air missiles by a terror organisation. The question gets passed on to another intelligence agency, which passes it to another. On its journey the question gets distorted, perhaps thanks to an inaccurate translation here and there, and, without any evidence to support it one way or another, it comes back to its point of origin in the form of an answer. Experienced analysts have an eye for such a result. And a warning for any analyst irresistibly attracted to a particular theory for whatever reason: 'If you look for something hard enough, you'll find evidence of it, even if it doesn't exist.'

Whatever was the case, the rumour was treated as highly plausible. Pretty much every Western government intelligence organisation began a search for the buyers and, most importantly, the weapons. The spiral-like patterns of the intelligence gathering system took a series of acute turns when someone working in the depths of the MI6 building on the Thames in London postulated that the shootings of the aircraft could well have been rehearsals. For something else. The theory had analysts sitting up all over the place.

A week before Stratton's visit to Washington DC a name surfaced, through British sources in Yemen. Someone had identified a possible missile provider. The name was Tajar Sabarak, a Saudi Arabian businessman. A name previously unknown to Western intelligence organisations. Sabarak was known to the Yemeni and Saudi authorities but as a petty smuggler who had so far eluded both countries' authorities. He made his income out of the legitimate transportation of khat leaf from Yemen to Somalia. And he was suspected of using his international network to traffic, on occasion, in blood diamonds.

The breakthrough came when MI6 sources in Yemen reported that Sabarak had met with representatives of people who a year earlier had shown up as being interested in purchasing ground-to-air missiles. Shortly afterwards, Sabarak began flying around the world, several of those trips to Hong Kong and Indonesia, nowhere that had anything to do with the buying and selling of the amphetamine khat leaf or blood diamonds. But when it came to places like Indonesia, plausibly everything to do with Muslim extremism. A sting operation was planned to try and entrap the Saudi into selling his missiles. And even though it failed, what it revealed, on secret recordings of meetings, was a man clearly obsessed with global jihad.

It was enough to trigger a reaction stronger than just the need for more clandestine information gathering, said the MI6 man. The SIS decided to bring Sabarak in for questioning. The decision was based on the feeling that it would be better to have Sabarak in custody than put him under surveillance in the hope of finding the weapons and then risk losing him. It was believed that whatever the jihadists were planning, it had in some way already begun.

While Stratton was landing in DC, Sabarak was flagged arriving by air from Saudi Arabia into Sana'a, Yemen's capital. From there he took a domestic flight to Riyan on the south coast. Before leaving Sana'a, Sabarak placed a call to a Somali in Riyan, a man named Mustafa Jerab, a man with strong ties to Al-Shabaab, an Islamic terrorist group. Stratton knew all about Al-Shabaab. Based in Somalia. No small-time organisation. In just a few years it had grown from a little-known gang of fanatics into a membership of tens of thousands and control of almost half the country.

Sabarak's phone conversation was recorded and sent to MI6 by a British spy operating within the Yemeni Secret Service. Sabarak and Jerab talked like business associates. They said nothing specific but the inference was quite clear to the British intelligence translator. Sabarak wanted to discuss the shipment of something highly sensitive.

Stratton's task was straightforward enough, the MI6 man said. He was to go to Riyan with one other operative and two Gurkha special forces support staff, snatch Sabarak and take him to the Oman border seven hours away by road, where British intelligence staff, with the nod from the Omani authorities, would take the Saudi away for a long rest and some very intensive interviews.

The MI6 man stopped talking. He picked up a phone and made an internal call. He needed a car out front right away.

Stratton's ride took him back to his hotel to pick up his belongings. From there it took him over the Anacostia river to Bolling Air Force Base, where he was met by a senior US Air Force officer whose job it was to escort him through the camp's bureaucracy and take him to a waiting aircraft.

Judging by the schedule Stratton had been given, he didn't have a lot of time to get to the UK to meet his next transit east. He climbed into a scuffed US Air Force van and as they headed for a line of huge C-141 jet transport aircraft he couldn't see how he was going to make the connection in time. So he wasn't surprised when the driver pulled the van past the transport craft towards a lone two-seater F-16 parked on the skirt.

Stratton stepped from the van as an aviation fuel truck drove away. After the senior officer's brief explanation of the flight – basically what not to touch and what to do in the event of an emergency – the man handed him a helmet and life vest and invited him to climb the ladder into the back seat of the dull-grey fighter. Stratton nodded to the pilot, who was already aboard. After a brief exchange the canopy closed and the engines roared as the bird rolled off the skirt.

As the pilot taxied the fighter, he called in to the tower and received clearance to go. He turned the F-16 on to the runway and fired the thrusters. Stratton's seat had been lowered to reduce the effects of the g-force but the take-off acceleration was exhilarating even for him. Especially since all he could see were the clouds through the poly-carbonate bubble canopy. Once they were airborne, the pilot raised Stratton's seat back up and after climbing to thirty thousand feet, they shot through the skies at around fifteen hundred mph, more than double the speed of a commercial jet.

After a while looking at nothing but clouds below and blue sky everywhere else, Stratton nodded off. Until a strange noise woke him. For a few seconds he wondered where the hell he was. A long tube with a bulbous end was hovering above him outside the cockpit. The far end of the tube was attached to the back of a large aircraft above and in front of them. The F-16 was being refuelled, a new experience for Stratton and he watched it with interest.

Three hours after leaving DC, five hours quicker than a Boeing 747, the fighter craft touched down at Mildenhall Air Base in Norfolk and Stratton got taken to an MoD civilianised Gulf jet, where he met Hopper, Prabhu, Ramlal and the ops team who were to give them the detailed briefing and provide the specialised equipment they needed.

Six and a half hours later the aircraft landed in Salalah, Oman, and after that the team rode in a Toyota Land Cruiser heading for the Yemeni border, which they crossed to follow the coastal road all the way to Riyan.

2

Flickering lights coming from the village snapped Stratton out of his reverie and he leaned his elbows on the edge of the wadi to look through a night-vision monoscope. Two Suburbans were making their way between the houses in his direction. It had to be their target departing the rendezvous.

He looked over at Hopper, who was on his knees holding the wire. The last house in the village looked about a thousand metres away. The vehicles would cover the distance in a couple of minutes on the rough road. The first vehicle emerged from between the perimeter houses and into the open, the second one close behind it, their headlights bouncing as they came over the undulating ground.

Stratton placed three small gas grenades on the top of the wadi and slid a hand inside his jacket to touch his holstered P226 pistol. It was a subconscious check. The weapon was already loaded. He had been ready for a fight from the moment they crossed the border into Yemen.

He looked once again at Hopper. 'You a happy man, Hopper?' he called out.

'I will be when we're on our way home.'

Stratton should have expected such a reply. He would bet fifty quid that Hopper was thinking about his family even then. But he took a moment to ask himself what he would feel like if he had the ideal girl waiting for him to get home.

Headlights suddenly appeared, coming from the coastal highway, and flashed across their position. It was a vehicle speeding along the track towards the village and the two Suburbans.

Stratton and Hopper dropped to the bottom of the wadi just before the vehicle, some type of 4×4, tore by, kicking dirt and stones into the wadi and on top of them. They knelt back up to watch it head towards the oncoming Suburbans.

'What the bloody hell was that?' Hopper called out.

Whatever it was, Stratton didn't like the look of it.

A sudden loud bang came from the direction of the two Suburbans. Not so much like a gun going off, more like the muffled burst of a tyre. Stratton and Hopper watched as the headlights of the leading Suburban bounced hard before turning sharply to one side like the vehicle had lost control. It came to a dusty halt and the second Suburban behind slid to a stop.

Stratton quickly took up the thermal imager and saw several figures running from a fold in the ground where they had obviously been hiding. There were four of them in total and they split into pairs as they went towards both vehicles. He could hear popping sounds as the figures reached the Suburbans. Then he heard a shot.

The red tail lights of the 4×4 flared as it came to a hard halt on the stone track right in front of the Suburbans. The sound of men shouting carried across the night air, the language impossible to decipher.

Hopper stood to get a better look but also out of mild shock. 'Is what I think I see going on what I think is going on?'

Stratton couldn't think what else could be going on.

'Someone's beaten us to them,' Hopper said.

Stratton didn't ask the question, who was carrying out the attack? All he could think of was what he needed to do about it. His team wasn't equipped for any kind of major firefight against numbers. They only had a pistol each. This was all now about coming up with the right reaction.

The 4×4 carried out a u-turn, its headlights pointing back the way it had come. They heard more shouts accompanied by the slamming of the vehicle's doors.

Stratton watched through his imager at what appeared to be the original ambush party: four or five men running across the rocky ground in the direction of the coast. The 4×4 accelerated along the track back the way it had come – towards Stratton and Hopper.

'Pull the claws!' Stratton shouted.

Hopper hesitated, looking for confirmation. He'd had the same concerns as Stratton – they weren't equipped for a firefight beyond a handful of pistols.

'They've got our target,' said Stratton. 'We're gonna take him back.'

Hopper yanked on the wire and dragged the multi-barbed snake out of its housing until it was stretched across the full width of the track.

'Nothing's changed other than we have just the one vehicle to take on,' Stratton called out. 'We also have surprise. They won't be expecting us.' He looked behind him and back up the mountain track hoping the Gurkhas would be ready to react as they had originally planned.

The 4×4 came fast along the dusty, rocky track, skidding on the bends, its lights bouncing violently over the ruts. Whoever was driving it was at the limit of his abilities. Stratton and Hopper pulled on their gas masks and braced as the vehicle closed on them. The driver was reckless, Stratton could see, the guy could easily skid into the wadi after hitting the claws. He hugged the edge of the riverbed, crouched below it as the headlights came on.

The vehicle shot over the claws, the teeth biting into the rubber and the links then wrapping around the front wheels as they were designed to, shredding the tyres. The driver fought to keep the SUV under control but he couldn't and slewed off the track opposite the wadi, the wheel rims gouging the ground. As the car stopped, Stratton and Hopper strode up and out of the wadi, pulling the pins from their grenades as they walked.

The front passenger door opened as Stratton arrived. He tossed a grenade inside. But as the cap fired with a loud pop and smoke hissed loudly from it the passenger climbed out. The man was wearing a gas mask. He was reaching inside his jacket. Stratton had several distinct thoughts in the space of half a second. Going for his own pistol could be the wrong move. The guy could be anyone. He was kidnapping a bad guy so he wasn't necessarily a bad guy himself. Stratton kept his forward momentum. He rapidly closed on the man, whose pistol came into view, and slammed into him, knee to crotch, palm to face, slapping the gun away with his other hand. The man dropped back into the vehicle with the force of the contact, his feet still on the ground. Stratton grabbed him by his front, ripped him from the vehicle and threw him to the ground.

On the other side of the car, Hopper had grabbed the driver, who was also wearing a gas mask, and pulled him out of his seat. The man crumpled to the ground and submitted the instant Hopper leaned his weight on him.

Stratton's man had no intention of giving up. As Stratton moved over him, the man kicked out, a hard blow to the torso that knocked Stratton back. The guy was some kind of a martial artist. He got to his feet, grabbed Stratton, swung him back against the 4×4 and gripped his collar with both hands in a judo-style stranglehold. Thick white vapour continued to stream from the gas canister, gushing out of the SUV's open door around the pair. Choking under the power of the man's grip, Stratton ripped away the guy's mask. He immediately began to succumb to the knock-out gas, loosening his hold on Stratton. The operative swept the man's legs out from under him and he landed hard on his side.

Stratton slammed the door shut to cut off the gas and placed a knee and his full weight on to the man while he removed his own gas mask and levelled his pistol at the guy's head.

'Hopper!'

'I'm good,' his partner called back, breathing hard. 'Driver's down. One man unconscious in the back. It's Sabarak.'

As he spoke, a vehicle came careering to a stop on the track. Prabhu and Ramlal. Ramlal hurried to help Hopper haul the prone Sabarak out of the back seat. Prabhu joined Stratton and they looked down on the man lying on his side breathing heavily as he fought against the effects of the gas.

He rolled on to his back, coughed and spluttered. He looked East Asian, his eyes narrow, a large, flat face. Stratton went through his pockets and produced a wallet and passport. The man was Chinese, or so the documentation showed.

'Who are you?' Stratton asked.

He remained expressionless, looked away like he had not even heard anything.

Stratton felt like his gut instinct had been right. This man was the vehicle's commander and he wasn't linked to terrorism, he was part of some organised security service like Stratton. He had used the same technique to carry out the kidnapping as Stratton. A controlled, sophisticated approach. But Stratton doubted he would volunteer any information about who he was and why he wanted Sabarak. Not without some help.

He aimed the pistol at the man's head. 'You attacked me and tried to prevent me from arresting a suspected terrorist. I'd be justified in shooting you. No one here's going to say it wasn't self defence.'

The man still didn't react.

'I don't have much time,' Stratton said. 'All I'm asking for is a reason not to kill you. Why do you want Sabarak?'

The man blinked. But that was all. Hopper came over to take a look at him.

'I think we're going to have to add a dead Chinese person to our report,' Hopper said.

'Unfortunately I think you're right,' said Stratton. 'Get Sabarak into our vehicle,' he said to the Gurkhas.

Prabhu and Ramlal dragged the unconscious Saudi into the back of their Land Cruiser.

Hopper looked through the thermal imager monoscope towards the village. 'Bodies moving this way. His ambush party have worked out what's happened, I expect.'

Stratton stepped back and clenched his teeth like he was about to shoot. 'Sorry, mate. You chose the wrong day to play the strong, silent type.'

'I work for Chinese State Security Ministry,' the man said quickly in halting English. Stratton kept the pistol pointed at him. There had been nothing in the brief about anything Chinese.

'What's your interest in Sabarak?'

'I cannot tell you that. Even on pain of death.'

'You sure about that?'

'You will eventually know the answer to that anyway. My life and reputation would be worth nothing if I told you.'

'Shall I engage them, sab?' Prabhu asked, looking to the approaching men who were less than a minute away. He'd unholstered his pistol and held it at the ready.

Stratton looked into the darkness towards the village, then at Ramlal behind the wheel of the idling Land Cruiser. 'No. Let's go.'

Stratton pocketed the Chinese man's passport, holstered his gun and climbed into the front passenger seat. Prabhu got into the back along with Hopper, and Ramlal floored the accelerator pedal.

Hopper kept an eye on their rear while Stratton studied the way ahead. He saw the foreign ambush team reach their commander. He saw the guy get to his feet. He saw them stand in the middle of the track, talking.

The Land Cruiser bumped heavily along. A lone car passed along the coastal highway in front, its headlights silently cutting into the blackness.

'What do you think the Chinese Secret Service wanted with this clown?' Hopper asked. The Saudi sat between him and Prabhu, his head lolling left then right, his tongue hanging out. He couldn't stop drooling. Hopper shoved Sabarak away on to Prabhu, who was equally unimpressed.

'No idea,' Stratton replied. His focus had switched back

to delivering their man to Oman. The threat had passed so short of any unforeseen accident, they would be at the border by first light. There was something niggling him though he did not know what. Whether it had been the fight or the close call that almost lost him his man, he didn't know.

He made an effort to unwind, shake off the uncomfortable feeling and concentrate on the drive. They would divide the journey into two watches. The Gurkhas were fresher than him and Hopper so they could take the first couple of hours. As soon as they were heading comfortably along the highway, he would grab a nap. It had been another long day.

The Cruiser bumped up on to the tarmac highway. Ramlal turned left and they headed north-east along the coast. It looked like the weather was closing in. The coastal highway did not hug the sea but paralleled it a couple of hundred metres away. An unending wall appeared on their right side, eight feet tall, a large property boundary made of concrete block and plastered and painted. It was a typical Yemeni construction. Stratton had heard of their love of walls. It was a national trait. He believed it. Even if there was nothing yet built on a property, or anything likely to be for years to come, they'd still build a wall around it.

The wall gave way to a view of the sea once more and the smooth two-lane highway stretched away from them towards Oman. The road was in good condition like it had been built not too long before. Stratton slid down a little in his seat, leaned his head back and got comfortable. As he was about ready to shut his eyes, a light reflected off the wing mirror on his side. He looked at the distant globes.

Headlights.

Stratton stared at them, his natural suspicion tingling. He hadn't been aware of any vehicle behind them when they joined the road. It must have come from a nearby house. The timing bothered him more than anything else. He wasn't a great fan of coincidences.

As they took a gentle bend, a second pair of headlights appeared close behind the first. That was enough to make Stratton sit back up. Harmless or not, it had to be proved it was safe before he could ignore it.

He considered the possibility that it was local security forces. They'd be interested in a lone car at night on these roads. Yemen had been placed on a state of alert after the increase in terrorist activity in recent months. He would rather avoid the authorities. He had the right paperwork and the numbers to call but the Yemenis would take for ever to confirm his right of passage. Particularly with his unconscious passenger. It would interrupt the final exfiltration phase from the country.

But as Stratton watched the vehicles he knew this was trouble.

He could feel it.

Everyone else in the car was by then on the same train of thought. Ramlal had hardly taken his eyes off the lights since he had seen them. He was at one-forty kph, which was standard cruising speed on these roads. He added another ten without noticing.

Hopper and Prabhu looked through the rear window.

'Trouble,' Hopper mumbled.

'I think so,' Stratton said.

'Tenacious buggers, the Chinese,' Hopper said.

'Clearly not easily discouraged,' said Stratton.

The two vehicles, smaller, faster 4×4s, had been moving at their top speed and once they closed the gap they slowed to match Ramlal's. It pretty much confirmed the suspicion that they were aggressors. Ramlal pushed on the accelerator but the Cruiser didn't have the power to do much more. He couldn't pull away from them.

The lead pursuer then accelerated and looked like it was going to ram them.

'Gun!' shouted Stratton, Hopper and Prahbu at the same time as a man leaned out of the passenger window with a pistol in his hand.

Ramlal swerved the vehicle, reducing the gunman's arc of fire. But another gunman leaned out of the other side.

Ramlal swerved again but he had been bracketed. The first guy fired, the round punching into the back of the Cruiser, erasing any possibility of them being overzealous highway or army patrol.

Now both shooters fired. No windows had been hit. They were trying for the tyres. Ramlal forced the Cruiser left and right, its tyres screeching.

Another stretch of long wall on the coastal side of the highway came to an end, revealing a broad stretch of ground that shelved gently down to the ocean five hundred metres beyond. Lights flickered a couple of kilometres in front near the beach. A village.

'Get off the road!' Stratton shouted.

Gripping the wheel like a vice, Ramlal swerved the vehicle to the edge of the tarmac and dropped it down on to the dirt shoulder. The lead pursuing vehicle followed like it was being towed behind them. But the dust kicked up by the Cruiser was vast and immediate, acting like a smoke screen between them.

As the Cruiser sloughed along the rutted shoulder, the second 4×4, still on the road, drew up alongside. Another man leaned out of the rear window and took aim with a handgun.

'Ramlal!' Stratton urged, as he aimed his gun past his driver's head.

Ramlal cringed and braced himself for the shot. But he didn't wait for it because he had to swerve to avoid a massive boulder right in front of them on the shoulder. The gunman fired at the Cruiser, hitting the door and doorframe. Stratton fired back turning the car's rear passenger window white.

Up ahead the shoulder was becoming rocky. Ramlal steered hard left, up the shoulder, back on to the highway. All inside hung on, except the Saudi. Sabarak was bouncing up and down like a rag doll. His head struck the roof as the Cruiser flew up on to the road and he opened his eyes with a gasp.

Ramlal aimed the front corner of the Cruiser at the rear quarter of the other 4×4, just behind the tyre. As the two vehicles brutally connected the Cruiser sent the 4×4 into a violent swerve as its back wheels tried to overtake the front wheels. On the second fishtail, they succeeded and the vehicle spun a full hundred and eighty degrees, its wheels smoking, coming to a stop facing backwards.

By now Sabarak, who had almost regained full consciousness, looked every bit like he was living a nightmare.

Ramlal had the old Cruiser up to its limit but the other 4×4 was more powerful and moved alongside. Stratton recognised the front passenger immediately through its open windows. It was the Chinese Secret Service officer. He had a semi-automatic in his hand and aimed it past Ramlal at Stratton. Another Chinese agent in the back held a sub-machine gun out the window.

The officer indicated with the pistol for Ramlal to pull over.

Ramlal glanced at his boss. He would do nothing without the OK from Stratton.

Stratton scanned the road ahead, searching for options. He had to assume the Chinese agent would rather not risk harming the Saudi or he would have done so by now. Like Stratton, no doubt the man's orders were to bring Sabarak in alive.

The other 4×4 had recovered and was closing on them. Stratton had limited options. He could try and pick them off while driving. Or he could have Ramlal stop and they could shoot it out. But the odds weren't in his team's favour and he wasn't about to risk the lives of any of his men for some low-life Saudi git.

The Chinese agent had probably worked out the same scenarios and appeared content to give Stratton time to come to terms with them.

Stratton looked up along the highway that cut between a distant hillside. He looked at the village on the coast. He looked back at the Chinese Secret Service officer with the semi-automatic. Then at Ramlal. There was another option.

'Right turn coming up,' he said. 'Brake hard so they miss it.'

'Hajur, sab,' Ramlal said.

The Gurkha saw the turn coming up and waited for the last possible moment. Ramlal slammed on the brakes and the Cruiser pitched and slid towards the bend, all four wheels smoking. Then he released the brakes and took the turn as the first 4×4 shot ahead and the one in rear swerved hard to avoid a collision.

The Cruiser bumped furiously over the edge of the tarmac and down on to a sandy track, and accelerated hard along it.

Stratton looked back and saw the pursuing vehicles manoeuvring to follow. He focused ahead. 'When we get to the village, Hopper and I will jump out with our man,' he said.

'You want me to stop?' Ramlal asked.

'No. Keep your speed. Maybe slow a little as you pass the first houses,' Stratton added, having second thoughts.

Stratton looked around at the Saudi who was wide-eyed with everything going on. He saw for the first time that the man was younger than him and somewhat athletic.

'You want to be a British prisoner or a Chinese one?' he said.

The Saudi didn't ponder the question for long.

'Keep them in pursuit of you for as long as you can,' Stratton said to Ramlal. 'If they start to shoot, pull over and show them your empty hands. Don't fight back. I don't think they'll harm you when they discover we're gone.'

'We would rather make a run for it into the darkness,' Ramlal said.

'We'll give you lots of time before that,' Prabhu assured him.

Stratton realised the Gurkhas didn't want to surrender to anyone, let alone a bunch of Chinese. Too great of an indignity. He regretted asking them. 'Sorry. You're right,' he said. 'Remember to toss the keys.'

Stratton opened his door slightly as the vehicle bumped heavily along the track. Hopper opened his directly behind Stratton and kept it open with his leg.

'Past this first house!' Stratton shouted.

Everyone braced. Hopper took a good hold of Sabarak while Prabhu grabbed him from the other side, giving him a look that stated unequivocally he was going out the door.

'Stand by!' Stratton shouted, looking back at their pursuers to gauge the distance. He was pleased to see the dust they were kicking up had obscured the 4×4s completely.

As Ramlal drove at speed past the first house on the edge of the village, Stratton shouted, 'Go!', and hurled himself out of the Cruiser.

He landed hard on his feet, which he kept together as if for a parachute landing, spun on to his back and shoulders and rolled several times in the dirt before coming to a dead stop against the wall of the neighbouring house.

The Saudi didn't fair quite as well. Hopper jumped out holding on to him while Prabhu shoved him with all his strength. More by luck than design, Sabarak ended up directly under Hopper. Every bit of air was forced from the Saudi's lungs as he hit the ground with the combined weight of Hopper and himself. When he finally came to rest, he remained where he was, unable to move. And had it been up to him, he would have stayed there. But Stratton and Hopper grabbed him under the arms and dragged him away from the track behind the house as the two 4×4s bounced past through the dirt.

Stratton watched the tail lights disappear.

'What's the plan from here?' Hopper asked.

'I'm working on it,' Stratton said, scrutinising Sabarak. The guy was sitting up holding his chest and looking like he might go unconscious again.

'On your feet,' Stratton said. 'I'll make this simple for you. I only have to get you back alive. No one said anything about unbroken. If you make life difficult for us, Hopper here will break your legs. He likes doing things like that.'

Hopper gave Stratton a glance that appeared to question the claim. When Sabarak looked at him, he adopted an expression that wholeheartedly supported the threat.

'Get up,' said Stratton.

Sabarak got unsteadily to his feet.

'Stay right behind me,' Stratton ordered.

The three of them walked quietly between the houses. Hardly any had lights on but that didn't mean they weren't occupied. It was hard to tell. The locals were very poor. They used their minimal resources sparingly. That meant going to bed and getting up with the sun to avoid using all their fuel on lighting.

The men arrived at a high wall, part of the harbour's perimeter, that kept them from the water. They went left and followed it to a large metal gate. The harbour entrance. It wasn't locked and they made their way on to a broad concrete jetty. A man-made boulder mole went out to sea at a right angle to the jetty and after a couple of hundred metres turned a sharp corner and ran on a few more metres, where it ended to face the end of the opposite mole a hundred or so metres away. This was the sea entrance.

They paused to survey the scene. The walkway was dimly illuminated by a spread of lamps. Dozens of small craft were moored to the inside perimeter or to each other. Mostly fishing boats of varying sizes, from little row boats to thirty-foot sailing boats. There were a handful of powered metal tugs, all of which could have done with a lick of paint. A building set back from the jetty and surrounded by the perimeter wall advertised itself as a fishery in English as well as the local dialect. They could see no sign of life other than a couple of scavenging dogs.

'Nice evening for a boat ride,' Stratton said.

Hopper noted the gloomy skies.

'All we do is follow the coastline to Salalah,' Stratton said. 'What can go wrong?'

Hopper rolled his eyes at the effort to tempt fate. 'Would be nice if we could find something with a bit of speed.'

'And comfort.'

Hopper moved to the edge of the jetty to look down on the boats. 'What about that one?' he said, pointing at a long skiff with twin outboards.

Stratton felt a twinge of guilt about taking any one of them. 'These people struggle enough to make a living without us coming along and nicking their livelihood,' he said.

'Right. What are those over there, by the entrance?' said Hopper. He jutted his chin towards the mole entrance and a couple of low-profile, sleek black semi-rigid inflatables.

Stratton's interest in them was immediate. They didn't look like fishing boats, more like some kind of security or military craft. And they looked fast. Hopper kept a hold of the Saudi and the three stepped along the concrete path at the base of the mole. They came to a building at the end, in the corner of the mole. The sign above the door said it was AUSTIN OIL TERMINAL SECURITY. The boats had twin 250 outboards bolted to the transoms.

'We don't feel guilty about borrowing one of these, do we?' Hopper asked.

'We don't. Check out the fuel. We need around forty litres. I'll look into starting this one up.'

'Give me a hand, Sabarak,' Hopper said, pulling the Saudi with him.

Stratton climbed down into the first boat and looked at the controls and battery housing. It appeared to be in good order.

By the time Hopper and Sabarak returned, both straining to carry a couple of large petrol containers each, Stratton had prepared the wires behind the ignition lock on the coxswain's consul. 'We'll need water,' he said to Hopper. 'Hand those down to me,' he said to the Saudi, who obeyed tiredly.

Beams of light suddenly flashed across the top of the mole. A second later they could hear the low rumble of vehicle engines and tyres on gravel.

'I suspect our Chinese friends have discovered the ruse,' said Stratton. 'Hurry up, Hopper.'

Stratton connected two wires then struck them with a third and they sparked and the starter motor turned over. They were spared the drama of having to wait for the engines to gun to life. The sound was loud and immediate and the two-stroke engines gave off a lot of smoke. Stratton released the stern line.

Hopper pushed Sabarak down into the semi-inflatable and jumped down himself, carrying a couple of bottles of water. 'I hope the tap water's potable,' he said as he untied the bow line.

Stratton straddled the jockey seat and reversed the long and powerful craft away from the jetty. As he did so, a 4×4 slewed up to the harbour gates, followed by another, their headlights shining through the barred entrance. A figure got out of the first vehicle and pulled the gates open. The two 4×4s swept into the harbour and came to a squealing stop. Doors opened. Men got out and started running along the walkway.

Stratton played the throttles. The powerful engines roared and Hopper and the Saudi held on as the nose of the boat came tightly around towards the harbour entrance. The Chinese agents had guns in their hands. Stratton heard the loud cracks of the weapons over the revving engines. As he lined up the nose of the boat with the mouth of the harbour he gave the engines full throttle. The boat lurched up on to its plane, the nose dropped and it tore out of the relatively smooth waters of the harbour and went partially airborne as it hit the choppy waters of the Gulf of Aden proper. The gunmen, who had run out of bullets, reloaded but by the time they came up on aim they had nothing more to shoot at.

The sea was heavy and Stratton eased the power back enough to get the boat into its rhythm, rolling over the waves.

'They might try and follow us,' Hopper shouted, looking back at the harbour entrance.

'Good luck to them in this. By the time we get into that lot, they'll need more than radar to find us.'

Hopper looked ahead and saw where they were heading: due south, straight out to sea, right into a massive bank of low, thick cloud. All sign of the land behind them disappeared as they hit the dark shroud that reached down from the skies to the sea. They couldn't see a single light, not even a shadow.

Using the compass on his watch, Stratton brought the tip of the boat around to the north-east, and set the speed at what he estimated was a steady twenty knots. With three hundred miles to go that would take around fifteen hours, if there was no tide of course. In the windless haze he had little chance of working out its direction or speed. Only daylight and the lifting haze would reveal that.

Stratton pulled his jacket together against the chilly air. Hopper sat in the bows looking unperturbed. He was a tough bird. But Sabarak was already feeling the damp cold through his thin jacket. He sat between them. He had lost the shemagh he had been wearing and his short, black curly hair framed a thin face, light-brown skin, dark eyes and thick eyebrows that came together above a large, narrow nose. His mouth was accentuated by a thin, manicured line of a beard that gave him a permanent grimace. It was either that or he hated the two Englishmen so much he couldn't hide it from his face.

As the hours passed the waters became even calmer and the boat motored along with only the occasional dip and bump. After a while the Saudi rolled himself into a ball on the deck and closed his eyes. Hopper hardly moved other than to offer Stratton and Sabarak a drink.

'Tastes pretty good,' Hopper said. 'A hint of chlorine but that's only encouraging. If we're not shitting through the eye of a needle by morning, we should be fine.'

Sabarak looked like he wasn't very well but Stratton suspected he was tougher than he appeared. The Saudi was trying to condition them. Stratton fully expected the man to act ill by the time they arrived in Oman. It might delay his interrogation by a little, but not much. It would be easy enough to determine the Saudi's true strength and condition.

Hopper raised his head like he had heard something. He turned to look ahead into the darkness. Stratton noticed the sudden interest and watched him. Hopper signalled Stratton to cut the engines. Silence fell over them like a heavy shroud. The swell gently lapping against the inflated rubber sides of the boat became the only sound. Sabarak sat up, alert.

'I thought I saw something,' Hopper said in a low voice. 'It was white. Another boat maybe.'

They all remained quiet, looking ahead and to the sides.

A noise came to them through the mist, like something heavy rolling across a deck. Then a creak. Then a man's voice. Hard to tell how far away it was. It sounded foreign, to Hopper and Stratton at least. But possibly not to Sabarak, who got to his feet as if in expectation. Another voice shouted a response from a different direction.

'Fishermen?' Hopper suggested.

'Maybe,' Sabarak said. 'But not Yemenis. They are not speaking Arabic.'

The voice came again. It sounded closer.

'The winds of fortune,' Sabarak muttered. 'How they change.'

Stratton had a feeling he knew what Sabarak meant and made ready to start the motors, when a big black shape appeared on their port side. It was the painted wooden hull of a boat. About a metre and a half out of the water. Stratton started one of the engines, gave it some power and turned the wheel to bring the boat hard about.

'Ahead!' Hopper warned.

Another vessel appeared, blocking their way. It glided out of the mist, a figure standing in the prow with a stubby brown and black rifle in his hands.

Stratton slammed the outboard into reverse and swung the boat around. As he pushed the gears into forward drive another craft arrived to block his way. Boats appeared from every direction, surrounding them. Stratton had little choice but to keep the engine in neutral.

The boats closed in, with men standing in all of them. They were all slender, dressed in grubby clothes, their dark brown skin smooth, their hair tight short curls. The kind of features hard to miss. Somalis, several carrying AK-47s, one holding an RPG on his shoulder. It didn't need a genius to figure out that fishing was probably a low priority for these men.

One of the Somalis shouted something as he aimed his weapon at Stratton.

Stratton put his hands up to show he was unarmed. Hopper did the same.

'He wants you to turn off the engine,' Sabarak said.

Stratton reached down and cut the motors. It all went

quiet again but for the lapping water and the boats gently bumping against each other.

A steel tug-like boat came out of the mist and nudged its way through the crowd of smaller craft. It was about twenty-five metres long, Stratton estimated, and covered in rust. It had Somalis lining its sides to look down on their unexpected catch. It was the mother craft to the rest of the pirate flotilla.

3

A Somali in a weapon harness scooped a hand over his shoulder at Stratton, Hopper and Sabarak and said something guttural-sounding. He pointed at the hooked ladder beneath his feet over the side of the tug. Stratton hesitated, as did Hopper. They had a few problems they needed to take care of, namely their equipment. Most importantly the guns. Stratton also had a spare knock-out gas canister. He could see no point in going on the offensive with the pirates. They had him seriously outnumbered and outgunned.

He and Hopper exchanged glances as Sabarak climbed up to the pirate boat. Hopper stepped on to the edge of their rubber boat and suddenly made a show of losing his balance. Stratton grabbed hold of him in an effort to save him and both men toppled into the water. Much to the amusement of the Somalis.

While both men struggled to get hold of the side of the inflatable, they dumped their holsters and guns, spare magazines and communications devices. No point in keeping any of it. They would be searched and all items of interest would be taken.

The two operatives finally managed to haul themselves back into the boat with help from a couple of the Somalis. Dripping wet they climbed up on to the pirate mother craft. The Somalis manhandled them down the side deck, which was a mess of rope coils and fuel drums. The pirates shoved them down on the cold, greasy metal deck area behind the raised superstructure that housed the bridge, galley and probably a couple of accommodation rooms.

A powerful-looking, well-fed Somali stepped out of the superstructure on to the deck and surveyed the three prisoners. Judging by the quality of his clothing, the jewellery around his neck and on his wrists, and his authoritative bearing, he was the man in charge.

Stratton watched him, hoping to get an early impression. But the pirate commander's expression was hard to read. He barked a command and a Somali began to search them thoroughly, then removed their belts and boot laces and tied their hands with nylon fishing line. The Somali handed his finds to the commander, who examined the three wristwatches – two practical timepieces, the third expensive. He flicked to the back of the passports, noting the two sodden ones were British. He eyed his captives again, now with a little more interest.

He handed the items back to the man who had given them to him and walked away along the side of the ship.

The Somali guard made the three prisoners sit among a pile of rolled nets, large fishing weights and stinking fish pallets. The smell cut through the night air. These guys obviously did some fishing, Stratton reasoned, probably just enough to feed themselves. He looked up at the rear of the boat, illuminated by a bright light at the top of the cabin superstructure. He could hear the rhythmic thump of the engines below the deck, the sound of the waves lapping against the side of the craft. Two of the pirates sat outside the back door holding AK-47s, smoking and talking quietly. They had no shoes, they looked unwashed. He noted that some of them wore what might have once been expensive clothing. But hard, constant wearing and no cleaning had taken all the value from them. They acted more business-like than unfriendly and didn't appear unfamiliar with foreign prisoners.

Stratton couldn't believe his bad luck. He was a prisoner of Somali pirates on their way, he assumed, to the Somali mainland. This wasn't going to go down well in London. The incentive to change the direction of events was immense. It was a duty of course, and a matter of self-respect. He had too many reasons to get away from these pirates.

Sabarak hadn't said a word since the pirates appeared. Which wasn't what Stratton had expected. But then again, he probably had his own reasons for not wanting them to know who he was. Before Sabarak could do anything, he needed to know a lot more about these Somalis. Most important was what kind of relationship they had with his Islamic brothers, the Al-Shabaab fundamentalists who controlled many parts of Somalia. Not all of the pirates had any great interest in the cause. Most simply saw themselves as businessmen. Sabarak didn't know where these guys fell yet. So he wasn't a danger to Stratton for the moment. While he remained unsure he would keep his mouth shut. The Saudi wasn't guaranteed a positive reception from anyone just because he was an arms trader to jihadists. He'd have to find an interested or sympathetic party and then prove he was who he said he was. That might not be so easy. They would have to know people in common.

Stratton hadn't learned much about the Saudi during the operational briefing because little was known about him. There had been a comparison made with the background of Osama bin Laden because like bin Laden, Sabarak came from a wealthy Saudi family and at some stage during his education, he developed a keen interest in the Wahhabi way of life. Sabarak's family made its wealth from retail as opposed to construction. Sabarak chose to hide his extreme beliefs no doubt because bin Laden had not and had been a hunted man even before 9/11. Sabarak enjoyed frequent trips to Europe and America, staying in fine hotels and spending serious money. What you could call the usual Western entrapments: fast cars, state-of-the-art electronics, generally appearing to fully embrace the secular way of life. The guy had clearly plotted to bide his time and wait for an opportunity to take part in the anti-Western cause. He'd made the move at some period in the previous two to three years. As soon as he did, it was always going to be only a matter of time before his head popped up into the sights of Western intelligence agencies. But Sabarak would have been aware of that and he would have prepared as much as he could before he stepped into the light. Stratton wondered how far the Saudi had got in his planning, if he had a clue before his kidnapping that he had actually made the wanted list.

As things stood, while the pirates didn't know anything about any of them other than their nationalities, Hopper and Stratton stood a chance of being offered up to the British authorities for ransom. But Sabarak only had to find the connection to Al-Shabaab.

Stratton decided to tests the waters. 'Well, Sabarak,' he said. 'It would seem as if fortune has indeed changed in your favour.'

Sabarak looked at him and in the dim light the operative could see the man grin. 'I am well aware of that,' the Saudi said.

'You think you'll be able to sell your story to these guys?'

'I'm as confident as you are that I can.'

Hopper leaned close to Stratton to whisper in his ear. 'Remember the rules. Make escape attempts early.'

Stratton looked through the anchor cable eye in the side of the boat beside him and down at the dark, cold water. The half-dozen small boats were empty and being towed behind the mother craft. Could they cut them loose and take one back to the Yemen coast? He doubted it. They would have to overcome a myriad of obstacles before they could even attempt it.

'Any ideas?' Stratton muttered.

Hopper had gone through a similar thought process and come to the same conclusion. Hopper leaned his head back against the metal side of the tug.

Stratton lay back and made himself comfortable against a pile of nets. He was cold, his soaked clothes and the chilly night air a bad combination. He decided it was going to be one of those situations when all he could do was wait for the right opportunity to present itself. And when it came he needed to be decisive.

The rhythmic thud of the engines went on and the rolling motion of the boat had a calming effect. After a while he drifted off into an uneasy sleep. He was awoken by a sudden rush of activity on board as several men ran past him. The engines had been cranked up to what must have been full power. Pirates were hauling in the speedboats ready for crews to jump down into.

Stratton sat up and squinted at the sun that had appeared low above the water on the port side. It confirmed to him they were sailing south. And from Yemen that meant directly towards Somalia.

Another man ran past and went up into the superstructure, leaving the door open. They could hear the speedboats revving up and skimming away over the water.

The chief stepped out of the superstructure and went along the side of the vessel towards the front without a glance at his prisoners, talking energetically into a radio. Several more men ran past the group, one of them kicking Hopper's legs out of the way.

Stratton got to his feet, feeling his muscles stiffen. He

looked around the vast, uninterrupted ocean. And he saw what all the fuss was about. Half a mile or so up ahead was a large cargo vessel. The pirates were going to work. He stepped along the deckside to see better. The leader saw him standing part of the way along the deck and shouted at one of his men, who aimed his rifle at the operative, moving the tip of the barrel repeatedly, urging him back to the stern.

Stratton obeyed but remained standing. Hopper joined him to watch the small boats go after their prey. As the mother craft got closer, they watched the half-dozen speed-boats, their former craft included, buzz the rear of the ship like a pack of hyenas. It was some kind of bulk cargo carrier nearly a hundred metres long, but it had a couple of significant disadvantages faced with the pirates: the bulker was slow, going little more than ten knots, and it had a low freeboard. The top of the stern itself looked to be only a couple of metres above the water. The bulker's sides, up until midships, were little more than three metres out of the water. Not enough to prevent pirates climbing aboard. For that the freeboard needed to be at least five metres clear of the water and the carrier would need to reach a speed in excess of fourteen knots. It hadn't because it couldn't.

The bulker began to swerve from side to side, as sharply as it could, creating large waves behind it, sending a churning wake towards the pirate boats. From what Stratton could see, the carrier had little or nothing else in the way of physical defences. No water cannon. No barbed wire or fencing. Short of any surprises, the boat looked like easy pickings.

The crack of gunfire could be heard above the thud of the mother craft's engines. The pirates were in full attack mode.

Stratton, Hopper and Sabarak weren't the only ones transfixed by the attack. So was their armed guard. Stratton looked at the back of the guy, calculating the possible phases after incapacitating him. He looked at the four or five Somalis on the prow. Guns in hand. The odds were not good enough.

He stood on a pile of fish boxes in order to get a better look at the action.

The bulker leaned steeply over with each desperate turn, its decks empty. No sign of any crew on board. Stratton could imagine them all inside, hatches battened down, locked inside the citadel, hoping desperately that it would be enough to defend against the pirates. No doubt they would also be wishng they had done more defensive preparation before entering the Gulf of Aden. But like wild dogs, the Somalis had a reputation for pressing the attack for as long as there was a chance of succeeding. Stratton had heard of Somali pirates boarding a boat and staying on its deck for more than a day while trying to gain entry to it.

The two longer attack boats each carried five or six men, the others three or four. As Stratton watched, one of the little boats accelerated along the length of the cargo carrier. A bang followed by a rocket with a smoking tail shot from the speedboat and curved over the top of the ship, narrowly missing the bridge and dropping into the sea the other side.

A second speedboat tore up the starboard side and released a rocket of its own. This one struck the bulker's funnel and exploded like a hand grenade with a sharp crack, leaving a dramatic black scar and indent on the red-painted metal.

A guttural shout went up from the Somalis on board the mother craft followed by a cheer from the others. One of the longer attack craft closed on the rear of the ship, which continued to manoeuvre desperately. But the experienced Somali coxswain mirrored the turns as he got closer to the stern. As he closed the gap to a mere metre from the back of the bulker, one of his boarding team raised a metal ladder a couple of metres long, formed into a large hook shape at the end. The carrier turned again. As it did so it leaned over. The pirate boat bumped the ship and the boarding team heaved the curved end of the ladder over the top rail, where it hooked on firmly. A Somali in back loosed off a burst of rifle fire while another scrambled up the ladder, quickly followed by others.

More shouts from the exultant Somalis on board the mother craft as they watched their comrades create a foothold. Within seconds, every pirate on the speedboat, except for the coxswain, had climbed aboard the cargo ship and was sprinting towards the superstructure.

The next long speedboat closed in for its turn. Stratton could hear the clatter of rifle fire increase as the Somalis already on board took their positions, tugging on doors, scaling exterior ladders and stairways all around the superstructure in an effort to gain entry. As the second boarding team attached its ladder and quickly clambered aboard, a burst shattered several windows on the superstructure. It looked like the Somalis were violently attacking a door with pieces of wood. Firing guns into locks. The cacophony went on. Smoke began to rise from a fire somewhere on board.

After a while, the vessel's erratic swerving ceased and its speed reduced. The bridge wing doors on one side opened and a couple of the Somalis stepped out, their arms waving.

The cargo ship was theirs. Once again a cheer went up from the mother craft.

After the leader went on board the bulker, he didn't return for several hours. By then the day had become warm and Stratton's clothes had dried out. He and Hopper and Sabarak had been given a dish each of rice mush. Sabarak had begun striking up small conversations with the guards. He seemed to understand the language pretty well but wasn't fluent, judging by the way the Somalis responded to him. Stratton and Hopper had listened, gaining what little they could. Which wasn't much. Except for one thing.

The commander was called Lotto.

Stratton watched as two of the raiders returned to the mother craft carrying a hefty backpack between them. They looked like two of the original boarders. As they stepped down on to the deck, one of the mother ship's crew who hadn't boarded the bulker stepped up to them, put a hand inside the backpack, apparently deciding that a portion of it belonged to him, for whatever reason. He came up with a pair of shiny binoculars. One of the boarders got angry but the crewman walked away to the back of the boat. The situation changed in a second. As the crewman stepped up to the superstructure, the boarder caught him and hooked an arm around his neck. The crewman pushed him off, drawing a knife from his belt. By now a gallery of interested Somalis had formed to watch him. A fight ensued. As the brawl came their way, Stratton and Hopper moved out of the way.

The fight didn't last long. The boarder went for the crewman's arm holding the knife but the crewman twisted free and they fell together and he drove his blade right into the man's guts. He stabbed him several more times, his final thrust going behind the boarder's ribcage where it skewered his heart.

The crewman got to his feet, his hands and clothing soaked in blood. As he picked up the binoculars and inspected them, Lotto stepped out of the superstructure. The chief shouted at the crewman, evidently looking for an explanation. The crewman's expression changed as he began to explain his side of the story. The man was frightened. Another Somali spoke but not in favour of the crewman, who argued with him. Lotto listened to the comments from one source and another. Then he withdrew a pistol from his side and shot the crewman in the middle of the chest. The man dropped like a lead weight and the binoculars fell on to the deck beside him. He opened his mouth a couple of times and started gasping.

Lotto shouted another command as he holstered his pistol and went back inside the boat and two Somalis lifted up the crewman and tossed him over the side. The dead pirate quickly followed. One of the crewmen took the binoculars for himself and Stratton and Hopper, with Sabarak close by, were left alone. A large pool of blood had formed in front of them.

By the time the sun set, the pirates had organised themselves, and the flotilla, along with its new and largest addition, continued south towards Somalia. By the next morning, they had changed direction and were heading east. The blood on the deck had dried and cracked across the deeper pools.

It had been a cool night but all of them had slept. Stratton looked over the side. He couldn't see anything but blue-grey ocean. But the air smelled different. And there were seagulls. Not in any great abundance. A handful flying close to the vessel, inspecting it from on high. The flying scavengers were going to be disappointed though. These Somalis were harvesters of the sea all right, but a much different kind.

Stratton got to his feet and stretched his stiffened body and checked the horizon the other side of the bridge house. The guards were watching him but it was like they had become used to his curiosity and took it to be harmless.

He couldn't see a distinct coastline but he knew it was there. A strong shadow divided the sea and sky. He looked back at the cargo vessel cruising behind them, attached by several thick steel cables. The speedboats were divided up between the stern of both mother craft and bulker.

Most of the pirates still appeared to be on board the carrier. Stratton could imagine the night they'd had looting the crew's belongings, the cargo and getting into the captain's safe, which always contained cash in several currencies. He leaned back on the edge of the boat looking at the water. He felt the urge to jump into it, but only to cool off. This was beginning to feel like it could be a drawn-out affair.

Stratton had been held captive many times before. But not by pirates. They were a new experience for him. On this occasion he was an economic commodity. He had a monetary value to them. They were going to put him and Hopper up for sale. That was unless the Saudi could change the stakes.

A craggy, arid scar of land became visible as the light improved, a lifeless spur of yellow and grey rock with few trees. As they drew closer to the coast, dozens of what had looked like bobbing seagulls hundreds of metres away became small fishing boats. When the pirate boat passed by them, the two or three occupants in each paused to watch, nets in their hands. There was the occasional wave of an arm. It wasn't an unfamiliar sight to them. A couple of younger fishermen watched with envious eyes, perhaps wondering when it would be their turn to gain a chance of becoming rich.

Stratton could make out buildings beyond a golden beach that stretched as far as the eye could see in both directions. A pall of smoke hung in the air above the habitats like a thin, floating carpet. The town was on a slight incline from the water's edge and at first looked like a sprawling caravan park until the structures became small single-storey brick and mud houses. A hundred or so in all, simple and square with flat roofs and nothing in between them but sand.

Dozens more fishing boats dotted the water in front of the town and along the coast in both directions. Several of the smaller, faster pirate boats left the flotilla and headed for the beachfront, their powerful engines roaring in pitches as they bounced over the heavy waves.

As Stratton looked further along the coastline, he counted three large commercial ships in a line, anchored a short distance apart and quite close to the shore. The seabed evidently fell steeply away from the beach.

The coastline curved sharply beyond the last of the three ships in the shape of a hook, turning back on itself to form a kind of cul-de-sac. It came to a point where it doubled back again to continue its course. The bows of the largest ship, a merchantman as long as a football field, were almost inside the entrance to the cul-de-sac that acted like a sea mole, providing a level of protection from the heavier seas coming down the coast.

When the pirate mother craft was a few hundred metres from the stern of the nearest anchored cargo vessel, it turned to head directly towards the beach. A stone's throw from the sand the engines went into full and noisy reverse to bring it to a halt. A couple of anchors were tossed over the side to prevent the waves from pushing the boat up on to the beach.

Stratton studied the cargo ships. They looked like they had been abandoned. So they were more than likely hijacked vessels. The town didn't look equipped to handle any kind of heavy cargo, that was for sure.

He wondered where the crews were and suspected he might soon be joining them.

4

A Somali hauled Stratton, Hopper and Sabarak in a line along the side of the deck to a waiting skiff. They climbed over the side, their hands still tied, and down a ladder to the small boat where they sat opposite armed guards. The skiff's pilot, an old man with greying head hair and beard, hardly looked at them. He had done this a thousand times.

The waves dumped heavily on to the sandy beach but the old pilot displayed a high level of skill and experience to take the little craft over the crest of a large wave and to a fairly smooth stop in the returning frothy surf. The water had looked dark and murky from the pirate boat but along the beach it was transparent.

Stratton stepped into the water expecting it to be warm to match the air and dusty surroundings but it was cool and fresh as it flooded his loose laceless boots, which he almost left behind in the sand as he walked up the steep incline.

The beach was littered in trash of all kinds. Mostly modern trash. Plastic bottles and cartons, pieces of old timber, wrappings, chunks of moulded polystyrene of the type used for packing electronic goods. The high-tide mark was a dark oil stain that ran the length of the beach.

They walked up the coarse, steep sand. It went from soft to compacted and near enough flat in about forty paces, halfway to the beachfront houses. The Somali guard halted them.

Stepping on land immediately altered Stratton's attitude towards escaping. He felt infused with a sense of opportunity. On the vessel he had been trapped, confined. It was no longer a case of if he would try to escape, but when. He considered the broader strokes at first, dividing his options between land, air or back to the sea. The latter was the more obvious choice. All he had to do was acquire a boat and sail it due north. Escaping across country would be more difficult. The only safe haven he could think of was Mogadishu. The United Nations had several bases in the capital but Stratton didn't know the locations of any outside of it. And Mogadishu was a long way south, close to Kenya. That put it at many hundreds of miles. Through hostile tribal areas where the locals would likely try to kill him as a matter of course. As for the air option, he had no knowledge of Somali airfields. But it wouldn't help that much if he did: he had no real idea where he was save on the north coast of Somalia, which was as long as the southern coast of Yemen at around six hundred miles.

A group of children ran from between a row of mud houses to see the new arrivals. They came at Stratton and Hopper from all angles but were driven back by the guards.

In front of Stratton, Lotto looked proud of his catch as he arrived on the beach and marched up the soft sand at their head and on to the firm packed hinterland and towards the town. The prisoners were pushed to follow him as a part of the display. The people of the town clearly revered him.

Everything about the place had a dilapidated and uncared for look about it. The beachfront homes were set back about a hundred metres from the surf. About a mile beyond the town the land rose up to a line of dark hills, running across them a prominent cliff edge like a faultline, a yellow ridge that became orange and brown as it angled up the peaks. They looked barren and dry and scorched by the heat of the sun. Everywhere Stratton looked the ground was hard, like it had been hammered solid and covered in dust.

The town was no better than the beach. The longer he looked at the houses the worse they got. All but a few were made of mud. The rest were of brick or both, constructed poorly with levels and angles clearly guessed at rather than measured. Trash everywhere. Not the kind of trash one would expect to find in a poor, isolated African village not all that far from the stone age. Modern cardboard packing, plastic wrapping, moulded polystyrene. For centuries the town had relied on the sea to provide everything it needed to sustain life. And it still did but there was a new kind of life support. Fishermen had become pirates. The backward, isolated and impoverished town was overflowing with the finest detritus of the developed world. A new washing machine being used as an outside table since there was no electricity or piped water for it to function as it was designed. One house had a collection of flatscreen televisions stacked outside its front door, just discarded – superfluous to requirements as there was no signal. A group of men were unloading boxes from a mule-drawn cart and taking them into a house. As Stratton watched he could see they contained brand-new laptop computers.

Each habitat was a standalone dwelling with gaps between them wide enough to drive a truck through. The Somalis led Stratton and the others along a wide, deeply rutted track through the town. The main thoroughfare. Stalls lined the route in places, offering a morsel of local vegetables, all dry and withered.

The local people stared at the two white men as they marched up the incline of the road. They had seen such people before but any newcomer was still a curiosity in their lives. A Suburban rumbled past, the fat black man behind the wheel wearing a tailored jacket and sunglasses. He glanced at the prisoners and gave a nod to Lotto as he drove past.

A quarter of the way into the town the pirate captain brought the cortège to a halt and had a word with a couple of lethargic armed men standing at the entrance to a street. When Lotto continued away up the main thoroughfare, Stratton and the others were pulled down the side street.

Up ahead, a group of scruffily clothed armed men loitered, mostly sitting and smoking between the houses, a couple of them dozing. As Stratton and the others reached them, the guards that had been dozing came to life to inspect the new arrivals. The escort guards spoke to them while Stratton, Hopper and Sabarak stood in the street under the hot sun and waited.

Lotto suddenly arrived from a side street and went to the door to one of the nearby huts and opened it. It was dark inside but Stratton could make out several grimy faces looking up towards the door. Lotto looked in on the hut, stood for a few seconds. Then he pulled the door closed, crossed to the hut opposite, opened the door to that one and looked inside. Then he said something over his shoulder and the Somali guards shoved the three prisoners over to the hut. Lotto indicated for them to go inside.

The room was about six metres square, its floor of dirt. It stank of sweat. There were no furnishings of any kind. About a dozen men were sat on the ground with their backs to the walls. They took up a third of the wall space. There were a couple of buckets in the centre of the floor full of water, a cup beside each.

The men looked up at them. They were grimy and miserable wretches, their boots also without laces, their hands tied with either string or heavy fishing line. 'Sit,' the pirate captain ordered. It was the first word of English he had spoken and it sounded odd coming from his lips.

Stratton and Hopper claimed an empty section of wall together. Sabarak selected an isolated corner on the opposite side of the room.

'You try escape, we break your legs,' Lotto said in a slow,

deliberate tone. His English had a heavy accent but otherwise it was clear. 'We get same money for you if you are broken or not.' He grinned. 'No escape. Nowhere to go. But very tiring to look for you.'

The pirate captain looked along the line of prisoners and stopped at one. He walked over to the prisoner, whose head was lowered, the face hidden by long, dirty black hair. Lotto kicked the prisoner's outstretched foot with his own but the prisoner didn't move, as if aware but refusing to look up. Lotto grinned and leaned down to say something that Stratton was unable to hear. He chuckled at the lack of response, straightened up and went to the door.

'Be good,' he said, pausing in the doorway. 'Everyone goes home if you are good. But we break legs and arms if you are not good,' he added.

He left, his guards closing the door behind him.

Stratton studied the sullen faces that surrounded him. Four were white and European-looking. The rest appeared to be Asiatic, Filipinos and Koreans perhaps. The long-haired prisoner sat back against the wall. To Stratton's complete surprise it was a girl. When she rested her head back, her hair parted to reveal her face. She was young, Asian and quite beautiful. Her expression was like stone as she glanced at him in response to his stare.

Stratton looked away at the walls and ceiling. Roughly hewn wooden rafters supported a corrugated metal roof. A metal pole in the centre of the room supported the apex. There was a single, narrow opening high on a wall that provided light and ventilation. He knew he could climb through it without much difficulty. He wondered if there was a guard outside and, if so, how attentive to his duties he was at night.

Hopper leaned close to Stratton. 'Wonder how she ended up here.'

Stratton took another look at her. She was gazing at the floor.

He had heard of women being crew on commercial vessels, though it was more common in Asia than anywhere else. But she didn't look the type to work and live on board a ship. Despite her appearance, there was something sophisticated about her. She looked educated. She looked delicate but exuded a kind of toughness. Stratton wondered what Lotto had said to her that had amused only him. He suspected it was something crudely sexual.

Stratton put his head back. London would by now know something had gone seriously wrong with the operation. Ramlal and Prabhu had hopefully escaped and informed them that Stratton and Hopper had looked for an escape option in a fishing village. They would assume a boat might have been involved in their escape. London would then have to examine the different scenarios. Stratton doubted anyone in MI6 would even consider they had been taken captive by Somali pirates. And if some bright spark did, it would hardly have been taken seriously. It was unusual for Somalis to operate so close to the Yemen mainland, but not unheard of. Yemeni fisherman had lost many of their boats to Somali raiding parties over the years. But even so, to suspect Stratton and Hopper had been victims of such an event was a stretch.

London would wait twenty-four hours after Stratton's last communication before beginning an investigation. And then it would be little more than a discreet enquiry through established channels. The kidnapping had been a high-level task and not common knowledge beyond MI6 in London and their partners in the US – this was in general a joint interest programme, but the Brits headed up the Middle East side of the operation. The British Embassy in Yemen wouldn't have known it was taking place for instance. But they would be alerted to the missing personnel and given the identities. The embassy would still not know what the missing personnel had been doing in Yemen. After several days of hearing nothing, investigators would be sent to the area where Stratton and Hopper had last been seen. They would find a way of including the Yemeni authorities in the search. A clever cover story would have to be created. And when that didn't produce any results, MI6 might confront the Chinese Secret Service, since Prabhu and Ramlal would have informed them about the intrusion into the operation. A lot of suspicion would be directed towards the Chinese. That could get interesting in itself. The Chinese agent who Stratton had brought to the ground suggested that the British would soon know why the Chinese were interested in Sabarak. But that had probably been on the understanding that Stratton would get the Saudi back to where the British could interrogate him. If the Chinese suspected that hadn't happened, they would go quiet.

Stratton wondered if London already had any clues as to why the Chinese would want Sabarak. The Chinese wouldn't be able to shine any light on Stratton and Hopper's disappearance anyway. The last they could possibly know of the British operatives was them riding out to sea in the boat. In the absence of any other explanation, London might well place a high priority on the suspicion that the Chinese were behind the disappearance of their people and the Saudi. The only other alternative would be that Stratton and the others had died at sea for whatever reason. Unlikely maybe but not impossible.

Stratton needed to let London know what had happened as soon as he could, not just to begin the process of his and Hopper's repatriation. He had to prevent the wrong accusations flying in the wrong direction. That would waste time and draw attention from the important focus, which was Sabarak and the weapons.

If Stratton couldn't get away himself, or get a message out of there by some other way, the first opportunity the Brits would have of discovering what had happened to them would be when the pirates eventually put out their identities and demanded a ransom payment.

Once that happened, MI6 would have to re-evaluate everything. It would be interesting to see how they would handle the ransom. Getting the men back would be a high priority because of the level of the task. They would want the men to be debriefed. They wouldn't want anyone knowing about the snatch on the Saudi. They would have to explain it to the Americans. The SBS might be sent in to try a grab. Stratton guessed that would be the first plan on the board.

But that would all take time. And there was a significant obstacle that remained, one that could destroy all other plans and bring a sudden end to any hopes Stratton and Hopper might have of getting home.

Sabarak.

Stratton looked over at the man. He was resting his head against the wall and his eyes were shut like he was asleep.

A dark thought crept into Stratton's head, and not for the first time in the last twenty-four hours.

Hopper whispered in Stratton's ear again. 'You know we have to kill that one, don't you?' he said.

'And the sooner the better, I think,' said Stratton.

Sabarak opened his eyes. It was like he knew what they had been thinking.

Sabarak wasn't a fool. The Saudi was well aware of the threat he was to the two operatives. He couldn't sleep because of it. But it was too soon to make his move. He still couldn't fathom the group. They weren't a devout bunch of Muslims, that much was for sure. He hadn't seen any of them pray nor heard a call to prayer. So they didn't take their faith seriously and neither did they care that he was a Muslim.

Telling them he provided weapons to Al-Shabaab might simply add a zero or two to his value as a hostage. And then what? They could sell him back to his family, to Al-Shabaab or barter him to the Somali authorities. Or try and sell him to the Western killers. But the way the Englishmen looked at him told him something: if he didn't move soon, he would be dead. Of that he was sure. It was a difficult situation.

An engine gunned outside. It sounded big, like a large truck, and it was labouring. They could all hear the gears crunching. Whoever was driving it gunned the engine again. Then it stopped as if it had died.

Stratton went back to his thoughts. After about half an hour the door burst open and an old Somali walked in, a long knife in his belt beside a holstered revolver. He had on cleaner clothes than the others as if he were prouder of his appearance. He looked at the prisoners like they were livestock.

He planted his feet and put a hand on the gun's grip. 'Get up,' he shouted. 'Rouse!' He kicked the nearest hostage's foot. 'Get to your feet, you lazy sailors.' They obeyed swiftly. Stratton and Hopper eased up off the floor.

'Out the door! Go!' said the Somali.

The group filed outside into the sunlight. The Somali pointed them forward and they trudged up the street, turned the corner into the main street, back in the direction of the beach. As they walked four Somali guards, assault rifles slung over their shoulders, stepped up to follow. The heat and humidity had intensified while Stratton had been inside the hut. He felt his clothes sticking to his back. He wiped the sweat from his brow.

Up ahead, he saw a large flatbed truck resting at an awkward angle, squatting to one side like a wounded buffalo.

When they got to it he could see its rear axle had collapsed. On the truck's bed were dozens of green-painted wooden boxes, all the same size, about a metre and a half long. It was pretty obvious to Stratton and Hopper the possible contents of the boxes. For those who could read Russian, the black stencilling described what each of them contained. And for those who couldn't, one of them had spilled on to the road and had broken open to reveal its contents: several PKM machine guns heavily greased and wrapped in brown wax paper.

The old Somali climbed up on to the bed and shoved one of the crates to the edge. He shouted at the nearest prisoners, pointed at the box, making them pick it up. Two stepped forward, dragged the heavy box off the truck, their hands still tied, and stood off awaiting instructions.

The Somali guards stepped into the shade of the nearest house and started smoking and talking.

The old Somali directed the first two bearers to wait to one side and ordered the next two men forward. And so it went, until Stratton and Hopper stepped up to pull a box off the back of the collapsed truck and stood with it at the end of the line. The box weighed about fifty or sixty kilos, Stratton guessed. The old Somali walked to the front of the line and waved for the group to follow him. The guards got to their feet and followed at the back.

The chain gang made its slow way along the hard-packed sand in the direction of the cargo ships. They got about two hundred metres before one of the Korean-looking sailors dropped the end of his crate into the sand. His buddy put down his own end of the box, and they both rubbed their fingers. The guards suddenly came to life, running right up to the two men and whaling on them to pick up the crate. Screaming in the Koreans' faces. The two Koreans looked tired, like they had no energy. Stratton wondered how long they'd been hijacked. The first Korean, overweight, listless-looking, stepped back from the Somalis. He should have stepped to the box because the Somali took it as a show of weakness and punched the butt of his rifle into the man's guts. The Korean went down to his knees in pain. The other Korean stepped away in fear, his arms up to protect himself. Another guard forearmed the stock of his AK-47 into the Korean's face and he went down.

The Somalis kept on shouting until the two Koreans, one bloodied across the face, got up and picked up the crate and started walking.

It was hard going in the heat, especially when they hit the soft sand.

There was already a large collection of crates and boxes of all sizes laid out on the sand in front of the vessels. Many had been ripped open to expose their contents. Scattered around were brand-new pieces of machinery spare parts, miles of plastic piping, tins of paint and sprays and all kinds of building material. It looked like the crates had been ransacked then discarded because they had no value to the Somalis.

Stratton studied the ships now that they were closer. The largest and nearest was called the *Oasis*. The merchantman had a Liberian flag hanging over the stern and a Dutch one above the bridge. It was over a hundred metres long and thirty wide. Easily forty-five thousand tonnes. The middle one, a black and white carrier with two jumbo booms, had a Greek name he couldn't read and the ship in front of that was a low flat carrier with vertical East Asian writing down one side. Furthest from him was the bulker the pirates had just hijacked.

The *Oasis* looked in fairly good condition but the others looked like they had either been abandoned months ago or the masters and crew had cared little for them. All showed signs of engine activity. Waste water came from exhaust holes close to the water line and the funnels leaked whiffs of smoke. Stratton guessed the Somalis put a skeleton crew on them to keep the engines turning over and the bilge pumps running or the things would sink. That would be the end of their value.

He could see men on all of the decks. On the new bulker, men were using ropes to lower boxes over the side into fishing boats. One was bringing its load towards the beach.

The old Somali guard indicated where he wanted the prisoners to stack the boxes. After the first pair had put down their load on to the sand, he ordered them back to the truck for another. He did the same with the others.

On the *Oasis*, several Somalis stood on the bridge wings and main deck looking over the rails. They weren't loading or unloading, they were just standing there like they were waiting for something. A couple were watching the sky through binoculars. Stratton looked at the other guards on the beach. Several of them were searching the skies. He sensed a definite atmosphere of expectancy but no fear, no concern.

They were clearly waiting for something to happen.

5

It took four journeys to unload the truck and ferry the crates to the beach, by which time Stratton and Hopper were tired.

The old Somali gestured to them to sit among the rest of the hostages who had slumped down on the sand beside the pile of crates that offered some shade. A Somali arrived with a bucket of water and a cup. On seeing the girl he seemed to have a second's indecision. He didn't put the bucket down, he went to the girl and offered the cup to her. She stared at him as he leaned close and said something to her. She remained grim-faced and didn't acknowledge him or take the water. He said something again. She didn't move. He pointed towards a separate stack of boxes.

One of the other guards stepped over and started talking to the water bearer. He stood listening, then he cut right across the guard. Obviously didn't agree with him. The two of them stood face to face, both talking fast, neither listening. Then the second guy started prodding the other with a finger.

The water bearer dropped the bucket and, still talking, grabbed hold of the girl's hair like she was his property.

She yelped, grabbing his hand, but he ignored her. She got up and kicked him from behind hard between the legs. As she did, a Chinese-looking prisoner, who appeared to Stratton to be her companion, jumped up and hurled himself at the guard. But the other Somali swung the stock of his rifle around on its harness and slammed it into the man's back. The blow was severe and immediately took the fight out of him and he dropped to the sand grimacing.

The Chinese girl fought even harder. But the Somali still had her by the hair and began to punch her brutally about the head with his free hand. Which brought another of the hostages to his feet: a tall white European who looked about fifty. He was shouting angrily at the guard in what sounded like Dutch, and he grabbed at the flailing arm of the Somali, holding it with superior strength.

A couple more guards stepped over when they saw the Dutchman intervene. The second guard, who had floored the Chinaman, set his eyes on the Dutchman, gripping his assault rifle like it was a club.

Hopper and Stratton couldn't keep their heads down any longer. They'd been maintaining a low profile because it was advisable in hostage situations like this. A fundamental wisdom imparted to students on hostage survival training courses: never stand out in any way or take on a leadership role. If you do, you run the risk of being singled out if the group needs to be punished.

But neither man was able to sit back and see the situation escalate after watching two other men take on the wrath of the guards. Hopper was first to his feet. As a young marine, before he joined the SBS and before he got married to Helen, he'd been a brawler. He didn't start them, being a polite and level-headed man, but he could finish them. If story-time among the lads ever got around to well-known brawls, the time Hopper took on four skinheads outside an Indian restaurant in Poole often came up. Hopper had simply been enjoying a take-away when one of the pinheads knocked his meal out of his hands. Hopper hit him so hard he broke his jaw. And then he took apart the other three. Then he lined them up in the recovery position in case they vomited and he called the police. Hopper even waited for the officers to arrive. He was the one charged with grievous bodily harm. But the restaurateur, who knew him, gave evidence in his defence and got the charge withdrawn.

With his hands tied, Hopper ran at the Somali about to butt the Dutchman and double-fisted him in his side with such force the man dropped his rifle and went down. Stratton focused on the Somali who was holding the girl's hair and who the Dutchman was trying to control. He dealt him a savage blow across the jaw. The man dropped to the sand and remained there in a daze.

One of the other guards brought his rifle up on aim as all the other hostages got to their feet. They were unsure and feared the consequences of running or staying. Then the guttural command of the older Somali stopped the guards and the old fighter stepped in between the converging groups. He screamed at the guard who looked about to fire his rifle into the Dutchman. The guard lowered the end of his weapon. The old Somali shouted at the other guards while indicating the girl. He appeared to be arguing in her favour. He clearly possessed some level of rank or respect.

The old man had achieved a pause. He had controlled his men, for the moment at least, and so it was time to direct his malice at the hostages. He looked at Stratton and Hopper. Directed his rhetoric at them because they were the most aggressive. He shouted and waved for them to step back.

'Move back,' Stratton said to the others. Beside him, the girl was still seething and stood her ground. He took hold of her arm. 'Easy. Just let it go,' he said as he guided her back.

Hopper moved to help the prone Chinese man to his feet but the old Somali walked swiftly over like he was going to strike him. Hopper stepped back to avoid any blow.

The Somali inspected the Chinese man without kneeling down or touching him. He shouted a command at a couple of the guards. They hauled the man up by his arms, pulled him to his feet and tried to get him to stand up on his own. But the man could not, he had something seriously wrong with his side, perhaps more than just a few broken ribs, Stratton guessed. The Somalis showed no interest in the man's condition and manhandled him away.

The remaining guards looked like they could care less about what had happened. All but two of them stepped off back to their spot in the shade. The one that Stratton had struck got to his feet in easy stages, feeling his bruised jaw. He sought out and found Stratton, looked at him like he was fixing the image in his head. The other downed Somali stepped beside him, looking at Hopper. He removed a long, crudely made blade from his belt and held it in a tight fist. He spat out some words to the other pirate.

The old Somali was still vigilant for trouble and did not miss it. He barked a command. The two guards showed no servility but decided to walk back to the shade. Stratton and Hopper glanced at each other, aware they had not made life any easier for themselves. Stratton wondered how much control the leadership had over its men.

The girl had watched her friend be taken away and stepped back into the shade provided by the stack of crates. She sat down, leaned back tired against them and stared into the sky like it could give her the answer to her problems.

Hopper and Stratton sat down in the sand near her.

After a glance at them and after some hesitation, she said, 'Thanks.' Then she looked away.

Stratton felt bad for her. This wasn't a good place for her. He knew how common rape was in hostage circumstances. In a place like Somalia it would be practically inevitable. And the most apparently devout jailers would be among the worst offenders. In Iraq and Afghanistan he had seen the results of the rape of prisoners, male and female. On top of everything else a hostage had to contend with – the psychological stress of pitiful confinement, the fear of torture every day, the pain of the beatings, the threat of death at any time – a girl had to live with the great possibility that her jailers would come for her like animals. And once they began, they usually did it again and again. Until death or release. If a girl survived, she had to cope with everything that came after, the physical and emotional scars, the possibility of disease, even death. And then there was the potential pregnancy and all that entailed.

'Where're you from?' Stratton asked. He didn't know why he was attempting to ease her anguish because there was nothing he could do for her. But she was sitting there beside him and he felt a kind of obligation to try and ease her suffering.

She took her time replying, like she was deciding whether or not she wanted to talk to him. 'China,' she said eventually.

Stratton couldn't help thinking how he had not talked to a single Chinese person in years and he'd met two in the same number of days. 'What ship you off?'

Once again she took a long time to answer. 'No ship.'

Stratton found the answer curious and wondered if she understood English that well. But something about the way she listened to him and responded suggested she knew the language well enough. 'How'd you end up here, then?' he said.

'A yacht,' she said. It was as though she felt guilty about it.

'You were sailing? Out there?'

She nodded.

It sounded like a pretty dumb thing to do. 'A regular sailing yacht, with a sail?' he said.

'Yes. With a sail.'

Stratton could only wonder why.

She looked towards the water and the carriers in front of them. 'I don't know where it is now,' she said. 'My friend and I were sailing around the world.'

'I guess it was just as risky going around the Cape?' he said.

She shrugged. 'Statistically we should have been OK. Something like seventy boats a day pass through the Gulf of Aden. Only a couple a week are attacked. Maybe one or two a month get hijacked. We were almost in the international transit corridor when they saw us. We were unlucky.'

Stratton sympathised. The international corridor ran east–west across the Gulf of Aden between Yemen and Somalia. It was a protected route patrolled by various foreign navies and regarded as the safest way to transit past Somalia. It obviously didn't guarantee complete safety from hijacking but it increased the chances of a navy vessel responding to a distress signal. Many pirate vessels actually hunted the corridor, knowing that it improved the chances of them finding a commercial vessel somewhere along it. The risk of running into a navy boat was all part of doing business.

'How long have you been here?' Stratton asked.

'It must be two weeks now.'

'You speak good English.'

'I learned in China. I spent six months in London. That was a year ago.'

She seemed intelligent and despite being petite, tough.

She'd carried the boxes without complaint and wasn't afraid to lay into the Somali guards. 'Do you know what's happening with your negotiations?' he asked.

She glanced at him for the first time like she was finally interested enough to want to see what he looked like. 'They have told me nothing.' She looked away again. 'I don't even think anyone knows I'm here.'

'These guys would've tried to make contact with someone. They're running a business.'

She looked at him again. 'You are English.' It was more of a statement than a question.

'Yes.'

'What ship are you off?'

Stratton hadn't prepared for the question, not in any great depth at least. The obvious story was that they worked for the local oil company that ran the terminal in Riyan, the company whose security ran the semi-rigid they stole. They could sing that song all day, until Sabarak decided to tell his story. Once he found the right people to talk to he would sound a lot more convincing than Stratton and Hopper. Stratton had expected the pirates to ask. But then what did they care? As far as they were concerned they'd netted three more potential pay cheques. What else did they need to know? He looked for Sabarak. The Saudi was squatting alone on the edge of the group and looking out to sea.

'They picked us up off the coast of Yemen,' Stratton said. 'We were doing a spot of sightseeing.'

'That's almost as bad as what I was doing.'

'No one told us pirates operated that close to the Yemen coastline.'

They heard a commotion coming from the town. They saw a man marching down towards the beach at the head of a boisterous retinue of gun-toting Somalis. It took Stratton a couple of seconds to realise it was Lotto, wearing tailored military fatigues, a green beret at a jaunty angle and wrap-around sunglasses. He carried an ornate walking stick over a shoulder and wore a pearl-handled pistol in a holster at his side. The men immediately behind him, judging by their dress and bling, had been exposed to a higher class of contraband than the run-of-the-mill guards and townfolk.

The group reached the beach and turned towards the anchored carriers, walking past the prisoners, largely ignoring them. There came the sound of electronic chirping and one of the men handed a satellite phone to Lotto. The leader stopped to talk into it, looking skywards after a few seconds. The guys around him did the same.

A shrill shout went up from one of the men standing on the bridge wing of the *Oasis*. It was echoed by others on the beach. Stratton looked up at the clear blue skies, along with everyone else. He could see nothing other than the occasional gull. But his ears began to pick up a new sound. A distant hum.

An aircraft of some kind.

Lotto was still looking up and he was still speaking into the phone.

Then the aircraft came into view, about a thousand feet

up, hugging the coastline. A small twin-engine propeller-driven craft. The sound got louder as it closed in. It was slowly descending, Stratton decided, as it approached them. Then the pilot adjusted its track and flew it over the line of cargo ships, then turned sharply away and began a wide turn out to sea.

It described a long, easy circle and it kept descending. When it reached the beach again, it turned sharply back towards the ships. But this time it came inland to fly over the sand. Right towards the pirate leader.

As he looked at it, Stratton noted something else about the aircraft had changed. Its baggage door was open. Just as it passed the bridge of the *Oasis*, a bundle the size of a laundry bag came tumbling out attached to a small parachute. The bundle hit the sand about twenty metres from Lotto and somersaulted along the beach, chased by half a dozen of Lotto's men. He followed them casually.

Stratton couldn't see the bundle because the group crowded around it but he had a good idea what it was.

They'd just witnessed the paying of a ransom.

'Hopefully some of these poor bastards will get to go home now,' Hopper muttered.

As they watched, a canvas-covered flatbed truck drove easily down from the town front on to the beach behind them and headed across the sand towards the *Oasis*. The driver pulled it up just short of the soft sand and a man got out the passenger door. He was Somali but he looked different from the others. He had a big dark curly beard, a white skull cap on his head and he wore a long white shirt, like a dishdasha, over baggy cotton trousers and sandals. A brown leather weapons harness tightened up the whole look. The man was an Islamic warrior.

He stood and looked at Lotto, the bottom of his shirt moving gently in the breeze. The driver stayed in the cab, his hands on the steering wheel. It was like they were waiting for something. Lotto said something to one of his men, a bespectacled and well-dressed individual who appeared to be employed in an administrative capacity. The man took several bricks of American hundred-dollar-bills from the ransom bundle. He handed one to each of the five hangers-on around Lotto. They all bowed and smiled and acted subservient. The bespectacled assistant tied the bundle back up and lifted it from the sand, eyes on Lotto.

Lotto left everyone and walked over to the Islamic warrior. Stratton detected a hint of distaste in the way the leader approached the Islamist. They had a brief exchange of words. Then Lotto signalled to one of his men, who in turn ordered a couple of the guards to go to the rear of the truck.

The warrior walked around with them, drew aside the canvas flap and indicated for the guards to go ahead. The men dragged a long, green-painted wooden crate out by a rope handle on its end. It was one and a half metres end to end and narrow, and whatever was inside was heavy – the Somalis strained to take its weight.

Stratton got to his feet. Once again, the shape, size, colour and construction of the box gave it away. It was another piece of military ordnance. But this one was different. The stencilling was in Far Eastern calligraphy. It wasn't a box of PKMs.

Stratton looked at Sabarak. The Saudi was also on his feet and staring intently between the Somali fighter and the box.

Stratton's interest went up a couple more notches.

The guards carried the crate down to the water's edge to a waiting skiff. The Islamic warrior followed them. The Somalis climbed into the small boat with the box, leaving the warrior on the sand watching as the coxswain backed the boat away and steered into the lumpy waves towards the centre of the *Oasis* and a staggered gangway that had been lowered to the water line. A couple of Somali men headed down the gangway to meet them. Between the four of them, they hauled the box out of the skiff and carried it up the gangway to the main deck.

The warrior walked back to the truck.

Stratton looked over at Sabarak again. The Saudi had focused his attention on the bearded warrior, who was climbing back into the cab. The driver backed up the truck and drove further down the beach. Several of Lotto's guards followed at a jog. The driver pulled up opposite the Greek carrier and the warrior climbed out again. The guards went to the back of the truck and heaved another long wooden crate from its bed. They carried it down to the shore and waited for the skiff. The boat took the crate to the carrier and then the warrior went back to his truck again. The driver drove him down the beach to the East Asian vessel. It all happened again, one final time.

Stratton looked back towards the deck of the *Oasis*. The men carrying the crate had gone along the side of the ship, past the huge storage bays to the very front, where they disappeared.

'What was all that about?' Hopper asked in a voice too low for the Chinese girl to hear.

'All very odd,' Stratton said.

As they spoke, the warrior's truck came across the hard-packed sand and headed for the town. Lotto, his man with the bundle and the rest of the Somalis came back up the beach towards the town, passing the prisoners. Lotto glanced towards them.

He stopped and lowered his sunglasses to take a better look at the girl. She was looking back at him, her expression cold.

He remained smiling. It was a knowing smile. He kept on walking towards the town and she lowered her head.

Stratton couldn't think of anything to say to help her. Perhaps if their leader himself fancied her, the others might leave her alone. But that wouldn't solve her problem.

'Up! Up!' the old Somali shouted.

The rest of the prisoners got to their feet and they were herded back to the town, past the broken truck, along the road to the hut. They filed in through the door, starting a line for the water buckets. After each man took a drink he went to sit back in his original place. The girl did the same.

A Filipino prisoner got to his feet, stepped to the door

and tapped it with the toe of his boot. 'Toilet,' he called out.

He waited for about half a minute. He kicked the door again and repeated his request.

They heard the Somali on the other side unbolt the door. The Filipino stepped out into the sunlight and the Somali closed and bolted the door behind him.

It was only then that Stratton realised the Saudi was missing.

'Where did Sabarak go?' he asked Hopper.

'He was with us when we came back,' said Hopper. 'I saw him. He must've held back and asked to get put in another hut.'

'He's made his move,' Stratton said. 'That jihadist character who arrived in the truck. Sabarak was very interested in him and those crates. Maybe something about that episode gave him the confidence to reveal himself.'

'He'll tell them who he is?'

'He's a jihadist. The warre bugger who turned up in the truck was too. Lotto has some kind of relationship with him. That would suggest that Sabarak could at least get an audience with Lotto. Once he did that he would begin the bartering game. And we don't know what he has to barter with.'

'He has us for a start.' That was very true. 'What do you think was in those crates?' Hopper said.

'Not sure. Weapons of some kind. At least that's what the boxes were designed for. But why were they taking them on board the hijacked boats?'

The Filipino returned and went back to his place.

'I don't think we should hang around here too long,' Hopper said. 'If Lottto lets Sabarak make contact with the jihadist, we're in the shitter.'

Stratton agreed, in principle. But there was something else on his mind.

They heard the bolts on the door go again and watched as a man walked in carrying a large cooking pot, followed by a filthy-looking boy with a stack of battered aluminium bowls. The cook filled one from the pot, handed it to the boy and the boy stepped to the nearest prisoner and gave it to him. He went back to the cook and took another bowl to the next person in line.

When Stratton was handed his, he studied the contents of the bowl in his tied hands. It looked like some kind of fish stew, with more bones than meat. But he was hungry. He crunched down on a fish head and chewed the bones to a pulp and swallowed. Someone in the room choked violently as he struggled to extricate a bone from his throat. The man beside him slammed his back repeatedly. The choking man managed to cough it up.

'It's Saturday,' Hopper said, eating his food as if it were an everyday meal. 'The wife would have expected me back by now. She won't be worried of course. Not if I'm late by a few days.'

Stratton sympathised. But it only reminded him once again of why marriage wasn't the wisest choice for someone in their business. Close relationships were almost as bad. Something Stratton had managed to avoid for the most part. And times like this proved him right. He wasn't missing anyone. And no one was stressing over him because he hadn't come home when he should have.

He had long since identified it as a kind of loneliness and he was well aware that it wasn't healthy either. The way his mind worked, no man could really be complete without a family. Surely that was the prime purpose, to find a partner and produce offspring in order to continue the line. But there was time yet for all of that. Right now he was a soldier and he needed to focus on that alone. Every lifestyle had its sacrifices. His was a lack of companionship, of love. He would do without for the time being and gamble that he could find it when he was good and ready. When he was no longer in this business.

'We were going cycling today,' Hopper said. 'Bradbury Rings . . . When do you think they'll tell her I'm missing?'

'If they thought we'd taken a boat, then they'd more than likely assume we'd been lost at sea before considering we'd been taken by this shower,' said Stratton. 'They won't rush into assuming the worst. First thing they'll probably tell her is there's been an extension to the op. They won't give her any bad news until they're certain.' He knew that much from experience. He'd had to pass on the bad news more than once. Watching a loving wife or girlfriend break into small pieces right in front of you is not something he was built to take, tough as he felt. He didn't have the tools to deal with it. Which only served to cement his belief that close relationships weren't worth the pain they could create, even for those not directly involved in them.

'If Sabarak barters us to Lotto, we're screwed,' Hopper said. 'Even if London agreed to pay a ransom for us, which I strongly doubt, Lotto might not take it. He might rather make a present of us to the jihadists. We should consider making a break for it, and the sooner the better.'

Stratton knew that was the right course of action. But the boxes on the ships were bothering him. Kidnapping Sabarak was one part of a larger operation. The big picture was about something else. They might have failed to bring in Sabarak, but perhaps they had stumbled on another and possibly larger piece of the puzzle. He couldn't let that go. If they concentrated on saving their own skins, they would be failing in their duties. They weren't just ordinary soldiers charging at an enemy. They were specialists. That meant thinking for yourself, changing course and making decisions, sometimes major ones, without consulting the head shed. He felt an urge inside him that was far stronger than the need to save his own neck. He couldn't leave Somalia until he found out what was going on.

'We can't leave,' Stratton said. 'Not yet.'

Hopper couldn't hide his surprise. He didn't know Stratton very well personally but he knew his reputation. Like everyone else in the SBS, Hopper hadn't been privy to the details of Stratton's operations for the SIS and, on occasion apparently, for the Americans. But the rumours went around. And Stratton would never reveal anything himself. If he had done half as much as he was supposed to have, he wasn't someone to ignore in a situation like this.

Hopper had initially thought there was no one better to get caught with after being captured by the Somalis. But cracks of doubt were beginning to appear in his confidence, cracks caused by Stratton's strength and his own weakness. He could think of nothing but escape and a return to his wife and children. Stratton hadn't mentioned it since seeing those boxes going on to the ships. The man constantly pushed the limits in order to succeed on an operation. Which was why he was a top operative. He saw success as a higher priority than his own safety, or at least close to it.

Stratton would probably never agree with that statement, but others who had worked closely with him were certain of its truth. Hopper was suddenly concerned. Like most other members of the service, he knew that Stratton preferred working alone. That was probably because few people could play by his rules. Hopper felt in his guts that it was looking bad for them.

'Those crates they loaded on to the ship,' Stratton said. 'I want to know what's in them.'

Hopper's heart sank, though he never showed it. He nodded, accepting that it had to be done. 'OK. Then as soon as we do that, we get out of here?'

'Then we get out of here,' Stratton agreed.

The guards allowed no more than two prisoners at a time to leave the room on a toilet break. After the meal, Stratton and Hopper took it as an opportunity to explore. When they stepped out, the Somali pushed them down the side of the hut opposite. The toilet, a hole in the ground, was at the back. All they could see were the cramped little houses left and right, front and back. And guys with assault rifles.

When Stratton walked back into the hut, the girl glanced at him. She did that every time the door opened. Like she was waiting for someone. Most of the prisoners had dozed off. Stratton and Hopper took their places against the wall. The girl remained awake, staring at the wall. She seemed to be in a constant state of anxiety.

The day dragged on and they all lay there in the hut. There was nothing else to do but think. Or doze. The evening meal when it came was fish stew again. The hours passed slowly until darkness began to fall. The girl had hardly moved. Her eyes were closed. The air became colder with the passing of the sun. Stratton firmed up his plans for the night's activities. He intended to be busy.

6

The moonlight shining in through the paneless opening high up the wall of the prison hut bathed the room in a grey wash. They could hear a couple of small generators chugging away somewhere not far from the hut. The privileged no doubt. The town had no mains electricity. They could smell kerosene lamps and hear the waves pounding the beach, a sound that had not been as obvious during the daytime.

They heard voices occasionally passing by outside. A round of laughter. A vehicle, probably an old truck, puttering along the main road. By now the limited conversations in the room had ceased completely. The sound of gentle snoring dominated.

Hopper lay stretched out on the floor. He was not asleep and was thinking, mostly about his family and what Helen was doing. He estimated the time at around nine or ten o'clock. That put it at six or seven back home. The children would be going to bed soon. Helen would then watch the TV or read a book, a mug of tea in her hands. She would wonder what her man was doing at that moment. But she wouldn't be concerned. Not yet. It was still too soon. He'd been delayed many times before. It was the nature of the job. They had got married two years after he joined the SBS. She'd grown thick-skinned, used to the long operations and him being away months at a time. He'd only been gone a few days so far and therefore the wait had been nothing.

He suddenly wondered what would happen if something went wrong. If he didn't make it back. He imagined them coming to her front door, one of the SBS officers and probably the Sergeant Major. She would probably have an inkling something was wrong as soon as she saw them. But she wouldn't react. She was the optimistic kind. Even when she saw their sombre expressions, at the worst she would expect to hear he had been injured and wouldn't be home for a while yet. And when they told her he'd been killed, she would suck in her emotion, for a while at least. The first thing she would ask was how he had died. They wouldn't go into detail. But then she would think the worst and crack up. She would burst into tears, her life would fall apart.

Hopper rolled on to his back.

'Hopper?' Stratton whispered.

Hopper looked up at his partner sat against the wall next to him.

Stratton slid down and whispered into Hopper's ear, 'Soon as everyone is settled, I'll make a move out of here.'

Hopper looked at him strangely, like he hadn't fully understood. 'You going alone?'

'I've been going over all our options. One person can

move more securely than two. If anything happens to one, there's still a chance for the other. Also, if any of this lot should decide to raise the alarm after I've gone, you can change their minds for them. I'll only be a couple of hours at the most if all goes well. I'll also be looking to our escape. When I get back we'll bug out together.'

Hopper understood Stratton's thought process. It was debatable but he saw the value in keeping the other prisoners quiet. He looked at the prone forms around him. He doubted any of them would make a peep if he and Stratton left together. But it could still work Stratton's way. And he was the ops leader. 'Have you got your hands free yet?'

'Almost.' Stratton had been working on the clumsy series of knots since darkness had fallen. He had untied most of them.

A whispered conversation started directly across from them. It was the girl talking with her friend. The guy had been lying there when everyone returned from the beach. He'd been conscious but looked like he was in a lot of pain. She had fed him his meals and made him comfortable as best she could but there was little else she could do for him without medical attention.

Stratton hadn't decided exactly when he was going to get out of the hut but a fundamental prerequisite was that everyone else in the room be asleep. He'd accepted that might not be easy, especially when they had little else to do during the day but sleep. But that was a chance he was going to have to take and why Hopper should remain.

Stratton attacked the final knot with his teeth and quietly unravelled the nylon line from around his wrists. It was a relief to get it off. He bit off a couple of lengths and threaded them through the empty eyelets in his boots and tied them up. He was good to go but he remained quietly where he was for another hour. The Chinese couple had finally stopped talking and seemed to have drifted off to sleep. Everyone else was equally quiet.

As he decided it was time to leave, there was movement in front of him. He thought it was someone turning over. But they slowly got to their feet. The figure went to the door and paused like they were listening. Stratton raised his head just barely enough to take a look. In the moonlight he could tell it was the Chinese girl. She took a hold of the door knob and pulled on it gently. The door was firmly bolted.

She stepped back through the middle of the room between everyone's feet, moving quietly and carefully, and went to the wall below the opening. She reached up but her fingers were a few inches short of the sill.

She looked behind her, around the room, checking to see no one was watching her. Stratton closed his eyes. She turned back to the wall and jumped for the sill. Her fingers hooked on to the edge and she fought to pull herself up. She was strong and determined and, trying to be as quiet as possible, managed to throw a hand through the opening to the other side. Slowly she pulled herself up. She was small enough to manoeuvre her legs through the opening while sitting on the sill. A second later she was gone.

Stratton listened hard for any sounds. He heard nothing. Not the girl landing, not any commotion. Which suggested no guard at the back. He doubted the Somalis had much of a guard routine going. She had clearly been as confident about that as he was.

He looked around the hut. No one had moved. If anyone was aware of her departure, they had, like Stratton, remained still and made no sign of it.

He sympathised with her completely. She'd made the right choice. If she stayed in that hut, there was little doubt about what would happen to her and probably by more than one of the bastards. It might not be any easier on the outside. But it was well worth the try. She would probably head for the water and find a boat. As a yachtswoman she had a good chance of making it once she got herself out to sea. He couldn't really see another option for her. Anyone who could sail around the world should be able to navigate the Gulf of Aden in a fishing boat. All she had to do was get as far away from the Somali coast as she could and wave down the first vessel that came by. Preferably a navy boat.

Stratton looked at her friend lying against the wall. His eyes were closed but his sharp breathing suggested he was in a lot of pain. It must have been tough leaving him behind. But the man would never make it in his condition. And she couldn't afford to wait. Stratton put her out of his thoughts. He had enough of his own problems. He waited a few minutes longer then he sat up and gently squeezed Hopper's arm.

'Have fun,' Hopper whispered.

Stratton thought he detected a slight edge to Hopper's voice but he ignored it. He eased to his feet, went to the wall below the opening, reached up, grabbed the sill and gently pulled himself up to get a look outside. The hut backed on to another, the gap wide enough to drive a car along. An orange light shone in the window of a house further down. The smell of kerosene was even stronger. He heard a vehicle rattle along somewhere, saw its headlights flickering between the buildings.

He reached up for a roof rafter and manoeuvred his legs through the opening. He twisted on to his front and slid outside, grabbing the sill and lowering his feet to the ground. He crouched to scan between the buildings. All he could see was junk and rubbish. As he was about to move off a nearby sound froze him. The scuff of a boot on hard ground. Coming from the gap around the corner of the prison hut.

Stratton went to ground and lay flat. In daylight he would have been exposed but in the shadows among rubbish and rubble, he could probably get away with being stepped on before anyone noticed him.

A figure appeared from the gap and paused. Stratton wondered if it was the girl returning for some reason. Whoever it was didn't wait for long and followed the back of the prison hut to the window. And another figure left the narrow gap to join the first. The two moved stealthily. Like they didn't want anyone to see or hear them. Both were too big to be the girl. When they turned to look up the street, Stratton knew immediately who they were.

They were the two who had fought over the girl on the beach. The two Hopper and he had flattened. It looked like they were going to climb into the hut. They wanted to avoid the front. They were either coming for him and Hopper or the girl. Perhaps all three. Once inside they would discover the girl was missing and Stratton too. Hopper would take them on but that might end badly for him, especially if he hadn't untied his hands.

One of the men reached for the sill and took his weight on his arms while his colleague crouched to give him a boost. Neither of them looked behind them. Neither saw Stratton pick up a chunk of concrete and ease himself to his feet. The one that had grabbed for the opening pulled himself up into it, the other still holding his legs.

Stratton moved at them. The man on the ground heard him coming but had little time to react. As he let go of the other Somali's legs and reached for the knife in the waistband of his trousers, Stratton brought the rock down hard on to his head. Enough to knock the man senseless. Stratton followed it with a knee into his side and, as the Somali rolled on to the ground, hit him again with the concrete, smashing his jaw.

Stratton straightened and grabbed the climber's foot as the Somali tried to scramble through the window. At the same time he reached down to the prone Somali's belt and pulled out the knife. It was fully in his hand as the guard dropped out of the opening on to his feet. As he landed, Stratton shoved the long blade all the way into him just below his lowest rib. The man jerked in a spasm and opened his mouth to yell but Stratton's free hand quickly clamped over it. The only sound that came from between his fingers was a muted squeal. As the Somali looked into Stratton's eyes, he recognised the Englishman. The life went out of his eyes and legs at the same time. Stratton lowered him to the ground beside his partner.

Stratton looked up at the hut window to see Hopper's face in the gap.

'Stratton!' he whispered.

'I'm OK.'

Hopper pulled himself out a little more to take the weight off his unbound hands. He saw the knife in Stratton's hand and the bodies at his feet. 'You need a hand with them?'

'I'll drag them out of the way. Hopefully they won't be missed until morning. We'll stick with the plan. Ensure no one in there makes a fuss. I'll get back to you soon as I can and then we'll get out of here.'

'And if you don't get back by first light?'

'Don't wait till then. But I'll be back sooner than that.'

Hopper disappeared back into the hut.

Stratton decided to keep the knife. He wiped it on the dead Somali's shirt, then removed the man's leather belt and quickly threaded it through the loops of his own trousers and tucked the blade into it. Grabbing a hold of the legs of one of the men, he dragged him into a narrow alleyway and went back for the other.

After piling enough trash on to the bodies to hide them from sight, while it remained dark at least, he set off in the direction of the beach. Stratton made his way across the town, using the darkest, least obstructed alleyways between dwellings, pausing often to listen. He couldn't afford to bump into anyone. He was the wrong colour to fool any local.

When he reached the last house at the corner of the town, he knelt to take in the ground ahead. The ships were well lit, the sound of their generators drifting on the night air. Laughter came from beyond some piled-up crates further down on the beach. He could see a glow on either side suggesting a fire. That all worked in his favour. It would be difficult for anyone to see into darkness from within a well-lit area.

Stratton headed away from the town, keeping to the higher ground, level with the beachfront houses. He followed a line parallel to the beach, keeping low to avoid being silhouetted. When he was well past the crates with the fire behind it, he headed across the beach towards another stack of boxes. He was exposed to the lights from the ships but knew he was pretty invisible.

When he reached the shadows of the crates he took his time checking the open ground between him and the water. He had twenty good paces of sand to cross. He edged to the end of the pile of boxes until he could see the light from the fire. A couple of guards stood between it and the water.

As he put his head further around the box to look for the rest of the guards, he saw a figure walking directly towards him and jerked his head back, moving into the darkest hole he could find.

The guard came around the corner, his rifle over his shoulder and mumbling to himself. He removed the rifle, leaned it against a crate and unbuckled his trouser belt. The Somali was barely a metre from Stratton, but he had walked into the darkness from the fire and had lost his night vision.

He dropped his trousers and squatted. As he did so he looked down and he saw what was there. A boot. He followed it up to a trouser leg. Then to a torso, up to Stratton's cold hard face looking down on him.

Before the man could react, Stratton swiftly gripped his shirt collar in both hands either side of the Somali's neck and twisted his wrists so that his knuckles dug deep into the man's throat. The effect was immediate and twofold. First, he closed the man's windpipe so that he couldn't make a sound. Second, he shut off the blood supply between the man's heart and brain. In about five seconds the Somali's eyes rolled up in their sockets, his hands hung limply by his side and his tongue hung out of his mouth.

Stratton lowered the dead man on to the sand and wondered what to do with him. If he left him where he was, he would be found by the next man who needed to relieve himself. Stratton dragged him away from the crates and up the beach for a distance before releasing him and making his way back.

The bodies were mounting. Hopper and he certainly needed to get out of there before the daylight exposed them.

Stratton decided not to take the Somali's rifle. It would

only get in the way and he needed stealth rather than firepower. He placed the weapon on top of one of the crates out of view and set his sights again on the largest vessel. Keeping close to the edge of the crates, he looked towards the fire again. The guards were huddled around it. Almost a dozen of them. He doubted they would miss their colleague. They would believe he had gone off for a kip long before they suspected anything bad had happened to him.

Once Stratton made it into the water, the next problem would be getting on board the ship.

An examination of the target presented him with two choices. The most obvious was the gangway. But although the bottom of it was in darkness, the top was exposed to the bright lights on the deck, the superstructure and the bridge wings. And he couldn't rule out the possibility that someone would be sitting on deck watching the top of the gangway.

The other option he had was to climb one of the anchor chains. He had scaled them many times before in his career and knew the technique required. He could not see any rat cones attached. Those were a bitch to climb around. He looked at the aft anchor. That would be the easiest option because of the low freeboard. But if he went up that way, he'd have to walk the length of the main deck to get to front of the boat where he'd watched them take the crate. He decided to avoid that exposed walk past the superstructure and climb the longer forward anchor.

Stratton looked over at the guards around the fire. Nothing had changed. He left the cover of the crates and walked briskly across the soft sand. He ran the last few metres and dived into the waves that were collapsing on the shore. He kept beneath the surface for as long as he could and when he came up he looked back to the fire for any signs that he had been seen.

The guards still hadn't moved and so he turned towards the front of the ship and swam. When he reached the huge metal links, he quickly pulled himself out of the water. He manoeuvred so that the chain angled beneath him and he climbed like a monkey on a branch using all four limbs and three points of contact at any one time. At first it was easy because the chain took much of his weight. But as the angle grew steeper, he had to climb the chain more like a ladder.

He took it one easy step at a time, keeping a watch above and on the shore, aware that from the beach he would be silhouetted against the night sky.

The last few metres were near vertical and required a greater effort as he eased himself up. The huge links passed through a large eye in the side of the ship that was big enough for him to climb through. He eased himself on to the deck and crouched in his wet clothes behind the anchor winch housing. No one could see him there and he took a moment to get his breath back and take stock.

The ship seemed fairly new, that or it was well cared for. The paint job was good and there appeared to be little rust. The superstructure was lit up like a hotel. It housed the accommodation, control room, galley and sick bay, with the bridge and radio shack on the top. The auxiliary generators that provided all of the *Oasis*'s energy needs maintained a constant hum.

The deck was greasy beneath his hands and feet. That was usually the case around the chains and cables. He studied the superstructure. Anyone on board would most likely be in it. He saw a shadow move across a porthole beneath the bridge. No other sign of life. He scanned the decks, like the rest of the ship exposed by lighting.

Keeping low, he moved across the deck between the winch machinery looking for any sign of the crate. But he found nothing. The most obvious location to store anything that big at the front of the ship would be the bosun's locker, a deep storage space that went from the main deck level all the way down to the bottom of the boat.

He looked at a large square hatch that was open. It had to be the locker. There was a light on inside. Which suggested that someone might be down there. The bosun's locker wasn't usually a place anyone hung around unless they were working in it.

He crept to the hatch and leaned over the opening to look down. Lights illuminated the locker all the way down, a good fifteen metres. The entire inside had been painted white. Metal stairs zigzagged part of the way down to ladders that continued to the bottom.

An oxyacetylene gas bottle stood upright just inside the hatch. He listened hard but he heard nothing. The hatch was the only way in or out. He took a quick look around and then he stepped into the hatch and down the handful of steps to the first landing and the gas bottle. A rope had been fixed to a strong point near the hatch and dangled all the way to the bottom.

The forward part of the bosun's locker was the sharp-angled inside of the bows that cut through the water. The welded steel plates had been reinforced by a series of ribs and bracings. These were used as storage shelves and were stacked with ropes, chains and rat cones.

He stepped carefully down the steeply angled staircase to the next landing. From there it was a series of vertical ladders to the bottom. He went down the first two and paused on the bottom to look around. The whole area was cluttered with ropes, old paint buckets filled with shackles, nuts and bolts and odd bits of bracing, pulleys and large pieces of timber. It all appeared to be covered in grease and grime. He stepped on to the final ladder to the bottom and then he listened again. He climbed down and stepped on to the hull of the boat.

A portable electric lamp had been clipped to a brace and aimed at an angle. The hull below the waterline was reinforced by box sections of welded plates. The light was pointed at a particular section, which had been cut open using a torch. The white paint along the cut had bubbled or burned away. An acetylene bottle lay nearby, the piece of metal that had been cut away beside it.

Stratton walked over to look at the opening. The long wooden crate lay inside the space. They had most likely lowered it down on the end of the rope. There was a tin of white paint on the floor with a paintbrush and cloth on top.

He reached inside the hollow hull and searched for the clips that secured the lid of the crate. He found three along its length, unfastened them and gripped the edge. The lid was a tight fit but after a couple of tugs it gave way. Stratton pulled the lid fully open to expose the contents.

He saw a layer of tough, black sponge moulding that ran the length of the box. He peeled it back to reveal a dark-green, metal and plastic weapons system. He knew exactly what it was – a Chinese hand-held HN series ground-to-air missile. He had fired the original Soviet version, which the Chinese had later copied. It was an effective and lethal man-portable missile system designed to shoot down any size aircraft between eight hundred metres and four and a half kilometres above the ground.

As soon as he saw it, several things fell into place that he had a very bad feeling about. The Somalis, or more to the point the jihadists who had delivered the missile, were smuggling the weapons out of the country. They must have muscled in on the hijacking business to use the ships to distribute their ordnance and to send anti-aircraft missiles around the world. When the ship was released by the pirates, it would eventually arrive in a port. All the terrorists had to do was wait until the ship had cleared the usual formalities and inspections and then get on board at their leisure and cut the weapons out. If they got a bulker to the US or the European mainland undiscovered, they could transport the weapons anywhere on those continents.

Stratton wondered how far along the jihadists were, how many ships they'd infiltrated, how many weapons had already been shifted. He saw a holdall tucked further down inside the hollow section and he reached in and pulled it out. He placed it on top of the crate and unfastened its buckles.

The bag contained half a dozen plastic bags filled with a dense white block. It had to be heroin and no doubt originated in Afghanistan. Weapons and drugs. A classic combination for smugglers. The same routes and techniques were used for both.

Stratton looked deeper into the hollow. There were several more holdalls in there. The street value was probably many millions of dollars. It gave the Somali pirate hijacking problem a new meaning. Governments saw it as a grave nuisance to commercial shipping but it was much more than that. He wondered which organisation was driving it, the pirates or the Islamists. Not that it mattered. Then he heard a dull sound from above. He wasn't in direct line of sight of the hatch and quickly put the bag back in the hollow, closed the lid of the weapons box and stepped away into the shadows of the cross-bracing.

Another noise from above, two noises. They sounded like the rasp of a boot on a metal plate. He tried to look up through the metal and bracing from his position. He could see a section of one of the ladders. There was movement on it. Someone coming down. They were moving carefully.

He felt exposed where he was and looked about him. A long, tapered bracing ran down from the main deck across from him. Behind it was complete darkness. He crossed the space and tucked himself behind the bracing. He needed to secure himself, secure his discovery. Get to where he could communicate with his people. His hand slipped to the hilt of the knife at his waist.

The figure stepped off the ladder and stood stock still, like they were looking around. For a second Stratton felt like they knew he was there. He tightened as he wondered if they were aiming a gun at him, waiting for him to move. He eased the knife from his belt.

The footsteps came again. The figure had moved closer. To the box. Stratton heard the crate open.

Suddenly, a loud clang came from high above, at the entrance to the locker, and reverberated around the chamber. What happened next was even more startling for Stratton. Whoever had been inspecting the cache shut the lid and hurried towards him.

He gripped the knife, tensed his body, ready to plunge it into the figure. A hand grabbed the side of the bracing and the figure turned around the edge. Stratton clutched the figure's throat, about to drive the blade fully into the small, slender body when he stopped himself. Just. He was looking at a pair of wide, frightened eyes.

It was the girl.

Another loud clang from above, this time accompanied by voices. Stratton pulled her in beside him, his hand still firmly around her throat, the tip of the knife against her heart. She grabbed at his hand as she began to choke, so Stratton eased his grip a little, ready to kill her if she raised the alarm. But at the same time he was confused by her appearance. 'One sound and you'll die instantly,' he assured her.

She fought to breathe, silently recovering from his choke hold.

The clanging grew louder. Someone, more than one, was coming down the ladder. Judging by the voices, there were two, perhaps three of them, and they were moving something heavy and made of metal and clearly unaware of anything else.

The girl stared into his eyes, blinking hard to fight back the tears caused by the choke hold. She shook her head, which was all she could think of doing to communicate to him that she would do nothing.

Stratton eased his head around the bracing to get a look at what was going on.

A Somali stood halfway down the last ladder before the bottom looking up. Stratton followed his gaze to see a gas cylinder being lowered on the end of the rope.

He looked back at the girl, his face inches from hers. 'What are you doing here?' he whispered.

'I could ask you the same thing,' she said. She was acting tough but her eyes and her breath revealed her true feelings.

Stratton's hand came back to her throat. 'I'll ask you one last time.'

A loud clang like the toll of a bell filled the space as the gas bottle banged against the ladder.

'The ransom drop was for this ship,' she said. 'They will release it soon. I came to hide on board.'

It sounded plausible enough, except for one important thing. Stratton took another careful look around the bracing. The Somali stood on the hull reaching up for the gas bottle above him. He guided it to the floor and shouted something as he untied it.

Stratton moved back and pulled the girl in closer to ensure she wasn't seen. The Somali untied the line, took the end over to the other bottle beside the weapons crate and secured it to the valve head. He gave a shout and the line went taut. As the bottle was lifted off the floor, the Somali guided it over to the ladder. He gave another shout and the bottle began to rise up. Grunting, heaving sounds came from above. The man climbed the ladder beside the bottle, guiding it as he went.

Stratton gave the girl his full attention once again. 'That was very resourceful of you. Now tell me the real story,' he said, his voice low and menacing.

'Why else would I be here?'

'You went straight to the crate.'

'I was curious. I thought it might have food in it.'

'Is that why you looked in the bag too?'

'Yes.'

'So tell me what you found.'

She swallowed, unsure of herself.

'Tell me what you found in the crate,' he repeated.

'I don't know,' she stammered.

'And what do you think I'm doing here, without my partner?'

'I don't know,' she said again.

'If you don't start telling me what you do know, your life will end here, and very shortly.'

She searched his eyes, looking for the sincerity, and she found it.

'By now you've decided that my story about getting captured was as much a load of rubbish as yours,' he said.

She blinked at him, smelling a trap but unsure where it was. 'Yes,' she admitted.

'Then credit me with the same intelligence. You knew, or at least suspected, what was in that crate before you opened it.'

Her eyes began to betray her but she refused to acknowledge him.

'I'm inclined to think you're not one of the bad guys,' he said. 'Mainly because you're their prisoner. But if you don't thoroughly convince me, I'll have no choice but to kill you. And I don't have a lot of time.'

He said it as much to convince himself as her. His gut feeling told him that she wasn't a threat. But he couldn't afford to risk everything on that feeling alone, not in this case. It was a risk he didn't have to take. And he wasn't going to.

She knew her time was running out. She could see it in his pale green eyes. She had one last card to play.

Stratton planted his feet like he was about to shove the knife inside her chest.

'I'm Chinese Secret Service,' she said quickly.

There were few circumstances where such an explanation would have been enough to save her, even if it was the truth. But there were some very clear links in all that was happening. It neatly combined with his other strings of thought. The Brits and the Chinese might be on parallel paths. The Chinese agent had tried to nab Sabarak in Yemen because the Saudi had somehow acquired a supply of Chinese missiles. If so, could it be these same missiles? There were pieces of the puzzle missing but Stratton felt sure they were not far away. Perhaps he had one of them in his hands at that moment.

'What are you doing here?' Stratton asked, his voice less threatening.

'Is this going to be all one-sided?' she retorted.

'Don't push your luck, sweetheart. I'm far from convinced. Tell me more.'

She looked at the floor, waited a few moments, then looked up again, like she had accepted she had something to prove. 'Nine months ago a consignment of Chinese weapons we sold to the North Koreans was hijacked while being transported,' she said. 'This happened inside North Korea on a train. A hundred HN missiles were among the consignment.'

'Who could have done that inside North Korea?'

'We believe Chinese Muslims. They have infiltrated elements of the military and defence department. They smuggled the weapons back into China and we traced them to a ship bound for Indonesia. But by the time we located it, the ship had set sail. Once North Korea took delivery of the missiles, they became Pyongyang's responsibility, but the North Koreans were unable to respond quickly enough despite the intelligence we gave them. These are Chinese weapons and we had to get them back.

'We were always days behind. In Indonesia they went on board a bulk carrier bound for Oman. But the ship never made it that far. It was never intended to get to Oman, although the captain and crew didn't know that. It was hijacked by Somali pirates who knew exactly what was on board and when and where it would be sailing through the Indian Ocean.'

She had been hoping for more of a reaction from Stratton. She got little.

'Is that weapon from the stolen batch?' he asked.

'To be certain, I would have to confirm the serial number is a match. But it has to be.'

'Did you know it was going to be on board this boat before you saw it unloaded on the beach today?'

'No. This was a surprise to me. We knew they were in this part of Somalia in the hands of the terrorists but we didn't know what they had planned for them.'

'Do you know who's behind it?'

She shrugged. 'Al-Shabaab.'

'Any particular individuals?' Stratton asked. 'Do you have any names?' He wondered if she knew about Sabarak.

'No,' she said, shaking her head. 'I shouldn't tell you if I did. But to save you from threatening me again, I don't know any names.'

'What about the destinations of the weapons? What they're planned to be used for?'

She shook her head. 'No. We initially assumed they wanted

to use them against Somali government forces. As I said. This was new to me.'

Stratton was beginning to believe her. 'What's your task?'

'To locate the missiles and report back to my superiors.'

Stratton looked at her quizzically. 'How did you really end up getting captured by these guys?'

She hesitated. 'Getting captured was a part of the plan.'

'You got caught deliberately?' he asked, surprised.

She looked defiant, like his tone implied that she was crazy. 'I found the missiles, didn't I?' she said. 'And now I'm going to get away from here and make my report.'

Stratton had to give her that much. But there was something missing. 'You found only one,' he said.

She didn't answer.

He stared into her eyes. He saw something. 'So where are the others?'

She still didn't say anything.

'Are your people going to be happy with just one missile system out of a hundred?'

She looked like she had told him more than she had wanted to, thinking it would be enough to appease him.

It turned out she was right. Stratton did leave it alone. He had learned a good deal anyway. They were on different teams but not necessarily on opposite sides. Not in this particular task at least. The Chinese wanted the missiles back. She, and the agent in Yemen, seemed to be proof of that.

'Will you tell me who you are?' she asked.

'Name's Stratton.'

'British?'

'Yes.'

'You knew about the weapons?'

Stratton could see no harm in some quid pro quo. There was always a need to make allies in his business, whenever it was safe to do so. You never knew when a friend would come in handy. And the best way to achieve that was to exchange useful information. 'We knew they existed. But nothing more than that.'

'Then why are you here?'

'A series of unfortunate incidents.'

She suddenly felt slightly superior. 'Then you didn't mean to get captured.'

Stratton took it on the chin. 'No.'

The hint of a smile softened her expression. 'What will you do now?' she asked.

'Get out of here. What about the man with you?'

'He cannot travel.'

Stratton understood. The information was too important and the man was too badly injured.

'You will leave your friend too?' she asked.

Stratton would have considered it only if there was a good chance Hopper could survive on his own. But he would most certainly die. 'No. I have to get him.'

She looked disappointed. Stratton suspected she saw it as a weakness.

'We would have a better chance together, you and I,' she said.

Stratton suddenly wondered if she had more useful information. But he wouldn't leave Hopper behind, no matter what she had to offer. 'Where are the other missiles?' he said.

'I'll tell you if you help me get away from here.'

It was a fair enough exchange. She was tough and might not be such a liability. She might even be helpful if they could find a boat. 'OK,' he said, stepping out from behind the brace to look up towards the hatch.

He made his way to the bottom of the ladder. He couldn't see any movement above and all was silent. The girl joined him.

'What's your name?' he said.

'Immy.'

'I'll go up first.'

'Or I can.'

'Get one thing straight. This isn't a partnership. You do everything I say, as soon as I say it, and without any chat. Got that?'

She shrugged.

He reached for a high rung and pulled himself up the ladder.

7

Stratton emerged from the bosun's locker hatch. He crouched, scanning the deck and the superstructure. Then he moved to the familiar cover of the anchor chain machinery. The girl paused at the hatch opening to look around for herself before following.

'Did you come up the anchor chain?' Stratton asked.

'Yes.'

'We'll go back the same way,' he said.

'I found something better,' Immy said. 'Follow me.'

Before he could stop her, she had stepped away to the other side of the deck. His jaw tightened with irritation, but there was little he could do in their exposed position. Keeping low, he followed the girl.

On the port side, a few metres down from the sharp end of the boat, a thick rope looped over a bollard and reached down to the water.

'Less exposed than the anchor chain,' she said.

He had to agree. 'Would you like to go first?' he asked.

Without hesitation she climbed over the solid perimeter, grabbed hold of the rope and let her legs swing below her. She was strong and shimmied down fearlessly.

Stratton didn't wait for her to reach the water before starting down. 'Follow me,' he said as he slid into the water and swam away at an angle towards the beach.

She swam close behind him.

He scanned the beach as they closed on it, in particular the fire. He could see the Somalis still gathered there, smoking as they sat around the flames. They didn't look like they had recently found a throttled buddy.

The waves had got bigger in the short time they had been aboard the *Oasis*. The wind had picked up. Clouds had gathered like a storm was on the way. Stratton was content enough with that. The darker and rougher the better.

The waves crashed heavily on to the beach. Stratton swam hard to pull himself through the surf. With metres to go, he lowered his feet and touched the sand. A swell raised him up and he floated in on it. The sea dumped him on to the sand and he crawled further up the incline on his belly. The water receded, leaving him high and dry. The next wave deposited the girl, who rolled on past him.

He looked at the men, and then he got up. 'Come on,' he said, grabbing her shoulder and dragging her to her feet.

They ran through the flood of ship lights up the beach until they reached darkness. They dropped on their knees to the sand and looked about them again. Then they moved stealthily towards the beachfront homes. A few had wood fires going inside or kerosene lamps. Several bright electrical lights shone somewhere in the town. They could hear the buzz of small petrol-driven generators.

Stratton saw movement between some houses and went

to ground. Several people, a family perhaps, hanging around in the street. The wind toyed with their wet clothes as they knelt to watch and listen. It was late in the evening but not everyone went to bed with the setting of the sun. The air had cooled but there was far too much to think about for them to feel the cold.

'Where are the rest of the missiles?' Stratton asked in a low voice.

The girl looked at him, surprised, not so much by the content of his question but its timing.

'If something happens to you, I need to know,' he said.

'If I tell you, perhaps you'll let something happen to me.'

Her answer amused him. She was certainly used to devious company. 'At least tell me if they're close to here or miles away in another part of the country.'

'They're close. A few kilometres from here.'

'How can you be so sure they're still there?'

'I'm not,' she said.

That was not what he wanted to hear.

She sighed. Then she said, 'It was Lotto's men who hijacked the ship carrying the rockets. He did it for the Muslim fighters. That was a month ago. He is being well paid for his services. I suspect they intend to send many more of the missiles abroad. If that is so then they will still be close by.'

Stratton hoped she was right. 'The drugs are his payment?'

'Yes. Al-Shabaab pays him with heroin from Afghanistan.'

'Do you think this is a new arrangement – between the pirates and the jihadists – drugs for their help?'

'I don't know. I think Lotto has been using hijacked ships to move drugs into other countries for several years. If it worked for drugs, it would work for weapons.'

Stratton found it disturbing. The jihadists could use the system to move practically anything they liked right under the noses of Western authorities. And they wouldn't know a thing about it. Today, portable ground-to-air missiles. Tomorrow, biological weapons, dirty bombs. Even nuclear components and devices.

'We have to stop those weapons from reaching their destinations,' he muttered, more to himself. 'I don't suppose you know how many ships have already left here with missiles hidden on board?'

'I only just discovered it today. Like you. It wouldn't be difficult to find every ship that has been released from here since the weapons arrived.'

'It will be if no one but us on our side knows about it.' Stratton took a look at her as another thought came to him. 'How were you supposed to communicate your findings back to your people?'

She took her time answering. 'I was not completely truthful with you,' she said. 'Like you, we weren't actually supposed to get captured.'

Stratton frowned at her.

'We were supposed to make landfall and hide equipment we had on the boat. That included a satellite phone. One of Lotto's boats saw us before we could get to shore. We dumped it all over the side. They would have taken it anyway and we wanted to look like simple sailors.'

'What was supposed to happen after you reported you'd found the missiles?'

'I don't know. I don't need to know, so I wasn't told.'

Stratton thought about the Saudi again. Perhaps Sabarak had something to do with the weapons being moved from Indonesia. 'Let's get going,' he said.

They covered the short distance to the first hut and then walked carefully up the street, hugging the houses. They criss-crossed through the town between the squat hovels until they reached the back of the prison hut. Stratton took a moment to study the window opening. 'I'll get my partner and we'll get out of here,' he said.

He jumped up and pulled himself into the opening enough to look inside.

He saw the prisoners lying on the floor. He saw Hopper in the darkness.

'Hopper?' Stratton said as loud as he dared.

Hopper didn't move. Stratton climbed through the window as silently as he could and lowered himself to the floor. He crouched beside Hopper and rolled him on to his back. Hopper's mouth had been taped over and his hands tied even more securely than before. A Somali who was lying on the floor across the room jumped up and shouted and aimed a rifle at Stratton. Another close by leaped to his feet brandishing a long blade.

The door burst open and more guards holding kerosene lights and weapons stomped in. The other prisoners parted before them, quickly back against the walls. Lotto walked in, swivelling his cane in his hand. He stopped in front of

Stratton. The man reeked of perfume, which overpowered the smell of the kerosene.

Lotto said something in his native tongue. A pause, then Sabarak stepped into the doorway.

'You were right,' Lotto said to the Saudi. 'He did come back for his friend.'

A Somali appeared in the windowless opening and said something. The leader nodded. The guard dropped out of sight.

'Where have you and the girl been?' Lotto asked.

Stratton had an urge to be flippant but he had seen Lotto's quick temper. He decided it was unwise to rile the leader. 'We were looking for a boat,' he said. 'We came back for our friends.'

'You know the punishment for trying to escape,' Lotto said. He barked a command and left the room. Sabarak followed him.

The guards had become much more hostile and two manhandled Stratton to the door, shoving him through it violently. Four others went to the injured Chinese man and Hopper and brutally hauled them to their feet. The Chinese man cried out but the Somalis showed no sympathy for his discomfort.

As Stratton stepped outside he saw the girl being pushed out of the gap between the buildings and falling to the ground, landing at Lotto's feet. The pirate chief ignored her.

Stratton eyed Sabarak, who was standing between four hard-faced fighters. All sported long beards and looked like clones of the passenger of the truck who had delivered the missiles to the port. They were heavily armed with AK-47s, spare magazines in pouches and long machetes dangling from their leather belts. They stared aggressively at the two Englishmen like they wanted to eat their hearts there and then.

Sabarak smiled thinly at Stratton. 'Now the tables have fully turned,' he said.

Lotto shouted an order and a couple of his men grabbed Stratton's arms and pulled them tightly behind his back, then securely fastened them together with nylon fishing line. One of the guards found the knife tucked into Stratton's waistband and withdrew it. He recognised it instantly and said something to his leader.

'Where's the man who's knife this is?' Lotto asked Stratton. 'He is not the only one who has gone missing tonight.'

Stratton could see little point in lying. The bodies would be found as soon as it was light anyway. 'They came looking for revenge for our fight on the beach. They also wanted the girl. You can find them behind the building. I'm afraid they're not in very good condition.'

Lotto seemed to be faintly amused by the account. 'If they came for the girl, they deserved it,' he said.

'You'll share their fate,' Sabarak said, using every opportunity to fill Stratton with fear.

'Only if the British don't pay for them,' Lotto interjected.

The comment angered Sabarak. 'You said I could have them.'

'I said you could have one of them.'

Sabarak clearly didn't have the control over Lotto that he wished he had. 'He's the leader,' he said, indicating Stratton. 'I want him.'

Lotto didn't appear remotely intimidated by Sabarak or his men. 'Then he is more valuable,' Lotto said. 'Take the other one.'

'He is more important to us,' Sabarak argued.

'What do you care which one you have? You will only kill them. You are at war with these people. I am in business with them. To you they are something to vent your anger at. To me they are a commodity. It makes no sense that you should cut the head off the most valuable one.'

'We will interrogate him. He will know more than his subordinate.'

'What will he know that you do not already know or you can guess? You can have the Chinese man too. How is that?'

'And the girl.'

Judging by Lotto's expression, Sabarak had clearly overstepped the mark. He turned to the Saudi, his eyes dark holes in his big face. 'Don't forget your place. You need me and I don't need you. I am giving you two men as a gift. Be grateful. Or I will give you nothing.'

Sabarak and his crew looked much fiercer than the pirates but they were greatly outnumbered. The Saudi was a businessman before he was a fighter and knew when to back off. He averted his eyes and nodded. 'Of course. Please understand that these people have murdered thousands upon thousands of my people.'

Lotto gloated over Sabarak's cunning apology. 'Take your gift away before I change my mind,' he said.

Sabarak gave one of his men a look. The man took hold of Hopper while another grabbed the Chinese man and they pulled them both away.

Hopper twisted around to look back at Stratton. The operative saw the fear in Hopper's eyes. He couldn't help wondering if he would ever see the man again.

Lotto looked down at the girl as a Somali tied her hands behind her back. 'It's time you and I got to know each other a little better,' he said with a raw smile. He shouted another command and one of the guards stepped up and took the girl away.

Lotto turned to face Stratton. 'Because you were trying to help the girl, I will not break your legs this time. If you try to escape again, I will cut off your feet. That's a promise. Your people will pay the same for half of you . . . I am not confident the British will pay for you at all. They don't normally, but perhaps you are special. If not, you will join your friend.' Lotto laughed and walked off after the girl.

The guard holding the knife he had found on Stratton grabbed the operative by his shirt and held the blade to his throat. Stratton could tell the Somali wanted to say something but knew Stratton wouldn't understand. The threat would have to satisfy them both for the time being. The message was clear enough. And in case Stratton didn't fully understand, the Somali kneed him hard in the groin. Stratton wanted to go down but the guard kept the sharp blade against his neck. Another guy decided to join in and slammed Stratton in the kidneys with a vicious punch. Once again, Stratton fought to keep his legs steady to prevent having his throat cut.

The Somali with the knife took hold of Stratton's hair and he ran the operative inside the hut, where he hit the floor, knocking over the water bucket. Behind him, they slammed shut the door and bolted it.

Stratton lay where he fell, concentrating on recovering. It was going to take several minutes of controlled breathing and focus to weather it.

When the pain in his crotch finally eased, it gave way to the one in his side, which also ached deeply. Eventually he rolled over and up on to his knees. He shuffled to a wall and eased himself back against it. He suddenly felt very tired.

Light from a kerosene lamp filtered in through the cracks in the door. A similar glow reflected around the edges of the windowless opening. Voices filtered into the room from both sides. The guards were obviously taking their duties more seriously.

Stratton looked at the roof of the hut. It had suddenly all gone horribly wrong.

8

They led the girl to a house at the top end of the town. It was bigger than the others and better appointed. She could see electric lights glowing inside. The dull hum of a generator came from around the back.

They pushed her up a short flight of steps on to a porch. They opened the door and took her in. On one side of the large room she could see cardboard boxes. Piled up the wall. All shapes and sizes, advertising booze and electronics, clothing and toiletries. On the other side there was a modern leather couch, worn but comfortable-looking. In the middle an ornate coffee table. A dresser with a mirror stood alone away from the wall. A large bed in the corner, its headboard made from boxes of liquor.

Lotto walked in and gave the guards a look. The men stepped back courteously and left, closing the door behind them.

Lotto regarded the girl, like he was assessing her, his eyes exploring her. She looked like a ragamuffin. But he could see beneath the bedraggled clothing and it gave him immense pleasure.

He removed his beret, placed his cane in a rack and the beret on top of it. 'Drink?' he asked.

She shook her head.

'Have a whisky?' he said.

The girl reconsidered and nodded.

He chuckled and walked over to a stack of boxes that acted as a drinks cabinet, reached inside one, brought out a bottle of Scotch and cracked open the top. He sniffed the bottle, took a short sip and rinsed it around his gums and tongue. He swallowed. 'Wonderful invention, Scotch.'

He removed a couple of glasses from another box and near filled them both. He went to a fridge and took a bowl of ice from it. He placed several chunks in each glass, returned the bowl to the fridge, walked over to her with the glasses and offered her one. She looked at him – her hands still tied firmly behind her back. She hoped he might untie them.

'Open your mouth,' he said.

She obeyed and he touched the edge of the glass to her lips and gently poured the drink into her mouth. She grimaced at the bite of the liquor. He tipped it all the way up, emptying the entire contents into her mouth, much of it spilling down her neck and inside her shirt. As he removed the glass, she coughed and spluttered.

Lotto took a long sip of his drink and put both of the glasses down. He stepped closer to her, his smile turning lustful. She looked defiantly into his eyes.

'I'm disappointed in you,' he said.

She did not react.

'I hope you're going to put up a bit of a fight,' he said, grinning. Then brought up his bony hand and slammed her across the face. She flew back on to the bed.

She went giddy instantly, found it hard to focus her eyes on him.

He leaned over her, turned her on to her front and untied her hands. He pulled one of them to a corner of the bed and secured it with the line to the bedpost. She started to struggle beneath his heavy frame. He put a knee into her small back and stretched out her other hand, tying it with another piece of line. She fought to get him off her, bringing her legs up to try and kick out. But he was too strong for her. He got off her and grabbed her left ankle, tied it to a post and then did the same with her right leg.

She struggled for long enough to realise how hopeless it was. She pressed her face down into the mattress, panting with the effort.

Lotto kept smiling as he reached for a knife at his belt. He inserted it at the bottom of one of her trouser legs and sliced all the way up to the top. He did the same with the other leg and then, with a magician's flourish, ripped the garment away leaving her in her panties.

He sat beside her and cut away her shirt, unwrapping her in a way that gave him great pleasure. She wore no bra and lay there naked but for her knickers. She closed her eyes tightly in an effort to control herself. She tugged at the bindings again but it was hopeless.

Lotto turned his attention to her panties and cut one of

the sides and then the other and pulled them off her. He got up from the bed and stood to admire her.

He took off his shirt, then his boots, then his trousers and he stood naked.

She expected him to climb on top of her but she was wrong. He had something else in mind. He took the heavy leather belt from his trousers and wrapped it around his fist a couple of times to leave a long tail. He cocked back his arm so that the end of the belt fell down his back. When he brought it forward, he did it with great effort.

The cutting thwack could be heard along the street. Her scream reached even further into the town. The guards outside the prison hut heard the shrill cry. One of them said something and the others laughed.

Stratton sat in the darkness of the hut, his eyes closed, but far from asleep. He couldn't see a way out of the predicament. The girl's screams bulldozed into his thoughts until he could only think of her and her suffering. He looked at the other prisoners. All of them could guess what was happening to the girl, more or less. He didn't feel responsible. Not for her. But he felt utterly sympathetic. His thoughts turned to Hopper again. His partner's position looked many times worse than his own. And it was Stratton's fault.

He could have taken Hopper with him. It hadn't been so important for him to stay behind. Stratton knew well enough why he had gone to the ship by himself. He just preferred operating alone. He always had. He achieved his best results that way. He could easily explain it. And his bosses knew it too. One man is never afraid to push it that extra step more when he operates alone. There's no one else to convince or debate with about choices or solutions. Instant decisions can be made, a direction can be changed without warning, and you don't risk leaving someone behind.

But on this occasion he'd been wrong. He had left his friend exposed to a great danger. The Saudi. Who had disappeared, which had been a clear warning. Hopper had known it. He said as much to Stratton. He ignored it. Hopper was probably thinking something like that right now. As well as wondering how long he had left to live.

The girl screamed again but she sounded weaker. The fight was going out of her. Stratton looked at the bonds around his hands. He tested them again. He couldn't stay where he was. That was impossible. He had to get going. But the bindings had been carefully tied this time. He needed an edge to rub them against. That would take a long time. He stood, walked to the wall under the window. His arms in the air, he stood on his toes and tried to scrape the bindings along the edge of the sill.

A prisoner across the room got to his feet and stepped quietly over to Stratton.

Stratton stopped to look at the man. It was the Dutchman who had made a stand on the beach when the girl was being attacked.

'My name is Vorg,' he said. 'I was in the Dutch Marines. Many years ago of course. I am very concerned about your friend. He will not survive long with those fellows who have taken him. You should be concerned about yourself too.' Stratton wanted to thank him for stating the bloody obvious. He also wanted to tell him to go away and mind his own damned business.

'The ransom drop today was for my ship,' Vorg went on. 'The *Oasis*. The biggest one. We should be going soon. In a few days perhaps. It's the only code these bastards have. They don't want to discourage the owners of all the other ships from paying. I'm telling you this because I think you should try to escape again. All you have to do is get on board my boat.'

It was a good idea. But getting just himself home was not a solution Stratton was open to at that moment. He had to get Hopper. The cold-hearted bastards among the Brit Secret Service would fully support Stratton getting himself out of Somalia and leaving Hopper to his fate. That was part and parcel of the job, they would say. But Stratton could not agree. Especially when it was his fault that Hopper had been left behind.

The Dutchman produced a strange-looking blade several inches long. 'I made it out of a small sheet of metal I found on the floor when I got in here,' he said. 'I rolled it over and over, the same way they make Samurai swords. I sharpened the edge on a stone in the floor. It's taken me three months. I hide it in my corner. I didn't know what I was going to use it for. I think you might have a use for it.'

Stratton looked into the older man's eyes and saw the sincerity in them. He turned to his side. The Dutchman sawed between his wrists. A moment later his hands parted. He removed the rest of the line from his wrists and rubbed the life back into them. 'Thanks,' he said.

'No need,' said the Dutchman. 'I'm sure what you're doing is very important and of benefit to all of us.'

Stratton glanced between the door and the window. Which one? he wondered. Neither would be easy. But he didn't have to mask his tracks this time. One way or another, he wasn't coming back. He gauged first light to be a couple of hours away.

The Dutchman watched as Stratton walked to the door.

Stratton moved his eyes from crack to crack in the door, the kerosene lamps outside allowing him something of a view. He could see a Somali squatting on a doorstep opposite. The man appeared to be asleep. If there was another nearby, he couldn't see him. But he might also be asleep.

Stratton looked at the Dutchman and beckoned him over. 'Your knife,' he said.

The man hesitated, clearly thinking about his knife being used on another human being. It was a bad thought to a man like him, even after all the jailers had done to him and to the girl.

'I need it to open the door,' Stratton said, reading the man's thoughts.

The Dutchman handed the blade to Stratton. The operative couldn't be sure if the Dutchman decided to trust him or if he had put aside his humanitarianism for the moment. Stratton put his ear to the door. He could hear nothing. He slid the blade through a gap between the edge of the door and the frame until it touched the bolt. He pushed down and sideways on the bolt with the blade and it moved a couple of millimetres. He did it again. And again, sliding the bolt over a little each time.

It didn't take long to draw the bolt out of its hole in the frame. The next move represented the real risk. He had to open the door without knowing what or who was on the other side, other than the sleeping guard across the street. It was the point of no return for him. If he failed here, they would cut his feet off. That alone would have been a strong incentive. But he didn't need it.

He pushed the door open gently. It swung easily and silently for the first few inches. Then the hinge protested so he stopped, but only for a second. Anyone looking at the door would know it was no longer bolted shut. He pushed it wide open and stepped out energetically, looking left and right, searching for a target, hand gripping the knife.

A guard stood with his back against the wall to his right. So close Stratton could reach out and touch him. The man lifted his head and saw Stratton and stepped back as Stratton leaned towards him, his arm reaching out. The guard went for his rifle leaning against the wall. He bent and grabbed the barrel and lifted it up and then he saw the blade in the operative's hand arcing towards him. And that was the last thing he ever did see. The tip of the blade went into the side of his neck and penetrated deeply into it with the force of the swing, severing both of the carotid arteries. Stratton grabbed the rifle before it fell from the dead man's hand. Blood spurted from his throat and he dropped slowly to his knees, Stratton holding some of his weight.

Stratton's eyes went to the sleeping Somali across the street, waiting for the slightest indication that the man was about to wake up. But he didn't stir. He was sound asleep.

Stratton leaned the dead man against the hut wall, moved away from the door, one careful step at a time, while he searched up and down the street, looking for any other sign of movement.

Vorg stepped into the doorway and looked at the dead guard and then he looked at Stratton.

'Back inside,' Stratton whispered.

The Dutchman handled the guilt he felt for his part in the Somali guard's death and did what he was told. Stratton closed the door and drew the bolt across. Then he moved around the hurricane lamp, careful not to cast a shadow over the guard, holding the weapon, ready to fire. Although he wasn't that confident it would work. The barrel had rusted, as had the magazine and trigger housing. The wooden stock and butt had dried and cracked. He could only imagine what the working parts inside were like. But the AK-47 was, if little else, a robust piece of kit and could generally be relied upon to operate no matter its condition.

He moved up the street, scanning in every direction as he went. The sleeping guard still hadn't moved.

Once out of sight of the prison hut, he focused his attention ahead, looking for Lotto's quarters. It dawned on him that he hadn't heard the girl scream for a while. He could think of several explanations for that, most of them not good, for him or for her.

In his case, he needed her help. She knew where the Al-Shabaab camp was located, or at least she said she did. And that was where Hopper was most likely being held. Rescuing him had become the most important priority. The information Stratton had discovered about the missiles hidden in the hijacked vessels was vital to be sure. But it was going to have to wait.

Stratton might have reminded anyone else in the same position of their duty to get the information back as soon as humanly possible regardless of the danger to other members of the mission. It was for the greater good. And in his younger days he might have done so. But his experiences over the years had reshaped him. He had lost too many friends. Hopper was more important to him than whatever the ground-to-air missiles were destined for. There were other chances to put a stop to that. Hopper had only one chance and that was Stratton.

He walked slowly up the side of the deserted street in complete darkness. The wind had picked up. Sounds came to him from every direction: a door banged, plastic sheeting flapped, a distant generator hummed. He paused at the corner to a broader street across his front. Two houses down, one of them had lights on inside. Stratton crept up the street to get a closer look at the front. He crossed over and stood at the corner of the front wall. He listened but he could hear nothing. He carefully looked into the front window, but he could see no one, just a torn old sofa, a table and chairs. He skirted the front of the house and waited, looking down the street. Movement on the porch of a large house back across the road caught his eye.

He studied the shadows on the porch. A figure sat near the front door. He walked down a narrow alley, around the back of a house and along another gap between houses, then back to the broad street where he was diagonally opposite the big place. A small flame flared on the porch and lit a cigarette. It moved to light two more before extinguishing. The ends of the tobacco roll-ups glowed bright as the men inhaled deeply.

He had an obvious problem. The house could well be Lotto's and he needed to confirm it. To do that he needed to get a look inside. That required neutralising the watchmen. Which might cause a disturbance and increase the risks. The burning question now, how important was the girl? Could he find the terrorist camp without her? What if she was already dead? On the face of it the risk calculation wasn't adding up.

He leaned back against the wall of the house and looked to the skies for inspiration. How could he find Hopper on his own? It was starting to look impossible. His mind began to drift to his exit strategy. The Dutchman's boat. Hopper kept coming to mind. He painfully pushed it aside.

The house's front door opened. Light streamed on to the street. The watchmen got to their feet. A figure stepped into the doorway. A large man wearing a towel around his waist. Stratton couldn't say for sure but it looked like the pirate leader. The man said something and one of the others stepped behind him into the house. A few seconds later he came out again, helping a small figure who was staggering. It looked like the girl.

The big man went back into the house and shut the door. The main light inside went out and then a lamp glowed in the window. One of the watchmen said something and the two others laughed. They helped the girl down the steps of the porch on to the street.

They took her around the end of the porch and into a broad alley illuminated by the light from a window. They let the girl go and she dropped to her knees. The three men talked in muffled voices. There was the occasional chuckle. It appeared that they were contemplating having some fun themselves.

One of them knelt down beside the girl.

Stratton took another quick review of the risk calculation. She was alive. Hopper could be found. There were three goons but they were occupied. It was dark. 'Bollocks,' he muttered to himself and gritted his teeth.

Stratton pulled the Kalashnikov into his shoulder, brought the end of the barrel up and strode across the street.

The two Somalis standing over the girl saw him at the same time. He pointed the barrel of the AK at them. They straightened and raised their hands, stepping back, their mouths gaping open. The one on his knees remained where he was, unaware of the intrusion. As Stratton walked, he reversed the rifle in his hands and swung it like a baseball bat at the kneeling Somali's head. He struck him hard on the temple. He landed on top of the girl and she collapsed under his weight.

Stratton swung the weapon back up on aim.

'Down,' he said softly but firmly, gesturing with a hand at the same time.

The two guards dropped to their knees, their hands still held high.

Stratton stepped around and behind them and pushed them forward to lie on their bellies. They kept their hands stretched out. Stratton stood between their prone bodies, decided what to do with them. There was only really one solution. He raised the carbine and brought the butt down heavily on to the neck of the first guard. There was a crack. Before the other guard could react, Stratton smashed the butt down on to the critical vertebrae of his neck and separated those too. He shuddered like the first one as the life left him.

Stratton rolled the third guard off the girl, who remained lying still. She appeared to be unconscious. Then a sound startled him and he moved to the side of the house, pressing his back against the concrete block wall beside the window. He was an arm's length from the porch. The front door had opened. It had to be Lotto.

Stratton heard a couple of footsteps move on the wooden boards of the porch. They stopped. Silence followed. Stratton held the gun close, ready to use it, either as a club or as it was designed to be used. The pirate chief's three guards lay at his feet.

But Lotto didn't venture to the end of the porch, he

looked out on to the street. He struck a match, his grim, toughened features illuminated briefly. He lit a fat cigar that he held in his bright white teeth and blew the smoke into the air.

Stratton waited. It dawned on him that killing the pirate was not such a bad idea. It might throw the rest of the gang into disarray. But then again in operational terms it would be better if their ground-to-air missile programme remained functional until the entire network could be brought down. A change in hierarchy might make everything less predictable. Stratton would take the man down only if he had to.

He heard the front door close and sounds from inside. The clink of a bottle like Lotto was pouring himself a drink. Stratton went to the corner of the building, dropped to a knee and looked between the rails on to the porch. He couldn't see any movement on the dark street. It was time to get out of there.

He turned his attention to the girl and rested his gun against the wall of the building. It was hard to tell in the poor light whether the marks on her skin were injuries or dirt. He felt her throat. Her heart was racing.

He quickly pulled off the unconscious guard's trousers and shirt. This was not the time and place to dress her. He stood the girl up, bent down and let her fall forward over his shoulder. He stood. She was light, something he was thankful for. He grabbed the rifle off the wall and made his way uphill between the houses and away from the pirate leader's house. The wind was strengthening. He got to the top of the town without seeing anyone. The houses stretched out to his left and right, straight ahead nothing but a black, arid wilderness.

He walked into the wasteland with the naked unconscious girl over his shoulder.

9

Stratton headed deep into the darkness, doing his best to go south. It was difficult to gauge by the stars because of the cloud cover. He had gone about a kilometre from the town when he came to a gravel road running across his front. It looked well used. He decided to follow it east. The higher ground had been in that direction as they'd approached from the sea. And he could see a few trees. Which increased the chances of finding water. He walked down the centre of the dusty road.

The girl was drifting in and out of consciousness. He had maintained a brisk pace, which couldn't have been comfortable for her. But they needed to put as much distance as possible between them and the town. Lotto would no doubt be fuming when he found out, with Stratton as well as with his guards. To escape yet again was a slap in the face. He would not be impressed with the final body count the pirates had suffered that night either.

The track they were on appeared to head parallel with the coastline. It was a tactical risk using it because it increased the chances of meeting someone. But this was an occasion when he was willing to take the chance in favour of the ease of movement. He came to the brow of an incline and paused to catch his breath and take in the view. The girl might have been light to start with but she was getting heavier by the minute.

A large body of water stretched across the panorama in front. It wasn't the ocean. That took up the entire horizon to his left. It was a broad river that came from the mountains in the south. But the river didn't flow into the sea because it had been blocked by a naturally formed dam. A seasonal phenomenon. During the monsoons, when the river was in full flood, it couldn't be stopped.

Stratton felt thirsty and hoped that the water hadn't been invaded by too much of an ocean backwash. He set off down the incline, his neck and back aching. He was looking forward to taking a breather. He felt the girl's muscles tense.

He stopped a few metres from the water's edge and lowered her to the ground, placing the trousers under her head as a pillow and covered her body with the shirt to preserve her modesty. She moaned and moved her head from side to side.

He went to the water, cupped a hand and tasted a little. It was brackish but drinkable. After a couple of mouthfuls he brought some over to her and dripped it on to her forehead and across her mouth. Her eyes flickered and her breathing quickened. She licked her lips. She opened her eyes and looked at him leaning over her. She suddenly became afraid and struggled to push herself away.

'Easy,' Stratton said, reaching out but without touching her. 'It's me. You're OK. You're safe now.'

She stopped, her whole body tensed as she came to her senses. Her eyes darted around before finding him again. She was still scared but he was a pillar of strength in a place where they were surrounded by danger. She realised she was naked and held the shirt to her.

'We're out of the town,' he said. 'It's just you and me. No one else.'

Her expression changed and she eased off a bit.

Stratton wondered if she remembered what had happened to her. Such a serious trauma could cause short-term amnesia.

But she suddenly remembered. The horrific memories of the past few hours flooded her mind. She fought to control an abrupt emotional reaction and rolled into a ball and began to sob.

'You know who I am?' he said. 'You remember me, right? I'm Stratton.'

She calmed a little and nodded.

'We can't stay here long. They'll be looking for us. We have to get further away. Do you understand?'

She didn't acknowledge him. He wondered if she was going to make it at all. Perhaps she had become unhinged. He couldn't help thinking about his next move if she was unable to keep going. He couldn't leave her of course.

'Immy?' he said. 'You need to get up. You can't stay here. I can't carry you any more. Do you understand?'

She still didn't move.

Stratton felt suddenly tired. He had to get on. Time was running out. She had to motivate herself. It seemed like she had gone into a catatonic state. He felt his patience wearing thin. He needed to find Hopper and get out of Somalia. It looked as if he might have to do it alone.

'Immy?' he said. 'I need you to wake up, right now.'

She remained motionless.

'Immy?' he repeated, getting to his feet and standing over her. 'I know you don't want to die. But if you just lie there, if you don't get up, your life is going to come to an end very soon.

'I'll spell it out for you,' he said, getting angry. 'I can't leave you here alive. If I did and they found you, they would eventually learn what I know, what we both know. I can't allow that information to be compromised. They'll move the missiles and find another way of getting them out of the country. So you see, if you don't pull yourself together, I won't leave you here to die. I will kill you myself.'

He held the stock of the assault rifle over her. 'Don't make me do this. You either get up now or it's over. You know I'll do it.'

He raised the weapon and aimed for her head, resigned to killing her. It seemed a terrible thing to do but the equation was simple enough. It was her or him. And she would probably die anyway, of exposure, or when she was caught.

He looked towards the beach, gauging the distance to the ships. Perhaps he could get her on board. Hopper was doomed. The girl sat up and looked towards the water, her back to him. Like she didn't know he was there. Stratton felt relief at his own reprieve as much as hers. She got to her feet, clutching the shirt to her, and walked to the water's edge. She walked into the water up to her waist. She started to wash herself. She took a long drink and then doused her face and her arms and shoulders gently.

She stopped what she was doing, lowered her head and began to cry again. He felt helpless and unable to offer any encouragement that might be of use to her. He decided to shut up and let her get on with it.

She didn't spend much longer in the water. She pulled on the shirt, turned around and walked towards him. She stopped to pick up the trousers a little unsteadily, pulled them on, rolling down the waist to shorten and tighten them.

'Sorry, no shoes,' he said. He looked at the welts on her neck and arms. She had taken a beating. He suddenly felt impressed by her. She had suffered enormously, in a way he could never really understand, but there she was, standing before him, unsteady, yet with a determined look in her eye.

'How do you feel?' he asked, grasping for something to say. 'We need to walk on.'

She looked at the ground, into the distance. Then at him.

'I can carry you for a bit,' he said, his guilt not fully receded.

She shook her head. 'I can walk,' she said, her voice shaky. She looked around again. 'Where are we?'

'East of the town. About six kilometres.'

'East?' She looked confused.

'South a kilometre and then east.'

'Away from the sea.'

'That's right.'

'Aren't we going to find a boat?'

'Not yet.'

She looked at him questioningly.

'I want you to take me to the Al-Shabaab camp,' he said.

Her gaze remained firmly on him. She seemed to be thinking, formulating a response.

'I have to get my friend,' Stratton said. 'Don't you want to help your friend too?'

She looked away again, like the question bothered her. 'How can we do that?' she asked. 'The camp will have many fighters.'

'I have to at least try,' he said.

'They are not like the pirates. They are more vigilant. More dangerous.'

He looked at her, waiting for her to narrow down her options until they equalled his.

She came to a conclusion. 'Is that why you rescued me?'

He did not need to answer her. It was obvious enough.

'I am thankful for that,' she decided.

'Where is the camp?'

She considered the question for a moment before returning to the water. She crouched to fill her palms and take a drink. Stratton felt his own thirst return and followed her lead.

'Did you see a road?' she asked.

'We followed it. It's just over there, at the top of the ridge.'

'It goes south?'

'Looks like it.'

She looked at the lake and towards the sea, comparing it to a map inside her head. 'The camp is south from here. Ten kilometres from the coast.'

'Have you been there?'

'No.'

She sat down again. Stratton watched as she tore the bottom of both trouser legs off. But instead of throwing the cloth away, she wrapped the pieces around her feet and tied them off.

She stood up, still a little wobbly. 'You think you can rescue your friend?'

'I have to try,' he said.

'And if you cannot?'

The answer to that was obvious enough.

'I think it's only fair I should know the plan,' she said.

Stratton felt like he had to accept her as something of a partner. She had earned that much. He also had an urge to trust her. She was an enemy in some ways, but she was also in the same hole he was. They were after the same thing.

'The same idea you had. The ship we were on is going

to be released. My plan is to recce the Al-Shabaab camp. Whatever happens, from there we head back to the ship. We climbed on to it once, we can do it again.'

The girl nodded as she considered the various phases he had proposed. 'OK.'

Stratton looked to the skies. The eastern horizon was growing lighter. 'It'll be dawn soon,' he said. 'We should go.'

He headed up the incline and looked back. She was following. He found the road again and they took it south. He set off at an anxious pace but after a short distance realised he was alone and stopped to look back for her.

She was still trudging along. 'Give me a moment to loosen up,' she said. 'I'll keep up with you.'

Stratton didn't doubt it and he moved off. Her determination grew and within a short distance she was walking alongside of him. He gave her a look. She looked right back at him.

The road followed the waterline but on higher ground and for the most part about a hundred metres away from the river. As they walked on, he began to see the strangeness of it all, walking through the Somali countryside with a Chinese Secret Service agent, and a woman to boot, kidnapped by pirates, her ordeal. Then he thought of Hopper and his mind came into focus.

'I'm thirsty,' she said.

He was too and they left the track and headed down the slope towards a line of thick scrub. They reached a wall of dense bushes and pushed through. On the other side the ground had levelled out and the roots of the plants had no doubt found the water table. After several metres of difficult progress, they came to the water's edge.

'You feeling OK?' he asked her as she took a drink.

'Yes.'

'I want to get to the camp before daybreak,' he said.

'I understand,' she said.

They pushed back through the bushes as quietly as they could, on to the road and walked along it at a faster pace. She was as good as her word and kept up with him.

They had been walking for just over an hour when they saw headlights. They were coming on fast behind them.

'This way,' he hissed as he ran off the road on to the plain and down into a small hollow.

She lay beside him. Both watched the vehicle come on.

The sound of the engine eventually broke through the quiet. It was an old truck. It jolted and creaked right by them, swerving left and right around the deep potholes. It kept on going, heading up the plateau, then disappearing over a rise. Stratton got to his feet. The girl stood too and they started walking.

It took a little while to get to the rise. He slowed as they approached and then he ducked just before the top, aware that he would be silhouetted against the skyline. She did the same, stopping alongside him. 'What is it?'

'Nothing yet.'

They could see the truck again a long way off, bouncing along the road, disappearing at times behind the scrub.

Finally it drove over a bigger rise and they could only hear it and see glimpses of its reflected light beams.

Stratton stood upright and looked beyond the point where the truck had disappeared. The wind blew gently into their faces. They could hear the branches of a rugged, stumpy shrub scraping together.

'It's stopped,' he said.

'I can still hear it.'

'Yes. But it's stopped.' He stepped over the crumbling rocks of the plateau and down the other side of the rise.

The girl followed but more cautiously, watching where she placed her cloth-covered feet. The horizon grew brighter by the minute. The breeze had been fairly cool throughout the night but they knew it would get hotter as the sun came up.

They reached the bottom of the slope and began up the crest of another. It was hard to tell the distance to the top in the near darkness.

When he reached it he lay on his belly to look down the other side.

She did the same.

They were looking into a large depression between the ridge they were on and another far beyond. As the ground descended into the basin he could see the way the dark, stunted trees huddled together. An encampment sat in the middle of the wood. He saw several fires and a sprinkling of oil and electric-powered lamps. Men's voices drifted up to them on the breeze. They could hear a generator, or perhaps more than one.

It didn't look like a village. It could have been nomads. They tended to use trucks as much as animals to carry their possessions. But it was too close to where the girl described the Al-Shabaab camp as being. 'What do you think?' he said.

'Do you think we're ten kilometres from the beach?' she said.

He looked back at the ocean to be sure. 'I'd say so.'

'Then this must be the right place.'

'They might have sentries on the high ground,' he said, looking along the ridge and beyond. But he would be surprised if there were any. In fact he would have been impressed.

'What now?' she asked.

He could tell she was uncomfortable being there and wanted to get it over with. 'I need to get a closer look. We should move in now before it gets any lighter, see if we can find somewhere to observe from. If we can't find anywhere, we'll have time to get back.'

They heard a cry of some sort from the camp. It had a rhythm to it, like a chant. He recognised it. The Muslim call to prayer just before dawn.

'Do everything I say. If I go to ground, if I stop, you do the same and without a noise or a word,' he said.

She nodded. 'I will.'

He gripped the rifle and, keeping as low to the ground as he could, stepped over the crest and down the other side. The girl moved as he moved, her eyes either on him or the camp.

Stratton stepped slowly and quietly towards a jumble of rocks halfway down the incline and a stone's throw from the first line of trees that formed the outer perimeter of the camp.

They crouched against the rocks and waited, listening. The voices became louder but he could not understand a word.

'I don't like this position,' he said quietly, looking around them. 'It will be exposed when the sun comes up.' He spotted a rocky outcrop further along the plateau with more of an overlook to the camp.

He set off, keeping low, careful not to disturb the loose ground. If he could hear them, they would be able to hear him. The girl followed a short distance behind.

A loud voice suddenly cut through the encampment and Stratton and the girl dropped to the ground. Stratton's first thought was that they had been seen. They waited but they heard only the distant voice rising and falling. He guessed it was the cleric exhorting his congregation. They crept to the rock formation using their hands to climb. Once there, Stratton felt satisfied with the cover. The boulders pretty much provided all-round protection from view if they kept well down. They waited again, on edge. If anyone had seen them, the action would soon follow. The minutes creaked by. Stratton felt happy enough that they hadn't been seen.

As the wind shifted a strange whirring sound became apparent. It was faint but constant. After checking around, he decided it was coming from a dip further along the slope. As he looked he thought he could just about see a rhythmic movement beyond the ridgeline, like something spinning. To get a proper look at it, he'd have to expose himself in the open so he decided not to, focusing instead on the camp.

He could see several long, low wooden huts, a single mud one with a sloping roof and dozens of makeshift shelters scattered through the trees, the ground littered with trash. Further inside he saw half a dozen Toyota pick-ups and a couple of large flatbed trucks.

As the first rays of sunlight broke over the horizon the insistent beats of the spinning, whirring object seemed to get louder. He still couldn't make it out and he decided to risk stretching his head a little above the rocks. As soon as he did so he knew what it was and ducked back down. The camp had a portable radar system, dispelling any possibility of it being inhabited by a bunch of nomads.

These people were not small players to be operating that kind of hardware. And they obviously had reason to fear an air attack. And if they were prepared to be alerted to an air attack, there was every chance that they had some level of air defence system beyond rifles and pistols.

As he examined the camp, several men carrying rifles and supplies of some kind emerged from the wood and began to walk up the incline towards the radar installation. Stratton studied them as they came on. By the time they were halfway to the radar, he had identified that two of them were carrying rocket launchers across their backs.

Stratton looked to the girl to see if she had recognised the hardware.

She was watching them intently. 'Those could be ours,' she said.

Stratton followed the men up the slope to a high point among the rocks.

As the sun fully exposed itself, he checked their position once again, in particular the route out. They had two broad escape options: uphill or downhill. If they headed up the plateau into the parched, treeless hills, they had little chance of finding cover. The ideal route out was back the way they had come and down to the river. The thick scrub along the bank would provide cover. At least the Toyotas wouldn't be able to navigate the riverbank.

The main problem with the location was its exposure to the sun. He didn't want to spend all day there, especially without water. So once he had formulated a plan, he decided to risk the move back to the first ridge and then down to the river.

The scope of the task to rescue Hopper looked daunting. The camp was large and probably held anywhere between a hundred and three hundred men. Which made any attempt to get closer during the day out of the question. To get inside at night would require a diversion of some kind. Ideally, something that forced the jihadists to evacuate the camp. Like a fire. The fuel storage. A serious explosion such as the weapons arsenal going up would be better. The rockets would make a big enough bang and solve a large part of the problem at the same time.

But just how he was going to achieve any of that he did not know.

Stratton glanced at the girl to see how she was doing. She was holding her head in her hands and looking exhausted. He decided to wait a couple more hours and gain more information if possible before making an attempt to get to the river. When darkness fell he would return alone and do what he could to get Hopper.

As he sat thinking about the problem, it occurred to him once again he shouldn't even be attempting it. The operations room back in Poole would be dead against it. He would be laughed at for even considering it. And if he died trying, he would be labelled a fool. His final epitaph. Someone back home would find out one day. The truth always surfaced eventually. The pair of them should get out of there right there and then, head for the coast and concentrate on getting themselves on to that cargo ship. It was the smart option to be sure.

Stratton reached out and touched the girl's shoulder. She snapped out of her daze and looked at him. He could see her better in the new light. Her face was bruised, her eyes and lips swollen. Scabs had formed at the sides of her mouth. Welts striped her neck and shoulders. He could only imagine the wounds on the rest of her body.

'Let's head to the river,' he said. 'Get some rest.'

Her relief at the news was evident. She nodded.

As they began to move a cry went up from within the wooded encampment. A roar of men's voices answered it.

The cleric shouted again. The faithful responded as one.

The shouting became unstructured, punctuated by angry voices raised as if in demonstration. It sounded like the congregation was moving through the camp. Stratton could make out figures among the parched, stunted bushes and tall spindly pine trees. He saw a large gathering of men, pressed together and moving as a single mass right towards them. The mob emerged from the wood into a level area at the foot of the hillside directly below Stratton and the girl.

There must have been a couple of hundred of them, all bearded, many with headdresses, most with AK-47 assault rifles slung over their shoulders.

Stratton and the girl instinctively pressed themselves further into the ground while watching the gathering through the gaps in the rocks around them.

The mob was close, little more than fifty metres from them. Stratton gripped his rifle in readiness. The girl tensed, her breathing short as fear enveloped her. The edge of the mob mounted the slope but stopped not far up it. The men's attention wasn't focused on the plateau, it was focused on the clearing. They kept shouting and formed a broad circle around the space.

Some men came striding through the wood hauling two figures between them and the mob parted to let them into the clearing. They threw the figures on the ground.

It was Hopper and the Chinese girl's partner.

They had their hands tied behind their backs and rag blindfolds over their eyes. They stayed where they landed in the dirt.

A warrior, wearing a black turban, pushed his way through the jeering crowd into the clearing and harshly pulled Hopper up on to his knees.

Stratton recognised the fighter. It was the Saudi.

Sabarak shouted something at the crowd, almost taunting them. He released Hopper who remained on his knees, although he appeared unsteady. Like a man who had taken a severe beating. Sabarak grabbed the Chinese man by the hair and brutally yanked him up on to his knees. Another taunt to the crowd, which responded with a roar.

'*Allahu Akbar!*' Sabarak called to the skies, his arms outstretched.

'*Allahu Akbar!*' the crowd replied.

Stratton felt utterly helpless as he watched his partner, grimy and filthy, on his knees. Hopper's face was bloody and swollen yet he remained upright and proud.

The Saudi addressed the crowd, who hushed enough to hear his ranting. They cheered each time he paused. Stratton felt surprised at how the man had achieved such an influential position so quickly. After a thunderous and climactic ovation, the mass of men went almost silent. The far side of the crowd from Stratton, nearest the trees, began to shuffle and part as a single voice cried out beyond them. A man, carrying a long, ornately ceremonial sword extended above his head, pushed through those not quick enough to move out of his way.

He entered the clearing and marched around the inner perimeter formed by the wall of men, angrily and enthusiastically brandishing the long thin blade.

The two prisoners remained where they were a few metres apart, oblivious to the swordsman parading around them.

Stratton glanced at the girl who was watching in cold horror. She looked at him for a second then back to the crowd.

If Hopper was about to be executed, Stratton could see no way out for him, not without including himself in the day's list of attendees. The man with the sword walked the circle a couple of times, stirring up the mob. Fighters stepped forward to spit on the two prisoners, men they didn't know and knew nothing about. Any one of the mob would have happily taken on the responsibility of killing the two foreigners. They didn't care that the two had families, friends, people who loved them. All the mob possessed was pure hate. They borrowed it, taught it or imbibed it from their own friends and families.

It was obvious that Sabarak was exulting in the menace and hate. He had finally taken the leap that he had looked forward to for so many years. He was among the fighters, the frontline troops of the jihad. Had Stratton been there, Sabarak would have thanked the Englishman for getting him to Somalia to be among the warriors. The Saudi was already planning for the future. The Somali front of the war on the West would expand. He had made a significant contribution by facilitating the plan that would signal a new offensive outside of the Muslim hubs in East Asia, the Middle East, Afghanistan and other parts of the world. He had been a major contributor to the hijack of the missiles.

It was a very proud day for him. He could hardly have been more pleased. The icing on the cake would have been Stratton. But he had that to look forward to. The fool Lotto had no idea who he was dealing with. Sabarak would simply march into the town one day soon and take whatever prisoners he felt like. And he would do to them whatever he wanted.

The jihadist came to a stop behind the Chinese man and slowly lowered the sword as he took the measure of the back of the man's neck.

The hate-filled crowd became silent and waited in excited anticipation.

The jihadist planted his feet and gripped the haft of the weapon, holding it firmly in his outstretched arms. Stratton could clearly see his face set into a determined grimace, his jaw clench in concentration. The jihadist shuffled his feet to widen his stance and slowly brought the sword up and back over his right shoulder. He held it there over the man whose head looked down and forward. The Chinese man had to be aware of what was happening, but he didn't move. He stayed absolutely still, just the tiniest sway as he knelt.

The jihadist held the position for several seconds, then he brought the blade down with all of his strength. It cut deep into the man's flesh and vertebrae. But the blade failed to sever the head completely, the edge of it jamming in the bone. The man fell forward and landed on his face and rolled limply on to his side. Blood began to flow from the partially severed arteries. The sword had penetrated his spinal cord and paralysed his lower body although it had not yet killed him.

The swordsman yanked out the blade and the crowd screamed as the man began to spasm. The girl looked away, unable to watch any more. The jihadist stepped quickly over him, hacking at the neck until the head came free. Then he leaned down and picked up the head by its hair and raised it high for all to see. The warriors roared again.

Stratton stared at the clearing, not so much seeing as thinking, his head buzzing with anguish and intention. The raising up of the head delivered him from inaction. He picked up his rifle and moved the safety catch down two clicks to the single-shot position. 'Get ready to run,' he said in a slow, determined voice.

The girl looked up at him. She looked towards the crowd. Then she looked back at him in horror. Panic spread across her face as she realised his intentions. She opened her mouth, wanting to say something, talk some sense into him. But she knew it was futile. She had been with him for little more than a day and already knew him well enough.

The jihadist dropped the head on to the ground and turned his gaze to Hopper. He walked around the Englishman, blood dripping from his sword. Stratton did not take his eyes from his partner. When the swordsman stopped behind Hopper and planted his feet, the crowd fell quiet again.

Hopper by now had a very good idea of his fate. He remained on his knees, back straight, shoulders back, chin out, his jaw tight. Impossibly still. His bloodied jaw began to quiver and then clench.

The jihadist pushed Hopper's head forward and down, then gripped the sword firmly. The way he shuffled and repositioned his feet suggested that he was determined to cut the head off with a single blow this time.

But Stratton had other plans for him.

The jihadist raised the sword over his head and held it as he had done before.

Stratton aimed the rifle. He prayed that the old carbine was accurate and that the piece of crap would fire.

The jihadist cocked the tip of the blade back a little, breathed in deep, gathered himself. He started his downward arc and Stratton squeezed the trigger of the Kalashnikov. The gun boomed in the operative's hands disintegrating the silence and the round spat from muzzle to its target, jerking the jihadist's head back as bloody detritus flew out of the exit hole and his body went limp. The sword fell from his hands into the dirt and he crumpled down on top of his own feet like a puppet that had had its strings cut.

The crowd seemed to freeze as it fought to comprehend what had just happened. Then as one they became aware that an enemy was somewhere on the slope above them. They reacted in panic, running in search of cover.

'Go!' Stratton shouted.

The girl scrambled up out of the cover of the rocks on to the incline.

Stratton adjusted his sights and quickly found Sabarak

but men were running across his front. The Saudi was looking in his direction. Sabarak began to run as Stratton fired. The round smacked past the Saudi, grazing his shoulder before punching into the back of a fighter.

The crowd continued to disperse in every direction. Into the wood or to the foot of the slope. Which gave the girl the crucial seconds she needed to pull herself over the top of their position and get across the open ground. She cared nothing for the soles of her feet on the stony, dry ground, expecting a bullet to smash into her at any second. She fixed her eyes on the edge of the first ridge and ran for all she was worth.

Sabarak pulled at the men around him in an effort to get through to the safety of the trees. Stratton fired again. The bullet slapped past Sabarak's face and struck a man in the neck. The Saudi fought desperately to get out of the line of fire. He knew it was Stratton and knew he was the target. He felt like he was running in molasses, the time between the shots painfully long. He pushed his way in between the men in front of him. Stratton shot the man directly behind Sabarak to clear his field of fire. The target dropped but another replaced him. Stratton shot him too but by the time he had fallen away, there was another where Sabarak should have been. Stratton lowered the weapon to get a better look. The Saudi had gone.

By then, many of the fighters had taken up firing positions in the dirt and were training their weapons up the slope. Stratton's eyes fell on Hopper, who had not moved, kneeling in the middle of the clearing, a lone figure surrounded by mayhem and bodies, with a headless corpse beside him. Hopper was clearly confused but doing what he knew was best in such a situation and that was to remain still. If it was a rescue attempt, the rescuers knew precisely where he was and in the absence of any instruction from them he would remain still and avoid getting in the way.

The only thing Stratton could now do for Hopper was obvious enough. The only humane thing he could think of doing. Hopper's fate had been truly sealed the second Stratton fired.

A round came Stratton's way, the first return of fire, thudding into the rock a foot from his head. He didn't move other than to raise the barrel of the carbine and set the sights on Hopper.

Another bullet screamed at him, ricocheting close by. As a another struck close to him, he placed Hopper's head in the sight picture. Hopper still hadn't moved but he was swaying. Stratton breathed out, then he pulled the trigger, dropping to the ground at the same instant he fired as a volley peppered the rocks around him.

He remained there for a few seconds. The jihadists loosed off wild fire in his direction. But he needed to know Hopper was down. Stratton wanted confirmation. The retribution Hopper could expect would be torturous and malicious. So he had to know he hadn't missed. He had aimed for Hopper's head when he fired. He was certain he had struck him. There was a possibility he had flinched as he pulled the trigger but he doubted it. But he realised he could do no more if he was to have any chance of surviving himself.

He gripped the rifle in one hand, moved the safety catch back one click into the fully automatic fire position and put a finger on the trigger. He took a deep breath, aware that it might well be one of his last, and scrambled around the back of the boulder. Without a pause, he stepped out from cover, held the rifle in his outstretched hand, aimed the barrel towards the clearing and fired, running along the incline.

10

The enemy's reaction to Stratton's charge from cover was slow, possibly because several of his rounds found their marks in the crowd of men. The clearing offered the fighters little protection. Shouts went up as fighters tried to warn of the enemy sighting but the majority of the jihadists reacted with unrestrained hysteria and anger and a lust for revenge.

It felt to Stratton like he had been running in the exposed open for minutes. He failed to see how they couldn't bring him down. Several rounds struck the ground around his feet, kicking up dirt and stones. He had expended his ammunition in the first few metres and ditched the weapon because it slowed him down. He felt sure a concentrated volley would hit him before he reached the crest. As another round struck close by, he threw himself to the ground and rolled downhill to break up his predictable direction. A cloud of bullets ripped up the slope where he had been an instant earlier.

Up he sprang. The crest was metres away. A bullet slammed across his back. He felt it burn like a branding iron. Another bullet hit his lower leg somewhere but his movement was not affected. He dived for the ridge and rolled over it. Bullets tore up the crest behind him. He scrambled to his feet and pushed on.

He could see the girl further down the slope running as fast as she could. She glanced back to see Stratton coming after her and as she faced the front again she tripped and went sprawling down the slope. Dazed, she clambered to her feet just as Stratton caught up with her. He grabbed her shirt and yanked her on, keeping hold of her until she was running with him.

They heard the crash of rifle fire in their direction and the sound of bullets slashing into the ground nearby. Stratton couldn't feel the pain in his back and leg, his adrenaline pumping hard through his veins. He wondered if the warriors would use the pick-ups. All the more reason for them to get to the river as soon as humanly possible.

They came to the bottom of the trough and ran hard to the top of the next rise. A handful of jihadists had made it to the crest behind them and opened fire. Stratton heard the girl make a grunting sound behind him. He quickly looked back to see if she had been hit. She appeared to have twisted her ankle but not enough to slow her by much and she soon recovered to keep up with him.

As several more rounds struck around them, they tore over the crest and down the other side. Out of sight of their pursuers. But not for long if they didn't keep up the pace.

Their next target was a couple of hundred metres away. The ground levelled out as they headed for the river. Dense scrub covered the broad lowland plain up ahead. Thin and patchy knee-high bushes grew on the outskirts but thick foliage was not far beyond.

They reached the low brush without a shot being fired at them. Stratton could feel his heart pounding in his chest with the effort but he would keep up the pace until it exploded. It was that or a bullet in the back.

The rounds came at them again but sporadic and poorly aimed. Only a handful of the faster warriors had made it to the rise behind them and these men were not great shots. The AK-47 wasn't accurate at long range.

The denser bushes looked like a dark-green wall and Stratton crashed right through, the brittle twigs painfully scratching and cutting his skin. The girl followed his path and although spared having to make the way through was whipped heavily by the catapulting branches he created.

Running quickly became impossible as the scrub density increased. They maintained as fast a walk as they could. Pushing their way through. The bushes were now above their waists but they were still targets. They finally made the higher foliage and went inside. The density only increased. They were making a lot of noise. Stratton was aware that at some point they would have to compromise speed for sound and reduced disturbance – the moving tops of the bushes would give away their position. He wanted to get closer to the river before they went to ground so that they could quench their thirsts. He knew that however bad he felt, the girl was going to be in a far worse state. He could feel and hear she was close by and still pushing on relentlessly.

Stratton crouched lower and they struck some really thick scrub so he paused to catch his breath and assess the situation. He could hear the jihadists crashing through the bush back where they had entered the mass. The thick bushes ahead of them were like barbed wire: hard to get through but still easy enough to see through. They didn't provide great cover from view. If anyone came within ten metres or so, they were likely to see them.

They had to remove the evidence of their train and Stratton got down on to his belly and began crawling between the bushes. The girl followed.

A sudden crash from a nearby flank and Stratton and the girl stopped moving. Several fighters were attempting to push through to their right. Voices followed. They were close. The snapping sounds increased but gradually began heading away.

Stratton examined the way ahead. 'How you doing?' he whispered.

She nodded. Her face was freshly cut in places and she looked exhausted. But the fight was still in her eyes.

'We can survive this,' he said. 'Come nightfall, we'll get back to the coast.'

She took encouragement from his words. 'I'll be OK.'

'Let's take it nice and easy and head for the river.' If the water's not far out in the open, he added to himself.

He looked for the sun through the branches to get his bearings. If they kept in an easterly direction they should cut across the river, which ran north–south.

Staying on their bellies, they manoeuvred around the

obstacles. They could hear movement around them and occasional shouts like the warriors had found their trail. But as time went on the voices and movement came from further away. Stratton's confidence increased, for the time being at least. The enemy obviously knew they were in the immediate area because there was nowhere else for them to go without becoming exposed. But the densely covered plain was large and as the jihadists broadened their search area, the chances of finding the pair would be reduced.

Stratton and the girl pressed on ahead at an easy pace, pausing every now and then to take a breather and listen. The sound of enemy searchers grew less. The air was warm and felt much more humid than in the town. Both were feeling desperate for a drink. Stratton crawled around the base of a tree and as he carefully parted a clump of bushes, it looked clearer up ahead. He hoped the riverbed was close, but more importantly, that it wasn't dry at that point. If so they were going to spend a very uncomfortable day waiting for the sun to go down.

As he crawled closer to the edge of the scrub, to his immense relief he could see water ahead, shimmering under the cloudless sky. He crawled to the edge of the line of bushes. The riverbank was within a few metres, the water's edge a few paces further beyond. The opposite bank looked a good hundred metres or so away. He got up on to his knees and looked as far up and down the river as he could, expecting to see evidence of the jihadists. There was none. But that didn't mean they weren't there. He would have placed observation posts at various locations to watch for anyone emerging from the scrub. The same dense bushes covered the ground beyond the other side of the river.

Stratton contemplated the risk of getting a drink there and then or waiting until darkness. The latter would be the wisest choice. But they would be in a weakened state by then. He did not think the Somalis were particularly diligent. But the risk was still too great.

He eased himself up on to his feet to get a better look around. The river, or lake as it was then, stretched out of view in both directions. It was indeed a large body of water. He wasn't encouraged by the smell of the air and hoped it wasn't the water.

Stratton gauged the position of the sun. It had to be close to midday. He looked at the girl to see her staring at the water. 'We can't risk it,' he said.

She didn't argue, knowing he was right. She would happily suffer the pain and mental anguish of thirst in place of the consequences of being caught.

'Another six hours and the sun will begin to set,' he said. 'We'll head back into the bush in case they patrol the bank. As soon as the sun drops, we'll get a drink and head for the coast.'

'Your back,' she said, her voice raspy.

Stratton had forgotten about his wounds. Both had stopped hurting. He went to check his leg and for a second had to think which one it was. He found the wound on the back of his right calf, an ugly cut but a large scab had already formed. As he examined it, the calf began to throb once again.

'Let me look at your back,' she said, noticing the bloodstain that ran down on to his trousers.

Stratton started to remove his shirt but it was stuck to his back. As he pulled it off, the wound began to throb near his right shoulder blade.

'It's bleeding a little,' she said as she used a corner of his shirt to dab it. 'You were lucky.'

'I have often been told that. But if I am lucky, how did I get into this mess in the first place?'

'You put a lot of effort into it,' she said. 'It will add to all the other scars you have.'

He pulled the shirt back on, impressed with her attitude. They were still in great danger and the odds on her getting out of Somalia alive were not good. 'Come on,' he said, preparing to make his way back through the bush on his knees. 'If we can sleep, it will help ease the pain.'

She followed him. When they were several metres inside the scrub, he dropped down in the dirt and forced his body to relax completely. She lowered her head on to the sandy soil and did the same. Her eyes closed and she fell into an immediate sleep. Flies landed on her face, exploring her eyes and the wounds on her mouth, but she didn't move.

Stratton watched and listened for a while. But fatigue gradually overcame him and he closed his eyes. He hoped to leave his ears to play sentry for longer. His training warned him to stay on watch and alert but it would have been impossible under the circumstances. He felt confident he would hear anyone approach even in his present state, but if not there was little he could do about it. His back and leg were throbbing and his throat felt like sandpaper. He knew he would drift off to sleep. There were times when things had to be left to fate and the gods.

Within minutes even the flies couldn't annoy him. His head eased over to one side and he drifted off.

The pair of them remained practically motionless for many hours in the shade of the undergrowth. The wind picked up at times and gently rustled the bushes around them. The sun moved across the sky and began to drop down on to the western horizon. A bird landed close by, gave the couple a curious look and moved on. They were dead to the world.

Bullets suddenly began to tear past Stratton. The air erupted with the sound of gunfire. His eyes were wide with fear as he grappled for the weapon. His face was sweating, his hands bloody and cut. He fired the gun and everything seemed to slow down as he followed the bullet from the muzzle of the weapon. It flew straight towards Hopper, who was on his knees looking directly at Stratton, his blindfold gone, his unshaven face wet with blood and perspiration. When he saw the bullet coming straight for him he began to scream. Yelling Stratton's name, like he hated the man who had betrayed him. The bullet went into his forehead and punched out the other side. Hopper fell back with the force of the strike and landed on his back where he remained, unmoving, the blood from his head soaking into the sand. And then, like he had become some kind of ghost, he got back up on to his knees and looked at Stratton. The head wound had gone. 'You missed, you bloody fool. *You missed!*'

Stratton sat up with a jolt and grabbed for the weapon that he momentarily forgot he had thrown away. He breathed heavy, sweat running down his face. He quickly glanced around before realising it had been a dream.

He looked at the girl. She lay in the same position she had fallen asleep in.

Stratton calmed himself and sat back. Hopper's image had been vivid. Stratton hadn't seen the bullet strike the man but he felt sure it had. Doubt suddenly shrouded him. It was possible he had missed. But again he dismissed it, not wanting to face the implications. He assured himself that he had killed his colleague. He had to have.

Stratton felt his throat. His thirst was painful. He couldn't see the sun and the evening had come on. He had slept longer than he expected he would.

As he eased himself on to his knees his entire body cried out in complaint, in particular the wound on his back. Every joint ached. He felt like he had been thrown off a cliff and landed on a pile of boulders. New pains, in his kidneys and his head, were indications that his body was dehydrated. He looked in the direction of the water. Time to get that drink.

Stratton decided to leave the girl to sleep a while longer. The more rest she got the better. He crawled through the bush to the edge of the scrub from where he could see the water. He checked left and right. There was no sign of danger. He was going to have to break cover at some time. It would get darker yet but he estimated it was enough for him to get to the water and back.

He moved out, keeping low, covering the open ground in seconds. When he reached the water, he laid down on his belly. It smelled OK although it was hard to see how clear it was. He couldn't hold back any longer, convincing himself that no matter how bad it was he would live longer with poisoned water than without it. He dipped his face into the cool liquid and gulped in several deep mouthfuls. He immediately fought to control a coughing fit, plunging his head into the water and coughing violently, the noise muffled. He came back up for air and with some difficulty managed to bring the fit under control. The sudden liquid had been too much for his parched throat. A moment later he felt ready for more.

Stratton made an effort to drink as slowly as he could. The water had a strange taste but he was past caring. It was wonderful to feel it flowing down his throat. When he'd had his fill, he doused his head again, rinsing his hair and washing his face. He could feel the life flowing back into him. It was magical.

Stratton made his way back to the girl and gently squeezed her arm. She woke with a start and was afraid for a moment until she realised who he was and where they were.

'It's OK. Everything's fine,' he said.

She took a moment to gather her thoughts, her hand going to her throat.

'Go get a drink,' he said.

She got to her knees and headed through the brush.

'Drink slowly,' he whispered after her.

He followed, suspecting she hadn't heard. As he reached the bank, she was already at the water. It was dark enough to almost conceal her from him. She began to cough violently but only for a few seconds as she muffled her mouth. She brought the spasm under control and put her mouth into the water once again.

He joined her for another drink. It would take several hours for them to recover from the effects of the dehydration.

When she had had her fill, she sat by the water gently dabbing her face with the bottom of the shirt.

'Better?' he asked.

'Better,' she replied.

'You ready for the next phase of this game?'

'The ship?'

'I still think it's our best bet out of here.'

'What if they search it?'

Stratton saw the fear in her eyes. It hadn't been there the day before. The memories of the previous night had clearly frightened her.

'We'll make an assessment when we get there.'

She took another drink before rinsing her hair.

'How're your feet?' he asked.

She threw back her hair and sat cross-legged to inspect them. 'I need to make myself some new shoes.'

She set about tearing more cloth from the bottom of her trousers and fashioning them into a sandal. 'Did you kill him?' she asked.

Stratton didn't answer.

'I wish I could have done that for Jimlen,' she said, like she knew he was uncomfortable with the question. 'Did you?' she asked again.

He believed he had. But he couldn't be sure.

'Do you feel guilty?' she asked.

He flashed a look at her. She was direct. 'What about?' he asked.

'You didn't need to leave him behind when you escaped to search the ship. Why did you?'

It felt like a punch. 'The job comes with risks,' he said. 'Hopper knew them. You know that too.'

'You would do well in my business,' she murmured.

He wondered why she had said that, feeling a tinge of resentment towards her. Like she had an arrogance, talking like she understood all the issues involved. But perhaps it was his guilt again. Something inside of him trying to defend it.

His ears picked up a sound and he stuck out a hand, warning her to be silent. She froze at the gesture. Then she heard the sound herself. A stick snapped followed by more similar noises. The dull crunch of footsteps in the dry, stony soil became a rhythm.

If they tried to head back into the scrub, they would most likely be seen. Stratton tapped her shoulder, an order to follow, and eased his way into the water. A reed bed growing out of the shallow water was not far away. They crawled through the water as quickly and as quietly as they could, their hands sinking into the riverbed, pulling at the muddy bottom. The ripples they formed mingled with those created by the gentle breeze.

They saw a line of men approaching, walking between the riverbank and the bushes. As Stratton made out the dark silhouettes, at first it looked like two or three men. But as the angle changed, the line grew longer and they saw more men. Maybe just less than a dozen. Stratton and the girl moved behind the reeds as the first man reached the bank where they had crossed from the bushes. They lowered themselves until only their eyes were out of the water. Not great cover but as long as the jihadists didn't stop and examine the location, they would be OK.

The first man walked past, his long shirt brushing the line of bushes. The second man stepped close behind. They all wore turban-like headdresses and all but the man in front carried their weapons slung over their shoulders. But as he looked at them, Stratton got the feeling that none was particularly vigilant, each watching the heels of the man in front as they trudged along. They looked like they were heading somewhere rather than patrolling.

They soon passed out of sight, their shadowy figures melding with the dark bushes and occasional straggly tree. It was going to be a long night.

11

Stratton eased himself to his feet, felt the water running through his clothes. He could see no further evidence of the enemy. Time for him and the girl to get going too.

It was much darker than the night before. Clouds had moved in to shroud the moon and stars. Dozens of small lights flickered in the trees on the lower hills where the Al-Shabaab camp was. A campfire burned on the highest crest beyond. A watching post perhaps.

Stratton turned slowly around in order to take a look in each direction. When he stopped, he faced the coast, far off out of sight. Lights flickered in the distance. Hand-held flashlights. Moving but too far away to be of a threat to them, at that moment at least.

His general assessment had been that the warriors were manning all obvious routes through the area. He could imagine how angry Sabarak must have been, not only with Stratton's assault on the camp and his attempts to kill him, but his subsequent escape. Sabarak knew Stratton was still somewhere in the immediate area and he would be desperate to get his hands on him. Sabarak would also be fully aware of the dangers to his operations if Stratton were to succeed in getting out of the country and back to his own people. That would make Stratton a very high-priority target.

'What do you think?' the girl asked. She knew the question sounded like an enquiry of the current situation but in reality she wanted to know about everything. He looked supremely confident, as ever, but it wasn't enough for her. Not right then. She felt in a weakened state and extremely vulnerable.

'I think we're going to have to take it very carefully if we want to get back to the coast without running into any of Sabarak's people. He cannot afford either of us to get away from here. He doesn't know what we know. And that's what's bothering him.'

'So what's the plan?'

He was eyeing a large piece of broken tree trunk lying at the water's edge.

'Swim.'

She looked like she was contemplating the proposal, then nodded to herself. 'Easier on the feet,' she said.

He walked further into the water. It grew deeper with each step. He stopped when it reached his chest and thought the idea through some more.

He stepped back out of the water and to the log, grabbed hold of an end and took the strain to test its weight. It moved fairly easily considering its size, suggesting it was hollow. He lifted up the end, shuffled it around so that he had it parallel with the water's edge and gently rolled it in. Bubbles came up as it absorbed the water and it quickly settled, a couple of inches of bark above the surface. He wanted to use it for cover as well as a flotation aid. He decided it would be adequate for both.

Stratton looked up at the thick, swirling clouds. He wasn't familiar with the seasons or weather patterns of Somalia but it looked like rain was imminent.

'I think we should stay in the water for as long as we can,' he said. 'You ready?'

'Yes,' she said softly. All she could think of was what would happen to her if they caught her. In truth, she was afraid to even move. But she was even more afraid to stay. It was a living hell. Getting to the coast unseen was only one part of the drama. The worst was yet to come. Getting back to civilisation seemed to be as impossible as getting to the moon right then.

Stratton took hold of the front of the log and pulled it into the deeper water. The girl followed, taking hold of the log, swimming within a few metres. Stratton lost touch with the bottom and he began to swim easily, one hand on the log, the other pushing the water behind him, his feet kicking gently below.

They swam the trunk soundlessly into the open water, keeping closer to the east side of the river to put as much distance as possible between them and the bank that the Somalis had patrolled.

He felt comfortable with the overall plan so far. Walking would have been quicker but it would have left them more exposed. There were risks with the waterborne option but after weighing them all, Stratton had decided it was safer than by land.

He estimated the beach to be around seven kilometres north. The town was another two or three kilometres west of where the river met the sea. He doubted they would be able to move the log more than two kilometres an hour. Add an hour to walk along the beach. If their progress wasn't interrupted, that would bring them within sight of the cargo vessels with enough time to swim out to sea, approach the ship from the opposite side to the beach and climb on board before dawn.

As they swam, Stratton kept a wary eye in all directions. He suspected the jihadists' efforts to contain the area would be focused on their own side of the water. But he couldn't afford to underestimate them. The camp was even more visible from the far side of the river, illuminated by a sprinkling of electrical lights, kerosene lamps and campfires. It also looked bigger than he had estimated from the rocky slope above it, spreading much further around the side of the hill. A conservative estimate of the number of men it contained, based on the crowd that had turned out for the executions and allowing for patrols and outlying control points, had to be approximately three to four hundred. He wondered how he would attack such a place, how many men would be required and the best way to approach it. Attacking the camp was certainly something to aim for to destroy the missiles. He wondered if the Yanks or the Brits currently had the appetite for such an adventure. The political and legal ramifications would be obvious. But if they didn't, many people would probably die. Stratton put his money on them mounting an assault – as long as he could get back to tell them what he knew.

If an attack did happen, Stratton could only hope that he would be a part of it. If so, he would make a point of finding Sabarak personally and tearing him apart.

As they progressed along the river, the dense bushes receded from the banks and the reed beds in the water became sparser. That all served to increase their exposure, which was a concern to Stratton. Because one of his contingencies on seeing signs of the enemy had been to leave the water and move into the scrub. That option appeared to be fast disappearing.

But as he thought, the dark clouds that had been thickening above them throughout the evening opened up and the rain started and came down in torrents. So heavy it looked like the water was boiling, the drops themselves like tiny pebbles hitting them.

'At least the flies have gone,' she called out above the noise.

And not just the flies would be taking cover, he thought. He very much doubted the Somalis would remain on exposed watch in this kind of weather.

'Let's up the pace,' he called out. There was no telling how long the rain would last and they had to make the most of it. Cover from noise and the disturbance of the water meant they could increase their activity and make as much headway as possible.

They pounded through the relentless rain, immune to the chill of the water. Soon the river began to widen. They pushed on at a good pace, enough for Stratton to alter their estimated time of arrival at the *Oasis*. But then they saw the enemy. Stratton wasn't in the least surprised. The first sign of the jihadists since they began their swim.

It was a distant light on the west bank.

He found it difficult to see beyond the banks because the surface of the water was well below the level of the land. The light seemed to be on the riverbank. As they drew closer, it looked more and more like a vehicle heading down to the water.

Stratton slowed his efforts and concentrated on it. They might have to get out of the water. The rain pelted them and they watched the vehicle come on. The single light gradually became two headlights as it turned a little more in their direction. When a few hundred metres away, the lights swept over the river as the vehicle made a tight turn to face right at it. The vehicle came to a halt with the headlights shining across the river and illuminating the opposite bank.

Stratton had two immediate thoughts. The enemy was setting up a control point or the vehicle was aiming to drive across the river. Then he remembered the track he passed on the approach to the jihadist camp, a track that headed in the direction of the river. He was probably looking at the same place. Perhaps the track led to a ford. Maybe it was a local truck, nothing to do with the jihadists.

They maintained their progress while they still had time to decide whether to pass it in the water or move to the land. The rain continued to fall heavily, providing good cover. In the absence of much scrub on either bank, they would be silhouetted even in the darkened conditions and so the water remained the best option.

The truck's headlights went off. Stratton could just about make out its silhouette against the distant lighter skies. He decided to remain on course and keep close to the opposite bank, a good football pitch's width from the truck at that point.

No sooner had he made the decision when small handheld lights appeared in front of the truck. It looked like men had been at the river and had emerged from cover when the truck arrived.

Stratton weighed the risks, which still remained in favour of the water option. If the people with the flashlights had been watching the river, they would be currently distracted by the truck. Their night vision would also be temporarily disrupted because of their lights.

The rain continued to come down in heavy sheets as Stratton, the girl and the log closed on the point where the truck faced the river. The noise made by the rain hitting the water continued to drown out all other sounds. They couldn't hear the truck's engine if it was still running. Judging by the flashlights, the sentries remained preoccupied with the vehicle. Stratton's confidence that they could get past unnoticed increased.

Then the truck's engine gunned loudly and its headlights came back on. Stratton and the girl were caught directly in the main beams. And the log ran aground at the crossing point.

It was a ford.

Stratton saw the line of tall sticks in the water that indicated its path.

The truck began to move forward into the river. Stratton cursed himself for relying so much on chance. All he had to do was come to a stop well before the crossing point and wait and see what they would do. But no. He had to be impatient, tempt fate. He recognised the arrogance on his part, the same petty disregard for caution that had resulted in Hopper's death.

Having been caught in the lights, they had no choice but to push on. If the men saw them, better to be going forwards than backwards. At least they would be running in the right direction.

'Leave the log!' he shouted.

Stratton crawled up the side of the ford and waded across it. The girl followed. They would be out of the way of the truck long before it reached them. Stratton could only hope the rain greatly reduced visibility and that the Somalis were looking elsewhere. Almost a dozen Somalis stood on the bank with only a couple of flashlights between them. The chance that none of them would be looking across the river, and into a light that naturally drew the eye, was a small one.

It was the driver who first spotted them as they hurried across the shallows. He pointed and shouted to the fighters.

The girl ran across the ford to catch up with Stratton. They managed to move out of the direct beams of the headlights and plunged into the deeper water once more.

But the Somalis caught them in the flashlights. Stratton braced himself for what he knew would follow as he pushed on as fast as he could. He heard the Somalis shouting, the hard-sounding guttural intonation. The sound of the pelting rain went on. Then came the staccato thunder of rifle fire, bullets strafing the water around them. The riverbed continued to fall away beneath their feet and they dived under the surface. They swam hard in the blackness in a desperate effort to put as much distance between them and the enemy.

The single shots became bursts as the Somalis let rip into the night. Stratton and the girl surfaced just long enough to take a breath. The Somalis caught them in the beams and the rounds quickly followed. But an AK-47 on full automatic is a difficult weapon to hold on to a pinpoint target, even at a short distance. The weapon had always struggled to fire high and to the right, no matter how strongly you held it. And in the undisciplined hands of poorly trained militia, the inaccuracy multiplied. A few rounds struck close but the rest flew into the far bank and the sky. He and the girl dived again. Then they came up again and he looked back and saw the log. It had followed them over the ford thanks to its momentum. The Somali guys must have thought they were hiding behind it because the fire all seemed to be aimed at the tree.

Stratton broke into a firm breaststroke, pushing himself beneath the water as much as he could. The girl elected to continue duck diving although she didn't have the breath to stay below the surface for longer than a few seconds at a time. When she realised the bullets were no longer striking close by and that Stratton was getting ahead of her, she switched to a crawl to catch up with him.

The gunfire petered out behind them and the sound of the rain hitting the water rose up again. They could hear shouts and the truck engine revving again. The alarm would be raised and the enemy would be alerted to the fact they were heading for the coast.

Stratton swam to the bank and clambered out of the water, his clothes hanging heavily from his body. The girl followed and staggered tiredly in pursuit.

'Time for a change,' he said, breathing heavily, as he dropped on to his knees to catch his breath and look back in the direction of the lights. She dropped to the ground beside him, breathing hard but at the same time thankful.

The gunfire became sporadic as the Somalis realised the log they been shooting at was unmanned. They started taking pot shots at anything that might be a person in the water or on the distant bank.

'We'll go on by land,' Stratton said. 'If we meet an obstacle, we'll still have the water as an option.'

She nodded in agreement. She would follow Stratton anywhere at that moment in time.

He set off. She adjusted her cloth sandals and padded after him. The rain had eased off by the time they had covered another kilometre. The river had also become much wider. Stratton thought he could hear waves crashing on a distant beach. The sound heightened their expectations, although these were tempered by the fear that the enemy was waiting for them.

They came across a small rise and Stratton climbed it to survey the scene despite the risk of being silhouetted. The smouldering clouds still hung low in the sky. It was dark in every direction except for a distant glow to the west.

'The town,' he said after studying it for a moment.

She joined him to take a look. 'Do you think they'd expect us to try for the ship?' she asked.

He had considered the same thing. But only the enemy knew when the ship would sail. That was under their control. Stratton had arrived at that thought from a different direction. She probably thought that the pirates and jihadists would prevent them from getting on board the ship if they thought it was the pair's intention. Stratton thought the *Oasis* would make a perfect trap and therefore the enemy would make climbing aboard as inviting as possible. 'We are assuming the ship will be leaving soon. It could stay here for weeks,' he said.

She hadn't considered that.

Stratton would make his decision when they had studied the ship and the activity around it. They would learn a lot from just watching for a while.

He stepped off the mound and walked along the bank at a brisk pace.

The ground had changed, become sandier, but the rain had hardened it and although the going was a little slower than on the compacted earth, the girl was thankful for it. They made good progress despite Stratton's insistence on halting every few hundred metres to listen. The closer they got to the town and the ships, he reasoned, the greater the chance they had of being seen.

The rain had reduced to a drizzle and the sound made by the waves hitting the beach dominated. By the time they could see the white surf folding on to the sand, the rain had ceased. They had lost a good source of cover but the clouds still remained to shut out the stars and reduce the light. Something at least, thought Stratton.

He faced the west and the distant glow from the town, now much brighter. They walked along the ocean side of the sand dam that held the river back. When they reached the end of it, Stratton halted to check around once again.

'We should move away from the beach,' he said. 'It's a natural line for a patrol to follow.' He looked towards the water as a heavy wave dropped on to the beach with a thunderous boom. Ideally, they should leave the land completely and cover the rest of the distance by swimming. 'You up for a swim?'

'I'd rather drown trying than stay in this land another day,' she said.

He believed her, but he also worried that she would soon get into trouble out there and he would end up having to help her. Which would be dangerous for both of them. He set off away from the water.

She followed.

They watched the ground ahead and towards the shore constantly. The glow from the town grew brighter with every step. When it separated to become two distinct sources of light, he slowed to an easy walk. The brighter glow to the right was coming from the ships.

The hazy radiance soon became distinct lights, the town sprinkled with white and orange, the vessels a tight collection of stark lights on top of large, dark masses. Electric lights had been placed on the beach in front of the carriers, a new addition since the night before. They had probably run cables ashore from the ships' generators. But that only worked in his favour. A well-lit beach would make it even more difficult to spot swimmers, especially beyond the ships.

Stratton kept staring at the vessels, aware of the girl's presence only by the light crunch of her feet in the sand behind him. He was constantly gauging when they should head into the surf. He had chosen to ignore the threat that there could be a trap waiting for them if they climbed on board. He decided it was too sophisticated for the Somalis. Which was a lot to chance on the Somalis' part because there were many places on board a ship large enough for a person to hide in.

He estimated they should begin the swim at four to five hundred metres from the ships so that they could get well out to sea. But the closer he got, the more he reduced that estimate. The lights around the bulkers would be more distracting to the guards on board and those on the beach.

As he looked at them, he saw something wrong with the picture of the vessels. From the angle of approach the ships were in a line and appeared as a single object. But as they drew closer, and the angle widened, he could pick out the individual ships. He could see three bulkers. Not four. He kept walking, his eyes fixed on the boats, hoping that one had been moved, tucked behind one of the others, or that it wasn't the *Oasis* that was missing. The girl had also been staring at the ships and came alongside him, transfixed and praying that what she suspected wasn't true.

They both slowed to a halt. Their vessel of hope had been the largest of the four and the largest of those that remained wasn't large enough. The Dutch captain's vessel had gone. It had sailed without them.

The girl dropped to her knees, more out of staggering disappointment than anything else.

Stratton sat down beside her and stretched out his feet.

She looked at him, trying to see into his eyes in the darkness, wondering if she would find the same distress and frustration that she was feeling. But she could see nothing of the sort in them. She wasn't surprised. Not any more. She found him to be a most unusual man. He got angry like normal men, showed petty frustrations and irritation at predictable times. But when most people reached the point where they were expected to lose hope, and could be forgiven for it, this one simply went cold and began to hatch an alternative plan, looking like he had missed a bus. He never seemed to tire of looking for options.

She wondered what he was thinking. Then she decided to search for an option herself. It was no surprise to her to discover the one that came to mind, something they had considered from the beginning, and probably the only other reasonable option available to them.

'I suppose we look for a small boat now,' she said.

'Out of land, sea and air that remains our best option,' he said.

He looked towards the cove in front of the first cargo carrier. She followed his gaze. Several small boats bobbed in the protected waters of the unusual loop in the beach.

He looked to the skies, the gentle breeze rustling his scraggly hair. 'I'd say we have five or six hours of darkness,' he said. 'We could be miles from here by dawn even with a poor sail.'

She felt like she could have cracked up on seeing their cargo ship gone. But his sheer confidence and tenacity prevented any chance of that happening. She got to her feet, doing her best to forget the cargo vessel and focus on the next plan. 'Let's do it then.'

He got up and they walked down to the beach and towards the boats.

12

Stratton and the girl reached the shore and studied the boats anchored beyond the surf. Stratton's first concern had been that a sentry might be nearby. It didn't surprise him to see no sign of one.

He saw several kinds of boat, the majority exposed skiffs, their empty poles sticking in the air, sails stowed, or simple rowing boats. They walked along the beach to get a better look at some slightly larger craft. In the darkness it was difficult to make them out but one appeared to have a kind of cabin.

'What do you think?' she asked.

'I was thinking sail earlier. But now I'm thinking motor.'

'A motor won't get us across the Gulf. Not without a lot of fuel.'

'We don't need to cross the Gulf. All we need to do is reach the transit corridor. Something like eighty ships a day use it. And then there are all the naval ships.'

'Could we even get that far in a motor boat? The Gulf is a couple of million square miles. That's a lot of ocean to get stranded in if we run out of fuel. At least with a sail we have power all the time.'

'We won't have speed though. There's little wind right now.'

'It'll pick up when we're out there.'

'I'd rather get as far away as I could from this coastline as quickly as I could.'

She decided he showed at least one sign of stress. He had no time for anyone else's ideas. Unless of course he was like that all the time.

'Let's take a look,' he said. 'If there's not enough fuel, then we'll sail.'

He walked into the surf and dived at a breaker and swam hard into the next set. She stood on the beach and prayed that once she stepped off the sand and into the water she would never have to return. She waded in until a large wave rolled in and she dived into it. The water was chilly and it felt good as she pulled hard to catch up with him.

Both were soon through the breakers and swimming over the deep swell. Stratton paused to get his bearings and find the boat he had been aiming for. He saw it and waited for her to catch up before setting off again.

The swim was further and more tiring than either of them had calculated, not that it would have made any difference. When they arrived at the boat, Stratton hauled himself on board. The girl grabbed the side and held on to catch her breath. Stratton took a firm hold of her hands and yanked her out of the water.

He surveyed the boat while he caught his breath. It was basic and untidy with all kinds of fishing equipment scattered around. It had a wheelhouse in the centre the size of a phone booth. A couple of outboard engines bolted to the transom with their props out of the water. Stratton went straight to them.

The engines were two different makes, one a one-twenty with an extra-long shaft, the other a seventy-five with a standard draught. They were an odd match but he doubted the fisherman who owned them cared for the equilibrium as long as they worked.

The girl made herself useful and checked around for fuel. The two working tanks seemed to be full, judging by the weight. She inspected the contents of a large drum lashed to the side of the wheelhouse, the fumes engulfing her. 'This is just over half full,' she said, closing the lid.

The engines looked well used but short of starting one up he had no way of knowing if they would work. He looked towards the only other motor boat he could see that might have been big enough for the proposed journey. But it did not appear to be as seaworthy as the one they were on.

'Let's take a paddle over to that one,' he decided. 'See what fuel it has.'

He found a couple of oars, handed one to the girl and went to the bows and untied the line attached to a buoy. They had to fight against the tide, moving at an angle across them. They pulled hard together, the girl leaning over the stern. The distance between the boats quickly shrank as they heaved with the desperation of escaping convicts.

Stratton dropped his oar inside the boat as the gunwales collided and the girl grabbed a line and looped it over a cleat. She leaned back and held on to it firmly and Stratton nimbly cross-decked.

He inspected the working tank attached to the single outboard engine. It was heavy and he carried it over and lowered it into their boat. He searched the vessel for more and found several cans beneath a large decaying canvas.

He couldn't find anything else of use and climbed back over.

'What do you think?' she asked.

'A wild guess . . . I'd say we have enough to get a hundred miles, give or take a few. That's if the motors are working OK,' he added.

'How far is this transit corridor?'

He looked at her. 'I thought you would know that better than me.'

'Why?'

'Weren't you sailing the bloody Gulf?'

'I knew about the corridor but I didn't plan on sailing that far north.'

Stratton took a moment to see the map in his head. He thought he remembered the Gulf being around two hundred miles across but the Yemen and Somali coastlines didn't quite run parallel. 'I'd say the corridor was around a hundred miles away, give or take.'

'And when we get there we just wait to be picked up?'

'That's about it.'

Trying to break the plan down didn't look like it had helped her.

'It's not going to get any better than this, sweetheart,' he said.

She knew he was right, once again. If he had asked her to swim back to the beach to try and come up with some other plan, she would have found it very difficult.

'How long will it take?' she asked.

He wasn't sure what she meant exactly. 'To find a boat once we get to the corridor? Hours maybe. Half a day max, I would've thought.'

'All together? The journey and everything. How long?' she asked, holding on as a swell rocked the boat. 'I don't really care. We're going to do it. I just want to know that's all. I want something to aim for.'

'My advice is to aim to wait for days.' He walked over to a five-gallon plastic container and unscrewed the top. He sniffed it quickly before picking it up and raising it to his lips. He took a short sip and then a long drink before putting it back down. 'We can live three weeks without food, three days without water and we have enough here for a couple of days if we ration it. So there's five days to aim for.'

She didn't look enthralled with the target.

He set about checking the engines. Whoever had rigged them had done it in a weird way. They were both pull-start with their control arms linked by a wooden pole so that they could be turned in unison by one person. The twist throttle control on each arm had a crude clamp device attached to it made of wood and fishing line. He could find no engine or steerage control of any sort from the small bridge house, the various cables intended for such use having long since gone.

'We need to get as far away from here as we can before we try and start these up,' he said, studying the beach and the waters around the cargo ships for any activity.

She picked up her oar again and waited for him to take hold of his. When he was satisfied, he grabbed up his oar. She released the line and they pushed away from the other boat.

Stratton moved to the front, where he could better control the steerage, and paddled hard. She took her position in the rear again. He aimed the small vessel towards the northern edge of the cove, which initially meant getting closer to the nearest cargo ship but it was the most direct route to the open sea.

The waves weren't very powerful within the cove itself and the pair of them managed to move the boat ahead at an easy pace. Stratton kept an eye on the golden spur of sand visible in the darkness on the starboard side that formed the northern edge of the cove's mouth. It was difficult to make out where it actually ended and every now and then he pushed his oar down as deep as he could in order to check the depth.

They put their backs into it, as much enthused by the fact they were quickly gaining on the mouth, towards the open sea, as they were by the reality that they were beginning the last major phase of the escape bar finding a rescue ship.

Stratton's oar suddenly found the bottom. 'Left,' he called out.

She did her best to compensate while he edged more to the front to bring the nose around.

The end of the spur was fast coming up.

'Almost there!' he shouted, aware she must be tiring.

As they reached the end of the toe of sand, Stratton saw the larger waves beyond it. They were rolling inland from the ocean unchecked and looking heavy.

'Keep it up!' he called out. 'We need to break through that.'

As they came around the end of the toe, the first big wave struck them remorselessly, spray breaking over the bows. The boat seemed to come to a standstill. Stratton increased his effort. The girl was tiring but she fought on, encouraged by the consequences of failure.

The next wave sets came at them relentlessly, raising up the bows each time as Stratton heaved against them, the nose then dropping down into the trough with a thump. His eyes darted to the finger of sand to gauge their progress. To his horror they were not only failing to make any headway, they were going backwards.

He couldn't put any more effort into it than he was already doing. And if that was the case for him, for her it had to be worse. They would only get weaker while the ocean's energy remained boundless. They had paddled into the main flow of the swell and at the rate they were going they would end up on the beach. Which was quickly coming up behind them. If that happened, they would get hammered in the surf. They would probably capsize. The brief dream was fast turning back into the nightmare.

There was nothing more for it. 'I'm starting the engines!' he shouted. 'Keep pulling all you can!'

She glanced at him between strokes. Suffering. Exhausted.

He dumped his paddle on the deck and hurried to the engines. She struggled to give him those precious extra seconds he might need, the thought of landing back on that beach more than enough to inspire her. She fought against the awesome power of the waves, putting all she could muster behind each stroke. Her life would be better spent dying of exhaustion trying to escape than getting captured again.

Stratton tilted both engines so that the propellers dropped into the water and squeezed the bubble valves on the fuel tubes attached to fill the carburettor chambers. When the bubble valves had hardened, indicating the fuel was all the way through the lines, he grabbed one of the starter cords and pushed the gear lever into neutral.

When he had planned it, he would be far out to sea before he started the engines. That advantage had evaporated. He had to get at least one of them going now or they were screwed. Stratton knew a bit about outboards, as he should have done being in the SBS. Both engines looked like they had recently been used, which helped his confidence, but not by a great deal. They were old and there was probably no great abundance of spare parts for when they went wrong. Somali fishermen often engineered the most extraordinary techniques for maintaining their engines, many of which would defy the understanding of those who had designed and built them. He prayed that no such method or technique was required to get either of this pair going.

He took a firm grip of the toggle and, as a large swell struck the boat, yanked it. The engine clattered as its working parts ground against each other but it didn't fire. No indication at all that an internal combustion of any kind had taken place.

The girl looked between him and the engine as she continued to row as hard as she could, snatching a glance at the sandy beach behind her.

The starter return spring was obviously broken and Stratton quickly ripped the cowling away to expose the guts of the motor. He spun the starter cable housing around until the toggle was all the way home and yanked hard on it again. The motor sputtered a little before dying. It was a spark of life, like a tiny glowing ember, though not enough. It showed a potential for life. But that was not enough.

'Stratton,' she called out, a warning in her voice.

He could clearly hear the waves breaking on the beach. If they got caught in the surf without the engines, it would be over. 'I know,' he said. A wave broke over the front of the boat, barging it brutally closer to the shore. One more like that would see them in the surf and overturned.

Stratton rewound the starter head and yanked it hard again. The engine burst into life. He grabbed the throttle and twisted it fully, aware that such a violent increase in power when it was so cold might stall it. But he had no choice. Without a burst of power right then, it would all be over for them. The engine responded and revved loudly without the cowling to smother some of the sound. Smoke spewed from it. He slammed it into gear and the revs dropped as the prop shaft clunked heavily. The propeller engaged and spun in the water.

The boat lunged forward. Stratton turned it sharply to face the next oncoming wave, which was almost upon them. They rose up over it as it slammed into the bottom of the hull. The nose dropped down into the trough and the propeller came out of the water for a moment, screaming shrilly as its revs increased.

The boat levelled off and accelerated away from the beach. Stratton's thoughts immediately went to the cargo ships and the beach. The Somalis had to have heard the noise. They would guess who it was. It was unlikely any fishermen were out at sea, certainly not at night in this weather. He could imagine fighters leaping up and sprinting down the beach.

'Take it!' Stratton shouted.

The girl dropped the paddle and hurried to obey. She grabbed hold of Stratton's hand that was gripping the throttle and he released it to allow her to take over.

'Straight out!' he shouted as he went for the second engine. One would be enough to get them out to sea but they would need both to stand a chance of escaping any pursuit.

She craned ahead, having to stand to see around the cabin and beyond the side of the gunwales that went up in the bows. Straight out to sea was simple enough but she knew she had to be careful not to hit another boat or the toe of sand on the end of the spur that formed the northern mouth of the cove.

Stratton yanked the starter cable on the second engine and, as with the first, it refused to start. He cursed the machine but at least the return spring worked and the toggle shot back against the top of the engine. He pulled it hard again. Nothing.

He glanced behind to see their progress. She was keeping the nose in the right direction. It was hard to tell if there was any activity around the cargo ships.

A powerful searchlight suddenly shone from one of the bridge wings of the nearest bulker. The end of the beam darted over the surface of the water like a desperate effort to find them. On the beach, flashlights flickered in the hands of men running hard along it.

Stratton got back to the task in hand and yanked the starter cable. This time the engine gave a teaser of a cough.

The sound of gunfire came from somewhere. He wasn't overly concerned though. The Somalis would have difficulty seeing the boat well enough to aim a shot. That was until the searchlight shot over them and came quickly back to illuminate the boat and the pair of them in it.

Stratton pulled the starter cord again and the engine came to life. He turned the throttle and the added thrust shunted the boat vigorously forward and out of the light.

Stratton stood beside the girl, a head taller than her. Together they looked ahead as they powered the boat over the heavy swell and out to sea. The light caught them again and since there was little or nothing Stratton could do about it, he ignored it. With the increasing distance and all the bobbing about it would be a lucky shot to hit them from either the vessels or the beach. And just as he finished that thought, a bullet slammed through the bridge breaking a window. Stratton and the girl ducked down a little automatically.

As they left the mouth of the cove and headed properly out to sea, Stratton looked back at the cargo vessels. His main concern at that point was any pursuit by the pirates. Their speedboats were much quicker than the little fishing boat. But the further Stratton could get into the darkness the more difficult it would be for the pirates to find them.

The firing appeared to have stopped although it was hard to tell being so close to a couple of screaming engines. He replaced the cowling to reduce the noise and fiddled with the simple throttle friction device to get them to hold the engine at high revs. The wooden pole lashed to both steering arms that acted as a coordinator worked fine and Stratton let go to allow the girl to steer both engines by controlling only the one.

He made a quick inspection of the fuel lines and containers and lashed down the ones that were loose using bits of the miles of fishing line scattered around the deck.

Then he went back to the lights to their rear. He looked at them for about a minute. They were growing increasingly distant. He held the side of the cabin to steady himself, the wind whipping at his clothes. He could see nothing that indicated any kind of follow-up. No other lights. The girl held the tiller firmly, her hair straight out behind her.

The boat cut through the swell nicely. Stratton looked ahead. The edge of the dark clouds that hung low above them wasn't far away and he could see clearer sky beyond it.

He looked at the girl. She glanced at him and allowed herself a semblance of a smile. Like she was grateful but also vaguely apologetic.

'I'll take it,' he said, crossing to her.

She was relieved to hand the tiller over to him. She felt exhausted. In the sea breeze, after the chilly swim, she could feel the cold working its way into her.

'Go inside,' he said.

She felt reluctant to take refuge by herself at first. But he was standing there, so strong and dominant. Like an automaton. A master in control. For a moment she felt like a girl, protected by her man, although he wasn't hers. It was a momentary feeling of partnership and it felt good, despite everything else.

She opened the small cabin door and sat on the floor inside.

'I saw some clothes bundled in there. You should find something to put on,' he shouted.

He watched her find them, pull on a large sweater. She needed to take care of herself, that was for sure. In her state he knew she could quite easily go down with hypothermia. But something had started to bug him. The girl was tenacious, gutsy, but she was also naive, vastly inexperienced for what she was doing. He asked himself why the Chinese Secret Service had selected her. Because if he hadn't been with her, he doubted she would have escaped. She would most likely already be dead. Whichever, she would certainly be in no state to continue the task she had been given.

He suspected the Chinese system probably had the same problems as his own, as many parallel Western ones. The so-called special operations organisations were never as good as they were cracked up to be. Too flawed, too many departments populated by fools. Too many mistakes, made all the time. Too much holding it together and hoping for the result in the end.

If they got out of this, she would return to her outfit a hugely more experienced operative. But he couldn't help feeling critical of her basic planning. Her bosses had to be heartless bastards.

He glanced back once again. The ships and the town beyond had become a single glow, the individual lights hard to pick out.

13

The small fishing boat eventually emerged from beneath the dark clouds and the stars appeared above them. Stratton searched for a constellation he knew. Any one of Orion's Belt, Cassiopeia or the Plough would lead him to the North Star, ultimately what he was looking for. He found the Plough, the end of it pointing directly at the North Star shining brightly in a space of its own. He hadn't been far off course and made an adjustment to put the star above the point of the bows. The vastness of the night sky was always humbling, especially in the wild and far from civilisation. The stars seemed brighter and more abundant.

For a moment, as he stared up at them, he forgot all his troubles.

He looked behind them again and the glow from the pirate town and its cargo ships had disappeared completely beyond the horizon. He looked ahead at the black sea and a great absence. He couldn't see a single light in any direction. Few ships would sail within a hundred miles of the Somali coast any more. And many of those that did preferred to scorn navigation lights in favour of remaining invisible to the evil eyes of the sea hunters.

The girl, who had put on several extra layers of dirty clothing to keep out the chilly night air, lay curled up in a ball, halfway inside the cabin, her head resting on a bundle of clothes, her eyes closed. Fast asleep.

Stratton felt good having slept during the day. He was hungry but ignored it. He had enough energy to keep going for days without food. It hadn't been the first time he'd had to fast on an operation.

The longer he stayed in the business, he knew the greater the chances were of experiencing a disaster he wouldn't survive. Stratton had often been lucky and that wasn't a good thing to rely on. He wondered how often Hopper thought he had been lucky in the past. It could just as easily have been Stratton's fate. The regrets piled up in his head. Leaving without Hopper. Not being able to kill Sabarak. The lingering doubt he had about Hopper and about whether he had succeeded in killing his own partner. The possibility that the man could be experiencing a living hell at that moment. Guilt flooded through Stratton once again and any feeling of relief he had of escaping that foul country withered.

He would have to report everything to SBS operations, exactly how it had happened. That would include an admission of his complete failure in regard to Hopper's safety, one that led to the man's death ultimately. If Stratton hadn't killed him, those bastards would have. But operational reports weren't forums for outpourings of personal blame and emotions. London wouldn't want to hear all of that tattle. That could come later if the operative wanted to reveal it. He could hear his boss in Poole telling him to go and get drunk, get it off his chest and get ready for the next job. If he really wanted one, they could provide him with a shrink or therapist. They would also watch him closely, concerned about any emotional baggage interfering with the job. If it did, he would be out.

Stratton thought about how he used to be. When he was young and full of piss and vinegar, it had been a simple process to fob off the deaths of colleagues. You accepted that it was all a part of the risk of the job. And if anyone got uptight about that, they should never have joined up. He recognised the sentiments of exuberant, carefree and ambitious youth, but also those of the mandarins at the top who ran everything. They could be even more ruthless. They had to be. Few of them had done anything more dangerous than run a desk or an ops room. Some had been exposed to the level of field operations Stratton had, but not many.

The more time Stratton spent in the field, the more operatives he knew personally died or ended up in wheelchairs, and the deeper the psychological wounds that cut into him. And not all of them healed. Not fully. The kind of wounds you never got rid of.

Like Hopper would be.

Stratton felt a chill run through him. He looked up at the North Star and made another slight adjustment of the tiller. Satisfied he was on course, he tied off the tiller.

He went to the cabin and reached over the girl to search through the bag of clothes, found a thick old sweater and pulled it on. The elbows had gone and it had a large hole on one side, but otherwise it would help keep out the night air.

He stepped out of the wheelhouse and looked behind them again. He couldn't help it. But until the pair of them were aboard a vessel and heading for civilisation he would always be looking over his shoulder. The edge of the sea had been black as pitch all around them for hours. He looked back again and something registered in his mind. Something insignificant to the point of being non-existent but he couldn't look away. The black sea met the lighter sky and the only light came from the stars. He thought maybe he had seen one shoot down past the horizon.

After a long hard look, he was about to face the front when he saw a tiny speck of light appear for less than a second. So faint that he still wasn't sure if he had actually seen anything.

He stared, suspecting his eyes of playing tricks on him. His mind began to run at the possibilities. If a vessel, it could have come from only one source: the pirate town. It was directly behind them. It could be from nowhere else.

The light appeared again. This time for a moment longer. It was real. It was a light. He hadn't imagined it. It had to be a boat of some kind.

He realised what it had to be, following directly in their track, and how it was doing it. It had to be the pirate mother ship. It didn't need daylight to see them. It had radar.

He felt a flush of fear run through him then he brought it under control. The implications were clear enough. Which amounted to nothing more complicated than death if they were caught again. Lotto had discarded the girl once and would not even bring her back to the town this time. And if the master wasn't on board, those would undoubtedly be his orders. Stratton doubted the girl would let herself be taken again only to go through the ordeal of a gang rape before being killed. As for him? Lotto had threatened to amputate his feet and Stratton didn't doubt for a second that the leader would do a lot worse this time. He wouldn't see land again if the ship got them.

It gave the chase clear parameters. Escape or die trying.

He continued to study the distant light and decided it had definitely become more visible. It had gained on them. The mother craft hadn't been a particularly quick ship but it probably had about a couple of knots on them at least. He could get little more out of the fishing boat. The mother craft cut through the water on the line of the horizon, which put it at three to four miles away. If the light he could see was on top of the boat that would make it a bit further away. He calculated the variables. He reckoned they had anywhere from two to four hours before the boat caught them.

He checked the fuel cans connected to the engines. Both nearly empty. He untied the knot in the short rubber pipe attached to the bottom of the fuel barrel. Fuel leaked out. He opened the cans, poked the end inside the first and let the fuel gush in. He repeated the process with the other can and when it was full, he checked the barrel. It looked like he could get four more working containers out of it.

He guessed they had covered around thirty miles by now. Not very much more. So his initial estimate of a hundred miles of fuel looked about correct. The bad news was that the pirate craft had enough fuel to cross the Gulf and back. Stratton would run out of the stuff long before the pirates did.

That left the single option of making it to the corridor and hoping to find a ship before they got caught. Considering the attitude the pirates had towards other ocean-going vessels, it would have to be a navy ship to help him and the girl. Or things wouldn't work out too well for them.

He looked in a wide arc across their front but he could see nothing, no sign of another ship. He felt certain they would come across another ship before long. But how long?

He looked back at the light. It had come over the horizon and no longer shimmered.

His mind started to work on alternative plans. Perhaps he could do something to confuse the pirate's radar or shrink the fishing boat's image. They could tear off the small bridge house and toss it over the side. But in the calm sea, it would probably make hardly any difference to their signature. Could he give the pirates another target to chase? That would require something tall and metallic. But it would need to move off under its own power in another direction. Impossible. Could he make the fishing boat go faster? He could if he made it lighter.

He went to the front and the heavy sea weights. He

picked one up with an effort and swung it over the side. The others soon followed and he stood there panting while he searched for anything else he could dump.

He looked to the forward horizon again. He could see a faint light on the port side front quarter. If it was on the top of a large ship, it could be ten or twelve miles away.

He went back to the tiller and pushed it over to turn the boat towards the light. If they were lucky, it would be a navy ship.

If they were even luckier, it would be sailing towards them.

The turn caused the boat to rock a little and the girl rolled over and nudged the edge of the cabin's door frame with her head, which woke her up. She sat up and looked at Stratton, watched him pick up a coil of chains and throw them overboard. She watched him pick up just about anything that wasn't attached to the vessel and throw it overboard.

She got to her feet and stepped into the breeze. 'Are you OK?' she called out above the wind and the tinny sound of the engines.

'I was about to wake you up,' he said. 'We need to throw the bridge house overboard.'

'Is there something wrong?' she said, concerned about the way he was attacking everything.

'Well, we have some bad news and we have some good news,' he said as he opened a box and rummaged through it, pulling out several old life jackets. 'Which would you like first?'

'I'll have the good news first.'

Stratton lifted up a tarp to find a collection of angling rods and weights and several heavy-duty fishing reels and harnesses. 'You see that light directly ahead?'

She found it and looked instantly uplifted and just as quickly her elation was tempered by the threat of the looming bad news. 'Yes.'

'That's a ship we're chasing. Look behind us and you'll see one that's chasing us.'

She turned to see the distant light, her heart sinking. 'You sure it's them?'

'Well, I'm generally the optimistic type but I can't see how it could possibly be anyone else,' he said, inspecting a knife he had found.

Fear crept over the girl as she stared at the light. She looked towards the light in front and back at the one in pursuit trying to compare their distance. It was a pointless comparison. One could be larger or brighter than the other, which would completely distort any estimation.

'Who do you think's going to win the race?' she asked. 'Us or them?'

Stratton came back to the stern and looked at the light behind them. 'That depends on the direction of the ship we're chasing, how far away it is and how fast it's going. And even then, what kind of boat it is. If it's a regular cargo carrier, Lotto will probably want to hijack it anyway.'

'And that's our only option? Get to that boat or get caught by Lotto while trying?'

'There are always other options. The trick is trying to find them in time.'

She looked at him. He had that same cold expression he usually seemed to have when there was little hope. He had no fear in his eyes, no panic. Just calculation. She could not even begin to imagine what other options they had. All she could think was how she was going to kill herself to prevent Lotto from getting his hands on her. Maybe that was the option Stratton meant.

Stratton walked back around the boat, looking at various pieces of equipment, inside boxes and on the deck. If he couldn't possibly imagine a potential use for it, it went over the side.

'What are you looking for?' she asked.

'Inspiration' was his business-like answer.

Stratton paused once more to gauge the sizes of both distant lights and compare the relative gains and losses being made. The front light continued to move to the port side of their track, which meant it was heading west. Which wasn't of any help to them.

Half an hour later another tight collection of lights appeared on their starboard side and Stratton took a moment to study them. The first light had grown very little since they first saw it but the pirate light had more than doubled in size. The new group of lights seemed to represent a much bigger vessel, that or it was much closer.

He elected to change direction and go for the new ship. After adjusting to the new track, he topped up the working fuel tanks and began to put the things he had selected into two piles.

The girl could hardly take her eyes off the following

vessel, partly in the hope that it wasn't the pirates, but mostly in fear that it was. Her nerves had begun to fray but she dealt with it. Coming to terms with everything helped her.

'I've decided how I want to die,' she said.

'Oh?' he answered matter-of-factly as he inspected a fishing reel harness.

'The best way is to drown.'

'Without a doubt,' he said. 'A friend of mine drowned once. He said it was the strangest experience. He was on a decompression stop after a deep dive off a barge somewhere in Africa. You know, hang around for ten or fifteen minutes at thirty feet to prevent the bends. One of the boat workers accidentally knocked a shackle off the edge of the barge. He was wearing a full-face mask and looking up at the time although he couldn't really see anything. The shackle smashed his face mask. He started to climb as quickly as he could but he just couldn't make it in time. He held his breath for as long as he could but the urge to take a breath, even when you know it's going to be water, is too strong. And so he did. He breathed in the sea. He said he felt the panic grip him and he fought like hell. But it didn't last very long at all. The stress and the gasping soon went away to be replaced by euphoria. He said it was ever so peaceful. There was even something pleasant about it. That lasted a few seconds and the lights went out. The next thing he remembered was lying on the deck of the barge coughing his guts up while someone heaved down on his ribcage. So, absolutely. Go for it. Has to be better than shoving one of these into your throat,' he added, raising the knife in his hand.

'Is that how you will go?' she asked.

'I haven't gotten that far yet,' he said, picking up a marlin fishing reel and inspecting the thick line. 'Do you know what the breaking strain of this is?'

She looked at the line in his hand, thinking it to be a strange question to ask when she was talking about their suicides. 'Around two thousand pounds,' she decided.

'That's right. You do a bit of sea fishing then?'

'My father. I was brought up in a small fishing village in northern China. Deep sea fishing was his favourite thing to do.'

'That the Yellow Sea?'

'Yes. Have you been there?'

'No.'

'He used to take me with him. When I was about twelve I caught a shark more than twice my size.' She smiled at the memory.

'So why are you thinking of killing yourself?'

The question snapped her out of her reverie. Her smile vanished.

'Don't you want to see him again?' he asked.

She avoided his eyes. 'I cannot see him again. He did not approve of my job.'

'You can't see him because you joined the Secret Service?'

'It's a little more complicated than that. He has very strong reasons for disliking what I do. I don't blame him.'

She seemed to want to tell Stratton something but she

was unable to get it out. Stratton chose not to dig. It sounded personal and he had a lot on his own mind anyway.

She watched him pick up another fishing reel harness and check the buckles to ensure they worked. 'What are you doing?'

'I have a plan. Not a brilliant one. Very cheeky. With little chance of success. But it's keeping me occupied.'

She wondered if he was losing it. She could see nothing they could do to prevent the pirates from catching them. Other than suicide.

She looked to their rear again. The dark mass below the light had taken on the form of a boat. She could make out the silhouette of the superstructure on top of a bulky, broad hull.

'It won't be long before they'll be in firing range,' she said.

Stratton took a moment to check for himself. 'Yep . . . You haven't looked ahead for a while, have you?'

She turned her back to the pirate vessel to see dozens of lights to their front and sides in all shapes and configurations. Each cluster represented a ship of some kind but they were all still so very far away.

'We won't reach any of them before the pirates catch us,' she said.

'I know. But we must be close to the corridor.'

She felt the optimism in his voice but still couldn't see why.

He put down the reel and studied the array of equipment he had laid out on the deck. 'They'll catch this boat soon enough, but there's no reason for us to be on it.'

Wherever his mind was, she was nowhere near it. She looked at the collection of life jackets, their use obvious enough. But the rest of the junk made no sense to her. 'We jump into the sea and let the pirates chase after the empty boat,' she said. It was all she could think of.

'That would give us a lot longer to live.'

'Then we hope one of those boats finds us.'

'Dawn will be up soon. Now we're talking hours of survival time.'

'How many days did you say we could live without water? Three?'

'Go on. Admit it. You think I'm brilliant.'

She figured it was an option, although nothing more than a delay of the inevitable, another desperate attempt to cling on to life.

'We might as well get on with it,' he said. 'If we leave it too late, they'll see us in the water. Put on as many life jackets as you can.'

'They'll see the bright orange.'

'Not if we put the sweaters over us,' he said, pointing to some clothing he had sorted out. 'They'll also keep us warm for longer. Truth is we'll die of hypothermia long before we die of thirst.'

He picked up one of the life jackets, pulled it over his head and tied the lines around his waist and between his legs. She sighed as she watched him. She had come to terms with ending her life there and then and been only minutes away from grabbing a hold of something heavy that Stratton hadn't already thrown overboard and diving into the water with it. She figured all she needed to do was hang on to it for as long as she could while she sank. Then even when she released it as she began to panic, as the man in Stratton's story had, she would never be able to reach the surface before succumbing.

'Don't hang about,' he said, pulling another life jacket over the one he already wore.

She picked up a jacket and put it on. He handed her another and helped her fasten it.

'Put this over the top,' he said, handing her a large sweater.

'Is hypothermia as painless as drowning, do you think?' she asked.

'It's even more pleasant. I've had it on several occasions. Once you get past the freezing cold stage, it's fine. Like drowning but without the freaking-out panic phase. Put this on,' he said, handing her a fishing reel harness.

'What for?'

'To hold it all together. If we get through this phase, I have another idea that'll keep us occupied for a while longer. Keeping oneself busy is the key to longevity they say.'

She thought he was acting a bit weirdly but nothing about him surprised her any more. She pulled the harness on while he donned one himself and after fastening up his buckles he helped her with hers.

When they were finished, the pair of them looked more than twice their normal sizes. She broke into a smile.

'I'm glad you see the funny side,' he said. 'I was beginning to think you'd lost your sense of humour.'

When he looked back at the pirate vessel he could make out the front mast and wisps of smoke from the exhaust stack.

'We'd better get into the water. I'm going to change the boat's direction to take them away from where we jump in. Soon as I set the tiller, we go overboard.'

She nodded.

It was an effort for him to bend down to untie the tiller with all the clothing he was wearing.

'Wait!' she called out.

He stopped, one hand on the tiller.

She quickly unfastened the drinking water container that was still half full and held it in her arms. 'OK!'

'Good thinking,' he said and yanked the tiller over. The boat turned sharply.

'Go!' Stratton shouted as he tied the tiller off with fishing line.

She leaped into the water. He rolled over the side. When he surfaced he watched the boat cruise away from them.

They then turned their attentions to the following vessel to see what it would do.

The mother craft continued straight at them. Stratton couldn't believe that no one on board was watching the fishing boat. Maybe the lookouts had seen them jump into the water.

Then the vessel turned in pursuit of the little fishing boat.

They bobbed in the water and watched the raiders come

on. The ship passed them some distance away. But it was the first time they could really confirm that it had been the pirate mother ship.

'Won't they just backtrack when they find it's empty?' she said.

'They won't know when we jumped off. Hopefully they'll come to the same conclusion you did about us getting captured and think we've killed ourselves.'

They watched the back of the vessel cruise into the distance. Without its lights, it would soon have become invisible in the darkness.

'I can see your life jacket on your right side,' Stratton said, inspecting her. She adjusted her sweater to cover it up.

'How do I look?' he asked.

She studied him. 'You'll do.'

Stratton turned to look in every direction. 'Quite a few boats about,' he noted.

'None within a mile of us, though,' she said, acting as the voice of doom.

'Dawn will crack in no time,' he said, looking to the east where there was a faint glow on the horizon.

She unscrewed the water bottle and took a little sip. 'Want some?' she asked.

'Thanks,' he said. She passed it to him. He took a couple of mouthfuls and handed it back to her.

'So,' she began, leaning back and looking up at the stars. 'We just wait here for a boat to happen by? Could be a while. But I guess we have all the time in the world.'

'Not exactly,' he said. 'My plan is not just to wait here for a boat to happen by. The odds on that would be very small indeed.'

He exposed the large fishing reel attached to the front of his harness. 'Turn around,' he said.

She didn't bother to ask why.

He pulled out a length of the line, looped it through the back of her harness and tied it off several times.

She turned to face him again, finding the line that went from her back to the reel on his chest. 'Good idea,' she said. 'We won't lose each other.'

'That's part of the idea. It's to keep us together, but from a long way apart.'

'I don't understand.'

'I'm going to go for a swim. Due north. You're going to stay here. There's about two kilometres of fishing line here. When I get to the end of the line, we're going to keep it nice and tight.'

'You're going to be two kilometres away?'

'Yes. Any boat that passes in between us will snag us. That gives us quite a large catchment area.'

She thought about the concept, trying to see the operation in her mind's eye. 'What do we do if we get snagged?'

'We get dragged behind the ship,' he said, like it was obvious.

'Yes, but. Then what?'

'Well. We try and get the attention of someone on board.'

'But if the ship snags the middle of the line, we'll be a kilometre away from the back of it.'

'Hence the reel,' he said, raising it out of the water for her to see. 'I reel us in, or me.'

She continued to stare at him, trying to see the plan.

'It has to be better than just floating here together,' he said.

She decided it was insane. But he was doing what he had done from the moment she had met him. He moved seamlessly from precarious step to precarious step with one perilous plan followed by another impossible one. This one was the craziest yet but he had pulled it out of the rubbish found on a beaten-up Somali fishing boat.

'It's brilliant,' she said. 'No, I really think it's crazy brilliant.'

'May I have another drink of water?'

She handed the container to him and he took a long slug before giving it back to her. He looked at the pirate vessel. The lights appeared to be the same size as they had been a few minutes earlier. He suspected they had caught up with the fishing boat.

'If this doesn't work out, we probably won't see each other again,' he said, his tone serious.

She looked into his eyes. She suspected it wasn't the first time he had said such a thing to someone.

'Hypothermia is as pleasant as drowning,' he reminded her.

'Without the panic.'

'And you wake up in another life.'

She found a little smile. She had been so close to death so many times in the last few days it no longer had such a disabling effect. She felt sad because he was finally leaving her. She had come to rely on him completely.

'I'll be on the end of the line if you need me,' he said, like he had heard her. 'Good luck.'

He decided he was going to miss her in a way. Companionships made in these kind of circumstances were unlike any others. They had forged a bond between them. If they both were somehow to survive this, they would never forget each other.

He leaned back, looked up at the night sky and kicked his feet.

'You too,' she said, though he couldn't have heard her. His hands joined in the stroke and he rode the swell as he moved away.

She never took her eyes off him. He remained visible all of the time at first, then only when he rode the peaks of the swell. Every few seconds she felt a tug on the line. Soon he had disappeared completely and she was all alone.

She looked around for signs of the pirate boat but could see none. The horizon was brightening, the sun about to emerge any moment.

She felt like she had passed through another significant porthole in her life. Maybe because she was on her own again. As she looked around her, she believed in her heart that it would be the final chapter in her story. She wasn't going to be surrounded by a loving family like she had always imagined. It was an ending she would never have predicted.

The fishing line tugged on her harness and she smiled. She wasn't quite alone. Not yet.

* * *

Stratton went into a zone as he lay back and kicked his legs while paddling his arms. He watched the reel slowly turning as the line paid out. He thought he might still see the girl beyond, the line showing the way before it went into the water. But she was long out of sight.

The reel still looked pretty full. With the tide and the swell he had no way of knowing how far he was from her. He amused himself with the thought of the possibility that after several hours he might even bump into her, having swum in a huge circle.

He looked to the east. The sun would be up very soon.

He dropped his head back and maintained an easy, relaxed stroke. It was a good time to think and take his mind off the problems. But as soon as he did, the same thoughts came nagging at him, the first of them being about Hopper.

He concentrated on clearing his head and focusing on his stroke as he moved easily through the water. It worked, for a while at least. He had no idea how much time had passed since he drifted off into a kind of trance. When next he looked at the reel, it was halfway empty and the sun had begun its slow rise above the horizon.

Then something else blew him out of his semi-dazed state of mind. He saw the silhouette of a vessel in the distance.

He let his feet drop below him and sat up in the water and stared at it, trying to figure out what type of craft it was and in which direction it was heading. After studying it for a good minute, he decided it wasn't getting any smaller and was in fact growing in size, quite possibly heading towards him.

He felt a rush of adrenaline. Their first chance. He suddenly felt confident that even if they missed it there would be others. It couldn't be much more than two or three hours since he had left the girl and a ship had already come into their vicinity.

The plan might not be as crazy as it seemed after all.

14

Stratton kept his eyes on the boat. It came on towards him. He realised he was seeing just a little more of the starboard side. Which meant it would pass by his right side, where the line stretched out towards the girl. He looked at the reel, still turning on his chest. It was about three-quarters empty.

There was a good chance the line would snag.

As the sun rose higher into the sky, Stratton could make out the shape of the superstructure. The bridge wings stuck out of the sides near the top like a stumpy crucifix. It had to be a cargo ship of some kind, a bulk carrier. Quite a large one.

He dropped his head back and paddled, deciding not to look at the boat for several minutes and just swim. Longer gaps between assessing its progress would provide a better picture.

He felt parched, not helped by the sea water that constantly splashed into his mouth. Sea water could turn a person insane before they died of thirst. If he missed this boat and all went wrong, he hoped the night cold would take him before that happened. There were so many ways to die in such a short period of time.

Another of which he was well aware of. He hadn't overlooked the possibility that he and the girl wouldn't be detected once they were trailing behind a snagged boat. He knew what it was like on board carriers like that. Minimal crew, and those on duty would usually be too busy to take the time to look outboard. The few people whose job it would be to look out to sea, namely those on the bridge, would concentrate forward. He hoped that this crew would be security conscious and have a lookout to the rear while transiting through hostile waters. But even then, if Stratton and the girl were being towed hundreds of metres behind the boat, they would be difficult if not impossible to see. And he wasn't as confident as he had sounded about being able to reel them in closer. He did not expect either of them to last very long if they were being dragged. The water would constantly pass through their clothing, sucking the heat from their bodies. They could succumb to hypothermia in a short time indeed. They might also drown while being towed.

Nothing about it was going to be easy.

But he would rather die making an effort than lying around in the water doing nothing.

When he looked for the vessel again it had closed the distance a great deal more. He could make out individual windows in the superstructure. It was definitely going to cut across his path, south of him where the fishing line headed towards the girl. He checked the reel. Still a couple hundred metres of line left.

He decided to stop paddling and stay where he was.

The set-up looked good enough. The bulker would snag the line in the next few minutes. No one in the bridge would be able to see him unless they had a pair of binoculars trained directly on his position. He estimated that he would be closer to the stern of the carrier than the girl would be.

He watched the oncoming vessel, counting the seconds, the life jackets tied around him, stuffed up under his chin.

He became aware of a distant hum. Engines. He took it to be coming from the oncoming cargo ship. Then he realised the bulker was too far away to produce such a sound.

He turned in the water and saw the pirate mother craft heading towards him. As he stared at it in horror, he judged that it wasn't in fact on a direct line towards him but to the cargo ship.

Stratton looked between the two vessels to gauge their relative tracks. Both were going to cut across his line but from opposite directions.

And it looked like the pirate vessel would snag the line first.

Stratton's choices were limited indeed. He could think of two in the time he had. He could cut the line and hope the pirates didn't see him as they pursued the bulker. But then he would be stranded. Or he could try stopping the pirate boat from snagging and take his chances from there.

Only the latter had an element of a possibility to it.

Stratton shot his arms into the air. He waved and shouted, and ripped away his sweater to reveal the bright orange life jackets beneath. He knew the Somali vessel would pass by him considerably closer than the bulker but the eyes on board would be focused on their prey. He untied the outermost life jacket, pulled it off and started waving it around in the air.

Almost immediately, the front of the pirate vessel dipped as its engines decelerated and the nose came around to aim directly at him.

He stopped shouting and watched it approach. An unqualified success, for the time being. He glanced at the cargo ship. It was still coming on. If its crew had seen the pirate vessel and were in any way suspicious, it showed no outward sign of it.

The pirate vessel slowed as it approached. Men gathered in the prow to look at him.

The engines suddenly roared as they went into reverse and the boat came to a stop a stone's throw from him in the light swell.

The fishing line ran away from Stratton only a couple of metres in front of the boat's path.

The Somalis had lined the side of the vessel, looking down on him. Stratton recognised one or two of them and suspected from the way they were gesticulating, that they had recognised him too. They looked surprised to see the Englishman. They appeared to be more curious than angry at the sight of him. They could afford to be.

A shout went up and passed to the back of the boat. Then a familiar-looking big man strode along the deck and stood in the prow to look down on Stratton. The tall, strongly built African wore camouflage uniform and dark sunglasses. He looked quite amused with his find. The grin didn't last very long though.

'Well, well, well,' the pirate chief said in his deep voice. 'You are a slippery fish to hold on to.'

Stratton had no immediate reply. All he could do was look at the man.

'You have nothing to say!' Lotto called out.

'It's a pleasant morning,' Stratton called back. It felt like the right thing to say under the circumstances.

Lotto grinned again. He said something to one of his men who came forward and handed him an AK-47 assault rifle. Lotto pulled back the working parts to cock it and as he did so a round flew out of the breach but another was reloaded.

He aimed the end of the barrel at Stratton. 'I hope you don't mind if I don't invite you on board,' he said.

Stratton glanced at the bulker. It suddenly seemed miles away from the line. 'I have a deal for you,' he shouted, not knowing what the hell he was going to say next.

'What can you possibly have that's of interest to me?' Lotto shouted back, keeping the weapon on aim.

'Information,' said Stratton. 'Valuable information that could save you a lot of money.' That was the right thing to say, Stratton thought. Lotto was all about money. Stratton tried to focus on Lotto's trigger finger. If he could see it start to squeeze the trigger, he might be able to move enough to avoid a lethal strike.

'I think you're wasting my time,' Lotto called out. 'I have

work to do.' Lotto made the weapon more comfortable in his shoulder and narrowed the sights on Stratton again.

'We know you're using the ships to move drugs around the world,' Stratton shouted. He didn't mention he knew about the weapons. 'You're playing a very dangerous game.'

Lotto pulled the carbine's trigger and the AK-47 bucked against his shoulder.

For a fraction of a second, Stratton thought he was a dead man and was stunned to find himself still alive. The round had smacked into the water close by his head. He glanced at the cargo ship. The front of it looked to be where the snag line should have been.

'Let me explain,' Stratton shouted. 'It will only take a minute and then you can shoot me if you want to . . . Hijacking ships is one thing,' he pressed on. 'It affects economies only a little and is more of a nuisance than anything else—'

Lotto fired the Kalashnikov again, this time the round striking the water even closer to Stratton.

Lotto chuckled, as did his men. They knew how their master often liked to toy with victims before he killed them.

The operative couldn't help wondering if it was best out of three. He kept up his tirade. 'Even smuggling drugs is small in comparison. But aiding international terrorism is a big deal. It's going to get you into a lot of trouble.'

Lotto fired for a third time. The round shredded Stratton's life-jacket collar an inch from his neck. Lotto made a show of moving the gun a little to one side to take a better look at his target. 'Did I hit you?' he called out, not in the least concerned.

'I don't think so,' Stratton replied with equal calm. 'Perhaps just a nick. A good shot if you intended to aim so close.'

'I was aiming for your ear.'

'Not bad at all then.'

'From your left ear. I was aiming for your right.' Lotto laughed and came back up on aim. 'Now unless you have anything of real importance to tell me, I need to go and catch myself a nice, fat cargo ship.'

Stratton felt a tug on his harness. The reel on his chest began to turn, slowly at first, then faster.

But he could also feel Lotto's cold eye on him through the rifle sight, his finger tightening on the trigger. In a second he would feel the bullet smash into him.

The reel spun hard. Lotto squeezed the trigger. 'Goodbye, Englishman. Finally.'

The reel locked. The line went taut as it stretched and Lotto fired as Stratton was jerked towards the front of the pirate boat. The bullet slapped into the water where he had been less than a second before.

Lotto looked utterly confused as he watched Stratton suddenly zoom unnaturally across the water on his front like he was Superman. The Englishman disappeared beyond the bows of the boat and Lotto hurried over to the other side. He watched open-mouthed as Stratton continued away at speed. All the Somalis joined their chief, all looking dumbstruck by the sight.

Lotto had no idea how Stratton was doing it but he

couldn't live with the man escaping once again. 'Full speed!' he roared. 'After him!'

Immy floated in the vast ocean, all alone but strangely not feeling alone. She had been more isolated in the prison hut surrounded by the others, the only girl, waiting in fear for Lotto or one of the others to come and take her away and rape her. There was no danger of that where she was now.

She lay back so that she could see nothing else but the wide open sky. The waves lapped over her, swamping every now and then. But she didn't care. She was in a zone. Alive for longer than she had expected to be. The reprieve from suicide had been somewhat emotional. It was quite something to come to the difficult decision to end your life and be determined to do it. She had become utterly convinced it was all going to be over in mere minutes. Then that character Stratton went and pulled yet another rabbit out of his hat.

She smiled at the memory of what they had done. Jumping into the sea to avoid being captured, adding a few more hours to their lives. He had finally gone out of her life, after a short but significant introduction. With him went any further chance of cheating death. In a strange way, despite the circumstances, she had grown used to his company. He was assertive and considerate, particularly in the face of adversity. An attractive quality most women never got to see in a man. She wondered how many people knew him that well or had misjudged him. Few people ever got into situations that exposed their true qualities.

She felt for the line as she considered his silly plan. He was still connected to her, but she knew she would never see him again. In an odd way she was sadder for him than she was for herself. The reason for it was simple enough. He had a noble purpose, she didn't. She could argue her case but it wasn't convincing. She had done what she did out of fear.

She could at least be pleased with how calmly she was taking her own death. She hoped she would maintain the same level of dignity until the end. Her body was beginning to chill but not too badly. Not yet. She suspected when her temperature did start to fall, it would happen quite fast. She wondered if she should try and fall asleep. That way she might not even know when she slipped into hypothermia. On the other hand, there was something wrong about spending your last hour or so on this earth asleep if you could help doing otherwise. She decided to stay conscious for as long as possible and she started thinking back through her life, starting as early as she could remember. Right back to when she was a kid. She expected to fall unconscious long before she got to the end. But it might not be such a bad way to go.

The water lapped around her ears and so she didn't hear the distant sound of gunfire. As she searched her mind for the earliest memory of her life, she felt a tug at the back of her harness. It frightened her at first, her brain unable to interpret what it was. As she began to accelerate away, she remembered the line.

Stratton's plan. They had been snagged.

Her speed quickly increased and she shot across the water, the life jackets taking the brunt of the bumpy waves. She spread out her arms and legs to remain as stable as possible and prevent from flipping over. She tried to raise her chin to look ahead but she couldn't get enough of an angle. All she could do was lie flat on her back and get dragged along.

It was all so bizarre. It felt extremely tenuous and alien. The waves set up a jolting rhythm. Her teeth rattled in her mouth with every bump.

She wondered how long she could last. The water was coursing through her clothes. She felt OK, as if she could ride like that for a long time. Stratton's insane plan was working, the first part of it at least. A hint of elation rippled through her. She suddenly saw a chance they could be rescued. She couldn't see what was dragging her, but she knew it had to be some kind of ship. That meant she was in touch with civilisation, be it remotely. All it took to be saved was someone from the ship to see them. It was a small chance, but suddenly a real one.

Stratton had managed to twist around on to his back so that the gushing water didn't drown him. Which was a far more comfortable way of being towed at speed. The swell bumped against his back and it was like being dragged across a corrugated roof. He had no idea how fast he was going. It felt like he could have water-skied at that speed.

Stratton leaned his head up to look for Lotto's boat. He could just about see it coming on after him, as he expected it would, the gap between them several hundred metres. He studied the picture, wondering if the pirate boat might be gaining. It was difficult to tell.

He made an effort to look ahead for the bulker but he couldn't. As he tried to manoeuvre himself to one side, he almost flipped on to his front again. He decided to leave it alone, for the time being at least.

The bumping suddenly increased markedly and he felt himself passing over a set of larger waves. Had to be the bulker's bow waves. He spread out his arms and legs to make himself a more stable platform. He was drawing in behind the carrier. When he was over the waves, the ride became a lot smoother. He wondered how far he was from the vessel and where the girl might be. He had been five or six hundred metres from the cargo ship when he was on his front. That meant she had to be a good fifteen hundred metres behind him. Well behind the pirates.

He craned up to see the pirate ship cutting across the bow waves and falling into the bulker's track.

A young British private security guard on the stern of the cargo ship was observing the pirate vessel through a pair of binoculars.

As he watched it cross the bow waves, he raised a radio to his mouth. 'Bob. That dodgy boat I reported earlier. It's even more dodgy now. It's moved in right behind us.'

'Roger that,' came the reply over the radio. 'Sound the alarm. All security hands to the stern. Don't forget your bloody weapons. You got that, Captain?'

'Yes, Bob,' came the captain's voice over the radio.

The bulker's alarms began to sound and crewmen working on deck dropped what they were doing, hurried into the ship's superstructure by the nearest door and bolted it shut. A security guard hurried through the carrier ensuring it was battened down.

'Full speed, Captain,' Bob shouted over the radio. 'Commence evasive action.'

As the stern guard continued to observe the vessel following it, two more security guards stepped from the bulker's superstructure carrying AK-47 assault rifles. They jogged along the decks and down steps, converging on to the poop deck to join their mate on the rear rail beyond a massive pair of anchor winches. After a couple of minutes the other security guard stepped down to the group. Another joined them. They now made five. The entire bulker vibrated as the engines reached maximum revolutions. A claxon joined in the general cacophony of bells and whistles.

The water directly below the poop deck churned up through the massive submerged propellers to create an even larger wake The carrier began to lean over a little as it started a hard turn.

An overweight, older-looking security guard marched out of the superstructure and across the deck to join the others looking over the rail. By his bearing and confidence, he was clearly the senior man.

'What we got here then?' Bob, the head of the security detachment, asked gruffly, grabbing the binoculars hanging around his subordinate's neck to take a look for himself.

'You reckon they're pirates?' one of the men asked, anxious. Apart from Bob, young guys made up the team, all of whom had military experience of a kind. Two were territorial soldiers who had missed out on any long-term drafts abroad and seen no action at all. One was a former fusilier who had done a basic three years with a short draft to Iraq but seen no action. The other two were ex-Royal Marine drivers and had done a couple of stints in Afghanistan with a little action but nothing to write home about. All had joined the maritime security circuit for two reasons only and they were the pay and a chance to travel. The men had all worked the maritime circuit for a few years but none had seen a pirate before.

'Where's all the other smaller boats they're supposed to use?' asked the bigger of the two ex-Marines.

'There's no usual when it comes to these fellas,' Bob said.

The other Marine nudged his mate and gave him a look like he doubted Bob knew that much about it. 'So just 'ow many pirates 'ave you actually seen, Bob?' he said.

Bob appeared reluctant to answer. 'These would be my first, laddy, like all of you lot,' he said. 'But unlike you lot, I've done over fifty of these runs and I've read all there is to know about the buggers and talked to loads of blokes who've run into them. And I can tell you they are somethin' to have respect for. They'll 'ave a go, I assure you. If they decide to go for this boat, then they'll go for it. If we make it difficult for 'em, they'll 'ave no worries about killin' any of us. We may 'ave to put a few of 'em away before they back off. That might mean they may put a few of us away too.'

For a few seconds none of them said anything. Like they had all realised something important. Like it was one thing to talk about pirates and the threat they posed, but something totally different to see them in person and know they were targeting you.

'Shall we get the 'oses ready?' one of the men asked.

'Yeah. Let's drown the bastards in their boat,' said the big Marine.

'We're not usin' 'oses when we've got guns,' Bob said calmly. 'You might want to take the more humane way right now. But if you end up an 'ostage of those wankers, you'll wish you'd shot a few of 'em first chance you 'ad . . . Everyone got their weapons loaded?'

The men moved as one, inspired by Bob's words. The rifles they used were not new but they had kept them well cleaned and oiled. The five men pulled back the gleaming working parts, loaded shiny magazines, released the breach blocks to fly forward on powerful springs and pick up bullets and slam them home into breaches. All five then put the ends of the barrels over the rail and aimed in the general direction of the pirate vessel.

'Somefin' in the water,' the guard with the binoculars said. 'About 'alfway between us and them.'

Bob grabbed the binoculars again, the strap yanking at the young guard's neck, and looked along the bulker's track until he found what the man was talking about. All he could see was something being dragged through the water.

'Don't worry about it,' Bob said. 'Let's worry about the job in 'and, shall we. If they've got RPGs, then they'll probably want to engage 'em around one-fifty metres. So as soon as those bastards come within two 'undred metres, we'll give 'em a volley to think about.'

'What if they keep comin'?' the big Marine asked.

'The closer they get, the easier they'll be to shoot,' Bob replied.

'Bob? Captain here.' The voice boomed over all of the men's radios.

'Bob, send,' the old team leader said into his radio.

'They've got about two knots on us and are gaining.'

'Roger that,' Bob replied. 'Just keep up the zig-zagging. We'll take care of the rest,' he added, before releasing his radio to dangle from a strap around his neck. 'I didn't take on this job to spend next Christmas as an 'ostage of those tossers. They close in another 'undred metres and we go to war. Is that understood?'

The men focused hard on the pirate vessel. Bob had said enough. They did not intend to be captured either. A war it was going to be then.

'Come on you bastards!' one of them shouted.

Stratton leaned up to look at Lotto's boat. He could tell the pirates were gaining on him. He could see men running along its sides. Preparing to lower a couple of speedboats into the water. He would be impressed if they could do it at speed.

They could. A boat dropped into the water off the starboard side, held there on a line by crewmen. A couple of men jumped down into it and the crewmen let the line go and the boat dropped behind as the men went to fire up the engines. More crew lowered the other boat into the water on the port side and it bobbed around as a second team jumped into it.

Stratton felt for the pouch attached to the front of his harness. Touched the knife that was still inside. He took it out and held tightly on to it, not sure what he was going to do when they came alongside him.

Then the tension suddenly went from Stratton's line like it had snapped and he slowed to a stop, no longer being towed by the bulker.

Stratton couldn't believe what was happening. He'd held on to the possibility that the pirates would eventually give up and pull off. That one of the ship's crew might spot him and initiate his rescue. But suddenly that was all over. The end of the road had arrived. The end that he had fought to avoid the past few days had arrived. The line had probably been stretched to its limit and the rough end of the vessel had worn through it. Whatever the reason, it was over. Lotto was going to win.

Stratton bobbed in the water and watched the pirate boat close in. He expected a bullet to the head. At least it would be quick. Arguably better than hypothermia or drowning and certainly better than thirsting to death.

Lotto had been at the front of his boat all of the time watching Stratton, willing the engine to get them closer, waiting for the opportunity that he knew would come to shoot the damned English. The sight of Stratton coming to a sudden stop, he truly considered a gift from on high. He gripped the rifle in his hands and brought it up into his shoulder. Held it there aimed square on to Stratton's chest. He hoped the first round wouldn't kill him so that Lotto could get two or three into the man before he died. But then he considered the wisdom of killing Stratton outright at all. Maybe better to let him die slowly in the ocean of undrinkable water. He quickly discarded the thought. He wanted the satisfaction of killing the man with his own hands.

Stratton stared into the end of the barrel coming right at him. He wanted to duck beneath the water but to do that he would have to get the life jackets off. No time. He couldn't keep ducking and diving for very long anyhow. Didn't want to add to the Somali's amusement, Stratton popping up all over the place for a second or two until the bastard finally shot him.

Lotto knew there was nothing else that Stratton could do. He would wait until he had a complete sight picture. Then he would pull the trigger and send a piece of brass-coated lead right through the irritating Englishman. And after that entertainment ended, he would pursue the cargo ship and capture it. It was going to be a good day after all.

But the fishing line hadn't snapped. It had simply worked its way down from the leading edge of the bow, popped off it, and slid along the keel as it passed over.

The sucking action of the propeller wouldn't allow the line to sink away. It pulled it into a vortex, towards the spinning blades along with the surrounding water. The twisted line wrapped around the turning shaft and swiftly gathered in the slack.

Stratton was staring at Lotto. The leader had a clear picture of him in the rifle sight. A plate-sized target any half-decent rifleman could hit from where he was, leaning over the front of the boat as it cut through the water towards the operative. Then the reel fastened to Stratton's chest whipped him around and he took off like a bungee jumper bouncing up from the bottom of his fall.

Just like before. Only this time much faster. The g-force wrenched at Stratton's neck and his limbs pulled against their sockets as he skimmed over the water like a jet ski.

As before, Lotto could not believe his eyes. He was filled with anger and extreme violence and acted on instinct, firing wildly at Stratton, emptying the carbine's thirty-round magazine in a desperate attempt to finish him off. 'Get that man!' he yelled, ripping away the empty magazine and throwing it down. 'Give me bullets!' he shouted. '*Kill him!*'

'Boss!' one of his men shouted from where he stood on the port side, pointing at the water beyond the stern of their own vessel.

Other pirates looked in the same direction, awestruck by what they saw. Lotto looked and was equally stunned. He watched the girl come shooting across the water towards them. She sped along the length of the boat, looking terrified, her legs and arms splayed like a spider.

As she looked at him, Lotto realised it was the Chinese

girl. 'Don't just stand there staring,' he screamed. '*Shoot them!*'

Every Somali with a gun ran to the front of the vessel and let rip.

On the bulker, the security guards had been watching the pirate boat close in. When Lotto opened fire, they assumed the bullets had been aimed at them.

'Right,' Bob exclaimed. 'They want a battle. We'll give 'em one. Section,' he shouted, reliving his days in the Royal Marines as a troop commander. Bob had never seen action although he had spent almost twenty years in the mob. He'd done a lot of training, numerous section attacks across Dartmoor in his early days and then much later in the Omani desert in preparation for the first Gulf War. Sadly nothing ever came of it for him and the action had ended by the time he arrived in Iraq. Before that he'd completed a couple of stints in Northern Ireland but it had all gone quiet by the time he arrived, apart from the occasional road-side bomb that he only ever saw the aftermath of. A year after he left the Corp to become a civilian, the Twin Towers in New York were brought down and the lads went into Afghanistan along with the Yanks. He had remained philosophical about it, telling his mates down the pub that life was like that in the military. Some people saw loads of action while others saw none. The luck of the draw. He hadn't been overly bothered about it on the surface. But deep down he always wished he'd seen at least one bit of real contact. His wife of twenty-five years was glad that he had left the Marines safe and sound but for his sake she wished he'd fired his gun in anger at least once, as long as he hadn't hit anyone.

Truth was, Bob regretted that he had devoted the best part of his life to the military and had never had a single opportunity to ply the trade he had dedicated himself to for so many years.

Things were about to change in that regard.

When the Somalis opened up on Lotto's orders, a couple of rounds zinged off the metal surfaces near the men. Bob felt a bullet ricochet somewhere around his feet. He didn't flinch, calling, 'Enemy front, rapid *fire*!'

The team let rip in unison, Bob blinking at the shock of the weapons clattering right beside him. He held his grimace as he stared back at the enemy. For a brief second he was in soldier's heaven. He was in command. The enemy coming at them. His men engaging them. It was a moment to live for.

The private security detachment fired directly into the pirate vessel, the weapons in the hands of men who knew how to use them.

Rounds peppered the pirate boat and hit several pirates before they could take cover. One fell overboard and disappeared beneath the water.

Lotto dropped to his belly on the deck behind the metal sides as bullets flew around him. Windows in the bridge shattered, the wheelman taking a round in the chest and dropping out of sight.

Bob wanted more than to simply stand and give orders.

'Give me that,' he said to the man nearest to him who was about to reload his rifle. Bob removed the empty magazine, took a full one from the man's pouch, loaded it on to the weapon, cocked it, aimed and loosed off a staccato burst of fire. He had never been quite so content as at that moment in his life firing at the enemy. Never again would he meet the question 'So, you see any action in your time then?' with a shrug before admitting that he hadn't. Now he could do the same as so many other old soldiers who had tasted battle when asked the same question. 'A little,' he would say, and then nothing else, knowing it wasn't a lie and letting the imagination of whomever had asked to run away with them.

'They've fired a bloody torpedo at us!' shouted one of the men.

Bob stopped firing to look down on to the water. Sure enough, something large was hurtling along towards the back of the boat.

Stratton ripped through the bulker's wake completely unaware of the firefight raging above. He couldn't hear it. He could hardly hear anything at all because his head was thrashing in and out of the speeding water. He had other more pressing issues to attend to. He had avoided being executed by Lotto one more time but instead he had sent himself hurtling towards the prop. He realised the line had gone around the prop and that he had barely seconds to do something to stop himself from going through the blades.

As he buffeted along he had kept a firm hold of the

knife. He fought to look ahead and caught sight of the stern. The seconds were running down. The truest indication of how close he was to the propeller came when all daylight disappeared and he got dragged under the water.

He grabbed for the line and drew the edge of the blade across it.

In an instant the prop thrust him upwards and he burst to the surface, launched up into the wake. He spun in the wash, gasping for air, with something running across his body. It was the line, cutting into his life jacket, with the girl on the end of it hurtling towards him. The second before she collided with him he yanked the blade across it and she rolled to a stop face down, her arms and legs thrashing in desperation.

Stratton grabbed hold of her and yanked her over. She choked and spluttered as she fought to catch her breath, instinctively clutching at him as if she might go under again.

'It's OK,' Stratton said. 'It's me. You're OK.'

She regained her breath enough to look at him through feverishly blinking eyes.

But it wasn't over. The back of the bulker was fast moving away. He thought he could see people on the stern and he waved in the hope that they gave a damn about who he and the girl were. As the carrier steamed away, Stratton continued to wave his arms at them.

The security guards had been stunned when the torpedo turned into a person, and then two.

'Bleedin' 'ell!' one of them exclaimed. The comment seemed to satisfy the moment for them all.

'Who the hell are they?' another said.

'They don't look black,' another offered. 'Maybe they ain't pirates.'

'Man overboard!' Bob shouted into his radio, keeping an eye on the pirate vessel. It had turned away and was still going full speed, its two speedboats alongside it. He knew it had been plastered by rounds and wasn't surprised to see it withdraw.

One of the guards grabbed a life ring from a rail and tossed it as hard as he could off the back of the boat.

'Launch a lifeboat,' Bob shouted and a couple of his men hurried away. 'Captain, this is Bob. You can slow the ship and cancel evasive manoeuvring. The pirates have had enough. We've got a couple of people in the water we need to pick up.'

'Roger. Understood,' the captain replied.

Bob and the remaining guards stared at the two people in the water who by then had become tiny specks.

'I wonder who the bloody 'ell they are,' one of them said.

It was what they were all thinking.

15

A steel, pyramid-shaped baggage cage, on the end of a heavy, twisted cable, rose up the side of the bulker as it cruised along at slow speed. The sun shone high in the sky, giving the ocean a deep and inviting look. A gentle breeze rounded off the tops of the waves that lapped against the huge orange-painted side of the vessel. Stratton and the girl stood on a narrow rim around the bottom of the basket hanging on to its rope surrounds as it ascended. The lifeboat that had rescued them rode the swell below, its two crewmen attaching the shackles to its ends before it would also be winched aboard.

The Chinese girl still felt in a daze. Once again she had been reprieved, having left her life in the hands of the ocean and been prepared to accept the inevitable. She experienced the same clarity of thought as she had after deciding against suicide before dawn that day. But this time it wouldn't be a temporary reprieve. She was free of that living nightmare. The ship was large and powerful. It had electricity, engines, food and warmth. Civilised people operated it and had aimed it towards a civilised port that would connect her with her home. She could hardly believe it.

But the euphoria didn't last long and even before she stepped on board, it had been replaced by a stark reality. Returning to her normal life also meant seeing through her responsibilities to the end. Because the only way she could have shirked her duties would have been to have died. While she had been faced with that possibility, she had forgotten them. So her reprieve was temporary after all. She had work to continue. She could never return to China if she failed to complete her task. Impossible. Before getting to Somalia she had considered running away to live somewhere else in the world. But those she worked for would not forgive that. They would find her, one day, eventually. She would then pay a terrible price. But worse still, if she did manage to escape, those she held dear to her heart would suffer in her place. Her family, back in China, would suffer the consequences.

She would rather die than let that happen.

The basket was winched aboard and lowered to the deck. Most of the twenty-five-man crew, a mixture of Western officers and Filipino hands, watched from some part of the bulker. The captain and bridge crew stood on the bridge wings. On the deck, waiting for the basket to descend, stood Bob and the rest of his boys, except the pair who had picked up Stratton and the girl. When they had radioed ahead that the two people were an English Caucasian man and a Chinese woman, the word had spread and everyone wanted to see for themselves.

Stratton and the girl stepped off the side of the basket as it hovered inches from the steel deck. They could practically hear the whispered questions about who they were and what they had been doing in the middle of the Gulf of Aden.

Among the crew there had been the usual round of the more obvious suppositions and explanations: they had fallen overboard; they had been in a small boat that had sunk; they had been in a plane crash. But no one could work out how they'd managed to be speeding through the water having somehow attached themselves to the cargo ship while being pursued by murderous Somalis. At this point the conspiracy theorists among the crew, and there were always several, had a field day. One suggested they were submariners who had ejected from their vessel. Yet the fact that one of them was a girl served to enhance the most popular theory: they were spies of some kind and more probably assassins. The lack of any vaguely intelligent explanation as to what they could have been spying on or who they intended to assassinate did not deter this theory. Even those who declared the whole idea preposterous couldn't help being lured to it in the absence of anything else.

'Thanks very much,' Stratton said with a smile. He held out his hand. 'John Stratton.'

'Bob Haldon.' A firm handshake. 'Pleasure to meet you.'

There was an awkward pause. They both stood for a couple of seconds. Stratton knew what he needed from the man but he waited. There were some rather obvious bureaucratic requirements.

On seeing Stratton face to face Bob had lost some of his confidence in regard to the questions he wanted to ask. He would have had no problem asking anything of a stranger under normal circumstances. Bob could be very direct. The same would have applied if Stratton had been an ordinary bloke, despite his anything but ordinary arrival. But there was something very unordinary about the man standing in front of him, soaking wet and looking at him with bright-green, intelligent eyes. Bob had never had anything to do with special forces, but he knew one when he saw him, or at least thought he did. This bloke, with his long hair, had the bearing and stature of someone who dealt with extreme adventures of a military nature. Bob felt certain of it. And although he had sneered at the stories going around about the couple, he couldn't think of any other explanation for such an outrageous arrival.

Bob had had time to think about and time to prepare a few questions. But after a glance at the girl, he realised something. 'I expect you could both do with a drink and something to eat perhaps,' he said.

'A wet would be fantastic,' Stratton said.

Bob gave his men a glance, like he had discovered something. 'This way,' he said, indicating one of his men to lead off.

The girl discarded her sweater and buoyancy aids. The security guys almost tripped over themselves to help her, fumbling with the oversized kit as she removed it. She smiled politely, which only caused an even greater quality of fumbling.

Stratton walked behind the leading guard towards the superstructure. Bob followed a few steps back, leaning close to one of the other security guards.

'I've sussed him,' Bob said. 'He said he'd like a wet. That's a naval term.'

'He's a sailor?' the guard said. 'You think he fell off one of the navy patrol ships.'

'No, you twat. Does he look like a bloody sailor? He's a boot-neck. A Marine. We say "wet" for a brew as well as the matelots.'

The line trooped into the superstructure and straight into the galley. But Bob paused outside and out of earshot of Stratton and the girl.

'So what's a Marine doin' out 'ere in the middle of nowhere then?' he asked, a rhetorical question. 'Think a little outside of the box. He's obviously no ordinary soldier, is he?'

'You reckon he's a super soldier, do yer?'

'What else?'

'Not SAS?'

'Exactly,' Bob said, looking at him. 'He's Special Air Service.'

'Bugger me,' the lad said.

'Keep it down,' Bob urged. 'They get very funny about it if they think you know. Just act normal.'

Bob straightened himself up and walked into the galley where Stratton and the girl sat sipping cups of piping hot sweet tea.

'How is it, then?' Bob asked.

'Nectar,' Stratton replied.

The girl nodded, then bit down on a biscuit.

'You must be starved,' Bob said. ''Ere, George, pop into

the kitchen and see what there is to eat. We're in between meals,' he added by way of an explanation to the strangers.

'You're very kind,' Stratton said. 'Thank you for everything.'

A man stepped into the doorway. He looked very much an authority figure. Bob straightened on seeing him.

'Sir,' Bob said to the man. 'This is the captain,' he announced to Stratton.

Stratton got to his feet and offered his hand to the portly, white-haired and -bearded older man. 'John Stratton, sir,' he said.

The captain shook hands with a smile, his whiskers stained brown from tobacco smoke. 'Welcome aboard. I trust you're being well looked after.'

'We're doing fine.'

'Well,' the captain started, broaching unfamiliar territory. 'When you've settled in, perhaps you can pop up to the bridge. Obviously we have some paperwork to do.'

'I'd like to crack on with that right away, if I may. I need to make contact with the UK immediately. I'm a member of Her Britannic Majesty's military.'

Bob gave the others another look.

'Right,' the captain said. He looked glad that some light had been shed on the mystery, if only a little. 'Let's get you upstairs and on the blower.'

Stratton glanced at the girl. 'This is a colleague. She works for the Chinese government. I expect she'll be needing the same.'

The girl gave a nod but she looked discomfited.

The captain could do nothing more than shrug politely, clearly in new territory. 'Whatever you need. Glad to be of service. I'll be on the bridge.'

He headed back into the corridor and Stratton walked out carrying his cup of tea between the crew that had amassed in the narrow passage and now parted like the Red Sea.

'Told you,' Bob said to his men.

The captain led the way up the steep, narrow staircase, past two landings before arriving at the door to the bridge deck. A small radio shack was on the left before another door that led into the bridge. A Filipino crewman in a smart white shirt and trousers stood on watch and he smiled broadly and nodded a greeting to Stratton.

The captain went over to the radio satellite equipment. 'Just punch in your number,' he said, stepping out of the way.

Stratton took the phone and inspected the equipment to familiarise himself with it.

'I expect you want some privacy?' the captain asked.

'A few minutes, if that's OK.'

'Not a problem,' the captain said. 'Jamail will have to stay on watch but he doesn't speak much English.'

'That's fine.'

'I'll be in my room directly below. Give me a shout when you're done. I have to make a report and explain what's been happening my end.'

'Thanks,' Stratton said as the old man walked out and closed the door behind him.

Jamail went to the wheel and concentrated ahead.

Stratton keyed in the number, going over what he needed to say. He wanted to be succinct but also cover everything. He thought about Hopper and how he was going to explain the man's death. He couldn't get into much detail over the phone but he had to give the broad strokes of what happened.

After several seconds he heard a gentle pulsing sound and shortly after someone picked up the other end.

'Hello,' a woman's voice said.

'SB Ops please.'

'This is not a secure line, sir,' the woman informed Stratton, robotically.

'I know.'

'One moment.'

The phone crackled a little and a few seconds later a man answered. 'SB Ops.'

'Is that you, Mike?'

'Bloody hell. Stratton?'

'Yes.'

'I can't say I'd given up hope just yet, mate, knowing your knack for always turning up, but I was starting to get a little concerned.'

'I should've left it a bit longer. I like the idea of you being concerned about me.'

'Well, there are some here who had given up. We thought the slopes had got you. Where the hell are you?'

'On board a cargo ship.' Stratton looked at the chart desk behind the ship's wheel. 'The *Orion*. She's in the Gulf of

Aden, heading west along the transit corridor. I've been on holiday in Somalia. We were invited over by a bunch of pirates. Great bunch of lads. Not to mention their jihadi mates.'

'Jesus. How'd you manage to end up there?'

'Trying to put some space between ourselves and the Slope Secret Service. They were after the same thing.'

'Yeah, we got that much from Prabhu.'

'The Gurkhas OK?'

'Yes. When they left you, they made it into Oman without a fuss. They weren't sure whether you'd taken a boat or not. I take it Hopper's with you?'

For a second Stratton couldn't answer. He hesitated. Then said, 'He didn't make it.'

The line went silent for a moment. Stratton had the impression others were near the phone listening in.

'That's not good,' said Mike. 'I've just got off the phone with his missus assuring her you'd both soon show up. How'd it happen?'

'Long story. Not the time right now. Basically, we ran into Al-Shabaab. The important news right now is Shabaab have what we came looking for. Dozens of them. And they're going international. Soon as you can get me on to a navy ship, I'll get you the details. But we have to move fast on this end. It's a big campaign. There could be dozens of the things all over the world already, or heading that way. The guy we came to interview in Yemen, he's one of the main players.'

'Right,' said Mike, his mind a whir. 'Let me pass all that

on to Ops and I'll get back to you. The priority is getting you on to one of our boats.'

'Roger that.'

'It's good to have you back, Stratton. This might sound odd, but, well, if anything ever happened to you, I'd start to think we might actually be losing.'

'You're not coming out of the closet, are you, Mike? Not that there's anything wrong with that, but—'

'Bollocks. Talk to you later.'

The line went dead. Stratton realised he was smiling and immediately wiped it away. He had no right to enjoy himself whatsoever.

He looked at the chart table to study the ship's track neatly inside the GOA transit corridor and heading north into the Red Sea towards Suez.

He suddenly felt exhausted. The thought of lying down was alluring. But that dogged soldier in him resisted, for no particular reason. It felt like he was in the middle of some kind of desperate battle and he didn't want to take the chance of going unconscious. But he decided to loosen up a little and grab some sleep while he had the time. While things stayed quiet because they could kick off again as soon as the nearest naval ship arrived. And it wouldn't be that far away. The Navy would know where the *Orion* was now. They knew where every vessel in the corridor was. The *Orion*'s captain would have registered with the UK Maritime Trade Operations office before arriving in the Gulf and again the moment he had made contact with the pirates.

Stratton went to the bridge door and opened it. The girl stood outside the communications shack looking up at him.

'Can I use the phone?' she said.

'Sure,' he said, stepping aside.

'All OK?' she asked as she walked in.

Stratton thought she looked more exhausted than he had seen her look before. 'Yes. I'm going to get my head down.'

'You deserve it,' she said.

'You need a hand with that?' He gestured at the radio equipment.

'I'm fine,' she said, picking up the handset.

'Catch you later.'

'Hey.'

Stratton paused in the doorway to look back at her.

'Thanks. For everything. You're an unusual man . . . that's as in great.'

'Needs must, that's all.'

'And all the rest,' she said.

Stratton closed the door and headed down the stairs.

When he got to the bottom, he found two of the private security lads hanging around in the corridor outside the galley.

'Anything I can do for you, sir?' one of them asked.

'You could steer me towards a bunk, if that's OK. Anything will do.'

'No probs,' the young man said. 'Name's Andy.'

'Good to meet you.'

'This is Spike.'

Stratton nodded a hello.

'Follow me,' Andy said.

He briskly led the way back up the stairs to the first floor and along a short corridor. He opened a door and stepped back to allow Stratton entry. The small space looked homely. The bed had been freshly made and a man's personal effects, including several pictures of the same woman in sexy clothing, adorned a mirror and built-in dresser.

'You sure this is OK?' Stratton asked.

'He volunteered it, sir. No probs.'

Stratton nodded as his eyes fell on the clean white sheets of the narrow cot. It was calling to him.

'Shower and heads are in there,' the security lad said, pointing to a slender door in the corner. ''Elp yourself to anything – shampoo, the lot. He'll have some spare clean overalls in that cupboard you can use.'

'That's very kind. Thank him for me please.'

'I will. You have a good kip, sir. You need anything else, just ask for Andy and I'll sort you out.'

Andy closed the door, a smirk on his face, Spike at the top of the steps looking at him. 'Does the first officer know you've put 'im in 'is room?'

Andy stepped over with a conspiratorial grin. 'No, but he's a wanker anyway. And SAS-man needs it more than 'e does.'

'Nice one,' Spike said, chuckling.

'What's he gonna do? Kick the SAS out of bed?'

The two men laughed heartily as they descended.

Stratton looked in on the coffin-sized shower room and turned on the water. Within seconds steam filled the room.

He pulled off all of his damp clothes and immersed himself in the hot water. The wound on his back stung a little. Several minutes later he pulled on a clean pair of overalls he had found in the cupboard.

He looked down on the bed. On the one hand he wanted to fall on to it. On the other he felt like he should be doing something to speed up the next phase of the operation. Someone had to go back into Somalia and sort out those missiles. Bombing them was his first thought. But it wouldn't be clinical enough. They had to be sure the weapons got destroyed.

He felt his eyes growing heavy. He lay down on the bed. Within seconds of closing his eyes, he fell into a deep sleep.

16

He walked in a dark and distant place, wandering through black, cold-looking hills but finding sanctuary among the gloom. Rain had soaked his straggly hair, his unshaven face. He pulled the thick coat he wore about him. He could hear a distant banging. It just kept on and on. Reached right into his subconscious. It began to irritate him and he looked back over his shoulder at the clouds rolling towards him. He stopped and turned to face them, certain he could see a figure hidden within their broiling plumes. Stratton controlled his fear, as always, and turned it into aggressive calculation. He took his hands from the deep pockets of the trench coat and squared up to the oncoming mystery.

As the cloud came on, a figure inside revealed itself. It was black, from head to toe, a man, his shiny skin taut, his head bald, his limbs and torso powerful. In his raised hand a whip several metres long. Lotto the pirate commander bore down on the operative, menace in his eyes. The whip lashed in the air. Stratton stood his ground, clenched his fists and teeth, eyes darting in search of an advantage. He could see none to hand.

He took a step forward. Lotto, who was twice as tall as him now, reached out a powerful hand to grab him and lifted the whip to strike him. As the commander's large hand touched Stratton, he awoke and sat bolt upright in his bed, his face sweating, his eyes wide.

'Sorry, mate.' It was Andy, the security guard. He had shaken Stratton and then jumped back as the operative reacted. 'I was banging at the door for ages but you didn't answer.'

Stratton stared at him as he came out of the dream, breathing harder than a waking man should.

'There's someone here to see you,' Andy said.

Stratton put the dream out of his mind, dropped his feet to the floor and ran his fingers through his hair as he got up.

'What time is it?' he asked, seeing the daylight through the porthole and wondering how long he had been asleep.

'It's just gone four. In the afternoon. You were dead to the world. You must've been knackered.'

Stratton still felt exhausted. A sound permeated the cotton wool that seemed to fill his head. 'Is that a chopper?' he said, looking to the porthole but not seeing anything but ocean.

'Yeah. Royal Navy. They've come for you.'

Stratton understood. He needed to get going. Still in a bit of a daze, he looked around like he knew he had something to put on but he wasn't sure what.

'Did you want any of those clothes back you had? They were pretty manky.'

Stratton shook his head and looked down at his bare feet. That's what was missing.

'You want some sandals?' Andy said, indicating a new leather pair beside the bed. 'The first officer won't mind. He said you could 'elp yourself to anything. He's a good lad.'

Stratton tried on the sandals. They were a perfect fit.

He went to the door and into the corridor. Andy stepped out behind him. 'They're waiting for you in the galley,' he said.

'Has the girl surfaced?' Stratton asked as he reached the stairs.

'She left a few hours ago.'

Stratton stopped and looked at the guard, wearing a puzzled expression. 'What do you mean?'

'She took a lifeboat.'

'I don't understand.'

Andy stood there.

'You dropped her off back in the middle of the Gulf of Aden?'

'It wasn't quite like that,' Andy countered. 'She was pretty knackered, more so than you were. She asked about you and we said you'd got your head down. I offered her a room but she said she wanted to look about the ship. The outside part. Then she asked about the lifeboats and how they were launched. Then we 'ad something to eat. She was quite hungry. Then she went for a walk on deck. She must've spent a bit of time loading the boat up with food and water. Next thing we realised, the boat was gone and so was she.'

'She lowered a lifeboat on her own without you knowing about it?'

Andy looked like he had been cornered. 'Not quite. You said she was Chinese government. We took it she was working with our side, because of you. So we let her pretty much do what she wanted. Plus she was very nice.'

'How'd she lower the boat on her own and cast off?'

'Well, it wasn't exactly on her own. I 'elped her,' Andy said, looking embarrassed. 'Are you saying we shouldn't have 'elped her?'

Stratton wondered if he was being serious. 'Where was she going?'

'I asked her that. She said she was going to RV with a Chinese ship. I asked her how she was going to RV with it without any comms. She didn't have a radio or anything. She then looked me in the eye, a bit fearsome like, and said she had unfinished business. I was in an awkward situation. I couldn't come and get you. She'd've been gone by then anyway. So I thought, Bollocks, she's a government operative, even though Chinese, and working with our side. So there you 'ave it. I 'elped her lower the boat.'

Stratton thought hard about the information, his immediate concern whether she could compromise his side's intentions, based on their respective goals. As far as he had understood her goals, he could see no real issues, no massive ones anyway. The two governments might clash on how they would handle the situation. The Chinese would be less concerned about human rights and international protocols. The UK might be sensitive to China's embarrassment at letting the weapons slip through their hands in the first place. Ultimately the two countries wanted the same thing, which was to put a stop to the use of the missiles. The two countries would go about that in different ways, but Stratton couldn't see anything to panic about.

The fact was she was gone and he could do nothing about it. He wondered where she was headed. If she'd loaded up with food and water, it wouldn't be to RV with any nearby Chinese naval vessel. And if she wanted to get to somewhere in the West, her best bet would have been to stay with the bulker, especially since she had no money and no identification.

So maybe she had gone back to Somalia. The comment about unfinished business could suggest that much.

The girl was without doubt ballsy. Stratton could only wonder what was driving her. Whatever, it was far beyond the call of duty, particularly after what she had been through. Maybe she wanted revenge. It seemed extreme to him, but he wasn't a woman. 'Did she have enough fuel to cover a hundred and fifty miles?'

'No,' the guard replied. 'But the boat's got a good sail system.'

She could get back to the Somali coast. But she would have to make her way to the village without being challenged. 'Did she take a weapon?'

'No,' Andy said with confidence. 'We've only got the five AKs on board and she wouldn't get her hands on one of them even if she took a turn for the lads.' Andy smiled at the crude quip but lost it when Stratton did not respond.

Despite the girl's motives, her actions didn't seem sensible ones to Stratton. And she never came across as stupid. The only other motive for her leaving the ship that he could think of was fear. But of what, he had no idea. Fear of failure perhaps. Fear of returning to her bosses without having completed her mission, whatever that was. He thought she'd done enough to be given a medal. Perhaps it was the fear of being questioned by the British. That might not go down well with her leaders. The Chinese Secret Service was clearly a strict outfit.

Stratton wished he'd had a moment to say farewell to her. He had grown to like her. He certainly respected her. She weighed nothing and was as hard as some of the toughest men he had known. He wished her well, whatever she was doing. He trotted down the steps to the main deck level. Through the open door he glimpsed a navy helicopter thundering by, a sleek, grey Lynx, the fastest chopper in the world and it looked like the pilot was putting it through its paces.

Stratton stepped into the galley.

Two young, intelligent-looking men in smartly pressed camouflaged fatigues stood talking. Stratton didn't know either of them. They stopped talking and faced the operative. They looked at him respectfully.

'Jasper Howel,' the shorter, blond-haired man said, holding out a hand with a smile. 'Lieutenant,' he added, without sounding superior.

'Hi,' Stratton replied, shaking his hand.

'Lieutenant Blythe,' the other man said.

Stratton shook his hand too.

'We've come to take you to HMS *Ocean*,' Howel said.

Just as Stratton had expected.

'You ready to go?' Blythe asked.

'Sure,' Stratton said.

Blythe put a radio to his mouth and pressed the send button. 'Sierra, this is hard stand. We're ready to depart.'

'Sierra, roger,' a voice boomed back.

Stratton followed Howel out of the galley and on to the main deck. The sun glowed low above the horizon and the wind had picked up.

Bob and the rest of his security retinue had gathered on deck. He stepped forward and offered his hand. 'It was good to meet you, Mr Stratton.'

Stratton looked him in the eye. 'Thanks for everything,' he said, shaking Bob's hand firmly. The look he gave Bob was a sincere appreciation for taking on the pirates. Bob, his men and the ship had saved Stratton's life and the operative didn't take that lightly.

Bob nodded, more than proud of his actions that day. He would dine out on the story, no doubt for the rest of his life. He had seen action, and he had rescued a British SAS man to boot.

'I sometimes go through Hereford. Perhaps we'll bump into each other one day and have a pint,' Bob ventured with a wink.

'Perhaps,' Stratton said. 'You take care,' he added.

The Lynx came into a hover by the side of the bulker

and held its position alongside. Blythe hurried along the deck to meet it.

The security guards held out their hands for Stratton as he passed. He shook each one of them before heading for the helicopter.

'You'd have more chance meeting him for a pint in Poole than Hereford,' Howel said to Bob in a low voice, before following Stratton.

'Bloody 'ell,' Bob said. 'Of course.'

'What's that?' one of the guys asked a vexed-looking Bob.

'Poole. He's not SAS. He's SBS,' Bob said. 'Bollocks. I should've known. The SAS can't swim.'

Stratton climbed the rails and stepped across into the thudding chopper. Howel followed close behind and as the men took their seats inside the cabin it peeled off and headed away low over the water.

Bob and the crew watched it disappear into the sunset. Stratton was living most of their fantasies.

'I suppose you've been on board the *Ocean* before?' Howel asked Stratton loudly over the noise of the engines. 'The SBS have used it a lot over the years as an operations platform.'

'I've been on board a few times before,' Stratton said. He hadn't been aboard it for several years, the last time off the coast of West Africa when he spent almost a week on it before a land operation.

The flight took less than half an hour but in that time the sun dropped beyond the horizon. The *Ocean* looked very much like a traditional aircraft carrier but it was a quarter of the size of the American supercarriers. Its island tower superstructure sat in the centre shoved over to one side to allow as much flat runway space as possible. A strobe light near the back end of the flight deck signalled the helicopter's landing point. Stratton could make out half a dozen large helicopters in a line along the deck.

He stared at the carrier through the window. Memories of his time spent on board it flooded back. They hadn't been particularly interesting ones. Life on a navy ship could be staid, especially when there were adventures to be had elsewhere in the world. He remembered the time the squadron had been waiting for some low-life criminals deep in the jungle along the Sierra Leone–Liberia border to negotiate the release of some British aid workers they had kidnapped. For some reason the kidnappers hadn't made contact on the satellite phone they'd been given. A couple of less experienced members of the operations HQ supposed the criminals would be conscious of having their positions vectored as soon as they turned on the phone. Others, like Stratton, put their money on the idiots not being able to figure out how to use it. It turned out he was right but for the wrong reasons. Whoever had organised the phone hadn't activated the pay-as-you-go sim card before sending it to the kidnappers. The card had been included in the package but the gangsters didn't know its relevance. And so the operation dragged on for another week before

Stratton and his team were allowed to swim ashore one night and move upriver until they found a position to lie up. They spent the following day watching the riverbank, where fresh human tracks came down to the water's edge. Sure enough, a couple of gang members eventually turned up to collect water.

Stratton and his team tracked them back to their camp where it all ended bloodily for the rest of the gang, but that had been the intention of the message – we don't pay ransoms but that doesn't mean we don't play the game. Stratton hadn't gone back to the ship but took a helicopter to Sierra Leone and a flight back to the UK.

He'd hoped he might not see the *Ocean* again but it looked like he was destined to spend a little more time on it after all.

The helicopter approached the rear of the flight deck like it was a fixed-wing aircraft, the narrow superstructure ahead and to the right, lit up like a dull Christmas tree, red, white and green. The wind had picked up even more after the sun went down and the little craft buffeted as it came into the hover above the deck. It landed with a heavy bump, the ship coming up to meet it. As soon as they touched down the engine pitch changed and figures headed out of the shadows towards it. One of them pulled open the door.

Howel stepped out and waited for Stratton to follow him. 'We're to go straight to the operations room,' the young lieutenant said.

On deck a tall, thin, hawkish-looking officer in a

camouflaged windproof eyed Stratton with a level of curiosity that bordered on suspicion.

'Lieutenant Winslow,' Howel said by way of introduction.

Winslow nodded, keeping his hands behind his back.

Stratton didn't dwell on it, used to the negative attitude from some members of the military. He knew all about how being special forces polarised opinion. People either held you in extremely high regard – more than you generally deserved – or considered you overrated.

Howel led the way through an open steel door into a red-lit corridor and up a flight of steps. Winslow followed. At the top another secure door that required a code-entry to unlock. Jasper tapped in the pass code and led them into a dimly lit operations room filled with a variety of humming electronic communications and technological equipment operated by several sailors. None of them took much notice of Stratton save a glance as he walked through in his boiler suit and sandals.

Winslow went ahead and opened a door into a small, gloomy communications shack packed with equipment like a compressed sound studio. A Wren, wearing a pair of headphones, sat concentrating on a complex-looking switchboard. When she saw the officer and the dishevelled man in the boiler suit, she got to her feet like she had been expecting them. She smiled politely and handed Winslow her headset and left the room.

'Your operations officer is on the other end of that,' Winslow said.

Stratton put on the headset and adjusted the microphone

in front of his lips. Winslow stood in the doorway and Stratton took the opportunity to return the man's cold glare. 'Close the door behind you,' Stratton said, deliberately omitting the words 'please' and 'sir'.

Winslow wasn't used to any level of insubordination and had it been any other subordinate in Her Majesty's armed forces he would have reminded them of their respective ranks. But at that particular moment he knew it was a conflict he would not win. He might have contempt for the man but the Royal Navy did not. He clenched his teeth and closed the door.

Stratton spent almost an hour inside the room talking to the SBS operations team in Poole over the secure communications system. He explained everything that had happened, in the finest of detail, leaving nothing out. As he had expected, they didn't react to his description of Hopper's death. He tried to be as clinical as possible, and if he had been describing someone else who had killed Hopper, he might have managed it. But the hints of his culpability and responsibility for what had happened seeped into the report. The ops team remained coldly automatic with their questions.

When Stratton finally put down his headset and opened the door into the operations room, the occupants spared him a glance or two, as though in his absence they had been told who he was. To him it looked like they had all heard his story, or, more to the point, his confession. That was impossible of course. No one on the planet but him and the ops team had been privy to that conversation. They were merely curious about the individual who had arrived on the boat from out of nowhere.

Stratton walked from the operations room back down the steps and outside for some fresh air. He'd forgotten how stale the ship's filtered air could taste in confined places like the operations room with all its heated circuitry and sweaty personnel.

He walked to the rails to look at the ocean and clear his head.

A matelot stood nearby having a smoke. He ditched the cigarette over the side when he saw Stratton. 'S'cuse me, sir,' he said.

'I'm not a sir,' Stratton replied without looking at him.

'Sorry. I'm s'posed to show you where to bunk.'

Stratton hoped they had given him a room to himself.

'The old man wanted to have a word but they thought you might be knackered and want to get your 'ead down first.'

Stratton still felt tired despite the few hours' sleep he had grabbed on the cargo ship. He expected it would take another day to recover fully.

'I'm to ask you if you need the sickbay for anything.'

Stratton thought about having his bullet wounds looked at. But he hadn't even thought about them since waking up on the *Orion*. The many hours he had spent in the sea should have cleaned them up but that didn't necessarily mean they would not get infected. 'I'm fine,' he decided. He knew where the sick bay was and if they started to become painful again, he would pay the place a visit.

Stratton followed the young man through the ship, down a narrow set of stairs to a wider, well-lit corridor. Part of the way along it he saw a pair of swing doors. Stratton remembered it was the galley and pushed one of them open. The place had been crammed with more chairs and tables than it was designed for.

'If you want a wet, you can 'elp yourself over there,' the sailor said, pointing to a counter with an urn on it. 'Your bunk room's down the end of this corridor. Number fourteen. Last door on the left.'

'Thanks,' Stratton said, aware of the man's eagerness to complete his duties.

'OK. I'm off watch so I'm going to get my 'ead down.'

'Have a good night,' Stratton said with a smile. He walked over to the urn and made himself a cup of tea. He heard the sound of aluminium trays being stacked somewhere beyond. A cook walked out of the back and placed a tray of food in one of the slots behind the counter.

As he sipped his drink, the main door opened and Stratton turned around to see Winslow looking at him.

The officer walked over to the table. 'Mind if I make a brew?' he asked. His tone had changed to light and chatty.

'Help yourself,' Stratton said.

As he was about to walk away, Winslow said, 'Do you live in Poole?'

Stratton didn't particularly want to talk to the man about anything but saw no reason to be rude.

'Just outside.'

'I haven't been there in several years,' Winslow said. 'I

expect it's changed quite a lot in that time. Quite a popular summer retreat for some.'

'Most of the locals wish it wasn't so popular,' Stratton replied, waiting for an opportunity to end the little chat and leave.

'Is there a Sergeant Downs still there?' said Winslow.

'Colour Sergeant Downs?' said Stratton. 'He might even be Warrant Officer by now. But I haven't seen him in a while.'

'He's a right son of a bitch. I didn't know him socially of course.'

Stratton wondered where the conversation was going with an introduction like that. 'Downs is a good lad,' he said. 'I know him quite well.' Stratton remained matter-of-fact. It didn't offend him if someone didn't like a friend of his.

'You probably don't know him the same way I do,' said Winslow, giving Stratton a sideways look.

Stratton sipped his tea, barely interested in the man or his dislike of Downs. Winslow went on: 'In fact he was a right bastard. He was in charge of the SBS phase of the selection.'

Stratton suddenly had a good idea where this was all going. It wasn't the first time he'd been cornered by someone outside of the service who had failed the selection course and felt they needed to explain it to him.

'He had it in for me from the start,' Winslow said. 'I think the moment he set eyes on me, he decided he was going to get me off the course. I'd done rather well during the combined SAS–SBS land phases. I'm a good map reader and was very fit. The map marches with the heavy packs were no problem for me. I passed all of that but when I got to Poole, Downs didn't like me, that was for sure.'

'He's not that sort of bloke,' Stratton said, not particularly wanting to get involved but deciding to stick up for his friend. He knew Downs to be not the kind to pick on someone for no reason.

'As I said, you probably wouldn't know him from my point of view. Let's put it this way, if he had been running your selection and had taken a dislike to you, you wouldn't have passed your course either.'

Stratton decided the officer was an arrogant prick. But Downs wouldn't have taken him off the course for being that way either. It was typical of many who had failed special forces selection to blame it on something or someone and not themselves. There were many valid cases. Injury often put people out. But at the end of the day, if you failed, for whatever reason, deal with it. Stratton wanted to ask why he hadn't gone back and done another course. Some members of the SBS and SAS had made more than one attempt before succeeding. But he wasn't interested in the man or his issues enough to ask.

Stratton took a long sip of his tea and put the mug down. 'The job doesn't suit everybody,' he said. 'Maybe you wouldn't have enjoyed it.' And if you had got through, he thought, you wouldn't have got along with anyone in the service with the attitude you have.

'I'm going to get my head down,' he said, walking away.

The officer watched him go. Stratton could feel the man's eyes on his back.

He pushed through the doors and went in search of his pit.

Winslow stirred his cup of tea then he put the spoon down, poured the liquid into a bin and sighed to himself. It was easy for those who had made it into special forces to write off those who hadn't. But the truth was many who failed were mentally scarred for life. Which was a risk few allowed for. There was the odd one who did attempt it knowing they would fail but wanted to give it a go anyway. But the vast majority of those who signed up for the gruelling course never planned on failing it. They had to believe in themselves. Winslow considered himself highly intelligent but he couldn't grasp what was obvious to those maybe less intelligent than he was. He knew that to dwell on his failure would be unhealthy and nothing could be done to heal him other than trying the course again and passing it. But that window of opportunity had closed for him. He had moved up in rank and he could no longer apply. He knew he should let it go, but he couldn't.

It was early morning when Stratton got prodded by a hand. 'Time to get up, mate.'

He woke instantly in the narrow bunk, recognising the young sailor who had shown him to the galley the night before.

'I brought you a cup of tea,' the sailor said, holding out

a steaming mug. 'I'm not a creep. But I reckon you deserve it.' He grinned.

Stratton rubbed his face and swung his feet down on to the floor and took the mug. 'Thanks.'

''Ope you like it sweet. I do.'

Stratton took a sip of the dark molasses that looked like it could absorb a pint of milk without getting any lighter in colour. He did all he could not to wince. 'You sure it's tea?'

'Tell you the truth, I made it for myself but decided to give it to you when they told me to give you a shake.'

Stratton handed it back to him. 'I'm wide awake now, thanks.'

'It does that to you.'

Stratton stood up, still in his boiler suit. There were several other bunks in the room, all occupied. He checked his wrist, forgetting he had no watch. 'What time is it?'

'Just gone eight. You slept well.'

'I need a doby. Where can I get a towel and a change of clothes?'

'I'll see the chief. Oh, I almost forgot the most important thing. The old man wants to see you up on deck.'

Stratton looked at the mug, took it off the sailor and had another sip. He shook his head as he tasted the strong tea and handed it back. 'I really don't think I could get used to that,' he said.

Stratton made his way through the boat and up a couple of flights of steps to a level where he could see daylight flooding in through the far end of the corridor.

He walked through a broad opening and on to a platform a flight above the main deck. The wind struck him as he stepped through the entrance and he braced himself against it, almost losing one of his sandals as he stepped back. The opening gave him a balcony view of the flight deck.

Six Sea King helicopters stood lined up in a neat row on the far side of the deck, their noses pointing forward, rotors folded back to form a single blade pointing towards the tail, where they were secured by a strap. The Lynx waited at the far end of the flight deck, where it had landed the evening before.

Crew emerged from the superstructure beneath Stratton and divided up on their way to all of the Sea Kings. They set about untying the rotors and making other preparations for flight. He searched the various clusters of men and individuals along the length of the deck for one who looked like he might be the captain. He saw two men standing at the front of the flight deck looking forward out to sea, one of whom fitted the description.

Stratton climbed down a ladder on to the flight deck. The wind whipped at him as he walked past the end of the superstructure and across the exposed deck.

The younger of the two men saw him and said something to the other. The older man looked around at Stratton as he approached. His cropped silver hair made him look older than he was.

The younger man gave Stratton an officious nod before heading away. Stratton wondered what the captain was going to be like. Everyone on board looked well turned out and he was walking around in a boiler suit with straggly hair and several days' worth of beard. No wonder he seemed alien to the regular military. He had spent so many years in SF and working with military intelligence that if he ever had to join the regulars for some reason, he doubted he would last a week before being court martialled for any one of a number of insubordinations. The service could be pretty laid back compared with the Navy and Marines, but it still had enough stuffed shirts within its ranks to make life difficult for field operatives when they spent any time back at the HQ camp.

The captain turned to greet him with a smile that was echoed in his eyes.

'Good to meet you, Stratton. I understand everyone calls you by your last name.'

Stratton politely shrugged indifference. 'Good to meet you too, sir.'

The captain looked him up and down. 'I see you've not had a chance to get some duds, or is it that you prefer the scruffy look?'

'One of the lads is finding me a razor and something to wear, sir.'

'Personally I envy you being able to wear what you want. When I go on leave I don't normally have a shave until the day I return to work. My wife likes that too. I don't think anyone would deny you your rest after what you've been through.' The captain checked his watch and looked in the direction his ship was sailing. 'I'm sorry about your friend.'

Stratton didn't answer. The captain had obviously been briefed by Poole or London. There hadn't been any hint of judgement in the way he said it. That was because it was unlikely he knew all the details. He wouldn't have been told anything other than the basic facts. He certainly wouldn't know that Stratton had killed his colleague. That kind of information would be kept in house, for a while at least. It would eventually leak out from Ops and into the ranks of the SBS. London could also be a bit of a sieve for that kind of gossip. So it would find its way into the general information mainstream, through wives and bar talk. It wouldn't be classified as secret, just sensitive. Everyone gossiped. Special forces and military intelligence were no different. It was a piece of information that ultimately did no harm if it was leaked. Helen, Hopper's wife, might be upset by it. She might understand when she heard the full details. But she would not be pleased if she discovered that Stratton was ultimately responsible for her husband's death. That the strategies he had employed were flawed. Self-seeking. That would leak out too. Eventually. She might wonder if it was a twisted rumour at first. If so, she might ask Stratton to clarify that himself. He would tell the truth. He didn't know her well enough to guess how she might react. He did know if she had a temper, she might hit him. He would have to take it. He would want to take it. Hopper's two children would eventually learn about it too. One day. They had all of that to come.

So the captain would eventually learn the whole story. He might reflect on their meeting. Stratton wondered how the old man would judge him. For the moment, at least, he would remain ignorant.

'You'll have a chance to avenge him,' the captain said.

Stratton wondered what he meant. It could have been a general 'you', as in the service. Or he might have meant Stratton personally. The captain had clearly been told about an operation of some kind.

'Scopus inbound one minute,' a voice boomed over the ship's loudspeaker system.

'That's your boys,' the skipper said.

Stratton looked in the direction the captain was gazing. The skies were cloudy but they were thin, streaky and very high. Typical for altostratus formations.

A helicopter started up. Stratton looked around to see the rotors beginning to turn on the nearest Sea King, several crew members climbing on board. Other Sea Kings came to life down the line.

'There they are,' the captain said above the growing high-pitched sound of engines.

The old man was looking skyward. Stratton followed his gaze to see a small, distant cluster of black. It wasn't long before it separated into three aircraft. As they drew closer they became large cargo carriers, too big to land on the ship. That could only mean one thing. They were going to drop something. And the Sea Kings would collect the delivery.

Before long all but one of the Sea Kings had started its engines. Stratton thought about asking the captain to elaborate but decided not to. He would find out in good time.

As the three aircraft got closer Stratton decided they were C-130s, flying at around a thousand feet. The sound of the helicopter engines increased. The turbulence from the rotors reversed the direction of the wind that had been blowing in the men's faces and whipped at the backs of their clothing.

The transport aircraft lost height as they passed down the length of the ship a kilometre away in a staggered formation. All had their tailgates open.

The lead Sea King lifted off the deck, turned its tail towards the superstructure, lowered its nose and moved away from the ship. The next craft carried out the same manoeuvre and the others followed in turn.

As the helicopters flew in a broad arc around the front of the vessel the sound of their engines and throbbing rotors decreased enough for the jet propellers that powered the fixed-wing cargos to be heard in the distance.

Stratton and the captain watched as the Hercules turned far beyond the stern of the ship before straightening up on a heading that would bring them down the port side. The two men stepped across to that side of the ship where they could see the drop take place.

All three aircraft had lost yet more height and were coming at the ship barely a few hundred metres above the grey, choppy waters.

When the lead cargo plane had got close enough to make out the pilots in the cockpit, a large parachute deployed from the back, which in turn dragged out a bundle the size of a small car. Closely followed by another and then a dozen more.

Seconds after each chute fully deployed the bundle swung down and hit the water with a foaming crash.

The following aircraft released a similar load in a line alongside the first. The last aircraft roared by a little further out to sea but just as low. As before, the first thing they saw appear out of the rear tailgate was a parachute, smaller than those attached to the other bundles. But this time, on the end of each, dangled a man. Over forty individual chutes, the first man hitting the water barely seconds after he had deployed and long before the last chute had exited.

The sound of other powerful engines came from below as several launches sped from the *Ocean* in the direction of the drop.

Stratton wondered what the bundles contained. He assumed the squadron would be heading into Somalia and he considered how he might carry out an operation like that based on everything he had reported about the target location. Which would have to be the jihadists' camp because that's where the missiles were. If you were going to assault the camp, you couldn't use helicopters. Not without pinging up on their radar. Choppers could be used to drop off teams far from the camp that would then have to yomp in. But that would take time and they'd risk being seen before they hit the camp.

As he thought about why they had chosen to mount the operation from the carrier, an option came to mind. He smiled to himself at the thought that Ops could have given the OK to such an audacious plan. He hoped it would be true. Something like that the SBS had never done operationally, to his knowledge. In fact, he didn't know any military outfit that had. He'd heard a story about the Israelis attempting something like it years before on a long-range desert assault. Whatever, you'd be well advised to try it only against a less sophisticated enemy. Like the Somalis.

He found himself suddenly looking forward to seeing if it might be true. And more importantly, if the plan included him in it. Because there was a chance it might not. But it would make sense to take him along because he knew the ground better than anyone else. That wouldn't guarantee him a seat but it had to go a long way towards helping. He felt glad he hadn't gone to the ship's hospital to have his wounds checked.

As soon as the transporters had dispensed their loads, their tailgates closed and they continued on into the distance, heading back to England no doubt, Stratton thought.

The Sea Kings roared around the sides of the ship low to the water, dividing up to collect the men and bundles, assisted by the launches.

'An adventurous scheme to say the least,' the captain said.

Stratton suspected that he might be toying with him. The old man would know that Stratton couldn't have been privy to any operational details as yet since his only communication with his people had been the night before when he gave his verbal report – and there was no way a plan had been hatched in that time.

'Sorry,' the captain said shortly after. It was a half-hearted attempt at admitting he was well aware he had Stratton at a disadvantage. 'I'm at liberty to tell you that your chaps are going to invade Somalia using powered hang-gliders.'

Stratton smiled once again. He had been right.

'I don't believe we've ever done anything quite like it before. What do you think?'

'I think it's a great idea,' said Stratton.

'I suppose you'd like to go with them?'

Stratton remained poker-faced, wondering if the captain was always such a baiter. Perhaps this time he wasn't playing games. Stratton decided not to answer.

'I hope you do,' the captain said. 'You're to attend the briefing.'

Stratton glanced at the man, who gave him a mischievous look in return. They had only just met but the captain appeared to have read the operative's character from the start and got his measure. Stratton couldn't help producing the thinnest of smiles that echoed the captain's.

'I'd better go and sort out my ship,' the captain said. 'You'll be taking off shortly after last light. Good luck,' he said as he started to walk away but stopped when he saw something on Stratton's back. 'Is that blood?' he asked.

Stratton hadn't been aware his wound was bleeding although it had started throbbing slightly after he climbed down the ladder. 'If it is, it's not mine,' he lied, looking the captain in the eye.

The captain nodded but Stratton could see in his eyes he was unconvinced.

Stratton watched him go and turned his attention to the first of the launches that was returning fully laden with men and equipment.

He looked to the horizon, towards Somalia. The *Ocean* was some fifty miles from the coastline but he could see the place well enough in his mind's eye, in particular the jihadist camp. He could see Sabarak, his features clear, his cold, hate-filled expression as he stared back at Stratton.

Stratton saw himself put a gun to the man's heart and, with cold relish, pull the trigger. He could only pray that his wish would come true.

17

Stratton stood on one of the small landings of the superstructure to watch the lads and their equipment arrive. Half the ship's crew had turned out to watch the spectacle, many of them young lads who hadn't seen special forces operatives before. In the past, HMS *Ocean* had entertained such personalities quite regularly, mostly for exercises and the occasional operation, such as Stratton's adventure in West Africa. But since the conflicts in Afghanistan and Iraq, there had been precious little time for playing war games, especially at sea. These days special forces spent practically all of their time doing the real thing.

There was the usual banter from the men as they mustered on deck in groups, small and large. Bursts of laughter regularly broke out, which was the norm. The occasional loudmouth could be heard above all others. Stratton enjoyed the men's company but his current position, watching them from a distance, proved an illustration of what it was truly like for him. He felt like he was on the outside looking in. It had always been that way. He had his close friends, but not many. It had been like that for him at school, as far back as he could remember. He had friends he would die for. Many of them were standing before him, with a good number of others spread about the world, and not all of them in the SBS. But that wasn't the same thing. It was bizarre that few of those he would truly risk his life for, and without hesitation, numbered among his close friends. It was a unique relationship for those who fought side by side in the face of death.

None of the men had noticed him, tucked against a bulkhead in the shadows. Which was the way he liked it, content to hang on to his privacy for a while longer.

He had another reason for holding back from greeting and mingling with them of course. Hopper. The man had been popular among the lads. He would have been down there laughing and cavorting among them already. He would have been waiting for the first lot to touch down on deck to greet them in his gregarious manner. He was never like that with Stratton, though. It was like he knew not to be, even though Stratton had never sent any kind of message of dissuasion. Stratton didn't mind boisterousness, but no one had acted that way with him in many years.

The last helicopter thudded down and a handful of the lads climbed out of it and headed over to the main group. He recognised the last man to step off the chopper. It was Downs. Stratton wondered if he was in charge of this crowd. He was certainly senior enough to be. There would be officers present but the key man of a squadron would usually be the sergeant major. He would take charge of the groundwork for the operation.

One of the young SBS faces walked up to Downs for a talk. Stratton recognised him as Lieutenant Phelps. The team leaders reported to their sergeant major as he made his way across the flight deck with the officer. The lads quickly lined up to be mustered and checked off to ensure everyone who had boarded the aircraft at Brize Norton had actually arrived on board the ship.

Stratton looked down on a couple of the ship's officers as they walked out of the superstructure. It looked like Howel and Winslow.

Winslow headed towards Phelps and Downs, no doubt to welcome them aboard. Stratton expected the ship's operations officer to recognise Downs. It had been five or six years since his selection course, but as a senior course instructor, Downs would have been a focal point for every man on that course, a face that none would probably forget. Downs would have been the last SBS face the failed rankers would have seen because it was his job to explain to the individual why he was on his way back to his unit. The officers would have been given a final let-go by a senior SBS officer. But they would have known it was Downs who had cut the umbilical cord.

Winslow walked up to Downs to introduce himself. It seemed to Stratton that Downs didn't know who the man was beyond his present role. That was probably because on the selection course Downs would have been looking at dozens of faces and not one in particular.

Stratton knew Downs very well. He had joined the service a year before Stratton. They were of a similar age and quite often ended up in the same section together. The man was generally cheerful, confident and forward. Had he recognised

Winslow, there was little doubt he would have mentioned it right away.

Downs smiled broadly as he shook the officer's hand and, although Stratton couldn't hear Downs's voice, in his head he could hear the rich Irish accent asking the officer how he was. Winslow would have realised by then that Downs had forgotten their previous relationship. Or he might suspect Downs of deliberately pretending not to know him.

Stratton wondered if Winslow would mention their shared past right away or wait for an opportunity to corner Downs in the same way he had done to Stratton. The officer might be disappointed if he did. If Winslow pushed Downs too far, the Irishman would quickly become indignant and brush the man's failure aside as having been for the best.

Downs, Winslow and Phelps went into the superstructure and the bulk of the lads ambled inside after them.

Stratton would have liked to stay where he was for a while longer but the operational briefing would take place soon and he needed to attend it.

As he headed into the superstructure and down the stairs to the main road, he didn't see any lads he was familiar with. He passed a group of younger SBS men in the gangway but they didn't give him anything more than a respectful nod. Stratton was known to everyone, even those who hadn't actually seen him before. That renown, however, had got tagged with the usual rumours and exaggerations. Because SBS guys were human and subject to the same rules of gossip and hyperbole. He had indeed been on several interesting operations during his time in special forces and while in the employ of the British Secret Intelligence Services. But only a handful of people truly knew the operations he had been involved in, and hardly any of those people were among the ranks of the SBS. But a snippet of a story would be enough to encourage suppositions and assumptions, parts of which generally stuck as fact. Nobody ever asked Stratton to comment. No one would dare. It wasn't because of any fear of him. You simply never made enquiries about a secret operation or anyone who had been involved in it. You were limited to asking only those people who hadn't been directly involved.

The men had a couple of hours to sort out their equipment and grab a meal before the operational briefing. They all knew in outline why they had arrived in the Gulf of Aden. The briefing would deliver the finer points and last-minute details.

Stratton arrived at the crowded briefing room minutes before it started and stood at the back of the dimly lit space. All the men sat in tight rows facing the operations officer on his podium set to one side of a large screen that had maps and images of ground-to-air rockets on it. The young officer, Phelps, gave his orders in the usual manner, beginning with the ground, situation and then the meat of the mission itself. All straightforward enough: destroy the Chinese ground-to-air missiles. The secondary missions included rescuing any hostages and repatriating them. All of the execution phases had to be visually recorded using digital equipment. To satisfy the usual legalities. Ops had prepared a legitimate excuse to kill as many of the jihadists as they could. It was an indictment of the times, the need for an excuse. It had been presented as a necessary strategy. The bad guys could not be given the time or space to regroup and mount a counter-assault while the men were distracted by the second phase of the task, which was the pirate village on the coast and the kidnap victims. Etcetera, etcetera.

The secondary pirate assault phase was intended to be less bloody and represented the humanitarian side of the operation. Which was partially because it would be the main cover story. As far as the media were concerned, the operation would be reported as purely a hostage rescue task, with no mention of the jihadists. Because they needed to keep the whole portable ground-to-air missile story secret. The al-Qaeda-backed operation was an international one and they had many players who had to be reeled in. You couldn't do that with global publicity of the attack.

An interpreter had been attached to the operation, an army linguist from Aberdeen who, by his own admission, could speak just about enough Somali to order a haircut and a cup of coffee. Not quite the level of expertise the MoD had been told about him. Someone had been misinformed. But Ops didn't look overly concerned about this oversight. His skill level would suffice for what they needed – his job would be simply to warn any Somalis who weren't jihadists to put down their weapons or risk being harmed. The man insisted he was up to that much at least and looked eager to give lessons in short phrases to any of the lads who were interested.

The most recent stomping ground for this particular squadron had been Afghanistan. They had lost four men in the last two months with seven others seriously injured and they didn't want anything to happen to anyone else, especially on this unscheduled backwater task. Stratton understood that.

Before Afghanistan and Iraq had kicked off, a job like this would have been subject to a real rush of men wanting to take part in it. Operatives would have been tripping over each other to get their names on the list. It had the hallmarks of a cracking adventure. But these days such a task, be it a different one in a different part of the world, merely interfered with leave or other equally dangerous work.

When the teams got announced, Stratton felt pleased to hear he would partner Downs for the flight infiltration phase. The powered gliders were two-seaters and although Stratton had completed an initial pilot course, he hadn't accumulated enough hours, and certainly not in recent years, to qualify as an operational pilot. But then, according to Downs, few of the lads had logged many hours either. Lucky the machines weren't that difficult to fly, the operative reasoned. Once you got airborne, it was straightforward enough to keep them that way. Landing could be a bit tricky for the inexperienced. But as someone pointed out, once the craft had touched the ground, crashing it would be little different from falling off a speeding motorbike. A few of the men raised suspicious eyebrows at the claim but several of the lads had indeed crashed on training landings and all had walked away without serious injury.

Stratton understood he hadn't been teamed with Downs because they were old buddies. Downs was the assault operations commander and it made sense to have the man who knew the ground best alongside him. Stratton would be more than content to sit in the back seat anyway and let someone else take the stress of flying the damned thing.

Phelps dedicated the final part of the briefing to contingency planning and emergency rendezvous and communications and signals. As soon as he had finished, most of the lads went to various map tables in order to cross-check their notes and confirm the GPS coordinates thay had been given.

The group had been broken down into two separate assault components or serials. Each was little more than a regular company troop and would operate in the same manner once they had landed and had mustered. A little air activity was intended to precede the ground phase. That was the bit the guys were most jazzed about. It was very much out of the norm and more akin to a First World War battle scenario.

Stratton was about to head out of the room when Downs caught sight of him, called his name and indicated he wanted a word.

Downs spent a moment talking with the briefing officer and the team leaders. Stratton watched as Downs's closely cropped red-haired head turned to face each question as it came at him. The man always seemed to be wearing a smirk on his face, as though it were an effort to appear serious.

Stratton remembered their early days in the service together and how Downs had often been reprimanded by one senior or another for grinning at an inappropriate moment. It took years before it became generally accepted that the man wasn't being impudent and that he had a semi-permanent smirk.

Downs finally broke away and walked over to Stratton. Both their faces broke into broad grins as the gap between them closed. When they met it was with a firm, bear-hug embrace borne of years of friendship and mutual respect.

'Ha! Ya bastard,' Downs said in a low voice. 'How come you wait till now to greet me?'

'You're the main man,' said Stratton. 'You have big responsibilities. I wanted to see you when you had a moment. It's good to see you.'

'You too. So you survived another one. I thought you'd bought it this time. I was on the verge of takin' your house keys from the safe and going up to Lytchett to see what I could prof before anyone else could get there.'

'I know. My wardrobe. You've always envied my dress sense.'

Downs laughed heartily as he eyed Stratton's boiler suit. 'That's better than anything you've got in your bloody house.'

They roared again together.

'Sounds like a fun op,' Stratton said.

'I was disappointed you didn't have anything to add to it.'

'No need. You have it smack on. Arrive. Wipe the bastards out. Go home.'

Downs nodded, his usually constant smile losing its grip as he thought of something else. 'Sorry about Hopper.'

Stratton had managed to forget about the man for a moment.

'You don't need to explain to me, mate,' Downs said. 'Any decision you make in the field is good by me.'

'No one's perfect. Least of all me.'

'Well. Not the time or place. We need a quiet pub and a tenacious barkeep if we're going to analyse that one, along with a few dozen other mishaps over the years, to be sure.'

One of the men arrived and hovered close by, looking anxious to ask Downs something but not daring to interrupt his conversation with Stratton.

'You'll be wanting some kit,' Downs said to Stratton, looking him up and down. 'Unless you're going in as an undercover shithouse cleaner. There's loads of spares in the stores. There's a bag with your name on it too,' he added with a wink. 'Scran's in twenty minutes. If I don't see you there, I'll see you on deck.'

Downs faced the young operator and Stratton stepped out of the room. He went to where the SBS stores had been assembled and set about selecting some kit for himself. All of the men had been wearing lightweight desert camouflage fatigues. Stratton supposed it was appropriate enough. But he felt it would be better suited to daytime operations. This task was timed to start by last light and be over by dawn. The best colour at night was black, anywhere in the world.

Stratton opened a large plastic container to reveal bundles

of combat clothing. Near the bottom he saw a pile of black outfits. He checked the sizes and pulled out a shirt. A pair of trousers quickly followed. He dug out some black jungle boots and socks and within a short while he was fully dressed.

A webbing box contained a belt and weapons harness with a variety of pouches attached. He laid out the belt so that the pouches were in a row and looked at the various weapons boxes in order to fill them.

Inside the first one was a box labelled 'STRATTON', courtesy of Downs. He opened it to find some of his favourite items, including a watch, a GPS and his P226 pistol with the front and rear sights filed away. Stratton regarded a pistol as a purely close-quarters weapon, which meant you didn't aim using the sights. So they were superfluous in his opinion. Shooting a pistol had to be instinctive. The gun had to become a part of your body. Milliseconds counted in a close-quarters pistol fight and anyone who needed to aim using the sights was always going to lose to someone whose gun was a mere extension of their wrist. They hit what they pointed at. But it was a much more difficult skill than it sounded.

Stratton held the pistol in his right hand and down by his side. He looked for a target to his front. A dull grey locker, the far side of the room, had a small white nameplate stuck to it. Stratton studied it for half a second before closing his eyes. He raised the gun in his outstretched hand so that it was pointing to his extreme right. With his eyes still closed, he traversed the pistol until it was in front of him and aiming at the locker. He opened his eyes and looked along the top of the pistol, which he kept still in a vice-like grip. He had aligned the weapon perfectly with the white name-plate – if he fired, he would hit it in the centre.

Stratton lowered the gun, pulled a loaded, extended twenty-round magazine from the bundle, placed it into the weapon, cocked it and released the slide so that it picked up a bullet and slammed it into the breach. He deftly nudged the release lever on the side of the weapon with his thumb and the hammer sprang forward without firing the weapon. It was cocked and ready to fire. He placed it into a holster, which he strapped to his thigh.

He opened another box to reveal a line of immaculate, new compact Colt assault rifles fully fitted with night scopes and infra-red spotlights. Stratton removed one of the weapons that had a combat harness strap attached to it, checked the working parts and looked through the sight. Happy with it, he picked up a pouch of magazines and stuffed a couple of spare ammo boxes into a small back-pack. He removed a scanning device attached to a laptop computer and scanned the barcode on the weapon and heard a soft beep. He pointed the same scanner at one of his eyes and moved it around until the same soft beep was emitted.

After recording the Colt magazines and the GPS, he opened a box of tracking devices and tested the one he selected. It was fully charged and he scanned its barcode, which registered the device to his name on the laptop.

Trackers were usually used by SF when operating against unsophisticated enemy who would be unable to crack the signal encryption. They were small and light and the battery could last for days on a ping to a satellite every fifteen minutes.

He replaced the scanner and checked the face of his watch. He had an hour to go before take-off. Everyone would be mustering on deck to prepare the gliders.

He picked up his pack, stuffed some food and a couple bottles of water inside, added a satellite phone, swung it over his shoulder and headed out of the room.

18

The light was beginning to fade as Stratton stepped from the superstructure into a stiff breeze. HMS *Ocean* powered towards Somalia, cutting down as much as possible the distance the powered hang-gliders would have to fly. Officially, the carrier could not sail nearer than twelve miles from the coastline to remain within international waters. But the plan required *Ocean*'s launches to be able to come into the coastline to cover emergency contingencies like a glider hitting the drink and to execute the main exfiltration phase. So the plan was technically illegal. So permission to carry it out would be granted by the Somali government in retrospect. You couldn't make them aware of the attack before it was complete simply because they could not be trusted to maintain secrecy.

The pyramid-shaped glider frames had been lined up in neat rows, their propellers mounted at the backs of the engines secured within them. On the uppermost point of each, where the tubular framing converged, a large bracket hinge would hold the wings. But because of the wind the wings hadn't been fitted. Two comfortable-looking, lay-backed seats had been arranged in front of the engines, the rear one above and behind the front. The back of the pilot's seat, in the front, would be part way between the legs of the passenger.

Ops was concerned about the weather. The overall forecast looked favourable but the winds were predicted to be on the high side of acceptable for the gliders. The wind wouldn't just make it hard getting the craft airborne. It was coming off the land and, with the gliders' limited power, a strong headwind could prevent them from reaching the target because they could run out of fuel. Which was the only obstacle so far that threatened to postpone the operation. Stratton could only hope the weather held. He was having visions of the last operation he had mounted from HMS *Ocean* and did not want to spend yet another week on board waiting for the opportunity to go into action.

The SBS operators had another concern: the final fighting weight of the small aircraft. Trials had been carried out using two fully armed men with complete field equipment and rations for ten days. These had pushed the glider's capacity to its limits but it had managed to take off using the length of the old parade ground in Poole and into a bit of a headwind. This assault wasn't going to need any long-term field equipment, but the craft would be carrying something just as heavy. Two robust pouches had been fitted, one either side of the passenger seat, with half a dozen 82mm mortar shells in each, rigged so that they could be dropped from altitude and explode on contact.

There were twenty gliders in total and, as take-off time

approached, the men began finalising their kit, putting on cam-cream and testing communications. Several shots came from the back end of the huge deck as a handful of the men tested their weapons out to sea. Dozens of crew members had assembled to help out where they could. Those that weren't needed stood on the periphery to observe. It was a unique sight, the like of which they might never get again. There was something of a festival atmosphere about the preparation, one tempered by a soberness at the possibility some of the men might not come back.

Downs stepped on deck with four other SBS operatives wearing full camouflage clothing, their faces blackened and carrying substantial backpacks. He had a brief chat with the men before patting one of them on the shoulder. The men walked away down the line of gliders towards the rear end of the flight deck.

'Good luck, Smudge,' someone shouted out.

In response, one of the four operatives raised a hand that clutched a loaded Colt assault rifle. They were the pathfinder team, whose job it was to mark the landing strips for the gliders. The operations room back in Poole, using satellite images, had identified several patches of level ground close to the jihadist encampment that would be suitable for the gliders to land on. The robust craft didn't need much room to land, depending again on the wind. But due to the numbers, they needed enough room to allow the tail-enders to land through the inevitable clutter of those who had already landed, or crashed.

The pathfinders made their way over to the Lynx, which was starting up its high-pitched engines. They would leave well before the gliders so that they had ample time to carry out the task. The plan was to drop them off a mile from the jihadist camp the other side of the range of hills. From there they would yomp to their respective pre-selected sites to prepare the landing markers.

The obvious question was, if pathfinders could get dropped off to yomp on to the target, why couldn't the other forty men do the same and save the risks involved with flying in? It had a simple enough answer. One small, low-flying super-fast helicopter might not be noticed. And if it was noticed, it wouldn't be considered a threat. A single Somali military helicopter flying across the plains wouldn't be unheard of in the area. A squadron of Sea Kings would invoke some concern and a warning message might be called into the jihadists. And two pairs of men could move practically undetected. If by some chance someone saw them, they wouldn't be considered a major threat to the four hundred or so jihadists. Forty men had a much higher chance of being detected and no matter how good they were at soldiering, they would soon run out of all of the ammunition they could possibly carry if the jihadists came out to meet them for a fight.

The final reason for using the gliders was the need for pinpoint pre-assault bombing. They needed to soften up the camp using air-delivered bombs. They intended to confuse and hopefully scatter the warriors before the ground assault – historically, such bombing operations, particularly in woodland, hadn't produced a significant number of casualties. A ground force would have had to use mortars. But they wouldn't have been as accurate as the same bombs delivered by hand from directly above by men who could see what they were aiming for. HMS *Ocean* didn't have guns large enough to hit the encampment. Stratton guessed London had considered Cruise missiles to be too heavy-handed and probably calculated they might work against them in the subsequent propaganda exchange. A more hands-on, surgical solution had been required.

The Lynx's engines roared to full power and it rose off the deck and politely reversed off the back end so as not to harass the men and their gliders with its downdraft. It turned to one side and dropped out of sight as it headed towards the coastline a few feet above the waves. Without any of its navigation lights, it soon disappeared from view and seconds later it could no longer be heard, the throb of its engines absorbed by the blustery wind.

Downs walked around the edge of the hustle and bustle and over to Stratton and the glider he was to share with his old friend. 'Bloody madness, if you ask me,' he said in his rich Irish brogue and wearing his usual grin. 'I'm talking about this glider lark. What do you think?'

'I think that about sums it up,' Stratton said. 'And you and I wouldn't be anywhere else in the world right now.'

'Ha, bloody roight.'

Lieutenant Phelps stepped out on deck and searched the

men spread out in front of him until he found who he was looking for. 'Stratton?' he called out.

Stratton turned to look at the man whom he hardly knew.

'A brief word, please,' the officer said.

Stratton left Downs and walked over to him.

The officer stepped away to a more private piece of deck as Stratton arrived and glanced around to ensure they were out of earshot of everyone else.

'I have a message for you from London,' Phelps said. 'The Chinese insist they don't have an agent in Somalia at this time and have not had in recent months. They have acknowledged the agent you confronted in Yemen. Given that, London is inclined to believe them. Why would they acknowledge one and not the other? They have accounted for all of their known citizens in Somalia and none fit the description of the woman in your report.'

Stratton felt surprised by the revelation. His initial inclination was to believe it but he wasn't immediately sure why.

'Good luck,' the officer said, before walking away and back inside the superstructure.

Stratton's head started to fill with questions about what the girl could have been doing in Somalia if she wasn't an agent. Maybe the Chinese were lying. That he could believe. Maybe she was connected to Al-Shabaab and the acquisition of the weapons. If so, something had clearly gone badly wrong for her. But that didn't explain why she would have been sneaking around the *Oasis* when he found her. None of the dots connected in a way that worked for him. He couldn't find a remotely satisfying explanation for it. He clearly didn't have enough information.

Despite the possibility that she had duped him, he couldn't dislike her. He never got the impression she was a bad person. Which was possibly naive of him but he fancied himself a fair judge of character.

He wondered where the girl was at that moment. Had she truly gone back to Somalia to finish whatever it was she had started there, madness though it had to be? Hopefully she had made it safely to another coast. If she wasn't a Chinese agent, it helped explain why she jumped ship. She knew Stratton would have included her in his report. She would also have expected him to go to the nearest British safe haven and would have expected her to accompany him. The Chinese authorities would also have been informed. She wouldn't have wanted to be interviewed by the British, and even less by her own people.

Stratton's thoughts were interrupted by Howel and Winslow stepping out on deck through a door beside him. The two officers headed over to Downs.

'The old man said you can go ahead and prepare for departure,' Winslow said. 'He's adjusting the ship's speed and heading to reduce the wind so that you can complete the assembling of the gliders.'

Downs looked into the wind and decided it had indeed grown weaker in the past few minutes. He brought a whistle to his lips and blew it. Everyone looked in his direction. 'Let's get the wings on,' he shouted.

Howel looked around at the preparations as he and Winslow walked back towards the superstructure, where Stratton still stood.

'God, how I envy you lot,' Howel said to Stratton.

'Well, you know where the door to true adventure lies,' Stratton said. 'You just have to get through it.'

He winked at Winslow and walked away. Winslow watched him go, his jaw tight.

Stratton stepped to his glider as a couple of the ship's crew were assembling the wing. The rest of the glider pairs, aided by sailors, were doing the same all over the deck area.

A tall, strongly built SBS operative preparing the glider beside Downs and Stratton's looked over at Stratton as he arrived. 'Hey, Stratton,' he said.

Stratton looked at him, recognising the face but unable to place him right away.

'Matt,' he reminded Stratton, aware the operative could not remember his name. 'We were in Helmand last year at the same time. I was in Blue Team.'

The man fell into place for Stratton. 'I remember. How's it going?'

Matt stepped closer. He was a head taller than Stratton with a pair of shoulders to match. 'So what's Somalia like?'

'I found it a tad unfriendly. But it would be unfair to taint the entire country. I only saw a small part of it.'

'I'm looking forward to punishing those bastards. Hopper was a good friend. Do you know his wife, Helen?'

Stratton had been wondering who would be the first to mention Hopper. 'Only in passing,' he said.

'You met the kids?'

Stratton could sense an edge to the man's tone. 'A couple of times.'

Matt nodded. Like he had no real interest in Stratton's answers to his questions, like he wanted to get to others he had on his mind. 'Do you mind if I ask you something?' he said. 'There's a rumour going around that you killed Hopper.'

The hint of confrontation Stratton had detected became suddenly far stronger. Hearing Matt's voice had improved his memory of the man. Matt had a reputation for being stroppy. He had a bit of the big-man syndrome. He used his size and naturally aggressive nature to intimidate. It worked on most people. Stratton remembered his behaviour during one set of operational orders in Afghanistan. During the questions phase, Matt had been sarcastic to the sergeant running that small op. Stratton suspected it was because he felt like he should have been running it. A childish response but some people were like that.

For Matt's part, Stratton didn't overly impress him. He felt he was every bit as good as guys like him. In Matt's eyes, the only difference between them both was that he hadn't yet had the opportunity to prove himself.

Stratton appreciated displays of confidence and didn't

mind if it bordered on arrogance or even discourtesy. But he drew the line at blatant disrespect. 'That's right,' he answered, a coldness easing its way into his own tone.

The men nearby who had heard the question and the answer stopped what they were doing to watch and listen. Everyone had heard and discussed the rumours but no one knew the truth.

Matt took a step closer to Stratton. Got close to invading the operative's personal space, a dangerous place to venture. Stratton would give him a lot of leeway though. Matt was SBS, but also upset about his friend's death.

'Was that deliberate or did you shoot him by accident?' Matt asked.

Stratton didn't react at all. He looked hard at Matt. He had a dangerous look in his eye. But Matt was afraid of no one. Few members of the service would dare to show disrespect to Stratton. Even fewer would threaten him. Matt believed he had a right to confront Stratton, regardless of the fact the man was the most accomplished operative in the SBS. He knew he was in dangerous territory but suddenly felt confident about it.

There were not many men on that deck who would have questioned Stratton's operational choices. Most believed that whatever he did was for a good reason. Stratton did have his detractors. There were men in the SBS who didn't approve of him in general. Most of those numbered among the older operators and officers. They believed London should not have favourites, that one man shouldn't get so many choice operations and be selected over others.

They also disapproved of him dividing his time between the SBS and the SIS. If he wanted to work for the London ghosts, then he should sod off and join them.

Matt didn't share those feelings. Deep down he wanted to do exactly the same things. But he wanted to be the man they came to, not Stratton. Over the years, that jealousy had twisted inside of him. Instead of doing something about making himself more attractive to the selectors, Matt became resentful. He wasn't helped in his dilemma by the fact that he didn't have a clue how to go about getting selected for those special ops. You couldn't just write in and ask. You couldn't fill in a form, you couldn't call a number. He knew, like everyone else, that just about every operator got gauged from time to time when the Secret Intelligence Service needed new recruits. He would never accept the possibility that the reason he hadn't been selected was because they didn't consider him good enough. That would have been too large a pill for him to swallow.

Matt would never be able to get away with abusing Stratton for no apparent reason at all. That would instantly be recognised as jealousy. And if he decided to get physical with Stratton and it was suspected he did it out of jealousy, he could find himself out of the SBS and on his way back to his commando unit for such a pathetic display. The unit didn't tolerate such things. They could ultimately find their way into an operation and negatively affect the outcome.

Matt wasn't that stupid, though. He knew the ground rules. So he also knew Hopper's death by Stratton's hand could be an acceptable reason to criticise him openly, show the man some disdain. He wouldn't miss an opportunity like that. Matt thought he could see a personal advantage in it. He might expose a severe flaw in the highly rated operative while at the same time turn the spotlight on himself. Elevate himself and at the same time shrink Stratton's stature.

'It was intentional,' Stratton said without any edge or emotion to his voice.

There were those nearby who hadn't known. Some of them had heard but could not believe that Stratton had wilfully killed Hopper. To hear the admission from Stratton's own lips left all of them confused. Even those who thought they knew him. A few immediately doubted that they could support him.

'I can't imagine a scenario where you would have to kill a mate deliberately,' Matt said. 'There's always a chance he might survive.'

Matt had a valid point. Stratton could never be 100 per cent certain Hopper would have died if he hadn't shot him.

'Who do you think you are? God?' Matt said.

Stratton was seething deep down inside. He harboured a great deal of guilt about Hopper's death, to be sure. But despite the element of doubt that Hopper might not have died at the hands of the fanatical terrorists if Stratton hadn't shot him, it wasn't the true source of his guilt. That originated with the events that had led to Hopper being taken away by Sabarak. Stratton's self-indulgent adventure to the ship was the reason Hopper had been taken to the jihadists' camp. That was his true crime and the cause of Hopper's death. But Matt was talking about something else. He didn't know about that side of the story, and perhaps if he did, he would not have seen anything wrong with it because it was precisely the kind of thing Matt would have done himself. Stratton not only believed Matt was wrong, he resented him for it.

'You don't know what you're talking about,' Stratton said, keeping a grip on his anger.

'Is that right? Why don't you explain it to us?'

'I would, if I thought you'd get it.'

Matt gritted his teeth, reading the insinuation that he in particular wouldn't understand while others might. He had been accused of being thick in the past, an accusation he didn't take kindly to. Banter in the SBS could get particularly barbed and personal but people were expected not to overreact and bite on the bait. Matt had been known to take a swing at anyone who ventured to illuminate his restricted intellect. But that wasn't the only thing that angered Matt this time. He also felt that Stratton had insinuated something else: that his inability to understand the subtleties of Stratton's actions was the reason why he had not been selected by the SIS for special operations.

Matt's jaw clenched even more tightly. 'You really do rate yourself, don't you?'

Stratton decided to ignore the man and get back to sorting out his glider. Matt's hands balled into fists. If anyone else had turned their back on him, he might have considered closing the distance and testing the waters further. But despite all his ill feelings towards Stratton, he knew better than to cross a certain line with the man. Matt had some weapons in his arsenal but he would not test them against those in Stratton's. But then again, there would probably never be a better time than this one.

'That's enough,' Downs said, stepping in. 'One more word, Matt, and you're off the op. And you know that ball will bounce all the way to the top by the time you get back to Poole.'

Matt might not have been the brightest light in the SBS but he could instantly figure out the consequences of being kicked off an operation. He not only backed off but gave Downs a look that was pure deference. He didn't even give Stratton a parting glance as he turned away and got back to his glider.

But anyone who knew Matt was aware he wouldn't let the issue go completely. He wouldn't risk injuring his career for anything but neither could he back off when he believed he was right.

Stratton focused on securing his equipment but he could feel the eyes on him. His wound was sorely exposed.

Downs wanted to say something to his friend but he couldn't. He knew as little about the incident as everyone else and was one of those who had forgiven Stratton immediately, feeling that if he had indeed killed Hopper then he had a good reason and that was that. But it still left something of a bitter taste in his mouth. He could sense Stratton wasn't exactly comfortable with it and suspected there was a lot more to it. He would ask Stratton, one day, but not at that moment. Perhaps over that pint they had talked about.

It was like the sun had taken advantage of the men's distraction to slip below the horizon. Darkness came quite suddenly. Which wasn't helped by the carrier going into full external dark mode, with only dim red lighting inside the superstructure's entrances. The men used low-light glowlights to finish off preparing the gliders.

The *Ocean* continued to cut through the water but at a reduced speed to control the wind.

'Is that Somalia?' one of the men asked no one in particular.

They could see a faint glow in the distance in the direction of the Somali coastline.

'Calula,' someone answered.

'I think that's too far east,' another operator said. 'Could be, I suppose,' he added, having a second thought.

The wind suddenly picked up a little, something each man was keenly aware of. Crewmen hurried to the wing ends to hold them in case a gust should arrive. With no one sitting in them, the craft were relatively light and could get blown about. The single thought that ran through every operative's mind at that point was how strong the captain would let it get before cancelling the take-off.

There was one other significant element in the equation that could stop the operation and that was any sign of mobilisation by the Somali jihadists. The ship's operations room carefully watched the terrorist camp via satellite. If they got any indication that the enemy were preparing for an attack, the task would be aborted, for the time being at least. The teams didn't have the manpower, equipment or firepower to mount an assault against a defended position. The satellite guys felt confident that the jihadists hadn't reacted unduly to Stratton's escape despite him knowing the whereabouts of their camp. The initial fear had been that they might immediately relocate. But all signs seemed to indicate that they hadn't. Not yet. It was the reason why the assault had been organised so quickly. They had to hit the camp before the missiles could be moved. The jihadists had to know that Stratton had escaped them but would they expect him to have escaped Somalia? Which was why Lotto had been upgraded to a significant factor.

They estimated that the pirate chief would have reached his coastal base by dusk that day. How he acted would depend on how seriously he took the possibility that the British would mount an attack right away or even at all. Lotto didn't necessarily know that Stratton had discovered the weapons secreted on board the *Oasis*. Once again, it was another good reason to mount an attack immediately.

A glider engine fired up and its propeller whirred. The glider engineer who had accompanied the teams was running a test after having completed some work on it. Stratton felt surprised by how quiet it was. He hadn't heard the engines since the new suppressors had been fitted. In fact most of the sound came from the propellers cutting through the air rather than the engine itself.

Before long, every glider had its wing fitted and appeared

ready to go. The wind hadn't increased significantly and everything looked good to go.

'You all set?' Downs asked Stratton.

'Yep,' Stratton said as he buckled up his fighting harness and adjusted the strapping.

'Seriously. You looking forward to this or not? You had a pretty hard time of it over there.'

'I'm ready to go,' Stratton said, with little emotion. 'More than anyone else here,' he added.

Downs believed him. He had the feeling there might also be more to it than just revenge for Hopper. He pushed the send button on his radio that was attached to his body harness. 'All stations, this is Downs, check.'

'Harry, check,' came an immediate reply.

'Dizzy, check.'

'Spud, check.'

And so on as each glider team responded to the communications check in turn. First or nicknames could be used instead of call-signs for a number of reasons. The communications system had been encrypted and even the Russians or Chinese wouldn't be able to decrypt it, let alone the Somalis. Another reason was that with so many teams it could be difficult to keep tabs on who belonged to which call-sign. The final check came from the ship's operations room.

'Oscar Zero, Downs, permission for countdown?' Downs asked.

'Oscar Zero, that's affirmative.'

'Roger. All stations, this is Downs, countdown five

minutes. No reply required unless you have a problem.'

Downs waited for a moment in case anyone did reply but the airwaves remained silent. 'Gentlemen, get seated and start your engines,' he said to those around him.

That had a ripple effect as the rest of the teams boarded their aircraft.

The ship's loudspeaker broke over the sound of engines starting up. 'All non-mission personnel move behind the flight lines.'

The sailors who had been lending a hand hurried across the deck in between the lines of gliders and over the thick white line that surrounded the superstructure. Some of the crew moved behind the squadron of gliders to the helicopters parked on the rear portion of the deck.

Every glider engine purred away, the craft positioned two abreast with several metres between the following rows. The take-off had naturally been discussed in detail but there had not been any time to carry out rehearsals back in the UK before departure. There had been a brief discussion about the practicalities of carrying out a practice run earlier in the day but that had been nixed immediately. Taking off was much easier than landing and accidents were only to be expected. A 10 per cent failure rate had been built into the take-off and target-approach phase of the operation, which meant they could afford to lose two craft and four men before the first assault stage began. A rehearsal that included a difficult landing on the flight deck, something none of the pilots had actually done before, was considered ill-advised.

Stratton got comfortable in his seat to the rear and above Downs and buckled himself in. He secured the strap of his Colt in case he had to release it from his grip for whatever reason, but otherwise it would remain in one of his hands. He had a pair of goggles but elected not to wear them unless the wind became too uncomfortable. Stratton disliked hats and sunglasses or goggles and only used them when he had to.

The propeller turned over behind him, vibrating the chassis. The bucket-style seats were snug and quite comfortable. Stratton checked his small backpack was secured to the back of Downs's seat in between his legs and that the mortar shells nestled tightly in their pouches either side of him. The safety pins remained in the heads to prevent them from going off should the glider crash. He looked over at the glider to his side. Matt sat in the back staring ahead. The man had not even looked in his direction since Downs's threat.

'Clear for take-off,' came a voice over the radio from the ship's operations room.

Stratton looked at the back of Downs's head and wondered how the man was feeling. He knew Downs to be a tough fighter and although he would be as nervous as everyone else, he was good at hiding it.

Stratton felt a touch of the butterflies in the pit of his own stomach as the seconds to take-off ticked away. The wind had picked up a little but it was being controlled by the captain to a large degree using the ship's speed and direction. The plan would be to have several knots blowing in their faces to aid the take-off because the first craft only just had enough runway to get airborne. That would improve for each following row of aircraft.

Stratton checked his GPS. The Somali coastline was eight miles away. There was a bit of a headwind but they hoped to be on target before 2200. The ideal time for an attack such as this would be in the early hours of the morning, around 0200 to 0300, when the enemy would be well asleep. But that would not have left them time to complete the other phases of the operation before first light, which was important.

'Hey, Stratton.'

Stratton looked at Downs who had his head turned to the side enough to talk to him but not to see him. 'Yeah?'

'I think we might be too heavy.'

'You just decided that?' Stratton asked, suspicious Downs was trying to wind him up, such was the man's sense of humour.

'No. Been thinking about it all day.'

'Why are you telling me now?'

'I didn't want to crash into the sea without you knowing I knew about it.'

'OK. Well, now I know, thanks for sharing that.' Stratton still wasn't sure if Downs was being serious or not. The Irishman had a wry sense of humour even during the most desperate of situations. But he wasn't a mental case either and clearly had some confidence they could get airborne or he wouldn't risk it, certainly not as commander of his first major operation. Stratton hoped so at least. 'I'm all fastened in so you might as well get going.'

'OK. Just what I was thinking.'

Downs eased the throttle forward. The propeller revolutions greatly increased. The framework vibrated much more as everything got a little louder though it remained much quieter than Stratton had expected.

The craft hadn't moved. Downs had intentionally kept the brake on until the revs reached maximum.

He released the brake and gripped the joystick and the glider lurched forward. The runway wasn't as smooth as it looked. Even though the wheels had a little suspension built into them, the little glider juddered and jolted along, rattling Stratton's teeth in his head so much he had to clamp his jaw shut.

As the glider picked up speed, the nylon wing panel above them ballooned into a tight curve as it caught the air. The framework creaked as it strained to hold everything together.

Stratton forgot everything else and stared at the end of the *Ocean*'s runway. They were quickly closing in on it and the wheels had not yet left the deck. He glanced to his side for the other glider that should have taken off with them but he couldn't see it. He didn't turn in his seat to look for it, concerned at that moment for no one else but them.

The engine was purring at full revs. Stratton could feel the wind not just blowing into his face but being sucked past him and through the propellers. He squinted ahead, wiping his eyes quickly as they started to water. He would have put on his goggles but he had greater priorities at that moment. His hands tightened on the rifle and framework. His thoughts flashed to his harness quick release. He considered releasing it there and then. If they took off, he wouldn't need it. If they hit the drink, he didn't want to be fighting with it, but crashing into the sea without it might be enough to knock him out. The problems of dropping off the end into the sea multiplied. They would have to get out of the framework as quickly as possible, not just because the craft would probably sink like a stone but also because the ship would run into them and they might get sucked below and through the propellers. These were not the best thoughts to be having seconds before reaching the end of the runway and he had Downs to thank for inspiring them.

Metres before the end of the deck the glider rose up and left the surface a few inches then dropped back down with a heavy bump.

They reached the end, the wheels still rolling along on the deck.

The craft went over the lip and dropped out of sight to everyone on deck watching it.

The pit of Stratton's stomach turned to mush as the glider dropped. He gripped the frame, his knuckles turning white as the sea came up to meet them. Downs pulled back so hard on the joystick it threatened to rip out. But the increased speed of falling off the end was all the craft needed to provide that extra lift and it levelled out a couple of metres above the wave tops. Stratton realised he had stopped breathing. He looked back to see the sharp end of the ship not all that far away. The important thing was that the wet stuff was still below them.

Downs gradually brought the nose up and increased the height until they got level with the deck of the ship again.

Stratton could hear another sound above the engine and the wind. It was Downs giving off a loud yell.

Stratton leaned forward. 'Did you enjoy that?' he shouted.

'If I hadn'ta crapped my pants when we went off the end, I might've enjoyed it more than I did!'

Stratton sat back and had to smile. It felt like a form of release. He looked back over his shoulder again to see another craft below them and dangerously close to the water. But it managed to level out and gain height.

Downs brought the craft up to about a hundred feet while making a gentle bank to the left. After a short turn, he reversed the manoeuvre, banking over to the right. After coming back on to the main heading, he did the turns again, the zig-zagging intended to slow the glider's progress without reducing their speed and to allow the tail-enders to catch up.

Within a few minutes all of the gliders had got off the *Ocean*. When Stratton next looked back, he could barely make out the others in the darkness. But they were all able to see his glider. Every craft had a navigation light on its rear, positioned in a device that only allowed it to be seen from behind and level with it or from above it.

Every pilot carried a GPS that provided a pre-programmed direction as well as a minimum height alarm.

'All stations, this is Downs, radio check,' Downs said into his radio.

One by one each pilot reported in.

'Downs, roger that,' Downs said at the end.

Stratton made an effort to relax. The wind whipped his hair about. His eyes no longer wept. It had something very tranquil about it. And surreal. What they were doing, or about to do, gave him a buzz at the same time as it sobered everything right up. People were going to die in the next hour or so. Hopefully that would be the enemy only but the chances had to be high that the squadron would lose someone. Maybe a few.

It was an innovative attack, that was for sure. They weren't in jet helicopters crammed with sophisticated navigation, communications and visual aids. They were in metal tubes under nylon wings and using engines about as powerful as a lawnmower's, with a wooden propeller behind it all pushing them forward at a cumbersome rate of knots.

But they were armed to the teeth and about to go into battle. It was great. It was beautiful. It was ultimately what Stratton lived for.

The GPS indicated the coastline to be less than two kilometres away. It was a perfectly black night. The clouds not far above them had formed on cue, just like the evening before when Stratton and the girl had escaped along the river. The stars and moon had been blocked out completely. The forecast had given it a 40 per cent chance of rain on the mainland. Which they didn't consider a massive problem. The gliders would fly almost as well, depending on how heavy the rain was. The landing might even be softer.

Stratton could make out a white scar running across their

entire front. The coastline. He could see a faint glow to the east. Lotto's town. The squadron planned to pass well to the west of it, head inland due south for a couple of clicks, before turning east towards the Al-Shabaab encampment.

The flight had not been without its little moments of drama. The wind had toyed with them and some crews had flown too close together which caused a bit of mild panic among those concerned. It was also impossible to judge the height by eye alone. That was difficult enough in the daytime without something like a boat in the water to provide a point of reference. But it was almost as difficult for the pilots to fly with an eye fixed on the altimeter. More than once Downs had suddenly pulled back hard on the stick to gain immediate height, an action that attracted every bit of Stratton's attention each time he did it. It was harder for Downs than for the other pilots. He was alone out in front with no other craft to gauge himself by. But if he hit the drink and the pilot behind wasn't watching his altimeter, they would probably follow. The gliders didn't respond particularly quickly to the controls because of the weight they were carrying.

Stratton hadn't discovered the precise type of radar the Somali jihadists had at their base but specialists back in Poole had advised a sea approach of a hundred feet, and less than that if possible when they reached landfall, would be good enough. Which was going to be tricky because of the way the ground rose into the hills beyond the beach. It was going to be pitch black and again they would have to rely on their altimeters. Confidence was high that if the gliders maintained the lowest altitude, they wouldn't be detected by the radar. But anyone on the ground would spot the large mass quite easily if it flew close by them. That was one of the risks they were prepared to take.

Downs carried out an all stations radio check every five minutes just in case someone at the back of the squadron had ditched without being seen. The emergency procedure for such an event was to press on and leave the crew to their own devices. A report would be sent detailing the incident and location to HMS *Ocean*. The ship would send out a rescue team. Each man carried his own SARBE emergency beacon so it wouldn't be considered a great drama if a pair did have to ditch. The impact was something none of them wanted to experience of course. The real fear was not being able to get out of the damned machine before it sank like a stone.

Stratton checked his GPS. The coast was less than a kilometre away. A sudden flash appeared up ahead. For a second he thought it looked like a device of some kind, his brain in full military mode, unable to decide what it was right away. Another flash followed immediately after in a different place and he realised it was lightning. The low rumble of thunder followed, which he could just about hear above the purring of the propeller.

Minutes later they crossed the beach line and Downs pulled back on the stick to increase their altitude as the ground started to rise.

They could barely see the dark hills up ahead, obscured by a mass of clouds. Another crack of lightning, this time much closer, and Stratton wasn't the only one who suddenly wondered what would happen if their craft happened to be struck by a bolt. It was not worth thinking about. Nothing anyone could do to prevent it if it happened.

Stratton peered ahead in the hope of seeing a hillside that he recognised. He knew that despite the dozens of satellite photographs everyone had studied, and the ones that every passenger held in his hand at that moment, and the metre-accurate GPS coordinates, there could be no better substitute for having someone who had actually been there. All part of the reasoning for bringing him along and placing him at the front of the squadron.

Stratton and Downs's GPSs both beeped at the same time, signalling the heading change to due east. Every other GPS in the squadron beeped in turn, just in case the pilot didn't see the craft in front make the change in direction. Something hardly likely to happen at this stage. Each man was concentrating hard ahead. They had minutes to go.

Stratton saw something he recognised. He could make out the unmoving river up ahead. He searched the black countryside just in front of it, looking for signs of the camp. On their right side the hills ascended, the tops high above them.

Another bolt of lightning striking close by startled everyone. It lit up the ground like the flash from a giant camera. For a second the terrain around them was exposed like daytime. The bad news was that people generally tended to look to the skies when lightning struck. But a few seconds later another element arrived that caused the reverse and induced those in the open to find cover.

Stratton felt a drop of water hit his face. Then another. They were heading into the rain.

Moments later the heavens opened up and it became torrential. The gliders buffeted heavily. Suddenly all of the confidence the crews had that the craft would fly normally in bad weather disintegrated. Those who had flown in the rain and who had declared it safe had never been in anything close to what they were experiencing at that moment. The danger was fundamental enough. If the rain beat down on to the tops of the canvas wings of the gliders too heavily, they could lose their shape. If that happened, the craft would lose lift and height and the rest was easy enough to work out.

Downs immediately pulled back on the stick to gain even greater altitude. If the wings did begin to flatten under the weight of the rain, he wanted them to be as close as possible to the camp when they went down.

The other crews did the same, or attempted to.

'This is Spud, having problems!' came a shout over the radio.

Stratton strained to look back and could make out a glider far lower than it should have been. And he could see a couple of others that looked like they might be struggling to hold altitude.

'We can't get any height!' Spud shouted, starting to lose his composure.

It was a private ordeal. No one could do anything to help them, other than pray that they could overcome the difficulty and get back up in the air.

The rain continued to lash against them all, biting at their faces like pea-shot. The heavy beating on the canopy almost drowned out the sound of the engine. Downs kept the stick pulled back. They weren't going up but then they weren't losing any height either. Not yet at least. He felt suddenly aware that the entire operation could quickly turn into a total disaster before the assault phase.

'We're going in! We're going in!' Spud shouted over the radio.

Stratton put a face to the name, a young stocky lad with stacks of enthusiasm. He didn't know who the lad's partner was.

A long silence followed.

'Spud, this is Downs!' Downs shouted.

Silence.

'Jordo! You still tail end?' Downs shouted into his radio above the cacophony around him and the rain slamming into his face.

'Jordo here. Roger that. I just saw Spud hit the deck. It looked pretty hard. I couldn't see anything else. I'm also having trouble holding on.'

'Christ.' Downs shouted back to Stratton, 'We're going to have to ditch these payloads!'

Stratton looked ahead, blinking through the rain. He was

pretty certain he could make out the camp area at the bottom of the dark slope. The heavy rain did not help.

He suddenly saw a light flicker. And then another.

'On the bomb run!' he shouted to Downs. 'You're on heading! Straight ahead!'

19

'All stations stand by!' Downs shouted into his radio. 'Hang in there another minute and we'll solve our weight problems.'

Which was precisely what every other crew was thinking. They were each carrying a dozen mortar shells which was, for most of them, the difference between staying in the air and crashing.

The rain hammered men and machines. But more and more lights appeared within the wood ahead. Some electrical, others kerosene-powered. Stratton could only hope that any sentry wouldn't be looking skyward. That they would all be under cover or heading for it in the downpour. That the sound of the rain hitting the trees would cover that of the glider engines until they got directly overhead.

'Dizzy here, not sure if we're gonna make it!' came a voice over the radio.

'Ditch your mortars!' Downs shouted. 'Or enough of 'em to keep you up. The rest of you, don't forget to pull the pins!'

Stratton didn't need reminding. He was already removing

the pins from the first row of mortars on each side of him.

'Anywhere in particular?' Downs shouted to his partner.

Stratton couldn't identify anything within the wood of more interest than any other part. Not yet at least. He hadn't seen inside the camp anyway.

As they drew closer, he could make out the dark clearing at the foot of the slope where he had killed Hopper. He suddenly had a flashback and could see the man on his knees waiting to die.

Stratton snapped back to the task in hand and took a couple of mortars from each pouch. Then everything seemed to slow down. A beeping sound broke his concentration. It was his GPS warning him they were on target.

A flash of lightning lit up the wood and for a second he could see signs of life: sheets of plastic glistening in the rain, several vehicles. He thought he saw someone running. He identified a hut directly in their flight line and decided that would be the target for his opening salvo. It no longer mattered to him if they were seen or not. In a few seconds he would open up the attack. This was the start of his revenge and he prayed it would be a satisfying night.

He sat back holding a bomb in each hand by its tail fins and dangled them either side of him as he concentrated ahead.

A bearded jihadist commander wearing a hooded raincoat left the cover of his tent and cleared both of his nostrils as he walked the short distance to the edge of the wood. He paused at his favourite pissing tree and hiked up his dishdasha to relieve himself. He looked skywards and a frown creased his brow as he saw a strange thing in the sky. He removed his hood to get a better look. A flash of lightning revealed the broad, dark wings of what appeared to be a giant bird approaching. He saw the two men beneath the single wingspan. He knew nothing about gliders. But he did feel that something very bad was about to happen and he turned and ran as fast as he possibly could.

The fighter charged between the well-spread trees, their lower branches having long since been removed for firewood or construction. He glanced back as he ran to make sure he hadn't imagined it. Sure enough, just above the trees and not very far behind him was the black beast with its purring growl which he could now hear.

He began to scream as he neared the closest hut. The door opened and a fighter stepped outside. The commander charged inside to grab his gun, yelling at half a dozen men lying around a cast iron stove.

A couple of seconds later the bird passed overhead and the hut exploded in a ball of smoke and flashing flames.

Stratton felt the shockwave pulse skywards. Bits of shrapnel and wood flew past him, a couple of pieces penetrating the glider wing. He looked over his shoulder to see the bright yellow flames light up the wood.

'A little more height, if you please, Mr Downs!' he shouted.

Downs laughed hard. It was like a high-pressure gas bottle of tension had been released. All the planning and preparations were behind them. All the worrying that he might have forgotten something had gone. The battle had begun. This is what it had all been about. Why he had joined the Royal Marines at sixteen years old and had trained for two years as a recruit until he had been able to win his green beret and join a commando unit.

Downs pulled back on the stick and turned it to one side to try and climb as well as get into position for another bomb run.

Stratton thought he saw some vehicles directly below as Downs made the turn and released two more bombs. The wood exploded behind them.

Downs continued to roar with joy. 'Come on you bastards!'

Another explosion came from elsewhere in the wood, followed by several more until there seemed to be one going off every few seconds.

As Downs yelled like a madman, Stratton released a couple more bombs and had to smile at his crazed friend. The glider appeared to be benefiting from the reduced weight as Downs turned and gained height at the same time.

'Truck!' Downs cried out.

Stratton looked ahead to see several vehicles parked nose to tail on a track that entered the wood.

'Let's go for it!' Stratton shouted as he removed the pins from several more mortars.

Downs lined up the glider so that it flew directly over the top of them.

Stratton dropped one bomb with a short delay before

releasing the next. They slammed into the beds of two trucks, one after the other, and the vehicles exploded.

Downs was clearly loving it. 'I'd do this bloody job for nothing!' he shouted.

Stratton's smile faded into concentration as he saw men running through the wood below him, illuminated by the fires that were cropping up all over the place despite the rain. They had caused total and utter panic. The Somalis had no idea what was going on. Those with any battle experience would know it was a mortar attack and not artillery but the sight of the gliders had frightened and confused them.

Downs took the glider in a gentle curve, his eyes everywhere, conscious that gliders could easily collide right then. The orders had been to keep all turns over the wood to the right only. It wouldn't prevent a crash but it did reduce the chances of one.

Stratton was hoping to see Sabarak. He knew it would be impossible to recognise the Saudi from the air but he couldn't help himself. He saw several men running along a track, illuminated by the flames. Stratton reached for the last of his mortars and held one either side of the seat as Downs took them above the men. Stratton staggered his release and the double boom filled the area where it struck with smoke and debris.

Another line of men ran out of the wood and into the black open ground. Stratton pulled up his Colt, shoved the butt into his shoulder and fired a couple of shots. The rear pair went down and the others scattered.

Downs turned in order to close in on another group of running men and lost a bit of height. As he flew alongside them, Stratton let rip with several short bursts. Three of the men went down and the rest scattered.

Downs pulled hard on the stick to gain height and headed away from the wood. Stratton looked back to see several explosions. A dozen or so fires blazed and a line of smoke drifted on the wind towards the coast.

Downs quickly checked his GPS and turned hard up and over a treeless slope. Several other gliders did the same and moved in behind him, all of the craft much more manoeuvrable since ditching their payloads.

'All stations, this is Downs, check!' Downs shouted into his radio.

The crews began to answer right away. There was a long pause after the last report. Two gliders were missing. It was an acceptable loss for that stage of the mission but only as a statistic. Downs could only pray that just the gliders were gone and not the men. The trackers would let the ops room know if the missing men were moving or not. But the tracker couldn't tell them if the men were still alive or that their bodies were being looted.

Downs would have to worry about them later. The teams still had work to do.

As the gliders crested a rise, they saw two straight lines of tiny white lights stretching away either side of them. A red line of lights at the far end indicated the limit of the landing strip. The pathfinders had done their job after being dropped off by the Lynx.

Downs didn't hang about and immediately lost height. He touched down hard and they bounced back up until he took the power out of the engine and the glider dropped back to the ground with another thump.

'Sorry about that,' Downs said as he steered the craft away from the middle of the landing strip to make room for the others.

They quickly climbed out, ditched their life-jackets and prepared their equipment for the next phase.

'I think I'd like the rain to stop now,' Downs said.

One of the pathfinders arrived from the darkness. 'All right, Downsy?'

'Thanks, Smudge. There's only nine left in this serial.'

'I 'eard. Get going. I'll clean up,' Smudge said. 'Got everything?'

'Yep,' said Stratton, pulling on his backpack.

'Go ahead,' Downs said.

Smudge tossed an incendiary into the glider and as Downs and Stratton walked away it burst into flames. Smudge ran off to help the next crews who had landed.

'We live in a very disposable world, don't we,' Downs said as he watched the glider go up in flames.

Stratton didn't answer, going to the edge of the small plateau to look down the slope at the glowing wood.

'I wish I'd gone for the black outfit myself,' Downs said, comparing Stratton's fatigues with his own. 'You're anxious to get down there, aren't you?'

'Sabarak will be on the run.'

'That's the idea. Our job is to take out the missiles.

Someone else'll get Sabarak, one day if not today.'

Stratton wasn't interested in another day. Only in this one. He looked back to see if the others were ready to go.

'But that's the bit that pisses you off, hey, Stratton. You want to be the one who does him in.'

'I owe him.'

'We all owe him. Hopper was my friend as well.'

'You didn't have to kill him!' Stratton said angrily, immediately regretting the outburst.

Downs couldn't remember ever seeing Stratton that upset about something. He decided to leave it alone. He also decided to keep an eye on his friend. He wasn't himself and they were about to step into a very hostile location.

Stratton stepped off the edge of the plateau and began down the slope that had turned into sludge in the rain.

Downs looked back for the rest of his men. 'Come on, you lot!' he shouted. 'There's a war on, you know!'

The men hurried over to the team leader as another glider burst into flames.

'We'll see you in the wood, Smudge,' Downs shouted.

'Roger that,' Smudge called back, dumping an incendiary into another glider and hurrying off to the next one.

The rain continued to fall in buckets. Stratton felt soaked to the skin but it meant nothing to him. He carried his Colt at the ready as he passed the redoubt he and the girl had hidden behind only two days before.

When he walked into the clearing on the edge of the wood, he stopped to look down at the spot where Hopper had knelt when he shot him. The ground was muddy with water pooling everywhere.

He heard Downs and the others coming up behind him. They spread out as they approached the trees. Fires still burned within the wood. They could see no movement. It was like all who had survived had scattered.

Milton, one of the non-pilots, stepped beside Downs with a video camera attached to a head cage that allowed him to look through the lens but keep his hands on his weapon.

'Oscar Zero, that's Tango One Foxtrot at Sierra Two,' Downs said into his radio.

'Roger, that's Tango One at Sierra Two,' came a reply.

Downs looked at the others either side of him to see if they were ready to move in but Stratton set off without waiting for the command.

'So used to working on your own, ain't you,' Downs quipped as he walked off after him.

They didn't have to walk far into the wood before they came across the first dead fighter. A fresh depression in the ground a few metres away and his missing leg suggested he had been killed by a mortar.

Milton stood over the body to film it for a few seconds. Downs and the others set off deeper into the trees.

By the time they reached a group of huts that appeared to be the centre of the camp, they had seen only a dozen or so dead. If there was a similar ratio throughout, Stratton estimated there could be no more than forty all told. Which was a small portion of the total numbers encamped in the location. It reminded all of them that they needed to do what they had come to do quickly and get out of there. If the jihadists regrouped and pressed a counter-attack, things could quickly go wrong for the teams.

They heard a moan from within a clump of bushes. A fighter lay on the wet ground, the rain dropping on to him from the branches above, his leg badly mangled. He stared pathetically at the faces looking down on him, as much in shock to see them as from his wound. He had no weapons and looked harmless enough. The operatives walked away, just left him. They didn't have the time or the equipment to be humane. The truth was, after so many years fighting the jihadists, the men didn't have much humanity left either. It wasn't something to be proud of, and if asked, most would have admitted that. But it was an easy fault to live with, or at least justify to a degree. If the jihadists caught a Western soldier, they wouldn't give him the finest medical treatment available and three square meals a day or leave him with the hope of one day seeing his family again.

The men understood why they had to be humane but they couldn't always maintain it.

Stratton walked to one of the wooden huts and pushed in the door. A fighter lay inside on the floor, killed by a piece of shrapnel that had blown through the thin plywood wall and hit him in the chest. A ceiling-high stack of long green boxes took up half the room.

Stratton knew instantly what they were. He unclipped the lid of one and opened it up. Inside he saw a brand-new HN series Chinese ground-to-air missile.

Downs stepped in behind him. 'Are these what it's all been about?' he asked.

'Most of them,' Stratton replied. 'Not all.'

'I wonder how many of the ones they've already shipped have been offloaded.'

'I expect London is trying to figure that out right now.'

Downs exhaled heavily. 'Right. Milton! In here. Film this lot before we burn it.'

The cameraman stepped inside along with a couple of other men.

'Make sure you get as many serial numbers as you can,' Downs ordered. 'Smudge, when he's done I want this lot done to a crisp.'

'We'll certainly take care of that,' Smudge said.

Stratton walked outside and looked around, unsatisfied. He stepped to the next hut. Nothing but dead bodies. The same with the one after. He stalked through the camp inspecting any dead he saw. The odds were against any being the Saudi but he had to check. He couldn't bear the thought of that low-life escaping. If the man did manage to get out of Somalia, London had only a slim chance of ever finding him. You only had to look at bin Laden. If that guy could stay hidden, then Sabarak surely could for a fraction of the price.

Stratton walked to another pair of huts, built out of wood just like the last. One had been partially destroyed but the other appeared untouched apart from a few shrapnel holes in it. The door stood open and he could hear movement inside. Voices.

Then two SBS operatives stepped outside and looked around like they were deciding where to go next. Stratton immediately recognised the bigger of the two. It was Matt.

Matt saw Stratton at the same time and stared at him.

Stratton had no interest in the man and turned away from the hut since it had obviously been cleared.

'Just another wounded in there,' Matt said to Stratton.

'No guns,' Matt's partner said. 'He speaks English. Asked if he could light a lamp. I told 'im 'e could set fire to 'imself if 'e liked.'

Stratton looked back at the hut. The only Somali he had heard speaking English during his visit was Lotto.

And Sabarak.

He walked up to the door and pushed it open. Sitting on the floor in the darkness next to a desk was a man holding a kerosene lamp. He struck a match along the side of a box and when it lit he touched it to the wick of the lamp. The flame glowed to expose his face.

It was the Saudi.

He sat with his legs outstretched, one of them bloody, disfigured by a gruesome wound on the thigh.

Sabarak raised his head to look at the new visitor. When he saw who it was his expression turned grey. When the glider attack had first begun and a mortar had struck the shed next door, sending a piece of shrapnel through the wall and into his leg, he had thought his end had come and had sat on the floor waiting for his executioners to arrive. When the two SBS operatives walked into the hut, Sabarak had fully expected them to shoot him. But they had simply looked around and checked him for a weapon. Sabarak had decided to risk communicating with them. It hadn't surprised him that the men spoke English. He knew the attack had to have been carried out by either the British or the Americans. When they left him on his own, Sabarak realised he was going to survive. The British were not bloody executioners. They had come for the missiles.

But as he stared into the cold eyes of the man standing in the doorway, his confidence in that last analysis withered. He swallowed, his throat dry, hoping there was a chance the man, whom the other one had called Stratton, had come to arrest him as he had in Yemen.

Stratton allowed the end of the barrel of his Colt to drift in Sabarak's direction.

The Saudi read the message clear enough. He had killed Stratton's friend. He knew Westerners weren't generally savage without a cause, not like his own people. He regarded it as a weakness in their race and a strength among his own kind. But he was well aware of the Westerner's appetite for revenge. This one had braved hundreds of fighters and risked his life in an attempt to rescue his friend. And he had failed. He then had tried to kill Sabarak. He wouldn't fail this time. Sabarak could see it in the eyes. There was no doubt there, just a cold hard reality.

'I have something for you,' Sabarak said.

He reached under the desk. Stratton applied a little pressure to the Colt's trigger as a warning.

Sabarak froze. 'You can shoot me after. But allow me the

pleasure of seeing your face when I present you with my gift.'

Stratton didn't move, suddenly curious about Sabarak's 'gift'.

Sabarak took hold of a heavy bundle covered in a towel. The effort caused him some pain, which he fought. He tossed the bundle towards Stratton while keeping a hold of the corner of the towel.

A human head rolled out and came to rest on the floor between the two men.

Hopper's head.

20

Stratton looked down at the head, Hopper's eyes half open, teeth visible and all of him, especially his hair, matted in dried blood, his neck in tatters where it had been hacked at. So the replacement executioner had his own problems cutting through it cleanly.

But the thing that struck Stratton most was something he couldn't see. Stratton had last looked at Hopper's face above the sights of the AK-47. It was not an accurate weapon and he could easily have been off by several inches. But he could see no damage to any part of Hopper's head. A bullet would have created a neat entry hole and a larger exit hole. So they had carried out the ritual. They had cut off the head because Hopper had been alive.

Stratton needed to confirm that. 'Why did you kill him?' he said.

'What else should we have done with him?' Sabarak asked, like the question was a stupid one.

It was all Stratton wanted to know. He hadn't killed Hopper, despite his efforts. Matt had been right in part. Stratton had decided Hopper's fate, like he had been God. If these bastards had only waited a couple of days longer, Hopper would most likely be alive and thanking the lads for rescuing him. But only because Stratton had missed the shot. Hopper might even have forgiven Stratton for leaving him in the prison hut. But he couldn't, because he was dead. And it was still Stratton's fault.

Downs stepped into the hut. He saw the Saudi first and then Hopper's head on the floor. 'Dear God,' he muttered.

Milton walked in with the recorder strapped to his head.

'Get out of here,' Stratton said coldly.

The cameraman either didn't hear or chose to ignore him. Milton reached for his recorder to unpause it. Stratton grabbed him by the neck and threw him outside and to the ground.

'Easy man,' Downs said.

'Leave us, please,' Stratton said softly. 'He's the one I've come for.'

Downs considered what to do. If he did his job, he should restrain Stratton and take him back to the town and then on to the ship. But that was easier said than done. He knew Stratton well enough to see the state he was in. He would need tying up and all sorts to get him back to the beach. So the wiser course of action would be to let him be. Downs looked at Stratton and the Saudi. Then he looked at the head on the mud floor between them. The man sitting beside it was surely responsible otherwise Stratton would not be looking at him like that.

'He was driving my guards crazy talking about his wife and children all the time,' Sabarak said, a smile on his face.

Downs's eyes narrowed, darkened, like a shadow had passed across them.

Sabarak seemed to see it and his smirk faded.

'Did you hear that, me old fellah?' Downs said to Sabarak. 'That was the sound of your own God turning his back on you.'

Downs walked out of the hut, closing the door behind him and leaving Stratton inside. He joined his men who looked between him and the hut. Some seemed to accept it, for whatever private reason they had. Some looked unsure, like they considered it to be wrong.

'What's going on in there, Downsy?' one of the men asked.

'Well, there's two men inside. One filled with uncontrollable hate, the other half mad with revenge. Thing is, I don't know which is which.'

Then they heard a shot. Then a crash. They saw the inside of the hut light up. The door opened and Stratton stepped out. The inside of the hut became engulfed in flames. Within seconds the entire room had turned into an inferno.

'Still playing God, are we, Stratton?' Matt said.

'We should've at least buried him,' Milton said. 'We should've taken Hopper home and buried him.'

Stratton walked right through them like they weren't there.

'He's mad,' Milton said to Downs. 'He's lost it, hasn't he?'

'We all live on the frontline,' Downs said. 'He just lives a little closer to it than we do.'

The hut that contained the missiles abruptly burst into

a massive blaze, one enhanced by several incendiary devices. Smudge came running through the trees towards the group, pausing to look back at his work. 'I suggest we're not anywhere near that lot when it goes up,' he said.

They all heeded his advice and started to walk away down the slope.

Downs brought his radio up to his lips. 'This is Downs. We're finished here. Call in the perimeter. We're headed towards Tango Charlie.'

'This is Harvey, roger that,' came the reply. 'All stations muster on the track towards Tango Charlie.'

As Downs and the others set off in the direction taken by Stratton, the hut with the missiles inside exploded with a tremendous thud. The rain seemed to fall harder then, like the blast had ruptured the clouds above. The downpour was temporarily joined by small pieces of timber and shrapnel returning to earth.

Downs's team exited the wood and were met by the other half of the assault squad that had covered the perimeter in small pockets to mop up any of the fighters who managed to regroup to mount a counter-attack. It had obviously been far from the enemy's minds or their ability.

The men broke into an easy jog while spreading out into a defensive pattern. Two of the fitter young men sprinted ahead to act as lead scouts.

Downs jogged towards Stratton and as he came alongside him the operative broke into an easy run to keep up with his old friend.

They said nothing as they made their way across country.

The rain eased off soon after the teams reached level ground and by the time they arrived at the outskirts of the town, it had practically ceased.

They kept up the pace as they made their way along the eastern side of the town. They couldn't see a soul about. Some lights. But the place wasn't deserted. It was late and most of the population had to be in their beds.

As the SBS operatives passed one end of a broad street that ran through the town, the team stopped and crouched on one knee in all round defence. Downs stepped into the centre and the other team leaders closed in for a brief confab.

Stratton remained standing and looking down the street, realising where he was exactly. It was Lotto's street.

Downs finished his brief and the team leaders took a moment to confirm the next phase with their own men. Then they got to their feet and continued down towards the bottom of the town and their respective objectives. They divided up, some going into the town while others went towards the brightly lit cargo ships anchored off the shoreline. Everyone knew what they had to do and focused on it like automatons.

Stratton looked at a porch halfway along the street. Lotto's porch. With a light on inside.

The interpreter had joined Downs's team for this next phase of the operation and they were about to set off when Downs realised Stratton wouldn't be joining them.

'More unfinished business?' he asked his friend as he walked over to him.

Stratton's bloodlust had ended with Sabarak but he had other things he wanted to know about. 'Just some loose ends,' he said.

'Be careful, my friend. And I don't mean with what you're about to do, whatever that is.'

'It's OK. I just have to find out something.' He looked back at Downs and smiled at him. 'I'm not mad. Least I don't think I am.'

'I hope not. I'll miss you if you are.' Downs returned the smile and joined his men and they walked down the side of the town.

Stratton waited, then headed along the middle of the street, his Colt held easily in his hands.

Downs led the way to the corner of a street, where his team spread to cover both sides of the entrance. It was the street where the hostages were being held. He wondered if news had reached the pirates that an attack had taken place against the jihadist camp. If so, they had two main scenarios to deal with. The pirates would either take to their heels and run or they would try to defend their stolen property. Since the Somalis had no idea of the size of the force that they might encounter, Downs hoped they would take the wiser option and flee.

The first two of his men moved forward to probe the possible enemy positions. Downs's main concern was their safety and it dictated his tactics. If the pirates were determined to defend their town, it could turn out bloody for the hostages, as well as for the pirates. His other fears, if the pirates had chosen to flee, were that they had tried to take the hostages with them or killed them before leaving.

The team spread out along both sides of the track in a staggered formation and advanced quietly along it. There was little sign of life other than the occasional sound from inside a dwelling. If word had spread that Westerners were coming, the local populace would probably hide in their houses until it was all over.

Downs's lead pair stopped a short way along the street. A small Somali boy was standing in a doorway looking at the lead guy. The operative waved. The boy shyly returned it. His mother snatched him inside and closed the door. The lead pair eased forward. They had seen men with rifles up ahead through their night-vision sights. The men didn't look like jihadists so were probably pirates. It looked like they hadn't heard about the attack on the camp because they hung around the street, smoking and chatting easily.

This and any other option had been discussed during the operational brief. The aim was for minimal casualties so the strategy had been adjusted to allow for this. The lead pair had suppressors attached to the barrels of their weapons and they both lifted the carbines, aimed them using the thermal sights and fired in quick succession. Fifty metres away four pirates died where they stood or sat and fell to the ground.

The team quickly advanced to clear the area of any other pirates who might be out of sight. The last thing they wanted was a panicked Somali firing in all directions. They got about halfway when a guy carrying an AK-47 did step into the street. He saw the bodies and as he grabbed his weapon off his shoulder silent bullets ripped into him and he joined them.

The team took up fire positions while Downs and Milton, still with the camera on his head, went to the front door of the prison hut. Downs drew the bolt across and opened the door. He looked inside and saw the hostages Stratton had shared the room with, minus the Dutch crew who had been released with their ship. Those who were awake looked startled at the new visitors but didn't move at first in disbelief.

Downs stepped inside with Milton and the interpreter and they set about keeping the hostages calm and telling them that they were about to be freed. When the hostages in the other building had been liberated, they were formed into a single group and led as quietly as possible to the outskirts of the town and down towards the cargo ships.

As Stratton walked along Lotto's street he breathed in deep to help bring down his heart rate after the jog from the jihadists' camp. His concentration remained at a peak, his Colt at the ready to respond to anyone who might challenge him. The rain had stopped but the roofs still dripped water on to the muddy ground. The potholes that covered the street were filled with water, which he avoided to reduce the noise he made. Apart from occasional lights in the houses, the place seemed to be deserted. He wondered if that was because the word had spread that the jihadists' camp had been attacked. It was possible the townsfolk didn't know. The rain, thunder and the distance would have done a lot to mask the explosions.

He came to the front of Lotto's house and stopped across the street to look at it. The dim light was on inside. He turned around in a circle. He could see no sign of any guards anywhere.

He turned back to the house, walked towards it and stepped gently on to the wooden porch. He stopped at the door. He could hear a soft voice inside. Followed by deep, gentle laughter. A man's laughter. Lotto's laughter.

Stratton slung his Colt and pulled his Sig Sauer pistol from its holster. He held it easily at his side. He was going to enjoy this immensely. Every time he had met Lotto in the last few days the Somali had had the guns, the manpower, the control. Now it was Stratton's turn.

Stratton still did not feel any great animosity towards the man, which was possibly strange considering the number of times Lotto had tried to kill him. The explanation was understandable enough, though. Lotto hadn't had any particular hatred for Stratton. His aggression hadn't been personal. Stratton had simply begun as a commodity to the pirate commander and later turned into a threat to the rest of his assets.

Stratton reached for the doorknob. More gentle laughter came from behind the door. This time he thought he heard a lighter tone mixed in with Lotto's. A woman's.

Stratton turned the handle of the door slowly, pushed it open and stepped inside, moving away from the opening.

The big pirate commander sat across the room from him with a glass in his hand and looking very relaxed. Right up until the moment he recognised Stratton. He almost let go of the glass he was so astonished. He looked hard at Stratton, from his boots to his face. His eyes locked on to Stratton's cold eyes for a long time. But then his qualities as an old fighter came through and he regained control of himself.

Stratton looked from the Somali to his companion.

It was the Chinese girl.

Her smile faded as she looked up at the Englishman. She didn't have quite the same control as Lotto and lost the liquid in the fine crystal glass she was holding.

All three remained silent for what seemed a long time.

Lotto's eyes went to his pistol, within arm's reach on a side table next to the single lamp that illuminated the room and the open bottle of whisky beside it. Then he looked at Stratton. The operative kept looking at the girl but was way ahead of the Somali.

Lotto sat back and took a breath, like he had an amount of respect for Stratton's ability to outmanoeuvre him. Like he had first-hand experience and didn't doubt for a second that if he chose the wrong moment to reach for the weapon, he would never live to touch it. 'Well, well, Mr Stratton,' he said in his deep voice, sounding confident. 'You are always full of surprises.'

'No more than you,' Stratton said, his comment aimed at the girl whose expression was coated in guilt. 'So who *do* you work for?'

It took several seconds for her expression to change. As though she could no longer see the point in playing games. She looked at Stratton, his pistol, his fatigues and they seemed to signal an end to something. She said, 'The Triads.' She looked matter-of-fact about it.

Stratton smiled inwardly. He was not expecting that answer. 'Would that explain the drugs?'

She nodded. 'Jimlen and I never sailed to Somalia. We got dropped off by a Chinese cargo ship. I was making the delivery.'

'What delivery?'

'The quarterly supply.'

'We've been in business a long time,' Lotto cut in.

'A long time? You two?' Stratton said. The girl didn't look old enough.

'Not her,' Lotto said. 'This was her first trip. The Chinese have been dealing through Somalia since before you were born.'

Stratton knew the Triads were international organisations but he knew nothing about a Somali drug connection. He thought again how drugs and arms smugglers used similar routes and techniques. And since nearly every terrorist organisation smuggled weapons, it didn't take a genius to work out that providing their smuggling services to drug dealers could be a very lucrative source of funding.

'What came first?' Stratton asked, curious about the set-up.

'Hijacking is not new to Somalia,' Lotto said. 'We've been doing it for hundreds of years. A couple of decades ago the Triads saw an opportunity and came to my predecessor with a business plan. In the early days we did not hijack many ships a year, only enough to transport the smaller amounts of drugs. I was a fisherman then, working for my father. When I was old enough, I joined the pirates and I watched the demand for drugs increase. That meant the need to hijack more ships. I knew that, even then. But my boss didn't see it. He was afraid to increase the hijackings. I decided to set up my own business. That old weakling said I would bring down the wrath of the international countries on all of us. So I took over all of the piracy on this coastline. You want to know something? We always made more money from the drugs. The hijacking has always been a sideline.'

Stratton found it an interesting history lesson. 'When did the jihadists get involved?'

'They first showed up five or six years ago. They wanted to get involved in the drug smuggling to fund their jihad and offered me product from Afghanistan. So we began to do business. I could make you a very rich man, Mr Stratton,' Lotto said. He took a deep pull of his drink. 'I have bank accounts all over the world. I could set one up for you by tomorrow morning. How much do your people pay you?' He smiled. 'How does five million dollars sound to you?'

Stratton eyed the man with contempt. 'When did you begin smuggling weapons for terrorists?'

'There's no money in that. I do it to keep them happy.'

'Was it your idea, combining their weapons with the drugs?' Stratton asked.

Lotto grinned. 'Of course. It is just politics, my friend.'

Stratton looked at the girl again. 'So how did you end up in his jailhouse along with the rest of us?'

'The Triads didn't like Lotto using the same system he used to move the drugs to smuggle weapons. They sent me to tell him not to do it any more.'

'I don't like being told what to do by anyone,' Lotto grumbled. 'So I punished her.'

'Why did you go aboard the cargo ship?' he said to the girl.

'I heard about the hand-held missiles when I got here. I knew it would lead to problems. Your kind of problem. I got a message to my people to confirm Lotto was putting the missiles on the ships with the drugs. That was when Lotto put me in his jail.'

'I put you in the jail because you accused me of cheating your Triad bosses.'

'I was also ordered to check the amount of drugs you were putting on board. You *are* cheating the Triads.'

'Cheating. A stupid word in our business. As long as everyone makes money, what is the problem?'

'If you went to China and told them that, you wouldn't live very long,' she said.

'And so let them come here,' he said. 'They would not because they are afraid to. Why do you think I keep Al-Shabaab happy? The Triads could not take on those guys. Not here in Somalia. And that's why I had to punish you some more. I wanted to send them a message. I'm sure you enjoyed it just a little. Isn't that why you came back?' Lotto asked.

She turned to Stratton. 'You've come for the jihadists, haven't you?' she said.

'That's all over,' he said. 'The camp and the missiles have been destroyed. We have the ships and the hostages will be free by now.'

Lotto opened his mouth slightly in horror at the news. His world was crumbling around him and it was all this man's fault.

'You avenged your friend?' she said.

Stratton didn't answer, he simply stared coldly at her. But she read a hint of satisfaction behind the veil of pain.

'I'm glad for you,' she said.

Stratton knew he should regard her with the same cold contempt he had for Lotto but still he could not. He suspected there was more to her story. 'You don't seem like the Triad type,' he said.

'I'm not a Triad. My father was.'

'I liked working with your father,' the Somali cut in.

'Too much unfortunately,' she said, not looking at him. 'The Triads found out that Lotto and my father were cheating them. That's how I ended up here. If I did not deliver the drugs and report on the weapons, they would kill all of my family. My mother, my sister and brother. Even my brother's wife and children. I had no choice.'

'I am feeling very bad about all of this,' Lotto said. 'There's a lot I have been blind to. I am going to give you a lot of money too.'

Stratton wondered if the man really expected anyone to take him seriously. And did he really believe that after this little talk he was simply going to walk out of here? Stratton hadn't decided what to do with the pair of them. He would take them down to the beach and introduce them to Downs. London could decide.

'When you beat her, did she tell you I'd been on the ship and seen the weapons?' he said.

'I don't think so,' Lotto replied.

'He's lying,' the girl said. 'He asked me where I had been. I didn't tell him at first. But the pain was too great and I thought he would stop. So I told him. He didn't stop. He asked me where you had been. I told him the truth. And he continued with me.'

Lotto looked like a cornered animal.

'So my next trip would've been to the Al-Shabaab camp?' Stratton said.

'In business terms, that was a long time ago,' Lotto said and shrugged. 'Now we can start again. I'll give you twenty million dollars US. I have money here. Lots of it.'

He reached for a large cardboard box. Stratton stiffened a little, but the Somali kept moving like a sloth and pulled the box over, tipping dozens of bundles of hundred-dollar bills on to the floor.

'It's all yours. There are more boxes filled with money. I have euros and pounds. You too,' he said, picking up a bundle and offering it to the girl. 'Take it all.'

She didn't move, her eyes fixed on his.

Lotto looked at Stratton for a sign that he was winning the operative over. He saw none.

'Why'd you come back?' Stratton asked the girl.

'For my family. I had to finish my work.'

'And Lotto?'

She was still looking at the Somali. 'To kill him if I could.'

Lotto could feel the walls closing in.

Stratton was enjoying the man's pain. 'A nice idea,' he said. 'But we'll have to leave that possibility for later. Right now you're both coming with me.'

She looked from the pirate to him, but not with anger in her eyes. Only sadness.

'I cannot go with you,' she said. 'If I do, I will fail and my family will die.'

Stratton appreciated her dilemma. But there was nothing he could do about it. The call was far above his station. To complete his job, he needed to deliver them both to Downs on the beach. From there on it was up to London.

The girl could see the operative's resolve. She knew what it looked like well enough. 'You know what they'll do, don't you?' she said. 'They'll let him go because he is a Somali. But the British will be happy to deliver me to the Chinese. Me and my family will die and he will live. All of my pain will have been for nothing.'

Stratton had to agree that her assessment was most likely correct. But he still could do nothing about it.

She slowly stood and faced him. 'You know how I am by now. You know I would rather die. I can't come with you. You will have to kill me. But please, I beg you, please kill him too.' Tears began to roll down her face. 'Please kill him,' she said softly. 'Do that for me. He is an animal and enjoys making people suffer.'

Lotto grabbed his moment. He threw the bundle of dollar bills in his hand at the table lamp and dived for the gun. The lamp toppled and went out before it hit the floor and the room went black instantly.

But Stratton knew the precise point that Lotto was reaching for, and adjusted the end of the barrel of his pistol to allow for the length of Lotto's arm and fired two shots. The Somali got to fire one, the muzzle flashes illuminating the moving figures for a split second. A body hit the floor hard.

Then silence.

Then a dozen long seconds.

The floor creaked like a foot had stepped on a worn floorboard. A switch flicked and the porch light came on.

Stratton stood in the doorway with a finger on the light switch, his gun in his hand. Lotto lay still on the floor, his eyes half open, blood seeping from a hole in his temple and another in his cheek.

The girl was kneeling beside Lotto with the Somali's gun in her hand and pointed directly at Stratton.

Stratton didn't have the Sig aimed at her but it wouldn't need to travel far to line her up. But even so, she still had the drop on him. It would be a close call and he would probably take a bullet. If he was lucky he would live, and if not he would die.

He looked into her eyes, evaluating her. He knew from experience that she had an ample supply of determination.

He also needed no further convincing that she would rather die than let her family become victims of the Triads. And the bottom line was he did not care enough about her paying for her crimes to risk his own life to see it through.

But she had one more surprise in store for him.

She lowered the gun and let it hang in her hand by her side. 'I cannot kill you. Not because you saved my life so many times, although I am grateful for that. Because each time you saved me you saved my family. And I don't believe you will waste all of that karma and kill me. I won't go with you and I will kill myself if you try and take me.'

Stratton wasn't entirely surprised by her decision. His gut instinct had been that she would not shoot him. He had failed to figure out her occupation but he had more or less nailed her character.

He sighed, holstered his pistol and shrugged. 'What the hell. I think the world might even miss one crazy Chinese girl like you.'

She smiled slightly and put the pistol on the table.

'How will you get out of here?' he asked.

'I have a few ideas,' she said, walking up to him.

She stood close to him, looking into his eyes. She put her arms around him and gave him a hug, her face against his chest. It felt completely natural for him to return the gesture and he wrapped his arms around her. For a brief moment, amid all the madness, he felt his heart soften.

She looked up into his eyes again, placed the palm of her hand on his face and gently kissed him on the cheek.

'Your friend's death was not your fault. You are who you

are. And things happen because of who you are, good and bad. I think you have much more good in you than anything else.'

She let go of him and walked out of the door.

He stood on the porch and watched her go down the street and disappear into the darkness. He looked back at Lotto lying in a pool of blood surrounded by his money. That will be a good find for someone, he thought.

He switched off the porch light and headed away.

When Stratton stepped on to the beach, he found Downs standing with his hands on his hips looking at the ships like he was deciding what to do next. Stratton could see the hostages all sitting in a group, waiting patiently. They looked more than content to wait all day. They were under the protection of the British military and on their way home. At that moment in time, life for them did not get better than that.

One stared at Stratton in the poor light, certain he had seen the man somewhere before. He asked the fellows either side of him and together they scrutinised Stratton until one of them twigged who it was. The news spread quickly and they were soon all in agreement: it was the one who had escaped and they had thought must be dead.

One of them whistled to catch Stratton's attention. When he looked at them, the collection of European and Asian faces cracked into broad grins, the first in a long time for some.

Stratton nodded at them, somewhat embarrassed.

'Brought your own fan club with you this time, did you?' Downs asked.

'Well, you know how it is. You reach my level and those are the perks.'

Downs started laughing and Stratton joined him.

'Is it my imagination or do you suddenly look more chilled?'

Stratton shrugged and looked out to sea.

'What happened back there in the town when I left you?' Downs said.

'I told you. I tied up a few loose ends.'

Downs knew he wasn't going to get anything more out of his friend and he shut up and looked out to sea alongside him.

By late morning the last of the Somali pirates had been cleared from the ships and the crews allowed back on to their respective vessels. Two of HMS *Ocean*'s launches had arrived to provide food and water and medical aid for the lads and the freed crews. All of the captured Somali pirates were stripped of their weapons and allowed to leave. The British were keen to avoid the complex legal hassle and publicity that would accompany the abduction of a Somali citizen from his own country even though they had proof of the crimes. A couple of hours after that the anchors were weighed and the ships turned out to sea.

The two glider crews that had gone down before the bomb run turned up at the beach as the sun was getting higher. Downs knew they were inbound because their trackers were still working perfectly and HMS *Ocean* could monitor their progress. Both pilots' radios had broken in the crash and their move to the beach rendezvous point had been slow because one of them suffered a broken leg. His partner had carried him over nine kilometres.

They couldn't resolve one minor issue. Shortly before the bulkers' anchors were retrieved, one of the SBS lads looking out through a porthole high in the superstructure of the East Asian carrier saw a figure climb through a stern anchor chain hole and dart along the deck and out of sight. Whoever it was had obviously swum to the anchor chain and climbed it to the top.

The SBS lad immediately assumed that a Somali was attempting to stow away. He organised a search but they could find no one. The operative who reported the sighting said he didn't think it was a local. In fact, unless his eyes had deceived him, the person's face hadn't been brown and they had looked very much like a woman.

The squadron arrived back in Poole within three days and after a short debrief they were disbanded to go on leave.

Matt didn't apologise to Stratton but neither did he try to denigrate him further. His final word on the subject, to anyone who cared to listen, was that Stratton had still tried to kill Hopper but the fact was he had missed. That was a dig Stratton could live with. Most of the service members who had been on the fence about Stratton's choice admitted they would rather have been shot through the head by him than have it cut off by those bastards.

Stratton left for his home in Lytchett Matravers to be

alone and unwind, but within hours Downs called him to report that he knew of a pub in the Wareham Forest with a particularly tenacious barkeep. They spent an evening putting the world to rights, mostly Downs naturally, and ended with a few choice Irish Republican rebel songs that both men knew well. Unfortunately for posterity, they were so trashed by the end of it that the details of the conversation were forgotten and thus those invaluable global solutions were lost to mankind for ever.

A week later a service was held for Hopper, and Stratton met his wife Helen and their two children. Downs urged Stratton not to mention his guilt about leaving Hopper in the prison while he went alone to the ship, not that Stratton had any intention of doing so. Downs felt that the subject belonged to the finer debate of strategy and should be left to those who dealt in that trade. Helen hugged Stratton and thanked him for being her husband's friend. Stratton said he was sorry but didn't explain what he really meant by that. And she didn't read anything else into it.

Epilogue

Dinaal Yusef and the six members of his team drove in a van along a deserted country lane, its full-beam headlights cutting into the night. The Colombian driver turned the van off the stone-crushed road into a narrower lane and immediately came to a halt beneath a stand of mature trees. Two men jumped out and ran off the road into the bushes as lookouts.

The headlights of the van went out and the Colombian switched off the engine. A heavy silence descended.

Dinaal climbed out of the front passenger seat on to the hard ground and looked in every direction across flat, agricultural country. He saw the handful of small farmhouses spread about in the distance. Some of them had lights on inside.

He looked at the night sky. It had been raining but the clouds had moved on and the stars now shone brightly.

He went to the back of the van and opened the doors. The two Saudis and the Indonesian climbed out carrying a long green wooden box between them. It had Chinese characters stamped down its sides.

Dinaal led the way across the wider track to a fence.

One of the Saudis hurried ahead and climbed over to receive an end of the box. The team made its way through the stile and carried on down the side of a freshly ploughed, gently sloping field to the bottom, eighty metres or so from the track. They could see a large patch of marshy water beyond the scrub that grew along the bottom of the field.

Dinaal's men placed the box on the soft, damp soil and opened it. They could all see the Chinese HN ground-to-air missile within.

Dinaal turned to look skywards, past a vast array of bright lights aimed upwards on the ends of long poles. Beyond them, the other side of a tall mesh fence, he could see the beginning of a long, broad runway. Lights spaced out on either side of it continued into the distance for ever, it seemed.

A bright haze on the far side of the great expanse of flat ground surrounded a collection of buildings, the offices, arrival and departure terminals of Bogota International Airport.

Dinaal turned his back to the runway and looked skywards again. In the distance, among the millions of stars, he saw another white light brighter than the others. It was coming on fast.

'Quickly,' he said.

His men had become a slick, well-trained crew who had carried out this procedure twice without live ammunition since the first rehearsal two months before. But this time it would be very different. This time it would be for real. Each of the men could feel a palpable tension among the group.

The Saudi weapon preparer lifted the rocket from the box. He handed it to the Indonesian. The Indonesian hoisted it on to his shoulder and positioned it comfortably, as he had done a dozen or so times back in their basement HQ since the weapon had arrived a few days before. His number two gripped him around the body to steady him and he aimed the pointed nose of the missile into the air in the direction of the runway.

Dinaal watched the progress of the aircraft, his back to his men. The plane had to be less than a minute away. He felt nervous but at the same time relieved that they were finally going into action. There had been times when he felt like it would never happen. It was only when the missile, disguised as farming machinery, finally arrived by truck, having been collected from the sea port of Cartagena, that he realised the operation would go ahead. This was it. His moment of glory. He had waited years for such an opportunity to prove himself. Each phase of the long, meticulous plan had finally come together. He felt masterful.

The engines of the A340 Airbus grew louder as it approached. It quickly took shape, its bulbous body outlined by its navigation lights like a constellation drawing.

The firing team could hear the craft approaching behind them and composed themselves as they maintained their aim. The Indonesian knew that in just a few more seconds he would release the rocket into the cold night air and its sophisticated electronic sensors would detect the heat pouring from the back of the airliner's engines and redirect the missile towards one of them. The missile would probably impact on the exhaust. Then it would detonate. The explosion would rip into the fuel tanks inside the wing and tear it apart. The huge jet would twist on to its side as its wing fell away and then it would crash down on to the runway, where it would break up into thousands of flaming pieces. Fire would engulf everything. Everyone on board would die.

Dinaal Yusef could see it all before it happened. It was going to be truly glorious.

Three figures in black stepped from the bushes that led down to the marsh. Each carried a silenced sub-machine gun. Dinaal caught their movement out of the corner of his eye. He saw their semi-crouched stances, the weapons in their hands, and for the fraction of a second of life he had left he knew he had failed.

Several brass-coated rounds slapped into his head and the life went out of him before he struck the ground. As the massive aircraft screamed overhead, the operatives put a dozen rounds each into the two Saudis, the Colombian and the Indonesian, the automatic weapons spitting death, the clicking of the mechanisms inaudible. The ground-to-air missile hit the soggy ground with a muffled clatter, swallowed up by the roar of the aircraft passing overhead.

The three assassins quickly moved forward to check the jihadists were dead. One of the operatives wore a recording device strapped to his head and ensured that he got everything.

They dragged the bodies by their feet through the bushes and into the marsh, ensuring each of them was fully under the water.

They returned to pick up the rocket launcher, place it inside its box, close the lid and secure it.

'Is that everything?' the team leader asked in an east London accent.

'All good,' the recorder said in a Lancashire brogue.

'Let's go,' the leader said, and they set off up the side of the field to the fence by the lane. They climbed over with the box and headed along the narrow track past Dinaal's van and into a field, which they trudged across. Past the point where they had shot and hidden the two lookouts.

'Wait a minute,' the recorder said, stopping to take the device from his head to inspect it. The leader and the other operative, who were carrying the box, slowed as they looked back at their colleague.

'What is it?' the leader asked, coming to a stop.

'I'm not sure I had it turned on.'

'You what? You were supposed to make sure it worked before we went on the ground.'

'I did.'

'When's the last time you checked it?'

'I checked it in Hereford.'

'Hereford?' exclaimed the leader.

'I mean, I did a diagnostics check in Hereford before I left and I checked it here in the embassy this afternoon.' He fiddled with the device.

'We can't go back and do it again,' the other operative said in a Welsh accent.

The team leader glanced at the Welshman with an irritated frown.

'No, it's fine,' the recorder decided, walking on. 'I thought it was off but it wasn't. We're good.'

The others set off after him.

'You positive?' the leader asked.

'Yes.'

The leader gave him a sideward look. 'How long you been in the Regiment?'

'Three years. Why?'

'You were RAF before you did selection, weren't you?'

'What's that got to do with it?' the recorder asked defensively.

'Everything. Come on. I want to be home before the pubs shut tomorrow.'

The three men trudged off into the night towards a waiting van.